The Time Gentleman

Ewen Hill

A catalogue record for this book is available from the National Library of Australia

Publisher:
Australian Self Publishing Group, Pty. Ltd. / Inspiring Publishers
PO Box 159, Calwell, ACT 2905, Australia.
Phone: 61-(0) 2 6291-2904
http://australianselfpublishinggroup.com

National Library of Australia Prepublication Data Service

Author: Ewen Hill

Title: **The Time Gentleman**
   A Solo Motorcycle Tour of Queensland

Book type : Non-Fiction

ISBN: 978-1-923250-87-1 (print)

Table of Contents

✦

Introduction

The story you are about to immerse yourself in is a mixture of both fact and fiction. Our main characters, the Bailey family, are indeed fictional, as you will no doubt work out soon enough. Their travels and discoveries are the basis for this novel.

There is however, a significant part of this story that is based on real events. Many of the characters are real, notably most of the officers that this story is woven around. Obviously, any interaction between our fictional family and these real people is fictional as well. There is absolutely no disrespect directed at these heroes of this country. Quite the opposite, in fact. The officers and men of the First AIF are due the undying respect and admiration from all Australians and in fact, most of the Western world. The battles and actions described in this story are correct and fairly accurately retold and follow the actions of the real 28th Battalion.

These men of the 1st AIF, over 400,000 of them, every single one of them a volunteer, left their country and travelled 12,000 miles in support of the "Mother Country" to help defend the Empire. All this sounds quite jingoistic these days, but that is with the hindsight of 100 years of progress, development and changes of attitude. A significantly large percentage of the 1st AIF were

British expats, and Australia itself was really no more than an outpost of the British Empire at that time. Australia had been a unified nation for only 13 years at the outbreak of The Great War. It did not even, officially, have its own flag yet. In many situations, the Union Jack (the British flag) was still considered our flag. The nearest we had in those days to a national flag was actually what is currently known as the Red Ensign, a red flag with the Union Jack in the top left quadrant, the Southern Cross in the right half and the States star in the bottom left quadrant.

The men of the 1st AIF were considered by much of the British high command as 'those damned colonials'; men of little discipline, respect, courage or skill. This impression was not without basis in some areas though, and the men often played on this misconception, much to the consternation of the British officers. Due to this disparaging opinion, the men of the 1st AIF had little time or respect for these officers, partly as a result of their perceived ineptness. We were, after all, a country founded by the resettlement of convicts. Development and living life in Australia at that time had produced a different outlook to that of the British Command. There was an almost complete disdain for the upper classes.

In battle, however, the Australians proved the exact opposite. Their kind of discipline was based on one of the cornerstones of Australian culture; mateship. You never let your mate down. Thus, as a fighting unit, they were a force to be reckoned with. Australia is a harsh country on the whole, with the majority of the population living around the coastal areas. Much of the interior is inhospitable, and to survive, one must have a great deal of fortitude. A harsh land breeds hard, durable people. It breeds the kind of endurance needed to take the fight up to a foe, with a never-say-die attitude. Put these two qualities together and imagine the sort of person we are looking at. One who looks after his mate and never says die. That sort of attitude breeds courage. Just ask any of the men these lads came up against, whether they be Germans in WW1 or 2 or the Italians or Japanese in WW2, or indeed the Koreans or North Vietnamese. Ask them if the Aussie soldier lacked courage. Australian soldiers were feared and respected by their opposition.

Australia considers itself a much more egalitarian society than the country of its roots. The AIF prided itself in being a force of equals. Officers were drawn not from the class structure like their British counterparts but by performance and experience. This was a practice frowned upon by the British command, as the officer class was considered a privileged class. In most cases, an Australian soldier would back his officer, in the same manner he would back his mate. Often as the officer was his mate. I say in most cases, as in any army, there are always those who manage to gain promotion without earning it, and they were despised.

If you had the attitude that you would do anything for your mate, you would fight with him, fight for him and protect him, come one, come all. In so many cases men would rather sacrifice their own lives to ensure the safety of their mates.

- Courage
- Endurance
- Mateship
- Sacrifice.

The four cornerstones of Australian society.

The purpose of this story is twofold, to entertain and to educate. It has only been in recent years that Australians have learnt of the achievements of their ancestors in this conflict we now know as World War 1. Australians made up a small percentage of the fighting forces in this conflict, but their achievements are a bit like the average-looking Aussie bloke who has the most attractive wife or girlfriend. We would say he is 'punching well above his weight'.

The 1st AIF punched well above their weight, and are largely responsible for the defeat of the German Army in this war, through innovation and tactics. This, of course, includes the New Zealand cousins with whom we formed the ANZAC Corps. And don't forget the forces from the other dominions either, from Canada, South Africa, West Indies and India. From Le Hamel and Amiens, where the German advance was halted and reversed, through to the Hindenburg Line and the Sombre Canal, until the Armistice was signed.

These men were sent home after the conflict and told to forget all about it and not to talk about what they had seen and done. They did that, and many suffered as a result of it. Not only the physical injuries but the mental ones as well. Ones we are only today becoming aware of. They kept their stories to themselves and their mates when they got together on ANZAC day each April 25th. They would only talk to their mates about what they experienced; the ones who were there. As a result, the Australian public was unaware, until the last 20 or 30 years, of what our heroic forbearers accomplished, unfortunately after most of them had passed on. Ironically, the people of France and Belgium were not unaware and knew more about our accomplishments than we did.

So this story is not about chest beating. It is not a celebration of war. Hopefully, it can go some way to redressing an oversight on the part of popular historians of this conflict, albeit in a strange way, and help us to understand the contribution of a small band of dedicated, legendary, if somewhat rag-tag bunch of my fellow countrymen.

Lest We Forget.

Please note that this story takes place in a different time, where different attitudes existed. This story may contain terms that these days could be considered offensive by some. They were however normal in the times that this story was set, so to change them would be to alter history. No offence is intended to any person or group of people, only the utmost respect.

Chapter 1
Questions

**The more you know,
the more you know you don't know.**

Aristotle

"Hey, Dad? Have you ever been to war?" Tim called out to his father, Frank.

"What was that, Son?" Frank called back as he lifted his head from his reading.

"Have you ever been to a war?" Tim repeated his question.

"Only with your mother," Frank replied in a deliberately tactful low tone of voice.

"Pardon?" Tim had heard him answer but could not hear what his father had said.

"No son, I haven't. Why do you ask?" Frank replied, this time loud enough to be understood. He smiled to himself.

"Well, today we had our ANZAC service at school for ANZAC day next week. The person talking to us said something about the Vietnam War 30 years ago. I was wondering if you were in that. What was it all about?" Tim pressed his father again.

"Oh, that. Your uncle went to that one. I was too young. I just missed out." Frank said dismissing the question.

Tim was not to be dissuaded. "If I asked him about it, would he be able to tell me?"

Frank immediately folded his newspaper and put it down on his knee. Tim had his attention now.

"Ah, I wouldn't do that, Tim. That's why we haven't mentioned it before. He had a pretty rough time of it when he was there. That's why he's not a very nice uncle, from time to time." Frank sat up now, trying to avoid Tim raising it with his uncle.

"I like him. He's a bit different. Kinda wild." Tim answered.

"Yep, that about sums him up," Frank agreed.

"So, what was it all about, this Vietnam thing?" Tim wasn't letting this one go.

"Well Son, I'm not a full bottle on it, but it started back in the early 1950s, I think," Frank commented whilst thinking about it.

"Wow, that was a long time ago," Tim replied.

"Yeah. None of us had even heard of the place then. I was still only just born. Vietnam is a country in Indo-China, straight north of us here in WA. From what I know, Vietnam was a French territory before WW2 and the Japs drove them out, trying to take it for themselves," Frank recalled.

"French? But France is on the other side of the planet," Tim was puzzled by this.

"Yep, that's right," answered Frank. "Many of the European countries, like England, France, Spain, Portugal, Holland, had lots of other countries or territories that they either discovered and settled, or took over, sometimes centuries ago. A bit like Australia being settled by the English and really, just being an outpost of England for many years. Anyway, after WW2, the French tried to take it back, but Vietnam and the locals wanted them out, so sometime around 1954, they started an uprising trying to kick the French out. Then China and Russia got involved," Frank scoffed.

"What did it have to do with them?" Tim asked.

"Well, I guess China is on Vietnam's northern border, and figured that if the Frogs, I mean the French, were out, then they would be able to push their brand of communism onto the Viets," Frank suggested.

"Cheeky sods," suggested Tim loudly.

Frank laughed and gently shook his head and then continued. "Yep, but they didn't get directly involved, they just supplied weapons and pushed their ideology. And to a bunch of poor peasants, communism looks pretty damn good."

"Why?" Tim now asked.

"Well, that could take weeks to explain," Frank said, "but basically, they believe that everyone is equal and should have the same."

"That kinda makes sense, doesn't it?" said Tim.

"Maybe, except it never really works like that. Put simply, what happens is that everyone makes the same amount of pay, whether they work hard or do nothing, so there is little incentive to do anything much.

"Oh, I see, I think," Tim replied.

Frank tried to explain, "You can imagine if you go to work for 40 hours in a week shovelling coal nonstop and earn $100 and your neighbour works for 40 hours and sits on his bum handing out a glass of water to those men shovelling that coal every hour, and he also earns $100, well..."

"Why would I shovel the coal? Hmmm." Tim nodded thoughtfully.

"Exactly. Plus, no one owns their land or house. It is all owned by the government and you pay rent. But if it works, it means no one goes hungry." Frank added.

"But if there is no incentive to work hard, who is going to make the food to stop people from starving?" suggested Tim.

"Now, you are starting to get it, Son." Frank smiled. "Anyway, the United Nations, the UN, saw this happening and said to China and Russia, 'You need to butt out,' which of course they didn't. So, they put together a little force of 'peacekeepers', from the US, France, Australia and NZ, plus a smattering of other SE Asian countries. Just like they did in Korea, in the early fifties. By about 1964, the whole situation escalated, and our Nashos, National Service, were thrown into it.

"National Service? What's that?" Tim was listening intently, and Frank could see he had a real need for answers.

"Wow, this is getting deeper. Let's see now," Frank thought for a moment. "Nashos was a programme where every twenty-year-old in the country, was compelled to do military service for two years. Usually, with National Service, it would be in done your own country, but with Vietnam going on, they changed the laws, and they were sent overseas. Actually, come to think of it, it wasn't all twenty-year-olds. They had a ballot, a kind of lottery, where every six months, a set of marbles were put into a barrel. Each marble represented a date and covered every day of the six months. So, if the date of your birthday was drawn, you went to war."

"Holy shit! I mean holy cow, that's a bit tough." Tim exclaimed.

"Unfortunately, Digger, your first statement was more correct. But don't let your mother know I said that. Okay?" Frank winked at Tim.

"Yeah, Dad. No worries here," Tim answered quietly.

Frank continued, "Of the one hundred and eighty or so days in the half year, I don't know how many were chosen, but you had a good chance of being selected. Uncle Ted's was pulled."

"So let me get this right," said Tim. "Let's say that Pete, Dave, Mike and me were in the lottery..."

"Mike and I," corrected Frank.

"Ok, Mike and I," Tim repeated, "were in this lottery. Pete and Dave could be called and Mike and I could stay here.

"That's about the strength of it, Son," answered Frank.

"Wow, that's not fair," complained Tim.

"No, but neither is taking all the twenty-year-olds out for two years either," Frank replied.

"Two years?" queried Tim. "Ya had to go, for two years?"

"Yep, and after that was up, you had to be in the CMF, or what's now the Army Reserve, for the next 3 years," Frank answered.

Silence for a while. Frank left Tim to process the information.

"So, Uncle Ted was called up, and went to fight, in a war, in Asia?" Tim said.

"He was, along with some of his mates," Frank answered.

"Oh, now I see why he hangs out with those guys. Also, a bit of a wild bunch. Were they all together in Vietnam?" he asked.

"They were, and from what I can remember, I think something like, 500 of our guys got killed over there?" Frank added.

"Hmm," Tim thought for a moment and then added, "Wow, I never knew that."

"No, he doesn't like to talk about it, so we just felt it easier to leave it alone. So please be careful with it, Son. Keep it to yourself," his dad suggested.

"Okay. I'd like to know more though," Tim answered.

"Well, I tell you who will talk, and that's your grandfather, my dad. He was in WW2, in North Africa and New Guinea, and in the last few years, he has started talking a lot more about it," Frank said.

"Cool," Tim replied enthusiastically.

"He never talked to us as kids about it much, they were told not to, but now that it's fifty-odd years ago, he has started to open up. I think it's something he should have done years ago," Frank suggested.

"What do you mean by that dad?" Tim asked.

"Well Son, you see ... war is not quite like you see on the TV or movies. It's mostly pretty damned horrible. It's about watching mates die in front of you, some of them in extremely nasty ways. It's about being put in situations where you may have to kill someone else," explained Frank, trying to paint a more realistic picture without getting too graphic.

"Yeah, but they are the baddies though, aren't they?" Tim countered with.

Laughing, Frank replied, "Well, that is only a matter of perspective. Sometimes, you may be right, but really, the other soldiers are just men, like your uncle, who are sent to war to fight for someone else's cause. How would you feel about shooting at someone like your uncle?"

"Hmm. I guess so," Tim answered. "But in Grandpa's case, weren't the Germans, and the Japs bad people?"

"Oh, good God, no son. They were just people. People like us, who got caught up in a fight, mostly not of their doing. You see, in Germany, there was Hitler."

"Yeah, I know about him," Tim said.

"He dragged the country out of a depression, following the Great War," Frank started.

"WW1?" asked Tim.

"Yes, but it wasn't known as WW1 then, as there hadn't been a WW2 yet. It was just known as the Great War," Frank explained.

"Oh yeah. I see what you mean," Tim said.

"So, it was the Great War or the Worldwide War. Also called the 'War to end all wars'," Frank said.

Tim chuckled a little, "Well that worked, didn't it?"

"Yeah, sure did." Frank agreed sarcastically. He went on. "Anyway, this Hitler character, managed to shift the blame, for all the country's bad situations, onto one group of people."

"Ah, the Jews," replied Tim.

"Yes, the Jews. In fact, there was more than just the Jews, anyone who didn't fit his Aryan race profile. So that included Gypsies, criminals, homosexuals, Romanies and the like. So, by blaming them, he could whip up a lot of public hysteria and hence support and sweep into power. Then he started exterminating those that didn't agree with him and expanding, taking back 'what was rightfully ours' as he said. By that, he meant those countries and bits of countries, that he believed had been taken from Germany after the Great War. But then he got greedy, and the rest of the world did nothing to stop him until he invaded Poland," Frank explained.

"So why did we go to war for Poland?" Tim queried.

"We didn't really," Frank said. "What happened was Britain, France, and the USSR (now Russia) had an agreement and told Mr Hitler that if he invaded Poland, they would stop him. He didn't believe they would, as they had been so weak in the lead-up to this. But this was the last straw, as far as these allied powers were concerned, so in September of 1939, Britain declared war on Germany and her allies after they did invade Poland. At that time, Australia was just like an outpost of Britain, so we declared war too, just like in 1914 for WW1."

Tim listened and just nodded.

"So, going back to why Grandpa didn't talk about it. He lost a lot of mates, in both North Africa and New Guinea, and I dare say, he had to kill a few of the enemy himself, although he has never said, and we have never asked."

"Yeah, I guess that would be like admitting you are a killer, wouldn't it?" Tim pondered.

"Yep! Completely legal, so it's not murder, but if you have had to kill someone else, I imagine it would be pretty difficult to come to terms with, don't you? Frank asked Tim this time.

"Yeah, I guess so," the answer came back. Tim sat there and slowly nodded his head.

"Not only that," Frank added, "but when it was all over, the Government said to them, "Just go home and forget about it.""

"Really? Forget you killed someone? That's crazy," Tim suggested.

"Yes, it is, Son. Yes, it is." Frank agreed. "Many of the blokes had a really rough time of it after that war too, and that caused a lot of problems in our society, with crime and suicides and violence."

Mum, who had overheard the bulk of the conversation, was by now listening in with great interest. She could see her son was really learning something about life here. He was having a good heart-to-heart with his father, which was something they had rarely done. She stayed out of it. She stood in the doorway out of sight of both of them and just listened.

"This is all pretty important stuff to understand, isn't it, Dad?" Tim suggested.

"Yes Digger, it is. What it does do, is it gives you a bit of an understanding of where we have come from. Hopefully, if more people understood that, it might prevent us from going back there in future." Frank was enjoying this conversation with his son too.

"You mean like in Iraq?" Tim asked.

Frank laughed. "Yeah Dig, like in Iraq. We haven't learnt much have we?"

"It doesn't look like it, Dad, does it?" Tim agreed.

"So, what about your grandad? Was he in WW1 then, was he?" Tim now asked.

"Yes he was," Frank answered, "but we don't know much about him at all. He died over there. My dad never knew his dad. He was born while his father was over there, in France."

"He was born in 1916 wasn't he?" Tim asked.

Frank was taken a little aback by this. He wasn't sure himself. "Yes, I think so."

"So, when did he go over? Was he at Gallipoli?" Tim continued.

"No, he wasn't. He went straight to the Western Front, France." Frank explained.

"Oh okay. Do you know how he was killed?" Tim pressed on.

"Ah, no I don't," Frank admitted. "I don't even know when he was killed. I'm not sure Grandad even knows."

"Well, if we have said that these things are important, shouldn't we try and find out?" Tim suggested.

"You know Dig, you could be right. Why don't we pay Grandad a visit next week and see what he can tell us?" Tim's questions had now stirred Frank's thoughts and he was now interested in these answers himself.

At that point in the conversation, Tim's mother, Lynne, walked into the room and joined in the chat.

"I was just hearing you two talking about Grandad and the war and stuff. What have you worked out?" she asked.

"Well, I didn't know, we had so many people in the family who were in the Army and stuff; people who went to war. To my thinking, it's not something to keep quiet, it's something to be proud of. We had some of the kids at school today, who said their grandfathers were at the war and they were heroes. Was Grandad a hero?" Tim asked turning back to his father. He was becoming quite animated as he asked now.

"I'm sure he would tell you that he was not a hero. He just did what he was asked to do," Frank said, and turning to Lynne, added, "We've decided that we'll take a trip to see Grandad next weekend and ask him a thing or two."

"Not a bad idea." Lynne thought. "I'm sure he will be glad to see us all. Are you going to ring him first?"

"Yeah. I think I will give him the heads up on the conversation. That way, he can prepare for it if he needs to," Frank explained.

"Good call, sweetheart," Lynne said.

Frank took the phone from the cradle and dialled his father's number. It rang a few times before a familiar voice answered. Frank then began.

"Hey, Dad! How are you?"

"Hello Son." His father replied. "Can't complain, for an old bloke. Hip's still playing up as usual, but we can't do much about that now, can we?"

"Too true Dad. How's Mum?" Frank asked.

"Oh, she's still…. Mum. Still fussing. She's off playing bowls with her playmates this afternoon," his dad replied.

"Oh great," Frank exclaimed. "You know, you should take it up again Dad."

"Too late now, Son," his father said, "Can't get down there now. Anyway, most of my mates are all gone. There's hardly anyone I know there anymore. You know how it is."

"I guess that's true," answered Frank. He then changed the subject. "Hey Dad, I had an interesting discussion with Tim this afternoon. Thought you might be able to help us with it."

"Oh, Yeah? What was that about?" he questioned.

"Well, they had their ANZAC service at school yesterday. You know it falls in the holidays now, so they hold it on the last day of term," explained Frank.

"Yes," came the cautious reply.

"Well, he came home asking what was Vietnam all about?"

"Yes," his father said, waiting.

Frank continued, "So, I tried to explain to him as best I could remember what it was all about and how it fucked Ted around, not in quite so many words of course."

"Oh Yes," he was still waiting for the inevitable request.

"Turns out, we have never discussed anything of our military past with him. So, I told him about your involvement and that of your father. So, I was wondering, if we could come round, say next weekend and you could fill him in on a few bits and pieces, from your point of view?" Frank then asked.

His dad sighed with relief. This would be an easy request. "Son, I would be delighted to. I have been hoping this day would come sooner, rather than later, as my time on this earth is now pretty finite. Even so, I can remember it all like it was yesterday. So, what did you tell him, Son?"

Frank then went through a point by point summary of what they had discussed about the Vietnam conflict, what he knew about his own father's service and what little he knew of his grandfather's involvement.

"Okay then, so he wants to know if I am a hero eh?" Laughed his father. "Well Son, it strikes me that I probably haven't told any of you very much, really. We were told not to you know."

"Yes Dad, I remember that. To be honest, I would love to hear what you have to say as well."

"Seems kinda pointless bottling it all up now doesn't it, after all this time? His father mused.

"It may help a little, understanding things; like Ted, for example," Frank said.

"I know Son. Ted might seem like a bit of a disappointment to you, but I understand. I mean I saw lots of stuff, but Ted, well, what he had to put up with; not knowing who your enemy was, whether the next patch of jungle was mined, the Yanks? Hell, we had enough trouble with 'em. By 1968, they thought they ruled the world." Frank could tell from this his father had a lot of experiences he needed to get out.

"Anyway, enough for now. I'll think up a few things to keep the lad interested. As far as your grandfather goes though, I don't think I'm going to be much use there. We simply don't know a great deal. I've got his medals, and his penny, but Mum never spoke much about it at all," his father added soulfully.

"Okay, Dad. Not to worry. I think your stories will keep him happy. How's Saturday arvo for you?" Frank then asked.

"Sounds good to me, Frank. I'm not going anywhere. I'll get Mum to ring and confirm it though, just in case she has something planned," his father added.

"Thanks, Dad," Frank said. "See you next Saturday."

"I'll look forward to it. Give my love to Lynne, Tim and Ellie, for us, won't you?" his dad concluded the conversation.

With that, Frank hung up the phone and sat back and smiled. At last, he might get his father to open up and divulge the Pandora's box that lay in his father's mind. He had often wondered about his involvement in the war. Sure, he had given them little titbits over the years, but never a full run down. Frank was looking forward to next Saturday as much as young Tim was now.

He sat back on the settee and looked around the room with a sort of warm feeling. He felt that today had been a breakthrough on several levels. His son was obviously growing up and was on the verge of manhood. He had made the leap from being a child to a young adult, as his summation of the situation as explained to him was revealed. He had made some really adult conclusions from that information. Yes, he was definitely growing up. Then there was his own relationship with his father. It had always been good, but there always seemed to be something missing. A gap, of some sort, something unexplained. He wondered now if indeed it had been his wartime experiences. Now, more than ever, he was looking forward to next weekend.

Frank's father, Albert Leslie Bailey, was born in 1916, so was now 84 years old, but still had everything going for him, except his left hip. That had been a problem for him for as long as he could remember. In fact, back in 1990, he had had a hip replacement. Now, 10 years on, it was starting to play up for him again. Alby, as he preferred to be known, had spent his life in a few jobs. Before the war, he had worked at the Midland rail workshops, working on the locomotive production line as a welder. He had been involved with building many of the locos used by the then WAGR, Western Australian Government Railways. After the war, he returned to that job but wasn't able to settle, so he moved on, to a position with the State Engineering Works in North Fremantle. He preferred being near the coast as well. "You got the Fremantle Doctor way before the rest of the city," he used to say, and in the summer, in Perth, that was definitely desirable.

The "Fremantle Doctor" is the name given to the afternoon sea breeze. It comes in from the southwest on summer afternoons and gives much-needed relief as it cools down the hot summer days. For Perth City, it blows straight up the Swan River from Fremantle, hence the name. People thought the doctor would bring relief from their symptoms of heat. In actual fact, it is not quite the correct name. It originates from the sailing ship days. During summer in Perth, the prevailing wind during the day is from the east or northeast and is usually hot and this wind prevented sailing ships from entering the Fremantle harbour. When the wind changed to the southwest sea breeze in the afternoon, the ships could sail into the harbour and dock, so it was called the "Fremantle Docker". Over the years, as we moved away from sailing ships, the name slowly morphed into Doctor.

He had liked his position at the SEW. Here, he got to work on a bigger variety of projects, not just locos. It could have been anything from park benches through to massive mining equipment. It helped that some of his old army chums worked there as well and that may have been a factor in him choosing to move there.

He met and married Patricia (Patsy) Florence Hudson after the war and they had two sons. Edward (Ted) and Francis (Frank). They lived in East Fremantle and passionately followed the East Fremantle Football Club, whose home grounds were just down the road from their home.

He often told the story of when he saw Patsy for the first time. He was not much of a one for socialising and talking, but a mate from his work had cajoled him into coming to one of the dances at the football club one night. He and his mate were knocking back a few bevvies, when Patsy and three of her mates walked in. Alby reckoned he was dumbstruck from the get-go. He turned to his mate, and said, "That one's mine, the blonde." His mate Ralph immediately answered, "Not a problem mate, I like the redhead myself anyway." The girls waltzed in and assumed a position on the opposite wall, while the crowd danced a Boston two step. The girls sat there, preening their dresses and checking each other's hair, in the hope that one of the gentlemen present would notice them. Alby wasn't much of a dancer by his own admission, but the next dance was a barn dance and that one he did know. Ralph elbowed Alby and said, "Come on then mate, put ya money where ya mouth is. Let's go give 'em a try," to which Alby replied, "Holy shit mate, I've never done this before," but with a surge of bravado as Ralph leapt up, Alby added, "but let's go." So go they did, and they each hit it off instantly. By the end of that year, Alby had asked Patsy to marry him and she accepted. Not only that, but Ralph and Marilyn had done the same. Quite an eventful dance was that one.

Alby and Patsy married in 1947 and Edward came along in 1949, with Frank following in 1953. Patsy had been unwell following both births, so they decided enough was enough. Two healthy sons was a blessing and whilst a daughter would have been nice, they were not prepared to go through all that again, just on the chance it would be a daughter. Both boys attended school at East Fremantle Primary School and John Curtin Senior High School, where they stayed until 5th year, the year they turned seventeen. Ted finished school in 1966 and did not know what he wanted to do, so he started a job at the local fuel station down on Canning Highway for a year, before deciding he wanted to be an electrician. He found a local sparky who was prepared to take on an older apprentice and settled into his routine. After 4 years, he would be a fully qualified electrician and, in a booming state like Western Australia, there was to be no shortage of work.

That same year, Prime Minister Robert (later Sir Robert) Menzies, announced the return of conscription. The country had had it previously, but there had been no need to keep it going, so it had ceased back in the '50s. Now, however, with the looming threat of war in Indo-China, specifically: Vietnam, it was felt necessary to reinstate it. A popular theory espoused at the time by the Americans was the "Domino Theory." It was felt, that if communism was established in any of the Southeast Asian countries, then the rest would fall like dominoes. The PM announced there would be two call-ups a year and that all people turning twenty in the first 6 months of the year first and then the second six months of the year, must complete a registration for the National Service ballot. They didn't need every twenty-year-old in the army; that was just too many, so there would be a ballot, a kind of lottery to decide who would be drafted. Every six months, they would draw marbles from a barrel, each one representing a date of that six months. If your birthday fell on the drawn date, you were drafted. That meant you were most likely bound for Vietnam. That was one lottery virtually no person wanted to win.

Ted's marble was drawn. He could have applied for an exemption or deferment due to his apprenticeship, but he decided it was probably better for him if he just accepted his fate. He felt like he needed a change right then anyway. He felt he was already getting stale, even though he wasn't yet fully qualified. The apprenticeship would still be there when he returned anyway, so he would be able to take it up on his return.

"Besides," he thought, "this could be a lot of fun, couldn't it? I get to see a new country and travel overseas." He had been in the Army Cadets at school, so he already had a bit of an introduction to army life. It wasn't all that bad. You got to shoot guns and trek through the countryside and camp out. Not all bad!

Later that year, he headed off to training camp in New South Wales. They trained there for 6 months before deployment to the battles in Vietnam. His previous training in cadets had indeed taught him a little of what it meant to be a soldier, and before too long, he found himself promoted to section leader, a corporal. That meant he was the leader of nine men.

He returned to Australia in the first half of 1970 and the family was so glad to have him home again, but he was different. He did not seem like the same old Ted who had left two years previously. He seemed distant, like his mind was elsewhere. He hardly smiled anymore and his choice of music had changed. It was like it was more aggressive. He did not return to his apprenticeship, much to his father's dismay.

"He just bummed around and we never knew where he went most of the time, or who he even associated with," recalled Frank in later life.

Frank completed his Leaving Certificate in 1970, gaining passes in all seven subjects, including two distinctions. Apart from English, he studied Maths II and III, Physics, Chemistry, Economics and his favourite subject, Technical Drawing. He decided to go on to WAIT (Western Australian Institute of Technology) and study Architecture. At that time, students had a choice of University of WA, or WAIT. WAIT was only five years old in 1971, and it would be another fifteen years until it gained university status, coincidentally taking the name of Frank's former high school name, Curtin University. John Curtin was Australian Prime Minister from 1941 to '45 and saw the country through the bulk of WW2. It would be another six years before Murdoch University would open and twenty years before Edith Cowan University would be founded. In 1970, Perth was still really just a smallish provincial city of about 700,000, so tertiary education had limited choice unless you wanted to travel to the Eastern States of Australia, three thousand miles away.

Frank too, was concerned about the draft coming up for him in 1973. He needed to register for the draft in the year he turned nineteen. He did not want to go to Vietnam, even though he too had enjoyed his time in the Army Cadets if it was responsible for turning his brother into the person he now was. By this time, however, the public was turning significantly against Australian involvement in the war, with many a protest march and call for a Vietnam Moratorium. There was a federal election in 1972 and the campaigning on the part of the Labor Party, the current opposition, focussed predominantly on the involvement in that war. Their campaign slogan was "It's Time". Labor was dead against the war and we would be out as soon as they got voted in, they promised. It really was "Time" for them, as they swept into power with Gough Whitlam as Prime Minister, and he immediately cancelled the draft.

Frank was able to breathe a sigh of relief. He didn't need to worry about Nashos now. (Yes, we Australians abbreviate everything). At the same time though, he did experience a pang of regret, that he had not been able to do his bit for his country, like his brother had or like his father had. This was a new generation, but there were still ties to the old allegiances and the old ways. You know, fight for your country and all that. It was only twenty-five years since the end of WW2 and the Korean war had finished, at least for the Western nations, the year Frank was born, so all this ethos was still greatly in the public mind. ANZAC day, 25th April, was still commemorated in a big way, as many of the old diggers from WW2 were still around, mostly only being in their forties or early fifties, and even the veterans of WW1 were still here, although most were in their seventies and eighties. Thus, his attitude to "missing out" was understandable, even though by now he knew, Vietnam was not a war like WW2.

Frank did well at WAIT and graduated in 1975, taking a position with the architectural firm, J R Buckman and Son, in Rokeby Rd Subiaco. It was a relatively easy commute for him in those days via the new Stirling Bridge over the Swan River just upstream from the old Fremantle Traffic Bridge and up Stirling Highway. He plied that route for 8 years to the same firm each day, until he was offered a more prestigious position in King's Park Road, West Perth. In this firm, Allerton, Buckley and Frobisher, he was told he had the possibility of partnership in the future. The present partners were looking to expand into other areas and had been watching Frank's work, for the last year. They were beginning to see the 'end of Architecture as we know it' with much of their previous work now being done by Engineers and Computer Aided Drafting (CAD) was in its infancy, but its potential was great. The principals at ABF, as they called it, said that they felt that within 10 years, Architects would be relegated to being just draughtsmen if they were not prepared to adapt and change.

Frank relished the new challenge at ABF. He found he had more reign to experiment with design, rather than just doing as he was told, like at the last place and over the next couple of years, he started with the CAD system on the computer. By 1986, Frank was indeed offered a partnership, and in that year, the company became ABBF and associates. The firm went from strength to strength, picking up both private and government contracts due to their progressive and aggressive business nature.

Whilst he was at Buckman's, through the 70s and early 80s, Friday afternoons usually finished half an hour earlier than usual, and the workers all went down the road to a local tavern about 200m away. This became a sort of ritual for the guys. Frank had noticed one of the other regular girls going to the tavern on those Friday afternoons, and after several times seeing her, he decided to pluck up the courage and introduce himself. He found out her name was Lynne Morton, and she worked at the Commonwealth Bank just up at the corner of Hay St. Despite his many, halting attempts at conversation, Frank didn't get much joy from his first meeting. He felt a little like an imposter, barging in on a group of giggling girls, out after a pleasant afternoon together, so eventually, he excused himself and went back to his mates. Two Fridays later, they were all back there at the tavern, when Lynne came up and asked Frank why he had not come back to see her again. He tried to explain how he felt about the exchange, to which Lynne replied, "Oh don't mind them. They are just a bunch of bitches." Frank decided there and then that he really did like this girl. Lynne sat down with them for the rest of the hour they were there. When it was time to leave, Lynne turned to Frank and said, "Well, are you going to ask me out or not, Frank?" He was over the moon. He had been trying to pluck up the courage to ask, but in front of his mates, he felt somewhat lacking in courage.

"Um, yeah, sure. Do you like the beach?" he asked her.

"Like it? I love it!" was her reply, so they made a date for the next day to go to Cott. (Cottesloe Beach). Frank learned that Lynne was 6 years his junior, that she lived in Tuart Hill, a northern suburb of Perth and that she had lived there all her life. From there, it was onward and upward with their friendship, until one day in September of 1982, Frank finally popped the question and asked Lynne to marry him. Her reply was initially somewhat deflating, as all she could do was laugh. That didn't exactly do much for Frank's self-esteem. He figured he must have grossly misread the situation. His mind was, however, quickly put to rest when she answered, "What took you so long? Of course, I will."

They opted for a spring wedding the following year. On October 15th, 1983, Francis Albert Bailey and Lynette Joyce Morton became Mr and Mrs Bailey. They set up home in a rental house in North Fremantle. It was an old house, not too far from where Frank's father had worked at the SEW. Once Frank moved to ABF, in King's Park Road, his salary increased incrementally until he was in a position to look at buying. They both agreed that Cottesloe would be a delightful place to build, but prices there were already rising quickly, so they decided to buy old place and rebuild. They found a suitable place in North Cott, put in an offer and it was accepted. They moved in, during January - 1986, at the same time as Lynne announced she was pregnant. All in all, 1986 was a good year for the Baileys. New house, new child on the way and a partnership. Life was rosy.

Their son, Timothy Francis, was born on 14th October 1985, just one day before their 2nd wedding anniversary. Over the next two years, they demolished their house and built a brand new "Architect Designed" house. Frank's design. During the time they were building, they all moved in with his father and mother, as there was plenty of spare room in the East Fremantle house. Alby and Patsy were extremely glad to have their grandson staying with them. In 1989, a daughter, Eloise Patricia followed, and the Bailey family was complete. A pigeon pair. What more could one ask for?

Chapter 2
The Spark

Call out to me and I shall show you wonderful things, that you do not know.

Jeremiah 33:3

Tim and Eloise knocked on the door in East Fremantle, and as Frank and Lynne walked up the front stairs, Patsy opened the front door.

"Come in. Come in. You don't need to knock, just come on in. Hello, my darlings." Patsy embraced the two children together. My, oh my, how you two are growing up so quickly. It's only been two weeks, but I swear you have both grown. Ellie, you are the same height as your brother, aren't you?

"I'm still just a bit taller than her Granny. But I'll beat her from now on, you just watch." Ellie just poked her tongue out at her brother and Tim shot inside, calling as he went. "Hello Grandad."

Patsy looked at Lynne and laughed. "He sure doesn't want to be beaten, does he?"

"No Mum. He doesn't. Just like someone else, I could mention," replied Lynne, with a sideways glance at Frank. "Hello, Mum. How are you?"

"I'm fine thanks, Sweetie. Still putting up with Alby's nonsense." They all three laughed.

"Hello Mum," added Frank as he reached through and gave his mother a kiss on the cheek.

The house in East Fremantle was an old house, built somewhere around the 'twenties'. It was a house typical of the post federation style of architecture. It was a timber framed and timber weatherboard clad house, with a roof of corrugated iron, that had been painted multiple times and was now royal blue. The walls and verandah posts were a stark white, giving a fresh look to the whole house. It was built on stumps raised about half a metre, with wide verandahs on four sides originally but the verandahs at the rear had been filled in at some time, to include the laundry and toilet inside the house. Originally, the wash house, as it was called then, had been detached from the house, about a metre behind the back steps. This had since been converted into a garden shed. The old toilet had been situated on the back fence along the rear night cart lane, but that had been removed many years ago, although its old concrete base and half height walls were still there, currently being used as a base for the compost heap. In the front yard was a huge Jacaranda tree, which dominated the yard, and it was surrounded by beds of roses along the front and two side fences. A brick driveway went down the right hand side to an added garage and workshop at the side of the house. The door of that was of the same blue as the roof. There were cane chairs on the front verandah, so that Alby and Patsy could sit out there and enjoy their afternoon tea looking at their garden.

In the area to the right of the old wash house in the back yard, Alby had built a large patio area, with a pavement of old salvaged bricks. Patsy had spent hours chipping old mortar off these bricks before Alby had painstakingly laid them in a sort of Zig-zag pattern. He was extremely proud of his accomplishment of this area, and often sat out here reading the newspaper in the mornings. The rest of the back yard was lawn, with garden beds again around the edges. Both Alby and Patsy were really happy with their little paradise, probably more so because it was their own place. Alby had grown up in the area, but as he had no father, his mother had to exist on a War Widow's pension, and whatever else she could bring in with washing and ironing. She had never been able to afford a place of their own, so Alby was brought up in rented accommodation.

"Come on through," Patsy said. "I tell you, since your phone call last week, Alby has been on edge waiting for today. He is really looking forward to this. He has told me a thing or two over the last few years that would curl your hair, and I have said that he is not to share those with young Tim. He's still a little too young for some of that." Patsy said as she walked them through to the back patio.

"Oh, I think Tim might surprise you now, Mum. After the talk we had last week, I think he is transitioning through to adulthood, and has quite an understanding," replied Frank as he guided his mother down the passageway.

"All the same Frank, I wouldn't want him to tell some of that. He said he will be careful, so let's hope so. But you know him, when he gets going," said Patsy, now opening the rear screen door.

"Yep, I guess we will see. I'll keep a good ear on things anyway," added Frank "Hello, Dad. How are you going?" Frank greeted his father as he swung through the back door and onto the patio.

Alby stood up and answered, "Hello, Son. I'm as fit as a fiddle if you're talking about a broken fiddle," as he let out a booming laugh. "Hello Lynne, darling. Have a seat."

"Thanks, Dad, but I'll go and give Mum a hand. Come on Ellie. You can come help too."

"Okay, Mum. Are we getting lunch ready?" prattled Eloise.

"That we are, my dear," answered Lynne.

"Okay, Grandad, what can you tell me about the war?" Tim jumped straight to the point. He was sitting on the chair opposite his grandfather, with his elbows on his knees and his hands clasped to the front.

"Whoa back there, lad. Not so fast. I think we might have lunch first and then we can discuss this," Alby replied.

"Ohh! Alright. But the women are not here now." Tim showed his obvious disappointment.

"Alright!" said Alby. "I'll tell you what we will do. How about you tell me now what you already know, and after lunch I'll tell you what I know, if it's any different? Is it a deal?"

That seemed to satisfy Tim, so he told his grandfather what his father had told him about Uncle Ted and Vietnam and also about him being in WW2. He then added that during the week, he had gone on the internet and searched what he could about both the European sector and the Japanese sector of WW2. He knew it started in 1939, with the German invasion of Poland, and the pact between the Allied powers to defend the rest of Europe from the Nazis. He told him that he wasn't sure of the difference between the Germans and the Nazis. He always thought they were the same thing. They were certainly portrayed that way in the movies. He said he knew about Pearl Harbour, the Kokoda Trail, and the Burma Railway, but not much more. He did know that the Japanese were a cruel lot though. That seemed to come out everywhere in his reading.

By the time Tim had finished telling his grandfather all that he knew, Lynne, Eloise and Patsy came out with the lunch, so the conversation went on hold for a while. They had a pleasant lunch in the warm, late April, last days of autumn. When the lunch, was over, they all sat around waiting for Alby to open up. Frank broke the ice by asking, "So Dad, what unit were you in?"

I was a part of the 2nd 28th battalion, Son. It was raised here in Perth in 1940. Everyone in the battalion were volunteers. There was no conscription in 1940, son," he explained, looking at Tim.

"Not like for Uncle Ted hey?" Tim commented.

"No Tim. Everyone for this and WW1 were volunteers. We wanted to go and fight for our country, for the Empire," Alby was clenching his fist and jabbing the air.

"The Empire? What's that?" added Tim.

"What? Don't they teach that in school now? Really?" Alby looked shocked. After a pause, he went on. "Australia was part of the British Empire then. It's called the Commonwealth now."

"Oh that," replied Tim. "I know about the Commonwealth. Just never heard it called the Empire, that's all. What I don't understand, Grandad, is why would we go and fight in a war 12,000 miles away in Europe, when it had nothing to do with us?"

Alby let out a little laugh and answered as best he could. "A lot of people have asked that question Tim, and still do, but it is a different time now. Times are very different now. In 1914, Australia, as a nation, was only 13 years old and still considered itself like an outpost of England. Over a third of the fellows from here that enlisted were, in fact, born in Britain, not necessarily England, but from all of Great Britain. They felt an obligation,

I guess, to defend the 'Mother Country'. Not only that, but I really think that as a really young nation, we wanted to prove ourselves to the home countries and the rest of the world. Prove that we could cut it, amongst the best. The Pommie attitude to the Australian troops was proof to the men that we needed to prove ourselves. I even think that was still the reason for us joining the 2nd war as well."

"Okay, that's a bit of history I didn't really know. It sort of does explain the feelings at the time though," Tim replied.

"So, the 2/28 was a Western Australian battalion, made up of blokes from all over the state. Not just Perth, but from many of the country towns and farms. We were part of the 24th Brigade, 8th Division initially, but it wasn't long until we were reassigned to the 9th Divvy. We did some training at Melville camp here in Freo, before shipping off to Palestine, for further training. We initially had the white on blue diamond unit colour patch, but that was changed a couple of years later to the red and black 'T'. I was sad to see the white on blue go, mainly as they were the colours my father fought under, in WW1."

Frank jumped in here, "What, was my grandfather in the 28th?"

"Yes, Son he was. He was 28th, I was 2/28th. Pretty cool, huh?" replied Alby.

"Well, I never knew that," confessed Frank.

"Yeah, I was proud to wear the white-on-blue patch. It was like a connection to him. You see Tim, I never knew my father. He was killed in WW1, the Great War. Ha! Great War, my fat .... ." He paused, remembering he was talking to his grandson here, and that he had been sworn to civility by his wife. "Oh well, you know what I mean. It was supposed to be the war to end all wars. They got that wrong, didn't they."

"They sure did, Grandad. I don't think they will stop them ever," replied Tim.

Alby looked at Frank and smiled and nodded.

"So anyway, we were eventually assigned to North Africa to fight against the Italians. They were an easy foe really. Most of them didn't want to be there, so those that we didn't beat the pants off usually surrendered. Mussolini was their president or something like that and he was in Adolf Hitler's pocket, but at least half of the country did not want to fight. They were pressured into it."

Frank broke in again, "So that's why when I was a kid, there were all the Italian jokes around."

"Yes, Frank. It was a hangover from the war years," answered Alby.

"What sort of jokes Dad?" enquired Tim.

"Oh, I can't remember them all, but how about this one? How do you tell an Italian tank? Four reverse gears and one forward. And this one; What does an Italian flag look like? A white cross on a white background."

"Oh, they are daggy, Dad," said Tim.

"Yes, they are Tim," Alby answered. "But that was what the times were like. The Italians didn't have much fight in them. That was until Mr Hitler sent the Panzers over. They were commanded by General Rommel. He was probably the best General Hitler had. Our boys hated but respected that man."

"How can you hate and respect someone?" asked Tim.

"Well, Tim, you see, it was like this. We hated him because he represented everything that we were there fighting against. He was the representative of a totalitarian system that was trying to take control over all of Europe, including England. He had to be beaten, and he was a lot harder to beat than the Italians had been. At the same time, we respected him, as the man was a tactical genius. He knew how to fight a war. There was no doubt this man was a worthy adversary".

"Okay, I think I understand that," Tim replied with a nod of his head.

"So, when Rommel came into the picture, we were holding a place called Tobruk."

"I've heard of that," Tim chirped.

"That's good. The rest of the 9th divvy had moved forward to Benghazi when Rommel started pushing them and the Brits backwards. He pushed them all the way back, through the hard-fought ground, to Tobruk. The 2/28 and a heap of other Brits and Aussies held onto Tobruk for 6 months, in what was known as the siege of Tobruk. We held Rommel off for so long he got really pi....., I mean annoyed and he pulled back to regroup."

"That must have really pissed him off, Grandad," Tim knew what he meant.

They all laughed, but Frank gave Tim a clip over the ear. But still, they all laughed.

Patsy then spoke up and said, "Hey Ellie, how's about you give me a hand, cleaning this lot up?" She could see that this conversation was perhaps not suited to an 11 year old's ears.

"Okay, Grandma," She was getting bored with the topic anyway and she jumped up and started collecting the dishes.

All this time, Frank was thinking and shaking his head. "So, what you are saying Dad, is that you were one of the 'Rats of Tobruk'."

"That's right, son, the good old Rats," Alby replied with obvious pride in the name.

"Holy …… I never knew. How did I not know that?" Frank was both embarrassed and proud at the same time.

"What do you mean by Rats, Grandad?" asked Tim.

He laughed and leaned forward in his chair. "Well son, there was this guy in Germany called Lord Haw Haw."

"That's a silly name, isn't it?" asked Tim.

"Yes, it is. His real name was William Joyce, but he had this silly laugh, that sounded like someone going, "Haw Haw", so the English called him that. He was actually British himself, but went over to the Germans just before the war. He used to transmit radio into Britain all the time, what we call propaganda. He would always try and convince the English that they were losing the war, and on this particular day, he was talking about us in Tobruk. How we were dug into the ground, surviving like rats. We all heard about it and thought, "What a great name!" So we became 'The Rats Of Tobruk'." Then turning to Frank, he added, "Actually Frank, I did tell you that, but you may have been too young. Do you remember a movie that they always used to play on the TV on ANZAC day, in the sixties? It was called…."

"The Rats of Tobruk and it starred Chips Rafferty. Yes, I remember that one well. I loved it," replied Frank, recalling the excitement of that movie.

"Well, I remember telling you at the time, that was my mob. My mates." Alby explained.

"Well, I'll be buggered. I do not remember that," admitted Frank.

"I wondered why you never asked me more about it. I know we were not supposed to discuss it, but by then, I felt it would be okay. I mean, that was twenty years on. Up until then, most of us just wanted to forget it."

"So, you were a hero then, Grandad?" Tim exclaimed.

"Oh, good God, no Tim. I was just as scared as the next bloke. We were all scared, but together we were determined that this bastard, ... oh sorry Frank, this sod, wasn't going to beat us."

"Don't worry about using that word Grandpa. I'm 14, and at school, the language is way worse than that," admitted Tim.

"I'll bet it is," answered Alby and they all had a good laugh, even Lynne.

Alby went on to explain about their withdrawal from Tobruk by sea at night, and the remaining British then losing Tobruk and their return to fight Rommel at El Alamein. At the first battle of El Alamein, he explained that most of the remainder of the battalion was captured and spent the rest of the war as POWs. He was one of about ninety that evaded capture, and they were withdrawn to Palestine, where the battalion was reformed, this time with the red and black 'T' as their Unit Colour Patch. 'T' for Tobruk. From an original size of nine hundred men, only ninety remained. Then, following further training to accommodate the new fellows, the reinforcements, they were sent back to El Alamein and whipped Rommel's butt. This time, under the leadership of General Bernard Montgomery. 'Monty'.

By this time, the Australian Government was getting justifiably nervous about the Japanese. It looked likely that they were working towards an invasion of Australia. They had already conquered all of SE Asia, including the Dutch East Indies (Indonesia) and had only recently been defeated at Milne Bay and Kokoda Track by the Australian Militia and AIF, and the Government wanted their troops, in the Middle East, back in Australia. Alby explained that they all loaded up and headed back to Australia, for retraining for jungle fighting. There could not have been a greater contrast of terrain as there was from the desert of Libya and Egypt, to the Jungles of New Guinea.

"But if we had to fight an enemy, we would rather fight one that was threatening our own homeland. By now, the Japs had already bombed Darwin multiple times, as well as Wyndham, Broome, Derby and Port Hedland, here in WA. The public were by now scared that the Japs would invade Australia."

Tim thought it was incredible that our state had been bombed, but it had never been mentioned in history at school.

Alby then explained that they spent six months in Queensland up in the Atherton Tablelands, on their retraining, when all the guys wanted to do, was to, "Get at those damned Japs". They all knew about Milne Bay, Kokoda, Buna, Gona, Sanandana, and they wanted their fair share of the fight.

"In August '43, we were mobilised to New Guinea, finally," Alby explained. "After a brief stopover in Gili Gili, in Milne Bay, we were dropped by barge up the north coast east of Lae to try and cut off the retreating Japs. They dropped us off east of the Busu River and we were supposed to make our way, across this small river and take Lae, cutting the Japs off from their supplies. That was a great idea, but the Busu might have been a short river, but it was far from a small river. It was extremely fast flowing and unusually deep. Also, we had to cross that river whilst under fire from the Japs on the other side, and we lost a dozen or so men, just from drowning, trying to cross the thing. There are heaps of stories around the boys, of rescues and saves of all kinds. Some men were gone for all money, when another just reached down into the water and grabbed a handful of hair and dragged them back to the surface to life. That was a horrible crossing that one. All the survivors remember that night."

"Was there no bridge anywhere to cross?" asked Tim.

"Oh, good lord, no Tim. This is New Guinea. It was back then nothing but a country of natives, really. No cars, only foot travel. If ever they needed a bridge over a river, they built one out of jungle canes and timber. It would usually get washed away in the wet season, so they would just build another one the following year."

"Oh, I see. So, they had to walk everywhere?" Tim asked.

"And so did we, as it turns out. It was either walk or take a boat by sea. We took Lae and mopped up the remaining Japs that didn't flee to the jungle. In fact, we did it so quickly, command wasn't sure what to do next with us, so our command decided that we should join with the push up at Finschhafen, out on the Huon Peninsular. This was really a mopping up operation. The Japs had already been soundly beaten in New Guinea, but those guys just didn't give up. They had this honour code they called Bushido. Really, all it meant was fight or die. No other alternative. Surrender was never an option. If they found out they could not win, they were to commit Hari Kiri, which meant to kill themselves. The traditional way was with a sword or knife to the guts, but many of them just held a grenade to their stomach. We saw lots of examples of both."

Tim just sat there, shaking his head. He had heard about Hari Kiri before but wasn't sure if it was true or not. Frank, by now, having had his eyes opened wide, was sitting speechless as well.

"Hey, you know there was no word in Japanese for retreat either. The boys on Kokoda, tell stories of Japanese orders, telling their troops to, 'advance to the rear' coz there was no word for retreat in their language," Alby laughed. He always laughed at that fact.

Alby went on, "So we marched up Finschhafen coast, following these Japs in retreat. You know Son, the one thing I remember about that march?" Alby glanced around to ensure that Patsy and Ellie were not yet returning. "By now, most of the Japs had dysentery, you know, the runs, explosive runs, and to make it easier to shit, they cut the seat out of their pants so they could just squat, shit and continue running. There was so much shit on the road, or track it was really. When the Jap aircraft came along to strafe the roads we were on, we had to dive to the side of the track and lie face down, but you just couldn't. You wouldn't lie on the ground. You just couldn't. It seemed preferable to take your chances with the machine guns than to lie in that shit. You just got down, like in a push-up position, and kept your face and body off the ground, and hoped for the best. Thankfully, they were pretty lousy shots, and we lost only a few men that way. Anyway, to cut a long story short, we took Finschhafen and were pulled off the line in January '44 and sent home for a rest."

"Holy shit, Dad, I never knew," Frank was still shaking his head. Lynne was in tears and by now, had her arm around Tim, holding him tight.

"You know, we then spent over a year up in Queensland on training. We had the Japs in all of Southeast Asia including what is now Indonesia, on our northern doorstep and we were 'training', not fighting. Why? Because that boofhead MacArthur was not going to have the Australian troops showing up his Yanks any further. As far as he was concerned, the Australians were useless and the only good fighting troops were Yanks. What piffle." Alby sat shaking his head. He was obviously still upset by this betrayal by South-West Area Command.

"That wasn't the end for the battalion though, although it was for a great number of us. Being the tropics, most of us either had dysentery or malaria, so we lost a heap to hospitals, including me."

"Malaria," said Frank.

"Yep. So that was it for me. For those that went on, they were discarded by that tosser MacArthur, and relegated to 2nd or 3rd rate mop-ups, in Morotai. They sent the boys up there in May of '45. Our General Blamey was basically neutered by the 'Bataan Boys' and was powerless to do anything. MacArthur was the golden haired Yank, as far as our government were concerned. They definitely suffered from an inferiority complex, next to that idiot."

"I'm sure MacArthur put us on those secondary jobs, so his gallant Yanks could forge on to the Philippines and Japan. He couldn't have the Aussies outdoing his boys again. Following his promise, 'I shall return' to the Philippinos, that's all he could think of. That man wasn't even a general's bootlace. Nor were his bloody Yank troops much chop."

"Dad, you said our boys weren't going to outdo his Yanks again. What do you mean by, again?" Frank asked.

"Hah! Yeah, when the yanks first came into the fighting in north PNG, they were under the command of a General Eichelberger. He wasn't a bad bloke, and he knew his boys were still green. He put his lads in with ours so we could teach them how to fight in the jungle. Geez, they weren't much chop. Our boys were way better soldiers, way better fighters than his lot. They were just better resourced and better paid. So many times, in PNG, the Aussies had to try and fix the mess left by, or even caused by the Yanks. Eichelberger understood that really and was so grateful his boys could learn from ours. But Boofhead would have none of that."

There was a sort of bitterness in his voice now. Frank and Lynne could hear it. If Tim did, he did not say anything. He just sat quietly. He had worked out when it was wiser to maybe not speak. They all sat, for maybe a minute, to allow Alby to collect his thoughts. Eventually, he spoke, this time in a low tone.

"So, you see Tim, I wasn't a hero, but together with a bunch of other not heroes, we managed to survive and do just what the country wanted us to do. Preserve our way of life."

"I don't know, Grandad. You sound like a hero to me," then he went over to Alby and threw his arms around him and hugged him.

Lynne looked at Frank and said, "Yep, he is growing up, isn't he?"

Frank just nodded. Was that a tear Lynne could see in Frank's eye? If it was, it was just like the ones in Alby's eyes, and hers.

Eventually, Frank spoke. "Well, Dad, I am so sorry I didn't take the time to ask you about this before. I might have been a little more understanding growing up."

"No Son, it's fine. These things happen a certain way for a reason. They come out when they are ready to come out. At another time, it may not have meant so much."

"Maybe," Frank said. "Maybe."

Patsy had noticed that the discussion seemed to be over, so she and Eloise returned with a tray of tea and biscuits. This broke the ice yet again and they all sat around chatting about anything but the war. The afternoon drew on, and eventually, it was Frank who brought the subject up again.

"So, Dad, you mentioned your father was in the 28th in WW1. What else can you tell us about him?"

"Very little, I'm afraid," he replied as he reached into his jacket pocket, and withdrew a small, somewhat battered blue box with a push-button clasp. He opened it and inside Frank could see what appeared to be some medals with coloured ribbons attached. Alby slowly fingered through them until he produced three medals and placed them on the table. One had multicoloured stripes of all the colours of the rainbow on its ribbon with a gold coloured medal. The other looked a little plainer, with just blue, white and orange stripes and a silver coloured medal. The third, had a blue, white and red ribbon, with a silver medal embossed with a laurel wreath, crown, and the letters GvR and the inscription FOR BRAVERY IN THE FIELD. "They are your grandfather's medals, Frank," and he left it at that.

Frank reached forward and took hold of the first medal and looked long and hard at it. It was the 1914 - 1918 War Victory Medal. He placed it reverently on the table as though it was fragile and picked up the other, the 1914 -1918 War Service Medal. This was the first and only tangible evidence of the existence of his grandfather he had ever seen, let alone held.

"Look at the edge, Son," Alby suggested.

Frank turned the medal on its edge and rotated it slowly, as he turned it slowly said, "Three, five, seven, seven, Lt F A Bailey 28 Bat. AIF. A lieutenant, was he?"

"Apparently, Son, he was. Mum didn't talk about it much. She did say he was a wonderful man and that before he was killed, late in the war, he had been posted as missing presumed killed a year or so before. She could never work out what that meant.

She used to write to him all the time apparently and he would write back, but the mail was so hit and miss that she would get nothing for months and then she would get ten or more letters in one bundle. That made it hard to follow what he was doing. She said the letters stopped around the time he was posted missing in 1917. She kept writing but she got nothing back."

"This third medal, Dad. It has nothing on the edge. Any ideas why?" Frank asked his father.

"Yeah," he answered. "That one is a replica. The Army told Mum that the original was issued in 1917 to my dad. It's the MM; Military Medal for bravery. As it was previously issued, they couldn't reissue it. So, I purchased a replica some years ago."

"I see," Frank replied.

Alby reached into his pocket again and withdrew a bronze medallion, about the size of a small saucer. "This is my father's death Penny." He handed it to Frank.

"A death Penny? What is that?" A puzzled Tim asked.

"It is a medallion given to the families of every man that was killed in the first war. Sometimes, it was called the 'Dead man's Penny'. It has the soldier's name inscribed on it. It was called a penny because it was the same colour and material as the penny we had in our money at the time. You've seen a penny, haven't you?" Alby asked Tim.

"Oh yes. I see," Tim replied, looking over his father's shoulder.

Mum was told his body was never identified, so his name is inscribed on the wall of the missing, at Villers Bretonneux. And that Frank, is about all I can tell you."

"Okay," Frank replied. "I understand. It's a shame we couldn't find out more than that."

Tim started thinking about this last statement his father made. In his mind, he churned over a few thoughts and then spoke up again.

"Dad," said Tim. "I was wondering; if I was able to find out some of that other stuff about the wars on the internet, maybe we could find out something about him. Maybe there's a page on that sort of thing we could find?"

"Hmm." Lynne cut in. "Tim might have a point there, Frank. Maybe it is a possibility."

"Could be. I might ask around the office on Monday and see if anyone there knows," Frank was running through the people in the office in his mind, trying to think who the best person might be to ask. "We do have a lad on staff who is a whiz at this internet, you know. Now that the fear of the millennium bug is past us, I might look into it. Yeah, good idea."

"Anyway, right now, I think it is time we left Mum and Dad to their space and head home, don't you think?" Lynne suggested.

"Yes, I have a couple of things I still must do before work tomorrow, so we probably should get going. Come on, you two," Frank called to the two children, "time to pack up and head home."

"Oh, do we have to?" was the chorused reply.

"Yes, we do. Dad has work to do for tomorrow, and I must get your tea ready. That is if you want tea, of course," Lynne said with a smile.

"Of course, we do," Tim said rather indignantly. "You don't want us to starve, do you?"

"After the lunch you've just had, I don't think you're in any danger of that happening," chuckled Lynne.

"Come on then, you two," said Alby. "I'll give you a race inside."

"Oh yeah, sure Grandad. Like you have any chance of winning that one," replied Tim.

"Ya cheeky little sod," laughed Alby. "You wait 'til I get my hands on you."

Everyone gave a good laugh at this exchange and headed inside.

They bid farewell and headed back towards Cottesloe.

"Well, did that answer many questions for you, Tim?" asked Frank, as he was driving over the Stirling Bridge.

"Sure did, Dad," Tim answered. "Still, lots of questions though, isn't there?"

"Sure is, mate," replied Frank.

"So, did that answer many questions for you, Frank?" asked Lynne, shooting him a sideways glance.

Frank was shaking his head. "I just cannot believe I never knew this stuff. All along, he held that, and a lot more I'll bet, inside, and I never asked. I feel really guilty."

Lynne spoke slowly, "I can understand that, but at the same time, I can understand why he bottled it all in. I don't think you should be feeling guilty though, Hun."

"Especially as he said he must have told me when watching that film. I remember watching it every year. I used to look forward to it being on. I guess I must have been about ten at the time, so must have been a bit young to appreciate it. I mean, I knew they were Australian troops and they were famous, but .... My own dad! Cheeezzzee."

"So, he really was a hero, eh Dad?" Tim said from the back seat.

"Yes Tim," replied Frank. "I'm with you on that one. I'm going to have a word with Jeff at work tomorrow and see if he can point me in the right direction to try and find out more about my grandfather. My namesake."

"Oh, was his name Frank, too?" asked Tim.

"Yes, son. He was Francis Albert Bailey as well," he said.

"That's something else I've learned today, then. What a day, hey?" said Tim with a smile on his face.

"What a day indeed son," answered Frank.

Chapter 3
Answers

The more I learn, the less I realise I know.

Socrates

The following day, Frank headed off to work as usual, but with maybe a little more spring in his step. He enjoyed the work he was doing these days; it involved a lot more project management than actual architectural drawing. As his partners had said when they took him on, architecture was indeed now a dying vocation. They had adapted early and changed the focus of the company and by now, most of the drawings were computer drawn. Today though, he knew he had a new purpose to fulfil. He was going to do everything he could to find out anything else about his grandfather.

He arrived at work just a little earlier than usual and went to see Jeff, who was already making his morning cup of coffee.

"Morning, Jeff," he said.

"Oh, good morning, Frank. How was your weekend?" replied Jeff.

"Well, it's funny you should ask that, mate. It was sensational," he answered.

"Wow that's quite a statement, mate. What the heck happened to make it so good?" Jeff was amazed at the reply.

Frank went into a brief discussion of what happened at his father's place on Saturday.

"Wow, so that makes your dad one of the Rats of Tobruk," Jeff said.

"He was indeed, and to think all this time, I never knew. Now it is my time to do something for him," Frank replied. "And hopefully, that's where you come in."

"Me? How the heck am I involved?" Jeff expressed real surprise.

"Well, you see, my grandfather, dad's dad, was killed on the western front in 1918, and he knows fuck all about him. He was born after his father left for France, so never met him, and his mum didn't tell him anything about him much either. I thought, with this internet–well, my son thought, that it may be possible to find out a bit about him now, if there is anything out there. So, I figured you would be the most likely person I know who would know how to go about it. You see where I'm coming from?" Frank asked.

"Okay, I get ya," replied Jeff. "It's not an area I have done anything in personally, but I know there is stuff now available that may help you. I know a couple of people who are into that stuff, so I'll send 'em an email and see if we can get something that way. Is that okay?"

"Brilliant. Thanks Jeff. Oh, and by the way, it's white and one. Thanks," Frank was laughing as he walked off to his office. He left Jeff shaking his head. He did make him that coffee though.

About 2 hours later, he got an email from Jeff. It stated in part, *…. Contacted those guys I mentioned and have heard back from* *them both already. Yes, there are a few places they recommend looking at. Firstly, the National Archives of Australia, and then the Australian War Memorial, addresses at the end of this email. In the NAA site, it's a bit difficult to navigate at first, but you will get used to it, they reckon. You are looking for a 'Name Search' page. Just enter the details you have and it will give you some options.*

There are also unit records, so if you know which battalion he was in, for example, you will be able to read the day to-day actions of that battalion....

By now, Frank was getting excited. There is stuff out there, he thought. The message went on... *but beware not all records are digitized yet and some of them are not yet available. Others are not released yet but by paying a fee, they will mail you a copy of what they have....*

Frank was unable to wait until he got home to search, and he figured that as he was one of the partners here, his time was at his discretion, so he could spend it how he liked. He jumped straight onto the web, and searched his grandfather through the NAA.

Within five minutes, he found the 'Name Search' page. He was getting so excited by now. Carefully, he typed in Bailey, Francis Albert; he clicked on the category tab, not knowing what it meant. It instantly became clear to him, so he selected WW1. Up jumped another field, Service number. His heart sank. "Bloody hell, I can't remember that. Dad did mention it, but I don't know. I wonder if it's really needed?" He thought. He just clicked search and hoped for the best. Bingo!

Bailey, Francis Albert, 3577, Lieutenant, 28th AIF KIA 3 October 1918. Access open.

A chill ran right through Frank's body. He had goose pimples from head to toe. He just sat there looking at the screen, thinking to himself, *"Unbelievable. All this time, knowing nothing and now, in five minutes, I already know more. 3rd of October 1918. So, Dad was two and a half then. Shit!"*

He scoured the page for any more information and saw on the right side of the screen an icon of a couple of pages with "view digital copy" alongside. Eagerly, he clicked it.

What opened before him, left him totally astounded. There, in front of him, were his grandfather's enlistment papers. In his own handwriting, what is more.

At the top of the page, he read, Bailey, Francis Albert, 28th, date of enlistment 23.11.1915 He continued down the page. He was born in Kalgoorlie, a British subject, was 25 3/12 old and listed his occupation as Boilermaker. Yes, he had been an apprentice to a Mr. J Johnson for five years. He was married and listed Margaret Bailey (wife) as his next of kin. At the bottom of the page was his attestation, signed by him personally.

"Holy Shit!" he said quietly, or maybe not so quietly, as his secretary came in and asked if he was alright.

"Oh, I'm sorry, Gloria. No, I'm fine. I'm just finding out some stuff about my family I never knew."

"Oh, I see," she said. "Good or bad?"

"I spoke to Jeff earlier today, about whether it would be possible to find out about my grandfather's WW1 service. He was killed over there. My dad knows virtually nothing about him. He never met him. I have just found his enlistment papers and I am beside myself," Frank admitted.

"Oh yes, a lot of that stuff is available online now, isn't it? My brother has done the same for some of my relatives," she offered.

"Seems everyone else knew about all this, except me," Frank chuckled. "I cannot believe I have his handwriting in front of me."

Gloria came over to his desk. "Mind if I have a look?"

"Not at all. Just look at that," he said.

"If you look at that there," she said, "You can see that this is only page 1 of 22 pages. If you click on next, it will take you through all pages one at a time."

Frank was laughing now. He really was a dinosaur, he felt. Even my secretary knows what to do. "So it does," he said as he clicked on next.

"Tell, you what, boss. I'll hold your calls for the next little while. Unless there is something important, as far as I know, you are out of the office. Just let me know when you get back in. Okay?" She gave him a wink and left him to it.

Over the next couple of pages, he discovered Francis enrolled at Blackboy Hill camp, was twenty-five years and three months of age, was 5 ft 10 inch tall. "Holy moly! He was about the same size as me," he thought. He weighed 140lb, had a chest measurement of 33 - 36in, had a dark complexion, blue eyes, brown hair and was a C of E. He started laughing. This description could be him or his dad. Apart from the religion bit, he did not go in for that stuff.

He moved forward to the following pages: statement of service. *"Oh Hell," he thought, "I can't make head nor tail of this."* It was full of abbreviations and dates. Some of it was in red pen and some in black. It seemed to make a difference to the entry. Some of it he could work out, like 'to Hospital sick' and followed by 'rejoined unit', but most of it seemed to be in some sort of code or shorthand he thought. Slowly, he started to work out some more entries. Embarked Fremantle, some illegible date in January 1916. Arrived Marseilles 21/3/16. He must have gotten sick in July of 1916 and returned to his unit that same month. He guessed Cpl probably meant a promotion to corporal, late 1916, and late 1917 Sgt, which he took to be sergeant. 'Paid in France' written in red? That was a strange thing to write. So much gobbledygook.

"Gloria," he was on the phone to his secretary now. "These enlistment papers, do you know anything about them? What I'm seeing here is just jumble."

"Hang on," she replied. "I'll be right there."

She entered and closed the door behind her. "I have seen some of the stuff my brother has done, so I know a little of what is there. May I look?"

"Please, be my guest. I have been able to follow some of it, but all the abbreviations leave me lost."

"Let's see," she said. "Um, that one, TOS means Taken on Strength, so that's the day he is officially part of his group. Was he …? Let's see … yes, he was 9th Reinforcements, so that means he was the ninth group trained as reinforcements for his battalion. If you see GSW anywhere, that is Gun Shot Wound. You hope not to find that one. Sometimes they wrote WIA and sometimes Wounded in Action in full. I found that a little strange. Oh, he got a promotion to acting corporal, I see."

"Oh, was it acting, was it?" asked Frank.

"Yeah, see the a/ in front of it?" she pointed out.

"Ah, I see it now. I couldn't work out what that was," he answered.

"Oops, nup, he got it as a permanent promotion later there. See that?" She pointed to the line on the screen.

"Oh yeah. Got it. Strewth, you need a translator for this stuff," he scoffed.

"True. It took us a while to work out a lot of the bits and pieces on there," she added. "Mind you, there are still things we haven't worked out. Must be army jargon, or admin jargon we think."

Frank pulled away and turned his head toward her and said in a fully mocking tone, "What? Administration with their own jargon? Surely not. It would never stick!"

They laughed, and she went on to explain a few more bits and pieces.

"You want to print these out and take them home boss and study them. The more you look, the more you will see in them. Most of it will become clear eventually."

"I'll do that now. Ah, how?" He could not see how to print it out. She took him through that and then left him to it.

Frank found it hard trying to concentrate on his work that day. Every few minutes, he would drag the papers out and pour over the next page. That was until he got to one page in particular. The date was marked as 1.10.17 and the entry KIA. Even he knew that meant Killed in Action. The strange thing was, it was crossed out with a single line and a following entry read, 'To Hospital wounded' and then 'Rejn unit' just over a week later. What the blazes did that all mean? He thought, maybe they thought he was killed, but he was later rescued and sent to hospital. He could not put the papers down after that, so he decided he might as well go home and read them, instead of wasting time in the office doing it. Gloria agreed with him and said she would take care of anything that came up for the rest of the day. Thankfully, the workload was light at that time, so it was simple enough to do.

Lynne got quite a shock when he walked in a little after 2 pm. "What on earth are you doing home at this time?" she asked, stopping her work. "Are you ill?"

"No, Sweetie. You are not going to believe this, but you just got to see what I've been able to dig up on my grandfather." He started rummaging in his briefcase.

"Really?" Lynne asked. "You have found something already?"

He thrust the handful of A4 sheets into her hand and said, "Look! That is my grandfather's writing. His handwriting."

"No! Are you serious?" came the astounded reply.

"Yep. These are his enlistment papers and his service record. A lot of it is sheer gobbledygook, but I have been able to decipher some of it. I just couldn't stay at work any longer. I had to come home and show you. As soon as I can decode some more, I'll go straight over to Dad's and show him and Mum too." Frank was showing his excitement as he explained.

"Unbelievable!" said Lynne. "And this was just from today?"

"Yep!" Frank answered. "I spoke to Jeff this morning when I got there and explained what I wanted and he said he had a couple of mates who would probably know and pinged them off an email, and within a couple of hours, he had replies from them, which he forwarded to me. Within five minutes, I had this. Five minutes and we have answers to eighty-year-old questions. Why the hell hasn't someone communicated this to us all before?" He threw his hands in the air as if pleading for help.

"I guess it's like your Dad said yesterday. Right time, for the right reasons. When you are ready for it, these things happen." Lynne was often the moderating influence, the voice of wisdom in the family.

"Well, thank heavens we have found this now, before Dad chuffs off. I'd hate to find it out after he had gone."

"Yeah, I get that, but it's too late for Margaret, isn't it?" Lynne remarked.

"Yeah. I guess that's true. Although, depending on your beliefs, she may already know," Frank answered.

"I'd like to think she does Darling, and that she is finally reunited with her Frank," she added.

"Oh, and by the way, apparently, he hated the name Frank. For him, it was always Francis. Dad said he was particular about that. His mum told him that," he explained.

"Okay. Francis it is," she said.

The two of them sat down at the table and browsed through the twenty-two pages. Some of them were just repeats of other pages or something with meaningless scribblings on them. There were only about a dozen pages of any consequence. He showed her the strange entry of KIA or not, and she agreed that Frank's assumption was probably correct. They followed it through then, to his final KIA, which was dated 3.10.18. Frank also worked out that his grandfather had been promoted to Lieutenant in February of that year. The two of them agreed that it was a shame it was so near the end of the war that he was killed.

"Oh, it's just dawned on me, Lynne. Where are the kids? I was forgetting it's still holidays for them," Frank had been so engrossed in his discoveries he had completely forgotten the kids should have been there too.

Lynne had a chuckle and then answered, "Ellie is over at Robyn's and Tim is up the street at Kevin's for the afternoon. They should be home fairly soon actually," she said glancing at her watch.

"Have been so engrossed in these pages today, I have been unable to think clearly about anything else," Frank admitted. "So much so, that Gloria even recommended that I just go home and go over it with you."

"Yes, she is a clever one, that Gloria. You're very lucky to have her there," Lynne commented. She also knew she had nothing to worry about with Gloria. She was head over heels in love with her beau, so had no need to do the 'secretary thing' with Frank.

"So, if Grandad was killed on the first of October in 1918, I wonder where that was? Surely, if we have been able to find out this stuff, we must be able to find that out somewhere," pondered Frank.

"What about your emails, if they told you where to find this was there anything else in there that might help?" Lynne asked.

"Oh, of course!" Frank exclaimed. "There was more info in that. I'll check that out now. There was something in there about unit records I remember that they mentioned."

Frank immediately opened the computer on the family room desk, pulled up his email programme and opened the appropriate email from Jeff.

"Yep! There it is," he chipped. "The AWM website for the Australian War Memorial in Canberra. Let's see what we can find out there."

Frank sat at the computer, waiting for the page to load, with Lynne hanging over his shoulder, watching and waiting as the homepage loaded. They fiddled around for a while with different links, trying to find their way through, until they found a lengthy list of records from the first AIF. They glanced down the list. It seemed endless. There were headings for schools, catering, salvage, supply, tunnelling, even veterinary and nursing pages. They scoured the list until Lynne pointed to 'Infantry'.

"That would be it, wouldn't it?" she said.

"I guess so," said Frank. He clicked it and waited to see where it went.

"Oh, my goodness!" Exclaimed Lynne. "It's a bigger list than the last page. Brigade? Do you know what that is?"

"Um, I think it's a bit like the battalion, but a bit bigger," he paused. "I remember Dad saying he was 2/28 battalion, part of the 24th brigade and ninth division, but that was WW2. I have no idea what brigade the 28th was in WW1. Oh, wait a minute, the list goes into battalions further down. There it is, 28th Battalion. That's what we're looking for."

Frank clicked on the link to the 28th and they waited again, for the next page to load. Both their mouths dropped open when the month-by-month listing of battalion involvements, unfolded in front of their eyes. Frank asked Lynne to pass him the papers he had printed out, casting his eyes down for the entry that was crossed out. His grandfather's first KIA record. He checked the date and said, "1.10.17. October 1917, let's see what they've got for that time."

"Oh, my goodness!" Exclaimed Lynne. "A hundred and sixteen pages. This is going to take longer than your first find."

"Does look like it. Let's see what it all is, shall we?" Frank suggested.

"Hi Mum, I'm home," Tim walked in the back door and called out.

"At the computer, Sweetie," Lynne answered.

"What are you doing here, Dad?" Tim asked as he walked over. "Are you sick?" His dad was never home at this time of day. Frank just shook his head.

"Well, Son, you were right about there being stuff on the internet about your great-grandfather. We've found lots," Frank told Tim. "I couldn't stay at work with all this, so I decided to come home early."

"Really?" Tim replied. "Already?"

As Lynne handed the bundle of papers to Tim, she explained, "These are his enlistment papers and his service record, from his time in the Army. It has a lot of information in it that none of us knew. Some of it doesn't make sense to us yet, but we are just following up on some of the leads. Dad's checking the unit records now for the time that he died."

"And there it is," sighed Frank. He read out what he could. There were lots of pauses as he tried to read what was written. It had been written in pencil at the time and the scanned documents were difficult to read in places. "October 1st. 28th Battalion ... divided into carrying parties.... did .... exceptionally fine work. Captain King MC wounded. Casualties, officers wounded 6, O/Rks, I guess that means other ranks, K 62, W 85 M5. I take it all that means, killed, wounded and M. What would M be?"

"Missing?" Lynne suggested.

"Oh yes. Missing, of course," Frank answered.

"So was Great-grandad one of the killed or one of the missing, do you think, Dad?" asked Tim.

"I guess we will never really know, Son," Frank answered.

"Unless there is a list in the remaining hundred-odd pages," Lynne suggested again. "Does it say where this was, Love?"

"No, it doesn't. Ahh, there is a reference here in the place column: Sheet 28 NE and another below it the following day: Sheet 28 NE, D23ac. I have no idea what that means. Let's see…. The previous day talks about a place called Broodseinde Ridge," Frank turned and looked at Lynne as he said, "Heard of it?"

Lynne shook her head.

"Google it, Dad," Tim was one step ahead.

"Good call. Let's see now. Oh, there we are, it's in Belgium, near a place called Zonnebeke. Oh, It's just south of Passchendaele. Bugger me! Passchendaele!" A shiver ran down Frank's body as he said it. "Everyone knows about Passchendaele, Son. It was a place of horror on the Western Front. Horrible mud and so much death. Even I know about that one. I've heard Dad talking about it. Dad!" He exclaimed. "I need to take this information to Dad."

"You go on over, Love. I'll have to wait for Ellie to come home. Do you want to go with Dad, Tim?" Lynne asked.

"Sure do!" replied Tim eagerly.

Lynne turned to Frank and added, "I think Tim deserves to be there when you tell him, don't you?"

"Absolutely," replied Frank. "If it wasn't for his questions, we would never have found this out." Tim smiled a big smile. *That is very true*, he thought to himself.

In the car on the way to his grandparent's house, Tim did a lot of thinking. He looked at his dad as they drove along and he was smiling. "You're pretty pleased we found this stuff, aren't you, Dad?" He asked his father.

"I sure am, Tim. You see, if we had not found this information, my dad, your grandfather may well have gone to the grave, not knowing anything about his dad. As you heard on Saturday, he has always had unanswered questions about him, and it has always bothered him. Now we can give him some answers. I am sure he will be happy to find this."

Frank was absolutely correct in his thoughts on his father's reception. In fact, as he showed him the enlistment papers with his signature on the bottom, he could see tears in his father's eyes. Patsy sat next to Alby and hung on his arm as he read the papers. She was in tears too, just watching her husband's reaction. Finally, he had some answers. When Frank told him about the unit notes, of the day he was incorrectly KIA and said it had mentioned Broodseinde, Alby immediately replied with, "Passchendaele! So, he was at Passchendaele." As soon as he said that, he let out a big sigh, sat back in his chair and closed his eyes. Now, the tears were unmistakable. It was no longer just a glistening around his eyes. There were full-blown tears, slowly dribbling down the lines and wrinkles of his face, until they reached the corners of his mouth. No one spoke for a while, until Alby himself broke the silence, "Thank you SO much for finding this. It answers a lot of questions for me."

"Don't thank me," said Frank. "Thank Tim, for bringing it up in the first place. If he hadn't done that, we would still be in total ignorance, and to think this information has been sitting there, for heaven knows how long."

"Tim? Come here, Son," Alby beckoned to Tim. Tim went to Alby and Alby held out his arms and gave him the biggest hug. They just hung on to each other. Patsy sat on the arm of the chair next to them and smiled. The tears were still flowing.

"I haven't followed everything through yet, Dad," Frank explained. "We just had to bring what we had to you immediately. By the way, you hang on to these papers. I'll print off another lot when I get home. Maybe you can explain some of the abbreviations and notations to us too."

"I've got to be able to see clearly first, Son," he laughed as Patsy passed him a tissue and he wiped the tears away. Frank had been used to looking at his father's lined, expressive face, but now he saw something different etched in those lines. It looked to him that his face seemed more relaxed, more contented. *Was that just imagination,* he thought or was that face finally showing healing after this long overdue information?

For the next half hour, Alby scoured through the papers, identifying what he could and showing Frank and Tim what some of the notations meant. He pointed out the acting corporal temporary promotion, and then the full promotion where he was made sergeant and then Lieutenant, both of which occurred after his false KIA.

Frank and Tim left Alby and Patsy to continue alone and went back to Lynne and Ellie late that afternoon, feeling a decidedly special golden glow and feeling incredibly pleased with themselves. As soon as they got home, Frank printed out a new set of his grandfather's papers and made some notes on them of the parts that Alby had explained. He decided that he would take his time with the unit records, as there was so much to go through. By now though, he had some key dates that he wanted to follow up on. His promotion dates and places, and where and when he was killed. He decided to work backwards from his death.

His records indicated he was 'Killed in Action' on 3.10.18, so Frank jumped forward to October '18, where he found he was in a detailed description of a battle of some kind. Often in these records, a single page may be devoted to a week's worth of activities, but here he found four pages of close handwriting devoted to three days action. He studied it closely. Each day's account started with the weather. He was reading it aloud to himself. "Very fine... Support line ... Artillery in vicinity of Bellicourt, don't know that one. Hot meal at 4 am. Right flank BANK COPSE. I guess those are map references. That would make identification easier, if I knew what that was. Advance to Lormisset. Don't know that place either. Beaurevoir line? Wonder what that is? Push on to Prospect Hill. Ahh, there we are. Three lieutenants killed."

Now, he had something to go on. He left his computer to find the trusty old Reader's Digest Atlas and look up Lormisset and Bellicourt.

"Hey Lynne, Tim, have a look at this. I think this is where Grandad was killed. The records show a big battle around here," he said, pointing to the map. "That's east of Amiens. Oh there, Bellicourt, that's the name in the records that the artillery was hitting. That's where they formed up, ready for the battle. There's also a name, Bank Copse. I can't find that."

"Who'd have thought, a week ago, you would be pouring over maps and war records to find where your namesake had been? Wow, we really are in the age of information, aren't we?" Lynne commented.

"So where in particular did he get killed?" asked Tim.

"Don't know yet. Still looking, but this was where they were two days before and this battle seemed to last three days," Frank answered. "They were in reserve for the first two days, then from Bellicourt, northwest to Lormisset, not that I have any idea where this Lormisset is."

"Right, can you pack it in for a few minutes, Darling? Dinner is ready. You can go back to it after dinner," Lynne didn't want to pour cold water on the investigations, but the kids needed dinner after a full-on day.

As soon as dinner was over, Frank was straight back into it. Lynne had never seen him so engrossed in a task, other than work, as he was with this. This was something that was really important for him, obviously. By now, she well and truly realised just how important this information was for him, more so, as information to pass on to his father.

"Looks like the 28th came from the reserve and took over on one part of the front. Looks like they ran into a heap of machine guns, at what looks like a map reference. Then, they took the machine gun positions and a heap of prisoners. Oh wait, it looks like there's a map attached here somewhere. Great! I'll see if I can find it."

He did not find it there. It may have originally been attached to the records, but not now. Having such specific map references would probably have allowed him to pinpoint where this action took place. For now, he had to be satisfied with the general area which had been identified.

Over the next few days, Frank was able to trace his grandfather's whereabouts back from Bellicourt, to Mont St Quentin, through Albert to Villers Bretonneux, Morlancourt, Amiens and to their arrival at the Somme region on 4th April 1918. Prior to that, they had been in Northern France and Belgium. Their time in Belgium in the latter part of 1917 had been divided between the Red Lodge area below Hill 63, Plug Street Wood and an area east of Ypres, near a town called Zonnebeke and an area a little further east known as the Broodseinde ridge. The latter two of these were a part of the third battle of Ypres, also known as the 'Battle of Passchendaele'. Frank had managed to plot his grandfather's journey, through the last year of his life. This basically, was the extra year granted to him after his false KIA. He would trace his grandfather's service back further, but this was the area of his service in which he was most interested, as he was unable to explain the quandary of his seemingly being killed twice.

Frank attempted to draw a map from the Atlas, onto which he traced his grandfather's movements on and off the front line. The first part of 1918, before their transfer to the Somme, the 28th Battalion spent a lot of time on either rest or retraining. He could tell from the weekly reports that the attrition rate within the Battalion was significant during battle and reinforcements were not keeping up with their losses. He could also tell why it was that when his grandfather started getting promotions, he went through to lieutenant fairly quickly. The role of a lieutenant (pronounced "left tenant" in British countries) was leading a platoon, which in World War I consisted of about fifty men. He had a 2 I/C (second in charge) of a sergeant, and there were three corporals, leading a section each of about fifteen men, with a 2 I/C of a lance corporal. The lieutenant was expected to lead his platoon into battle, so was the officer level most often killed or wounded. Most other officer levels, apart from maybe captain, oftentimes remained behind the action. This was not a reflection of their courage, as most of these men had already progressed through the lower ranks and had survived. It was just that above the level of captain, the ranks were more involved, at an organisational level. Also, there were also a lot more lieutenants than any other officer rank. An infantry battalion would have at least sixteen second lieutenants, four lieutenants, four captains, a major and a lieutenant colonel, just in the basic structure. There would be ancillary lieutenants as well.

Many of the smaller towns and villages that were mentioned in the unit records did not show up in the Atlas, but in this day and age, with the help of the Internet, he was able to find where these villages were and get a fairly accurate image of his path to the Somme.

It was still not clear to him, even at this point, how his grandfather had been listed as KIA and then returned to duty a week later, after having been noted as injured. Reading the unit diaries was one thing, but the appendices that supported those diaries was another altogether. Each month from here on in had around four hundred pages of appendices and wading through those, looking for any information on his grandfather, was a mammoth task. Most of these appendices were just boring day to day operational tasks, but occasionally they contained information on the operations the men were involved in, as well as the casualty lists and reports. Unfortunately, to his disappointment, he could find no reference to answer this strange occurrence. Still, he figured, they probably could not record everything, even though this seemed to be rather strange.

By the time Frank had been searching the records for a month or so, Lynne was becoming concerned about the amount of time Frank was spending on this quest. It was like it was becoming an obsession to him, which, in all fairness, it probably was. He often said in discussions on his findings, that it was a bit like being a detective on the trail of the fugitive. Piecing together little bits of information, in order to build a bigger picture, to trace the actions and whereabouts of that fugitive. He was, in his own words, "having a ball", at the same time furnishing his father with more information.

As time went on, it became clear to Frank that the only way he was going to be satisfied with what he had found was to actually go to Europe and retrace his grandfather's steps.

"Lynne?" Frank uttered one evening. "What do you think about the idea of us heading to Europe during these coming school holidays? I have so many bits and pieces, that I just can't seem to put together and I'd like to see the places he was."

"Well, Hun," Lynne answered, "I have to say, I'm not the least bit surprised by your suggestion. I've been expecting it for a couple of weeks now. I have already started making enquiries about how to go about it. Our passports are all in date, so if you think we can do it, then I agree."

"You never cease to amaze me, woman," Frank said with a smile on his face. "You always seem to be one step ahead of me. Love you, Sweetie."

"Love you too, Darling. You want to tell the kids yet?" Lynne asked.

"I guess we'd better, hey?" Frank sighed.

"Hey kids, do you want to come in here for a minute?" Lynne called to the lounge room.

"What's up, Mum?" Tim said as he came into the room.

"You two have any idea what you want to do for the holidays next month?" Asked Lynne.

"Ah, not really," said Ellie.

"It would be nice if we could all go on a holiday, somewhere warm," Tim suggested.

"Well, Dad and I were just talking, and Dad has an idea about what we can do, haven't you, Dad?" Lynne taunted them.

"Well, you both know I have been researching this stuff on your great-grandfather, so I wondered if maybe, we should go over there to France and Belgium and have a look," Frank told them.

"Are you serious?" Tim crowed, his mouth remaining open in amazement.

"Yes! Yes! Yes!" was all Ellie could say.

"That would be awesome!" Tim added.

"That means I'll get another stamp in my passport," said Ellie excitedly.

"Yes, my dear, you probably will," Lynne said smiling. There were only three years between the two children, but there was a big distance between their maturity. Time would change that fairly quickly, though.

"Will we get to see Paris?" Asked Tim.

"We haven't worked it out yet, Sweetie, but I imagine we will. I would think that's where we would start. Either there or London," Lynne told him.

The remainder of the evening was spent looking at possible itinerary choices and flight arrangements. The Bailey household consisted of four ecstatic people that night. The next day, Lynne organised the flights to Paris for the four of them and started to check out accommodation in the city for the first night. They had decided to hire a car to give themselves more independence, to be able to go when and where they needed Frank to follow his grandfather.

$$\diamond$$

Chapter 4
Down On The Somme

**Wars are not paid for in wartime,
the bill comes later.**

Benjamin Franklin

The second week of July saw them on their way to the airport. Alby and Patsy drove the family to Perth International Airport for their departure. There was a great deal of excitement in the car on the way to the airport. Tim wondered aloud what movies they would get to see on the plane. Ellie was more interested in wall-to-wall cartoons. Lynne knew that she was more likely to fall asleep.

"So, Son," asked Alby. "What's the plan? Time in Paris first, or straight to Belgium?"

"We'll probably need a day in Paris first, just to acclimatise, get over the jet lag, then head up to Amiens, which seems to be pretty central for the Somme part of the story anyway. I guess we will spend a couple of days there, then head up to Ypres. I don't want the whole time to be spent on following Grandad. I've got a wife and two kids here to keep happy too." Frank sent a wink to Lynne.

"Yes, he'd better remember that, Dad," laughed Lynne.

"Yeah, it's going to be great to follow in his footsteps, but don't neglect the rest of the family, Son," added Alby. "I take it you have all the paperwork?"

"Sure do, Dad," replied Frank. "Probably got way more than I need, but I decided to take what I had, just in case. I'm hoping to get a few maps over there, so I can overlay my rough ones onto real scale ones. That way, I'll be better able to explain it to you when I get back."

"I have to say, Frank, I can't wait to see what you get. Take lots of photos, won't you?" Alby asked.

"We will, but I guess eighty-two years since it finished, there won't be much to show for it," added Frank.

"You may well be surprised there, my boy. I understand, both the French and the Belgians have preserved a lot of sites of importance," Alby informed him.

"That would be nice, Dad. One can only hope so," Frank replied.

Alby dropped them all at the terminal and went to find parking. By the time he returned, the four of them had checked in and were headed for the coffee shop.

"Bloody expensive parking here, isn't it? I remember when the airport was first built here in, oh, must have been about '62, parking was free. There was a bloody great big Lancaster from the Second War parked over there. I think it's now in the Bullcreek Museum now," Alby said.

"What, one of the big bombers, Grandad?" asked Tim.

"Yes, Tim," Alby answered. "When you get back, we should make a day and go there. It's really rather good."

"Have you been there, Grandad?" Tim questioned.

"That I have Tim. It's predominantly an RAAF museum, but there is more to it than just that. We'll make it a date, hey, Son?" Alby promised.

"Cool!" I've never seen a Lancaster up close," Tim added excitedly.

Once they had finished their coffees and milkshakes, it was time to go through immigration and passport control. They all said their goodbyes and the four intrepid travellers headed off through the doors into the depths of the airport. Once airborne, Tim got to watch his movies and Ellie had an endless choice of cartoons. Frank and Lynne took it in turns to sleep, or if the children were asleep, they both did.

The following day, they arrived in Paris, landing at Charles De Gaulle Airport. Once through customs, it was onto the train to the Gar Du Nord, followed by taxi to their accommodation. Lynne had found them a little place in the backstreets of Arrondissement 1, that was central and convenient, but not cheap. Still, it would only be for two nights, just long enough to recover from the flights and to see a few of the Paris sights. They would have a few hours to catch up on sleep that afternoon and use tomorrow to see a little of the main attractions. The children wanted to climb the Eiffel Tower, but Lynne knew the queues would be long. That would be a wait-and-see job.

The following day, Notre Dame, Arc de Triumph, Champs Elysée, and the Tuileries, would all be within walking distance of their hotel, as would the inevitable markets. The day they had for their walk around was nothing short of spectacular. A lovely mid-summer day in Paris, strolling down the Seine, admiring all the artists and artisans, then wandering up through the Place de la Concorde and the Tuileries gardens to the Champs Elysée. The children were astounded at how wide the road was. They had never seen anything like it. Cars everywhere honking and ducking and diving up the tree-lined avenue. It was a long walk up to the Arc de Triumph, but Lynne and Frank broke it with a stop along the way for coffee and cake. Lynne had studied French at school, but that was a long time ago. It proved to be enough to get by though. She surprised herself how easily it came back to her. She laughed every time Frank asked if they spoke English; the answer was, of course, "No", but when she explained they were Australian, suddenly, they did speak some English, and they were warmly welcomed.

"It is incredible, that the same old prejudices exist today, isn't it? The French really do despise the English, even today. You think they would be so grateful that they came to their aid to protect them from the Germans in two world wars. Not just one, but two," Frank commented softly.

"True, but I think the resentment goes way back beyond just the last eighty years. There are centuries of history behind this attitude," Lynne remarked.

"Yes, but you think there would be a bit of gratitude, wouldn't you?" Frank was genuinely puzzled by the overtly anti-English attitude in Paris.

"Let's face it, Frank, the English are a fairly arrogant lot," Lynne added. "Born to rule the world and all that. So, I guess it's like two similar magnetic poles coming together."

Tim, laughing, commented, "Yep, like poles repel. We learnt that in science. But I thought you were talking about the French, not the Poles."

Both Lynne and Frank groaned as Tim laughed.

"It will be interesting to see what reaction we get from the French out of the city area to us being Australian," Lynne commented. "I understand Aussies are warmly welcomed in some areas, particularly Villers Bretonneux, I believe."

"Yes, they have a school there, that has "Remember Australia" in their main quad," Frank said.

"Really?" Queried Ellie. "Why would they have that?"

"Well, Ellie, you see, back when your great-grandfather was at the war over here, Germany had taken over the town of Villers Bretonneux and destroyed everything. They kicked the locals out and took the town for themselves. When Great Grandad's men came through, they kicked the Germans out and gave the town back to the townspeople. They were so grateful they have named lots of places in the town after parts of Australia," Frank explained.

Lynne went on, "A lot of our men, engineers and troops helped rebuild the town too. They gave them back their town and their dignity. That was extremely important to them, so they are incredibly grateful. I'm sure you will see what we mean when we get there."

"I can't wait," Tim added, rubbing his hands together.

"We will go there, don't worry, but not straight away. We are going across to Amiens first, then Perrone and we will come back through Villers Bretonneux, so you won't have long to wait," explained his father.

They finished their walk up to the Arc de Triumph and just stood in awe at its size. The children could not believe the traffic there. How no one collided with another was beyond belief. Frank guided them over to the tunnel and they heaved a sigh of relief at not having to try and cross that road. Once they made it to the Arch, it looked even bigger than before.

"Are we allowed to go up it? Asked Tim.

"Sure," answered Lynne. "We just need to go over there to the stairs and up you go."

"There's the Eiffel Tower, Ellie," said Tim, pointing it out to his little sister.

"Oo, it's big, isn't it?" she replied.

"Are we going there, Mum?" asked Tim hopefully.

"We will go there from here, but I think you will find it's got very long queues to go up. We will have to see," Lynne explained to them.

The view from the top was a little disappointing, Tim told them. He thought they would be able to see more.

"There's not many big buildings here, are there, Dad? There's bigger buildings in Perth," he said.

"Yes, Paris is very big and spread out but they are not so much into high rise," Frank explained. "I think the soil here is not suitable for tall buildings. But look, you can see the Eiffel Tower." Then, pointing to their left, "And over there is the Sacre Coeur."

"We've seen the Eiffel Tower, Dad. What's the other one?" asked Tim.

Frank pointed to Tim's mother, and she explained.

"It is a famous church, over in the Montmartre area. Do you see how white it is? That's because of the stone they built it from. It sits high up on the hill overlooking the rest of Paris. The name Sacre Coeur means Sacred Heart. If we get time when we come back next week, I'd like to take you there. It's beautiful."

The children had never seen an intersection that had twelve roads coming into it, as they did here at the Arc de Triumph. It looked chaotic and yet the cars all missed each other. After about twenty minutes, they headed down to the tree-lined Avenue Kleber, back towards the Seine River. There was so much for the children to see, and to make it more interesting Lynne taught them a few French words from along the walk. In no time at all, they found themselves at the Jardins du Trocadero, the Trocadero Gardens, with a massive vista of the Eiffel Tower.

"Wow! Will you look at that," yelled Tim. "That's even bigger than it looked from the Arch. Wow, it's massive."

"It's pretty isn't it, Mummy?" chorused Eloise. "With the gardens in front of it, it makes it look pretty."

"It does, doesn't it, Sweetie," Lynne answered, then turned to Frank, grasping his arm with hers. "Oh, it is spectacular Frank, isn't it?"

"It certainly is impressive," Frank agreed. "Even more so that it was built one hundred and ten years ago,"

"Can we go over there, Dad?" pleaded Tim.

"Of course," Frank answered. "Just stay together until we actually get there. We still have a bit of traffic to navigate."

They made their way through the Trocadero gardens, across the Pont d'Lena and into the courtyard at the base of the tower. Tim just stood and stared in awe at the mighty structure, whilst Eloise was more interested in the many busking acts around the park. She had seen the tower already. Frank made enquiries about the elevator climb and brought back some not-so-good news. Indeed, the Eiffel Tower climb had a queue of well over an hour, so they just looked and moved on. Disappointed as they were, the children were old enough to understand there was better use of their time at hand. But not before purchasing one of the many models of the famous tower. That would indeed be a useful prop back at school, to show the other kids.

The day was slipping by rather quickly, and they turned and headed back to their hotel. Along the way, they slipped into a street market off one of the main streets. It sold all kinds of wares, from clothing, fruit and vegetables, jewellery, toys, electronics and just about anything you could name. Of course, Ellie wanted everything she saw. They did indulge in a few trinkets and decorations for their home, as well as some refreshing cool drinks, which by now had become a necessity. By this time, the little legs among the small party were beginning to wear out, so they all headed for their lodgings.

The following day, they took the train to the outskirts of Paris, not all that far from the airport, to pick up a hire car for their stay. Frank took a while to get accustomed to driving on the wrong side of the road and the wrong side of the car, but as soon as he joined the motorway, he picked up the pace and headed northeast toward St Quentin. Frank was expecting this trip to take a few hours but soon found distances in Europe are not what they are at home. He only had about one hundred and fifty km to go, so in fact he made it there by lunchtime. They hunted down a place to stay for two days. Frank thought that would be enough at this location. Anyway, if they needed to extend it, they were told there would be no trouble. Already, they were starting to see the regional admiration for Australians. The hundred-metre-high Mount St Quentin, which had been a German stronghold in 1918, had withstood many an attempt to capture it, but when Lt General Monash and the Australians tried, they took it in a little over one day. Such was the tenacity of the Aussie troops and the brilliance of Monash that British General Rawlinson described it as possibly the greatest single achievement of the entire war. The Mount had been guarded by parts of five divisions of crack German troops and in the end, it was taken effectively by two battalions of the second division, both of which were undermanned, simply by daring and blind courage. Four Victoria Crosses were awarded that day. Frank was looking forward to exploring this place, but first, they would find the last area that Francis had been. Somewhere on the Hindenburg Line.

In the afternoon, the family explored St Quentin, and Frank found several shops dealing in WW1 memorabilia. Included amongst their wares were reproductions of the old trench maps. He had not given this a thought previously, other than to say he wished he could get his hands on some of these maps. He purchased a series of maps that covered this area. Once he laid them out, he could see the explanation of how to read the references, something he had been unable to fathom before. It all made sense now. Each map had a sheet number, like 28 NE, which meant map 28, northeast quadrant. That map was divided into lettered sections A, B, C, etc., across an entire area, not just on the one map. It meant, for example, that on a map, it could contain D, E, and F, sectors in the top half, and J, K, and L sectors in the lower half, each of which was then divided into 30 numbered squares, each 1000 yds x 1000 yds, (900m) which were then divided into four further squares, a,b,c &d, (500 yds square) which could then be divided by imaginary lines into ten divisions vertically and horizontally. Thus, a map reference may look like this. 28NE, D, 23, c, 2,5, and be accurate to within 50 yds (45m). Using this reference above would indicate a crossroads in the town of Broodseinde. For further accuracy, the last two numbers could be one-hundredths, rather than tenths and be accurate to within 5 yds (4.5m) Using the above example, if the reference was given as 28NE, D, 23, c, 25,51, it would be indicating the SE corner of that road intersection.

Now, Frank could take the references in the unit notes and pinpoint precise positions on his map. Mind you, he figured that these were from over eighty years ago, so things would undoubtedly be different now. He was, to his amazement, about to find out otherwise. He sat down with the unit diaries of the 3rd of October 1918 and traced the 28th movements from the beginnings of the battle to the end of that day, drawing all appropriate positions as given by the map references. He then got out his present-day map, to see if it was possible to plot those positions today. Lo and behold, virtually nothing had changed. The roads were still in the same positions and many other landmarks he could compare were still in the same places. He could not believe his luck. He told Lynne and she had a simple explanation for him.

"In Australia, we are only 200 years old," she said, "and still developing our infrastructure, so it is changing often. Here in Europe, they have had many hundreds, even a thousand or more years to lay down theirs. Why would they change it now? They just rebuilt everything exactly as it was."

"Well, when you put it like that, I suppose it makes sense. I have never given it any thought. I guess these countries are fully developed, as far as land use goes, so it is already all there. Hmm, makes sense, I suppose," Frank admitted.

He then worked on how far away all this was and got yet another surprise to find it was only twelve kilometres away.

"I was going to leave this until tomorrow, 'cause I thought it would take a couple of hours to get there and back. I can't get used to these short distances between places. It is always a half-day trip at home to get anywhere. This Bellicourt place is only twelve kilometres away. Why don't we do it now?" Frank suggested.

"So, what is the place we are going to, Dad?" asked Tim.

"It's the last known place where your great-grandfather was alive. So, he had to be killed somewhere near this place up the road," he replied.

"Oh, I see. Well, what are we waiting for?" Tim asked.

"Well, it's not just us, mate. There are two other people here who need to have their say too, you know." Frank answered. "What do you think, Lynne?"

"It's okay by me," she replied, "so long as we get a chance to rest this arvo. I think Eloise is a bit tired, eh, kiddo?"

"Yeah, I'm getting a bit tired now, but it's okay," Ellie answered slowly.

"Right, into the car," called Frank.

Once they were on the road, Frank started a running commentary, as by now he realised stops would come up fairly quickly. They had to start by finding route number D1044, then drive north, out of town. At about the 6 km mark, he advised them they had just crossed the San Quentin canal, which, prior to October 1918, formed part of the Hindenburg line defences. 2 km later, they were travelling alongside the canal and shortly, pulled up next to the Riqueval Bridge.

"Come and check out this bridge," Frank called to them. "It's a famous bridge. It's called the Riqueval Bridge and it was famously captured by the British Army on the day before the day we're going to look for. You can see by the steep sides to this canal that it would be extremely hard to cross, and the British managed to capture this bridge before the Germans destroyed it."

"Destroyed it? Why would they destroy it?" Asked a puzzled Ellie.

"Well, Sweetie, by this time, the Germans were running back towards Germany and needed to slow down the attacking troops, which were English, Scottish, Canadian, American, French, New Zealand, and Australian. What the retreating troops used to do was to blow up the bridges so that the ones chasing them had a much harder job keeping up. It gave them more time to escape and set up defences," Frank explained to Ellie.

"Oh, I am so glad they didn't destroy this one, it's beautiful. And so high. You wouldn't want to fall off that one, would you, Dad?" Ellie commented.

"No, Darling, you would not want to fall off that one." Frank went on, "On the Australian War Memorial website, there is a photograph taken from here of one of the English generals talking to all his men, who were sitting on that bank over there on the other side. It's a very famous photograph. Apparently, no one expected them to take this bridge intact, but they advanced so rapidly that the Germans just turned and ran."

"So, was great-grandfather here, Dad?" asked Tim.

"No, Son, his division was further north of here. We're about to go there now. I just thought you might like to see this bridge first. Just up ahead of us," Frank explained as they were heading back to the car, "this canal goes underground for a few kilometres, and it was here that General Monash planned for the Australian divisions to attack the Germans and drive them back to Germany. Your great-grandfather had to start from the town you can see in front of us, it's called Bellicourt. That town is at the top of this canal tunnel and it was through this town that your great-grandfather walked on his last days on this earth."

"You know Tim, talking about it all and reading about it is one thing, but to be able to look at and walk over the actual ground that he fought so hard for is really quite amazing," Lynne explained to them. "You two are very lucky to be able to do that, and you will be able to go back to school and tell all your mates and your teachers about it."

The two children smiled and nodded in agreement.

They drove into Bellicourt and had a quick look around the town, before turning down to Nauroy, 1.5 km southeast, then 3 km northeast and then a further 1 km northwest. These roads were all so narrow, hardly room enough for two cars to pass, let alone park, but Frank found a little pull-off next to a line of trees. There, he stopped the car and got out. He stood there for a moment or two, surveying the farmland to his left. It was hard to imagine that this area was home to one of the worst wars in human history. It all looked so peaceful and pleasant on this beautiful day.

He pointed to the area in front of them and explained, "It looks like this tree line just here, formed the southern edge of the 28th Battalion starting point. Here in Europe, a patch of trees like this is called a copse and this particular copse is known as Bank Copse," Frank paused to look at his notes. "The full Battalion strength is somewhere around nine hundred, but on this day, all that remained was about 350. Those 350 men were stretched out in front of you, covering a distance of just under a kilometre, so that would be about one person every two and a half metres. Your great-grandfather was in A

Company and they started against this tree line, then, at 6.50 in the morning, the artillery situated back towards Bellicourt opened up bombing this area in front of them." Frank indicated the area by pointing north-east of where they were standing. "Once the artillery started, these troops then started marching forward, and the artillery increased its range as they marched. That is called, a creeping barrage." Frank again consulted his notes, then peered to the northeast. This whole time he was talking, the other three stood silently, hanging on every word, looking in every indicated direction. "They managed to advance a kilometre or so to the northeast, where they encountered machine-gun fire and return artillery from the Germans. We don't know precisely where my grandfather was killed, but it was probably in that area to our right, just over there, near the top of that small hill."

"Are we able to get over there, Dad?" Asked Tim.

"Not sure, Tim, just let me have a look," Frank answered. Frank checked the old trench map against his present-day map, and then said, "I think we may well be able to, Son. Let's give it a go."

They all hopped in the car again and headed north-west, nearly two kilometres east, then south-east half a kilometre. Once again, this road was unnervingly narrow. It felt like it was no more than a driveway. Frank pulled the car off to the side as best he could, and they all got out again.

"This is highly likely to have been the place where he died," Frank said. "At the top of this hill were three machine-gun nests, which the Battalion was successful in taking. I think by now, in the war, the average German soldier had had enough and didn't really want to keep fighting. Apparently, two of the three machine-gun nests were taken quite easily, and the Germans surrendered."

"You said, two of the three, Frank. What about the third one?" Asked Lynne.

"It put up more of a fight, according to these notes and all the Germans in that pit perished," Frank replied. "So Tim, one or two questions that you asked, after three months of searching, has led us to this place in France, on the other side of the world, and has answered a lot of questions that a lot of people have had over the years, that we didn't even know about. You see, you don't know what you don't know." Frank put his arm around Tim's shoulder and the two of them just stood there looking at what appeared to be just vacant farmland but was, in fact, sacred ground, where many Australian and German men lay dead and dying, eighty-two years before.

As they stood there in silence, they could see a local farmer walking along the road to them from the farmhouse, three hundred metres up the road. When he reached their location, he said, "Est-ce que je peux t'aider? Es-tu perdu?" to which Lynne replied, "Oh, pardon Monsieur. Nous sommes Australiens, regardant les sites du guerre."

"Oh, welcome, my Australian friends. Did you have family in the war?" He asked excitedly, with his arms extended at right angles in front of him and his hands facing each other.

"Yes," replied Frank with relief that he spoke English. "My grandfather, we think, died right here."

"Mon Dieu," the farmer said, clasping his right hand to his heart. "It was a terrible war, and all for what? I thank you, sir, for your grandfather's sacrifice, on our behalf. You have no idea how much we in France appreciate the sacrifices of your countrymen, thousands of kilometres from their homes. France will never forget, believe me, good sir." The farmer extended his hands and grasped Frank's, with both of his wrinkled, calloused hands and shook it vigourously, and then gave Frank the traditional European kiss on each cheek. Frank felt rather uncomfortable, not quite knowing what to do, but his embarrassment was short-lived, as the kind gentleman then did the same with Lynne.

He was an elderly gentleman, probably in his eighties, not at all tall, a little stooped, with a mass of curly grey hair. His face was lined with years of experience and time in the sun. He had the largest red nose that Tim reckoned he had ever seen. It was a kindly face, however, and when he smiled, his face lit up from ear to ear. Frank figured that all his years of living and working on the farm had kept him still quite nimble, as had been evidenced by the way he bounced along the road on his way to meet them.

"You like café, sorry, coffee?" He added.

"Er, yes we do," replied Frank.

"Good! You come. You meet my wife, that house just there. Please." He said, ushering with his hands toward the house.

"We would love to. Thank you so very much," Lynne answered. "We'll bring the car up to clear the road."

"Bon, Bon. I go, I see you there." He said with a huge smile on his face and he turned and hurried back towards his house.

"Well, there you go kids! Do you see what we were talking about in Paris now? About how Australians are considered here in France." Lynne said to the children.

"He's a very nice old gentleman, isn't he, Mum?" Ellie added.

"Yes, my dear, he certainly is," Lynne answered. "Now we'll go up to his house and have coffee with him, so you two be on your best behaviour, won't you now?"

"Of course, Mum. We will," answered the children.

They drove up to the farmhouse and parked in the driveway. It led past the house into a large four sided courtyard, with sheds on three sides and the house at the front facing the road. The house was typical of the many farmhouses they had seen already in their short time in France. Red brick outer walls, two stories high, with a slate shingled roof. It had a quaint wooden front door, painted mid-green, and wooden window frames of bright white. It was adorned with perfectly manicured gardens either side of the front path.

As they got out of the car, the front door opened and the old man stepped outside and motioned them in. They were met at the front door by him and his wife. She shook hands with all of them, including the children, and beckoned them through to the kitchen.

"Oh, thank you for dropping in. Thank you so very much. Please, please sit. Coffee for you both?" She was so excited to have them there and it showed.

"Thank you, yes, please," answered Lynne.

"And the children? I have juice. That is good?' The lady of the house went on.

"Thank you. That would be lovely," Lynne said.

They introduced themselves as M. and Mme Boulanger and M. Boulanger was born just after the Great War. His father had farmed this land before and after the war, but all its buildings had been destroyed in the conflict. His father had rebuilt this farm from scratch. The house, the sheds, the fences and the fields. There were so many trenches and shell holes all over the property, which needed filling before the land could be returned to productivity. M. Boulanger said the trenches and shell holes persisted for years, as he used to help fill them in as a child.

Not only that, but the large amount of unexploded ordinance that they continue to this day to dig up. They term it 'The Iron Harvest'. Farmers stack the newly upturned shells on the side of the road each year and they are then collected and disposed of safely. That made the job of farming just that little bit more dangerous. He then asked about Frank's grandfather, so Frank explained what he knew.

"Those machine gun posts you talk of were right here. There was one in this house, or what was left of it and two more toward the top of that hill," M. Boulanger remarked as he pointed to the hill next to the house.

"So, it was more likely he was killed here, rather than over where we were stopped," Frank commented.

"I would say that was definitely possible," M. Boulanger added.

They enjoyed a pleasant afternoon with the Boulangers and after taking quite a few photographs, they bid them au revoir and drove back to the hotel in St Quentin. Frank pulled out his maps and adjusted them to indicate the change in position of the machinegun posts. He was well pleased with his first day's expedition. Already he was a day ahead of schedule, due to his miscalculation of distances in France.

That evening, he worked on the previous campaigns Francis had been involved with. He already had a basic outline, but now he was armed with the trench maps, he would be able to be more precise. He plotted their next moves back along the Somme River, to Le Hamel and Villers Bretonneux. The actions at the end of September '18 were right here next to St Quentin, he thought, so he would try and find a point to see there first and then work their way back along the river to Amiens, which would follow in reverse his grandfather's movements. He was getting confused by the grid references and his knowledge of where the different places were. It was not until much searching and confusion that he worked out there are two St Quentin places. One was the town of St Quentin, where they were currently staying, and the other being Mont St Quentin, which is situated over next to Peronne. That answered his confusion over the name of the battle, which was known as "The Battle of Mont St Quentin" and equally, 'The Battle of Peronne.' It also answered the question in his mind, that he had been unable to see any 'Mount' near the town. What that meant was that the sites he wished to see around St Quentin, were actually around Peronne. Peronne was thirty kilometres to the northwest. As they would be working their way westward, they made plans to move to Peronne tomorrow.

This time, Frank would not be caught out by arriving and having time to look around. He planned to check in at Peronne and head up to the "Mont" that afternoon. Their drive up to the mount did not take long. In a way, they were all a little disappointed at the size of the hill; that it was higher than the surrounds was certainly true, but it was only one hundred metres high. Not really a mountain by anyone's measure. Atop the Mount sat a church, which was the stronghold occupied by the Germans through most of the war, although the British did hold it for a few months, before losing it again in a German assault. Many attempts had been made to rest this position from the Germans, and all had failed until the 2nd Division AIF assaulted it with an undermanned force. General Monash instructed his troops to scream at the top of their lungs as they attacked, and the Germans, underestimating the size of the force, just surrendered.

When the family arrived at the top, they found a memorial to the 2nd Division AIF. Frank was studying the information on both the memorial and the information board. He called the others over and said to them, "Hey, this setup here is to the 28th and the other battalions of the 2nd Divvy. That's to your great grandfather, kids."

"Well, how do you like that?" replied Lynne with a soft chuckle.

"So, this is what we have been looking for then, Dad, eh?" Tim added. "Recognition that we couldn't even find at home."

Frank laughed an ironic laugh and added, "Yes Son, as usual, you are absolutely correct."

"It seems to me, Dad, that our soldiers are more recognised here in France than they are at home," Tim commented. He thought about it for a few seconds, then added, "I wonder why that is? I mean, why aren't we told about this stuff at school, instead of some of the other stuff to do with other countries?"

Frank just looked at Lynne and gently shook his head. She could read his mind on this. *"This kid of ours is way ahead of his age. He understands more than most."*

He then spoke aloud, "So Francis was dug in, on this exact spot, at the end of this particular battle. They occupied this hill until they were relieved the next day." He wandered off in silence and Lynne let him have this time to himself. She knew he needed time to ponder what he had just said, and just what it meant to him to be standing in this place. He turned briefly, looking all around him and Lynne could see there were tears in his eyes. This had meant more to him than he could have ever imagined. What he could not understand, was why. Why did this mean so much? He never even met this man he was following. He died 35 years before he was even born. His own father never even met him. Regardless of all these internal questions, Frank just knew that it meant something, and it was important.

He rejoined the family, which by now was moving around the site and checking out the view to the north. He stood alongside Lynne and put his arm around her and looked out. "Are you okay, Darling?" she asked.

"Yeah, thanks." He answered softly. "I Just had a bit of a moment. I don't understand this at all. Suddenly, there has been a huge change of direction in my life, following something or someone I know nothing about. I never had any inkling that this was so important."

"It's family. It's your father. It is plainly important for you to find answers, maybe more for him, but you need those answers, too. He is a part of who you are. He's in your DNA. It's only natural for you to want to know," Lynne tried to give him some comfort in his quest. "Anyway, I'm proud of you for taking up the mantle on your father's part. It's just a shame his mum never found this stuff out."

"Too true," he answered. He paused, "Maybe by now she has. I hope so."

Lynne just nodded. The children were by now at their side.

"If you look carefully over there in the distance, about 4 km away, there is a small canal, you can see the sun reflecting off it. Once the men had finished here, they were rested back at that canal. They marched from here to there, and then a further six km the next day."

"What? They had to walk, Dad? Why didn't they drive?" queried Eloise.

"Yes, Sweetie, they walked," Frank answered. "In 1918, there were very few cars or trucks, and they were terribly slow and rough, and I dare say rather expensive, so the men mostly walked or marched. They were used to walking long distances in those days."

"Yes silly! They didn't have many trucks then. They had only just been invented," Tim admonished his sister.

"Well, I didn't know that, did I? But I do now," Ellie replied indignantly.

"Come on you lot. Let's go back and have a look around this town, shall we?" Frank said.

As they jumped in the car, Ellie called out, "Hey, look at that road sign. It's got a word on it like Australians, but spelt different."

Lynne spoke up, "Yes, Darling. That sign says Avenue des Australiens. It is the name of the road and it means, Avenue of the Australians, or Australian road."

"You mean they named a road after us?" replied Ellie.

"Yes, Ellie. They named it after the men from Australia who saved them from the Germans. Men like your great grandfather," answered Lynne.

"Wow. They must have been important," crowed Ellie.

They all laughed as they headed back down the hill to town.

Peronne had all but been levelled in the war, so the whole town had to be rebuilt. There was not a building in the town older than eighty-two years old when our travellers arrived. Even so, the town had a quaintness to it that suggested it was much older than that. The rebuilders had tried to recreate the age of some of the buildings but also took the opportunity to modernise and upgrade the town as well. Since 1918 it had grown, to now fill the gap between Peronne and Mont St Quentin, which had been some distance apart. It was now just one town, with the mount on the edge of town. The town was built on the confluence of the

Somme River and La Cologne, the latter being not much more than a creek. The Baileys were also a little surprised at the size of the Somme River itself. They were expecting a substantial river, but instead, they were presented with what looked more like a series of swamps joined together. To keep the water flowing, a canal had been built in the riverbed alongside the river.

Whilst driving around town, Lynne noticed a rather impressive and old looking building, which happened to be a museum of history of the Great War. They made plans to visit tomorrow, as by now, it was approaching closing time.

The following morning, the family spent an hour and a half wandering around the museum as they had planned. Here, they all got to see the types of weapons that the two sides of the conflict used on each other. They got to see the uniforms they wore, the equipment they carried and now, Frank was able to show Eloise the types of truck, or lorry as they were called then, that our troops were moved around in. It was a well laid out museum, with lots of space to walk around and instead of having exhibits on tables, they were set into the floor, with bench seats around so anybody, of any size, could sit, observe, and reflect. There were interactive displays where you could listen to stories, in your choice of language, from many of the men who were there. Not only did it help Tim to understand, but it also helped Frank and Lynne as well. But it all felt rather mechanical to Frank. It was about stuff, not so much about the effect on people. He felt he needed more. When they had finished at the museum, they loaded up into their car again and headed south and west to Villers Bretonneux. Francis had been part of the attack that rescued Villers Bretonneux from the Germans in July 1918, according to Frank. He explained this to the family, to prepare them for what they were going to see here. The residents of that town will never forget Australia. Shortly, they would find out why. The museum in Peronne had referred to their equivalent in Villers Bretonneux, so that's where Frank thought they should go next. The museum was attached to the school.

Villers Bretonneux is really only a small village in the Somme region of France, so it was not difficult to find. Even before going inside, they found the connection to Australia displayed outside in the form of two plaques on the front wall, one in French, the other in English. Frank read aloud.

"This school building is the gift of the school children of Victoria, Australia, to the children of Villers-Bretonneux, as a proof of their love and goodwill towards France. Twelve hundred Australian soldiers, the fathers and brothers of these children, gave their lives in the heroic capture of this town from the invader, on the 24th of April 1918 and are buried near this spot. May the memory of great sacrifices in a common cause, keep France and Australia together forever in bonds of friendship and mutual esteem."

"So that's why there is such a bond here," Lynne commented. "Now I am beginning to get it."

"So, the school kids of Victoria paid for the reconstruction of this school after the war, did they Mum?" Asked Ellie.

"Yes, Sweetie, they did. It shows how someone's small idea can build huge friendships around the world," Lynne answered. "It needs to happen more often, I think."

"So, hang on," Frank broke in, "These notes say the battle here was in early July. Strange!"

"Really?" answered Lynne. "Perhaps all will be explained inside."

"Hmm. Guess so!" replied Frank. "Shall we go in and have a look?"

The four of them went inside to find a small, but really quaint display. It consisted of a lot of photographs, interactive displays, uniforms of the time, dioramas, flags and plaques everywhere, and a few salvaged relics from 1918. They wandered around checking out all the displays until Frank found what he was looking for.

He found Lynne and Tim and explained to them, "Okay, it looks like the Aussie troops did wrest Villers Bretonneux from the Germans, on about Anzac Day 1918, but they had to battle for a couple of months, to hang on to it. My grandfather's efforts in July were the final efforts to push the Germans into retreat and keep the village in Allied hands. It makes sense now. He wasn't in the initial take back, but the follow-up."

"Not any less important, I would have thought, Dad," Tim suggested.

"Good God, no Tim, just as important," answered Frank. "No good pushing them out just to let them back in again."

"Hey Frank, I've just read something that got me thinking. You know how the Germans were fighting both the allies on the Western Front and the Ruskies in the east?" Lynne asked.

"Yeah!" replied Frank.

"Well, what happened in 1917, when the Bolshevik revolution took over Russia? Did that fighting stop? I don't think Russia were involved in the Treaty of Versailles, were they? If the fighting did stop, wouldn't they have had a lot more troops to redirect over here?" Lynne asked.

That is a lot of questions for one question, he thought. But a good one anyway. "If they did stop on the eastern front, that would release a lot of troops, alright. I might find someone to ask. You better come with me in case they don't speak English," Frank suggested.

They found the person supervising that day and Frank posed the question. Thankfully, they did speak English.

"Yes sir. They did stop all fighting on the Eastern Front. That released something like fifty divisions of Bosch troops to fight on the Western Front. That had the Allies very worried in late 1917, and it did have an effect, with them being able to take back some lost ground. Then, in March of 1918, the Germans commenced the "Spring Offensive" down here and pushed a long way west from St Quentin, almost to Amiens."

"I see. So how did they get it back so quickly then," asked Frank.

"Well, the joint allied command realised the Bosch were overstretching their supply lines too quickly, and just waited for the right moment, and we were fortunate to be where the allies struck back. On April 24th, 1918, troops from your wonderful country pushed the Bosch out and held them out. Then, on July 4th, US Independence Day, your General Monash accomplished one of the finest victories ever, to that point, just over at Le Hamel, just 6km northwest of here, where he claimed the battle would take ninety minutes. It took ninety-three. That was the commencement of the 100 day offensive that saw the end of the Germans. But I guess you knew most of that."

"Not at all, Monsieur. We have been taught so little of this. That is why I am here now. My grandfather was in the 28th battalion," Frank explained.

"The 28th? They were here in July. Oh, good sir, I thank you for his service. Did he survive the war?" the gentleman asked.

"Unfortunately, no, he did not. He lost his life over near Bellicourt," answered Frank.

"Oh, I am so sorry sir. He is a hero to us," he added.

"Thank you, sir. He is to me, too. This is a journey to find out more about him. Until two months ago, we knew nothing about him," Frank explained.

"Ah, I see. Do you know about the Australian National Archives?" He asked.

Frank chuckled and answered, "Yes, I do now. But not until two months ago."

"Ah, now I see," and they both laughed.

"Have you been up to the memorial just up the road to the north yet?" The man asked Frank.

"Ah, no sir. We have not. I do not know of it," Frank replied.

"For an Australian, that is a must-see," the man became quite animated. "It was unveiled just before the second war and contains the names of 11,000 Australians who died in France, for whom there is no known grave. You must see that."

"Really?" Frank exclaimed. "My grandfather was never found. I wonder if he is named there?"

"I would say he is very likely on that wall, Sir," replied the attendant, placing his hands together as in a praying action.

"Thank you so much, my friend. Your information has been invaluable. We shall go there immediately," Frank offered him his hand to shake.

As they shook, the gentleman asked, "It is less than two kilometres to the north. After that, where to then, Sir?"

"After that, I think, we head up to Flanders in Belgium. He was there just before coming down here. We will continue the journey of discovery up there," Frank explained.

"Well, good luck, friend," and the gentleman bid them goodbye.

They all went straight up to the memorial recommended by the gentleman. It was indeed only just up the road.

"Wow, Dad," Tim called out. That is pretty impressive, isn't it?"

"You can say that again, Tim," Lynne answered.

Frank was just staring at it. "Why have I not heard of this place either?" he quietly said. Then he started to walk up through the rows of headstones, with so many of them, once again, engraved only with the words "Known Unto God" below the rising sun emblem.

The area of headstones was dominated by a large white stone cross, adorned with a bronze sword. Beyond that was a large, grassed area and at the top, a large walled area with what looked like a tall bell tower in the middle, all made from the now familiar white stone of the area.

"That wall up there must be the one the man at the museum was telling me about," Frank told Lynne. "I need to go there and look for my grandfather's name."

Frank could see the names were listed by unit and then alphabetically. They set out to find the 28th Infantry Battalion. It was not long before Frank and Lynne were standing in front of that panel. Frank scanned his eyes down the long list of names. There it was. Bailey F. A. Frank reached out and ran his fingers across the name. Suddenly, he felt a massive relief. He felt like the weight of the world had just decided to up and fly away. A massive weight had been lifted from his shoulders and he could scarcely believe what he was seeing. A wave of emotion flowed through his body and he felt the goose bumps rise from head to toe. He found it exceedingly difficult to hold back the tears.

"He really is here," he said with a sigh. He dropped his head and looked at the ground. This was hallowed ground.

"Yes, Frank, he is," Lynne answered, as she stepped forward and took his free hand. They stood in silence for at least a minute, hand in hand, saying nothing. There was nothing that really could be said. Lynne felt the surge of grief run from Frank's hand. At least, that's what she thought it felt like. Then Tim came up to them. "Have you found his name, Dad?"

"Yes, Son. We have," replied Lynne.

"Fantastic," is all Tim would say and he too, gazed at the inscription on the wall.

"To think we nearly missed this," Frank remarked. "I'm so glad we stopped at that museum and spoke to the man there." Frank did not say it, but he felt as if he was being led from one place to another. It was inconceivable to him that these discoveries were coincidental. There had to be some force drawing him to the appropriate connections.

Lynne took out her camera, and photographed the name, along with some of the others from the 28th. She also drew from her bag a piece of plain paper, and a pencil she had for just such an occasion. She spent a few minutes rubbing that pencil across the paper as it was stretched over Francis' engraving. When finished, it gave a perfect impression of his name engraved on that wall. They spent some time there just gazing and reading the other names, thinking some of them were probably Francis' mates.

"How do you get 11,000 unidentified men, just from the one country and just in France?" Tim asked his father.

After a short pause, he replied, "Beats me son, beats me," it was all Frank could say.

"I guess some of them were so badly damaged by bombs or something like that," Lynne said to Tim, "that they could not be identified. Also, not all of them were able to be buried straight away, so, well, there might not have been much left of them by that time."

"I guess so. But that is still an awful lot," Tim responded, still a little confused.

Frank looked at the inscription on the tower building. He read it aloud to the family. *"To the glory of God and in the memory of the Australian Imperial Forces in France and Flanders 1916 – 1918 and of the eleven thousand who fell in France and have no known grave."*

"I thought the war started in 1914, Dad." Tim queried his father.

"It did Son, but the Australians were only fighting at Gallipoli before 1916. The first Aussie forces didn't arrive in France until part way through 1916," Frank informed him. He had only worked this out himself a few weeks ago.

They walked around the cemetery now and looked out across the countryside. How beautiful it was, they all thought. Standing there, with the warm July sun soaking into them, it was hard to believe that this was the site of such a terrible war. As they gazed around at the beautiful green countryside, slightly undulating with patches of brown and red here and there and carefully sculpted tree groves, Frank wondered if he was standing on ground his grandfather had trodden on.

The rest of the afternoon was spent exploring Villers Bretonneux and Le Hamel. Frank had no specific sites to check out here, rather just a general overview of the area. He had some information gained from the museum but nothing specific from the unit diaries. The two months prior to the action at Villers Bretonneux by the 28th battalion were spent in and around Albert, Amiens and Dernancourt. They planned to take these towns in on their way to the Flanders region in Belgium. They would commence that part of the voyage of discovery tomorrow.

Frank tried to explain to the children, that the greater part of the move from Flanders to the Somme region, was done on foot. Yes, they had some bus transport and some train, but a fair proportion of the "march south" was just that, a march. The children were amazed that the men would be asked to walk halfway across the country. Once the men arrived at a destination, usually the following day or two were allocated for rest. The march south, of around one hundred and twenty kilometres, commenced on the 2nd of April 1918 and was completed by their arrival at Corbie at six pm, on the 6th of April. The next day, 'A' Company continued the march to Dernancourt and to the front line.

Chapter 5
Up To Flanders

The best way to find yourself is to lose yourself in the service of others.

Mahatma Gandhi

The plan, once they arrived in Belgium, was to stop in Ieper (Ypres) and to find the place where Francis was first noted as KIA. That would be near a place called Polygon Wood, just east of Ieper. From there, they would follow his progress until his move to the Somme, a period of approximately six months. The following morning, they set off through Albert (pronounced Al-bear), then up to Armentieres on the French-Belgian border and onto Ieper through Mesen (Messines). Little did they know at that time they travelled through the centre of one of the areas Francis had been involved in, around Ploegsteert.

After checking into their accommodation they all went walking around Ieper. Frank again explained to the children that everything they were looking at had been built since 1918. Whilst the town had been in existence for centuries, everything had been destroyed by the constant shelling during the war and as such, was all rebuilt following the armistice.

"How long did it take to rebuild, Dad?" asked Tim.

Frank replied, "I have no idea Son, but I guess it took decades. I'm sure we will find something that will tell us."

They wandered into the central square and gazed with amazement. Before them stretched the wonderful façade of a long, old-style, three-story building, with dozens of gothic-style arches, a grand central spire and smaller spires at the ends.

"That's only built in the last 80 years?" queried an astonished Tim as he gazed around the central square.

"Yes," answered Tim's mum. "That building is known as Cloth Hall. It is a famous building, which was originally built seven hundred years ago. It used to be the centre of the cloth trading industry in Europe but was totally destroyed between 1914 and 1918. It took over thirty years to rebuild it piece by piece, from 1933 to 1963, but they managed to do it and have it look just like it did before it was destroyed. Probably even better I imagine."

"Wow," Tim replied.

"You're suddenly an expert on this, aren't you?" asked Frank.

"Oh yes, I'm a fountain of knowledge," Lynne said nonchalantly. "Actually, I just read it on the way here, but I did know a little about it before. Apparently, there is a museum inside it that is classed as a 'do not miss this' place. Shall we go for a walk around outside first? The cathedral behind was also rebuilt just the same."

"It's a very pretty building, Mum," Eloise commented.

"That it is, my dear," replied Lynne.

They walked around, through the mews and around to the cathedral, all the time marvelling at the scale of the building. The gardens around the cathedral were all impeccably kept. The roses were in full flower, and Lynne was impressed by the range of different varieties, some of which she had not seen before.

They could see where parts of the original building were retained and the rebuild added to it.

"They have done a beautiful job getting this back to its former glory haven't they, guys?" Lynne asked the kids.

"Yes, they have, but I thought there would be bomb marks or something on it," Tim answered.,

"Well, I guess they got rid of all the damaged parts and used fresh stones and bricks," Lynne remarked. "I suppose you will see explanations on it inside the museum, when we get in there."

"Okay. We will see," Tim replied.

They continued their walk around the precinct and then entered the museum. They planned to meet at the front desk if they got separated, then went to look around. Ellie stayed with her mother, and Tim stayed within vision of his father.

"This has so much stuff in here, Dad, I don't know where to go next," Tim said to his father as he passed him ducking from one display to the next.

"There sure is a lot. Did you see the photographs of this place after the war?" Frank asked Tim.

"Sure did. There wasn't much left of it was there?" Tim answered. "They didn't have much to start with to rebuild."

"Looks like the whole town was totally destroyed, eh?" Frank commented. "I have also found out that at 8 pm sharp they have a 'Last Post' ceremony, down at the Menin Gate. They tell me it's just a couple of hundred metres down from the Grote Market here. There is more information on it just over there." Frank indicated the area for Tim to check out.

"Okay, that's easy. What is a 'Last Post' ceremony?" Tim asked.

"According to the board there," Frank answered, "the Menin Gate has a list of Commonwealth soldiers that died here in

Flanders for whom there is no known grave. Like the wall in Villers Bretonneux, but this is for here in Belgium. That means they were unable to either find a body to bury, or they were unable to be identified. Every night since 1929, except throughout the German occupation of WW2, at eight pm, they play the Last Post under the gate. It says here, there are over fifty-four thousand names on the gate."

"That sounds like something we need to see; don't you think Dad?" Tim asked.

"Definitely! It's only a short walk so I think when we are done here, we should go and look," Frank suggested.

They wandered around for two hours, marvelling at the variety of displays, both static and interactive, before heading back downstairs, where they found the girls waiting for them. Ellie had seen enough and wanted to do something else, so they sat and had an ice cream each. Both Frank and Tim admitted that they had not seen everything yet, but figured the girls had probably had enough. Frank told them about the 'Last Post' ceremony, and they agreed to go down to the Menin Gate, after dinner. They all headed off now, through Grote Market toward the Menin Gate, just to have a look. The walk took them past rows of quaint little shops selling books, art, memorabilia and all manner of things, to cafes, restaurants and pubs. To look at these buildings you would never know that they were only 80 years old. The rebuilders had done a magnificent job, regaining the earlier look of the town. They continued past dozens of these shops before reaching the Menin Gate.

The gate itself was constructed through the mid-1920s and unveiled in 1927. It is an imposing structure containing the names of the missing from British and Commonwealth countries up to August 1917. Any missing after that, are to be found on the walls at Tyne Cot cemetery, near Zonnebeke. The Menin Gate Memorial is administered by the Commonwealth War Graves Commission.

"That is one impressive looking gate," Lynne remarked when she saw it.

She looked up at this large Flemish brick and white stone building in awe. It was about 50m long, by maybe 40m wide and lies on the Menen Road, at the entrance or exit to the town, with the moat at the outer edge. The entrances at either end are high, vaulted, archways, maybe 15m high, she thought. Four massive, white stone columns support the top section, which contains beautiful stone carvings of wreaths and laurels. Sitting atop the structure at the outer end was a huge lion.

They crossed the road and wandered inside the gate.

"Wow!" Tim echoed the reactions of the rest of them. "This really is impressive, Mum." Once inside the gate, the size became evident. The arches reached right up to a curved ceiling, in which were three circular holes, maybe three or four metres in diameter.

They wandered around slowly looking at all the inscriptions. British, Australian, South African, Indian and West Indian names, all listed by unit.

"Here's the 28th Battalion list," Frank called. He cast his eye down the list of names just to check to see if his grandfather was listed. It wasn't. He knew it shouldn't be there, as he didn't die here, but he just wanted to check. They wandered around for a little while, taking in the views from the upper levels of the moat around this part of town, and the gardens. They decided to go back to one of the restaurants they had passed, and then come back for the 8 o'clock ceremony.

Not knowing quite what to expect at the ceremony, they walked back to the gate at 7.45, only to find quite a large crowd already in place. They found a position, but the children were not able to see a great deal until they worked their way through the crowd. They stood quietly, through the roughly twenty-minute ceremony and when it was over, came back to their parents and suggested that they come again another night, much earlier to get a better position. Both Frank and Lynne had found the ceremony so moving and definitely worth going to, but had also realised it was much bigger than they thought, so had decided the same as the children; get here early and get a good position.

They all walked slowly back to their accommodation, where Frank prepared for the following day. He had gotten all the necessary maps and worked out the best way to go. They would head out the Menen Road, through Hellfire Corner and straight on up to Zonnebeke, where they had a re-creation of the underground dugout and trench system, typical of the Great War. After that, it would only be a few minutes south to Polygon Wood in the area where his grandfather went KIA for a short while. After that, they would go north to Tyne Cot cemetery, between Zonnebeke and Passchendaele.

The following morning, the family loaded up the car again and struck out east, through the Menin Gate. Frank took this slowly, with them all again gazing in wonder at the gate, as now they were driving through it. It was a normal road twenty-three hours a day. Soon, they passed through the roundabout that was Hellfire Corner. Frank explained to them that this was an infamous corner along the Menen Road that suffered almost constant shelling throughout the war. Here they turned onto the road direct to Zonnebeke, where they arrived some ten minutes later and parked outside the Passchendaele Museum.

"Not another museum, Dad?" cried Ellie.

"Sorry Sweetie, but I think you will like this one. It's a bit different. Here you get to go underground and see how they lived and worked there," Frank tried to console her. *"Maybe not too many more museums", he thought.*

They entered the museum and had a quick look around the exhibit hall, marvelling at the different guns they all used, including the artillery, and the hundreds of different artillery shells. Frank was able to get a little more information on the different attacks made in this area, then they headed down into the underground displays. They walked through the tunnels and looked into the workshops, cookhouses, accommodation and even into the multiple-seat toilet arrangement. It was only a re-creation, but it was tight and cramped and gave them all a little of what it must have been like in these underground spaces.

"Boy that must have smelled really bad in here, eh Dad?" Tim asked his father.

"Sure would have. Hope they had good ventilation for that," came Frank's reply.

Soon they exited the underground into the different styles of trenches that were made in the area. As they wandered through, Ellie started huffing and puffing and seemed to be getting frustrated.

"What's the problem Sweetie?" asked her mother.

"Oh, it's all this zigging and zagging," she replied. "Why couldn't they just build them in a straight line? Would have been easier and quicker to dig and to move through."

All three of the others chuckled. "Yes, Darling. It would have been easier, but they were done this way deliberately. Just imagine you were in your trench, say here, and one of the enemy jumped in up there, he would be able to shoot at you immediately and you would have nowhere to go, would you?" Lynne explained. "This way they can only see six or seven metres, and be able to shoot only that far, and you would have a corner to jump around for safety. Do you understand that?"

"Oh, yes, I see. That makes sense I guess, but it is still very annoying," Ellie answered.

They all laughed. "Yes dear, it is," Lynne replied.

"Shall we all go and get a coffee and ice cream now?" Frank asked as a peace offering.

"Oh yes please!" yelled Ellie, relieved at last.

They went to the cafeteria, back in the main building and sat for a little while. The children chatted and looked out at the lake and ducks and other water birds, whilst Frank consulted his notes. They were about to head directly to Polygon Wood, which was near where his grandfather disappeared in October 1917 and he wanted to have a few facts clear in his mind. It did not happen at Polygon, but from his notes, it had to be nearby. That would have to do for the moment.

Polygon Wood was only two kilometres south of Zonnebeke and consisted of a large, wooded area, the Buttes New British Cemetery, and a Memorial atop what used to be a rifle range, stop butt. It was believed the Germans used the butt to dig into and under to provide accommodation and officers' forward planning rooms.

They hopped in the car now and commenced the drive to the butt. Once the car was parked, they walked the short distance to the entrance and then walked through the avenue of freshly sprouting trees, leading to the base of the butt. It was a lovely walk through the mottled summer light Lynne thought. In front of them, was a wide, set of white stone stairs, climbing to the top of the butt. The path they were on led around the base of the butt to the right and into the Buttes New British Cemetery. The children ran straight up the stairs, but Lynne and Frank walked around to the right. As they rounded the corner, they both stopped and said nothing at first. They just looked around, as in front of them lay the headstones of over two thousand soldiers of the Allied forces. They were neatly arranged in rows and beautifully tended. Flowering plants abounded and many shady trees were spaced throughout the cemetery.

"Holy moly," Frank commented. "Will you look at that?"

Lynne could say nothing. She just slowly started walking along the rows, pointing but not saying anything each time she saw the emblem of the AIF, the rising sun badge.

"According to the guide booklet I picked up in Ieper, there are over 500 Aussies buried here, and 160-something New Zealanders," Frank mentioned.

"Look," Lynne finally spoke, "Nineteen years old. That's only five years older than Tim." She shook her head slowly. "And here eighteen, here forty-two. My goodness, what a waste."

They wandered around for a few minutes before Ellie joined them with tears in her eyes.

"What's the matter poppet?" Lynne asked.

Ellie replied, "Tim said these are all dead soldiers. That's not nice."

"Oh Sweetie, these are called headstones and they mark the graves of the brave soldiers, who did in fact die here, at about the same time as your great-grandfather died," Lynne tried to explain to her.

"So, they are dead soldiers?" Ellie asked.

"I'm afraid they are, Sweetie. They died a very long time ago. Long before even Mum and Dad were born," Lynne said.

"Oh! I thought he was trying to be mean," Ellie said.

"No Darling, I think he was trying to explain, what this place was. You okay now?" Lynne asked.

"Yes, I guess so. It looks pretty here, doesn't it?" Ellie observed, now changing the subject.

"Yes Sweetie, they do a very good job of looking after these places. The gardens are beautiful," Lynne answered.

Tim had by now worked his way over the butt and down the other side and was coming over to his mother. Frank had decided to go and check out the memorial on top of the butt. It was a memorial to the 5th Australian Division, responsible for capturing this place from the Germans in 1917. It reminded him of the cenotaph in King's Park back in Perth. The same shape, the same purpose. Frank's information sheets told him that the 55th Battalion AIF had captured this place on the 26th of September 1917, only a few days before his grandfather's KIA incident. He walked around the monument, reading each side, before finally sitting down on its steps, facing the wood rather than the cemetery. As he sat, he gazed out into the wood, noticing just how serene the whole scene looked. The trees were like vast sentinels, standing guard over the cemetery. A vastly different outlook to eighty-three years ago he imagined. It was difficult to imagine that a war had taken place in this beautiful place.

As he sat, he was approached by another man, who just stood looking out into the wood as well. It had become eerily quiet. No bird sounds, no traffic sounds. It was strange, Frank thought, as he had not seen anyone approaching. He was not a tall man, impeccably dressed in a light grey suit, white shirt and with a red tie. He was wearing brown polished shoes and had a kerchief in his top pocket the same colour as his tie, and his pocket was also adorned with the red Flanders Poppy. He was wearing a grey Fedora style hat on his head and he seemed to be ever so slightly stooped. The man turned and looked at Frank and Frank's first thought was, that this man looked rather familiar, but he could not place where he had seen him.

"Good morning, good sir," the gentleman said cheerfully.

"Good morning. How are you today?" answered Frank.

"I am very well, thank you, but then again, I am always very well. No use complaining is there," the man answered. Frank noticed that he spoke beautifully, with no discernable accent.

"Too true," replied Frank. "No one listens anyway."

The gentleman laughed. "Where are you from my good man?"

"I am from Australia. That's my family down there," answered Frank.

"And a beautiful family they are, sir," the gentleman added.

"Thank you," replied Frank. He thought this was a rather strange interaction. The man's use of language was different from normal, almost like he was from a different earlier era; and yet he spoke so incredibly well.

"Have you a relative buried here sir?" the gentleman asked.

"No. Not that I know of," Frank replied.

"On that, you might be surprised," the man added.

"My grandfather fought near here and was initially listed as killed, but he turned up a week later and rejoined his battalion, the 28th, and continued to fight with them through to the Somme. He was killed down there, although they never identified his body," Frank explained.

"Ah, so he is immortalised on the memorial at Villers Bretonneux," the gentleman said.

"Yes, he is," answered Frank. "We stopped in there and had a look at it on the way here."

The gentleman then asked, "What was his name, may I ask of you?"

"Francis Albert Bailey. I'm Frank. I am named after him," Frank answered.

"Oh, he never used the name Frank, he was always Francis. He hated being called Frank," the gentleman explained.

"How did you know that? Did you know him? Oh, what am I saying you couldn't have known him could you?" Frank was confused now.

"Do you mind if I sit with you good sir, Frank?" the man asked.

"No, please sit," Frank responded. He was intrigued.

The gentleman sat next to Frank and gazed out into the woods in front of them, as Frank had been doing previously. He paused for a few seconds before continuing. "It is difficult to imagine, that this vista in front of us now, was nothing but bare, pockmarked battleground mud, being fought over by men of many different countries, each trying to kill as many of the others as they could." Again, he paused. "Your grandfather was an extremely brave man. His actions saved a lot of men in his section. He was a corporal you know."

Frank was getting a little concerned about the nature of this conversation by now, but he answered the man's comment with a slow, "Yes, I did know."

"And I suppose you are wondering what happened to him here aren't you?" the man asked.

"Ah, yes and what happened after this too," Frank answered slowly and deliberately. "I don't understand how someone can be listed as KIA and then turn up a week later," Frank added.

"Hmmm. Yes, well, there may be an amazingly simple explanation for that. It depends how much you want to know about it all?" the man remarked.

This was getting a little freaky, Frank started to think. *"Who the heck is this guy? Why does he look so familiar? How does he know so much about my grandfather? He speaks like he knew him, but he has been dead eighty-two years and this guy only looks to be in his fifties."*

"I don't understand what is going on here, but I want to know all there is to know, about Francis," Frank said.

"Are you sure?" asked the man.

"It's why I came halfway around the world. I need to know," Frank answered.

"Alright then," and the man reached out and placed his hand on Frank's shoulder. Before he had any chance to react to this, Frank found himself unable to speak or move and he drifted into unconsciousness.

Chapter 6
Captivity

The great questions of the day will not be settled by means of speeches and majority decisions but by iron and blood.

Otto von Bismarck

Frank awoke, to find it was dark and there were sounds of gunfire and explosions; and the smell, *What was that?* he thought. *It smells like rotting flesh.* There was a man standing over him in a grey uniform armed with a rifle.

The man yelled at Frank, "Komm Englander, nimm deine hande hoch. Jetzt! Hande hoch," Frank had no idea what he'd just said, so just shrugged. The man repeated, "Komm. Up. Schnell!" Frank had seen enough movies to know that Schnell meant fast, get moving. He started to get up and the man used his rifle to indicate for Frank to raise his hands. He looked around and found he was standing on the butt still, albeit an exceptionally damaged version of the butt and it appeared to be in the middle of a firefight. The cenotaph was, however, not there. The man in the grey uniform pushed him down the bank and he rolled to the bottom. Frank lifted himself up at the bottom and looked around in the dark. There was an unmistakable smell of; what was that? Death? The cacophony surrounding him made him wince. "Rasch, schnell," the man yelled at him and he motioned him into a gap in the wall of the butt.

"Well, what have we here? An Englander eh?" Said a voice from the dark. He spoke briefly, but authoritatively, to the man in grey and the grey man saluted and left. The voice that had spoken English now approached Frank, and now in the dim light of the kerosene lamp, he could see that this man was also dressed in grey with a little red piping and insignias. Frank recognised the uniforms, from the museums he had visited, as those of the German army from WW1. This man was an officer. He wore a black leather belt around his tunic with a black holster complete with sidearm. *But what was he doing here?* He thought. *Where has everything gone?*

"And just who would you be?" the officer asked. "And why are you dressed in so little?"

Frank had gone out today wearing black shorts and a white T-shirt, as it was a warm summer's day and on his feet, he'd worn a pair of grey Crocs. He needed to stall to think, so Frank cast a slow eye down his attire. He was muddy from the tumble down the butt and his Crocs must have flown off then as well, as he was standing there barefooted.

"Um, I don't know," Frank now answered. "I can't remember. I have no idea."

"Oh, like that is it?" asked the officer in a heavy German accent. "Maybe you lost the rest of your clothes in an artillery explosion."

"Ah, maybe," Frank replied. "I just don't remember." He thought to himself, *did I fall asleep up top and I have been moved to a re-enactment maybe? But the gentleman up the top, who was he? Maybe he did this?*

"Just what is going on here?" he asked the officer.

"Oh, so you are asking the questions now, are you? I have got news for you my British friend," the officer gloatingly said. "All in good time."

"I'm not British I am Australian," Frank stood higher when he said this. It wiped the smile off this officer instantly.

"Oh, so you are Australian, are you? Well then, that is different. What are you doing here? This is not your fight. Why did you not stay at home?" the officer scowled now.

"When people's freedom is threatened, good people must stand up for it. I can tell you now, you do not win this war, so it is you who should go home if you value your life." Frank was getting pissed off with this little upstart's attitude and thought he needed to be told a little of the truth. This may be a re-enactment, but he was not going to let this twerp get on top of him.

"Oh, this one has spirit, does he? So, who are you and what unit are you with?" the officer demanded. He was in Frank's face now and his jovial attitude was gone. Frank thought "One to me. I've gotten under his skin. This has got to be some kind of game." For the moment he decided he would give nothing until he could work out what was happening here. He would use this opportunity to get some information for himself. He moved towards a chair at the nearby table and sat himself down.

"And just who gave you permission to sit?" asked the pompous officer.

"I did," answered Frank, "and if you wish to talk, you will do likewise and talk like civilised human beings."

The German officer mumbled something to himself in German but then sat down. "Alright then if we are going to be civil, how about you tell me who you are?"

"My name is Frank Bailey, and I am from a place called Perth in Western Australia. Now then, who are you?"

The German coughed and said, "You are the one captured here. I ask you the questions."

"Not if you want to find out any information. This is a two-way street buddy. I see you are the 49th regiment, so what is your name?" Frank tried to keep this civil, in case he upset this man too much.

"Alright then, I am Hauptman Joaquin von Feldt, and I am from Hamburg in northern Germany. See, we can both be civil. Now, what regiment are you with?"

Frank had to think quickly now. *"Play along with this little upstart captain,"* he thought.

"Well captain, I am from the 55th Battalion AIF, that is going to drive you from this place."

"Oh, are you now?" the captain laughed. "And just how do you propose to do that? So many others have tried."

"Were they Australians?" asked Frank.

"Well, you should know. Of course, they were not. They were Englanders," answered the captain.

"There's your answer then captain," Frank explained. He then asked, "By the way, I can't remember what today's date is. Can you tell me? I'm still a little disorientated by that artillery explosion."

"I see no problem there my friend," Captain von Feldt answered. "Today is Wednesday and it is the 26th of September, and the time is four o'clock in the morning."

"The year is 1917?" Frank asked.

"Stop playing games with me, prisoner. Of course, it's 1917, but you know that don't you?" von Feldt barked.

"Well, I do now, and I also know that you had better pack your things because you are about to go on a long trip backwards." Frank recognised the date from that on the memorial at the top of the butt, where he was only an hour ago. *Or was it? There was no memorial on the top when I woke up,* he thought. *Strange? Just what did that gentleman up top do?*

"Oh, had I?" scoffed von Feldt. "So, you and who's army are going to dislodge me from here then, Private Baily?"

"Corporal actually," Frank reacted instinctively. *Oops, let that one out.*

"Ah so you do remember something then, do you?" crowed von Feldt.

Frank reacted quickly. "I seem to be remembering a little more. Maybe I'm getting my memory back." He chided himself for letting that out, but it was a good lesson to him, to watch what he said and take it slowly. He thought to himself now that if it was four am on the 26th the 55th would be forming up on their front tape as they spoke. He needed to draw this out as long as possible, without giving the game away. *Wait a minute,* he then thought. *What am I saying? This isn't real. This is only a re-enactment. He already knows what is going to happen.*

At this point, another soldier entered and spoke briefly to the captain. He gave him some orders and dismissed him. "We will be staying under here for a little while. Our artillery is about to give a little touch-up to any of your friends that might have wandered close to our lines, just like you did."

As he spoke Frank could hear the tell-tale signs of artillery explosions not too far away.

He knew from his reading that the artillery used here was of the 5.9" calibre, so he commented. "So, that sounds like 5.9s captain, or perhaps I should say 150 mm."

"I'm impressed Corporal," came the reply. "You know your artillery. I shall have to watch you."

"It won't do you any good. There's no one there. Yet!" Frank knew, there in fact were troops there, but he thought it might help to cut the barrage short.

At that moment, the soldier that came in earlier, returned and placed a bundle of clothing on the table. The captain again spoke to him, he saluted and departed.

"Some clothes for you Corporal Bailey. You must be rather cold right now, the captain said.

"Thank you. Yes, it is rather cool isn't it?" Replied Frank and he pulled on a pair of German uniform breeches and a jacket.

"Shall we go up top and watch the display? They have their range now and it should be safe for us," the captain showed Frank to the door and up the makeshift stairs to the top of the butt. Crouching down in a trench, Frank could see the artillery exploding in the morning half-light. *Holy shit! This is real stuff,* thought Frank. *These are real explosions. What the fuck is going on here?* One of the shells fell a little shorter than the others and some of the dirt from the explosion made it to the men on the top of the butt.

"So, you see, Cpl Bailey," said the captain as they walked back down to the dugout, "If any of your friends are out there, they are all dead by now."

"We'll see captain. We'll see," replied Frank. This comment seemed to unsettle the captain.

A few moments later the barrage ceased.

Sitting back underground the captain continued to try and get information out of Frank, but he kept falling back on the memory loss from the artillery story. He could see the captain's patience was wearing thin. He had to come up with something to appease him.

"I can tell you something captain," Frank said. This made the captain sit up.

"And what might that be?" he replied.

"Well, the Russians won't be in this war much longer," Frank told him. "There will be a revolution there very soon, and they will sue for peace. That will release fifty divisions of your troops to reinforce your army over here."

"So, are you Nostradamus now are you Corporal Baily?" The captain smiled as he said this.

"Let us just say I have some ability, in being able to tell you what goes down in the future," Frank explained.

"Goes down? What is this, goes down?" he demanded.

"Oh sorry. That term hasn't been invented yet. It means, what happens in the future." Frank followed this explanation with a little chuckle.

"So, you think the Ruskies will give up then do you." Von Feldt asked Frank.

"Oh, I don't think they will give up. I know they will," Frank told him. "There will be a revolution and they will throw out the Tzar and eventually kill the family, and a new style of Bolshevism will arise and rule the country for seventy years. Actually, it will wreck the country in my opinion."

"You really are a sooth are you not?" laughed the captain.

"You just watch, captain. I give it two months." Frank smiled. Like he was ever going to see him again anyway, after today.

As he finished his sentence, shooting broke out from above them and explosions started ripping through the butt. The soldier that had brought the clothes in dashed in and rapidly spoke to the captain. He grabbed his helmet and dashed out briefly, shouting orders to the men around him. He spun around and glared at Frank. "No one out there you say. Are these your Australian 55th?"

Frank just sat there and smiled and folded his arms. He knew that most of the men at the butt had gone back to sleep after the earlier artillery barrage was over, as the place had gone so quiet, but not now. There was shouting and men running in from further behind the butt, at the same time as explosions sent many of these men sky high. He could hear the yelling of the advancing Australians, just as von Feldt dashed in with the earlier soldier, who stood Frank up roughly and tied his hands together. "You, soothsayer, are coming with me."

"We wouldn't be retreating, would we captain?" Frank asked with a knowing smile on his face.

"Fear not corporal, we will counterattack, as soon as we are reorganised," yelled the captain. "Get moving." The soldier behind him prodded him heavily with the muzzle of his rifle and Frank set off, with the captain leading the way and a rifle pointed at his back. As they ran, he looked around him at the devastation going on. The stench of death was unmistakable. The human bodies, as well as horses, lying all around.

In his twenties, Frank had been to visit the whaling station in Albany, on the south coast of Western Australia. He remembered the stench from that was almost unbearable, but this; this was something else altogether. Bodies and pieces of bodies protruding from the upper trench walls. Detritus everywhere. Equipment, scraps of timber, shell-hit sides caving in. It was a sensory overload for Frank. At one point, there was a mostly decomposed head and shoulders, protruding from the trench walls and his gaping mouth was partly filled with cigarette buts. His mouth was being used as an ashtray. *"What have these men been through here, to cause them to overlook the dignity or fate of one of their own in this manner?"* Frank thought as he moved swiftly along.

"All these explosions are real. People are really dying here. This is no re-enactment. This is for real. Who the hell was that gentleman? Could I really be in 1917?" These and a million other thoughts raced through his mind. He had stopped smiling now. This was serious.

They had run about five hundred metres when the captain slowed down to a walk. He felt safer now back here. They went down into a backup trench system and the captain ushered him into another dugout. There were two other officers in that dugout. They snapped to attention, so Frank guessed they must be lieutenants. They looked at Frank with bewilderment. Von Feldt spoke to them briefly and one of them left. The other soldier was standing guard outside the entrance.

"Corporal Bailey, Leutnant Rudner." Frank saluted the lieutenant as best he knew how.

"So, Corporal Sooth I shall call you," the captain said mockingly. What else do you not remember?"

"I'm sorry I don't remember," Frank replied.

"Fear not corporal," von Feldt scoffed. "Our counterattack will soon have your 55th on their heels and retreating again. I have to give you this much; your Australian troops fight a better fight than their British counterparts."

"No doubt about that captain," Frank replied.

"So Corporal Sooth, how will our counterattack go then?" asked von Feldt.

"You won't get past the beginning, our artillery, will stop you in your tracks. You may try a few more times, but you will not make any progress." Frank replied. He was giving this advice from memory, from what he had read in the Cloth Hall museum, and the Zonnebeke, Passchendaele museum.

"Hah!" von Feldt scoffed. "That shows how much you know. Our glorious German army will crash its way back to the wood and your Australians will be in retreat."

"We'll see, captain. We will see," Frank repeated. Once again the smile disappeared from von Feldt's face. He spoke to the lieutenant in German. Rudner turned and looked intently at Frank and asked, "So, how is it you know what happens in future if you cannot remember?"

"Oh, I guess it's called selective amnesia, Rudner," von Feldt commented, glancing at Frank.

"Well, I guess if you have been close enough to a big bang to blow your clothes off like I apparently have, then you would have some loss of memory, wouldn't you?" Frank suggested.

"Maybe. Maybe not," Rudner replied. "We will see corporal. We will see."

Von Feldt smiled at this mocking of Frank. Frank refused to react. Instead, he opted to wait and see.

"So leutnant, in the meantime, what are we to do, with our guest?" asked von Feldt.

"Perhaps, we should hold him a small longer and see his predictions fail. Our counterattack should answer that one very quick, do you think?" Rudner smiled as he remarked. His English was not as good as von Feldt's.

"A little longer. Yes, I think that is a very good idea, leutnant," von Feldt replied. "Would you please arrange for him to be 'accommodated' nearby? That way we will be able to show him he does not know everything. Goodbye corporal."

"Until we meet again Captain von Feldt." Frank saluted and turned to follow Rudner.

Rudner indicated for Frank to precede him and then walked him twenty metres down the trench and around to the reserve sap, where he showed him into a small underground room.

"You should be quite comfortable in here corporal. Escape is not possible. Guard is on door and door is locked. I will arrange for food to be brought to you. I take it you have not eaten today?" Rudner asked.

"Thank you, lieutenant, that would be lovely," Frank replied.

Rudner left, after lighting the kerosene lamp. Frank looked around his cell. It was about 3 metres square. The walls were timber planked, to hold the dirt back. It was less than 1.8 metres in height. He was glad he was not that tall. There was a wooden plank table with a bench seat on one side and a double-decker bunk on the other, which left him with less than 6 square metres to move around in. There was a layer of hessian, draped across the doorway and a large wooden door, securely bolted, across the opening. It was full daylight by now and he could see daylight streaming through the slits in the door. At least he would not suffocate in here, he figured. He had to stop and think at first, but he worked out that if the daylight was coming through the door at that angle, it had to be facing south. The opposite of what it would be at home.

Shortly, the door was unlocked and a soldier came in with a plate of something. He placed it on the table and turned to walk out. Before leaving, he looked at Frank and spoke, "Schweinehund," was all he said, before leaving and locking the door.

"Love you too," Frank said as he left, then he smiled. The smile did not last long. He sat with the 'meal' and contemplated his predicament. "*Somehow, and don't ask me how, he thought, I have ended up in 1917*". His rational brain tried to tell him that this was not possible, but what other conclusion could he draw? He has just watched real artillery explosions; real people, dying in front of him, and now this food? "*If that's what it is,*" he thought. He took up the spoon and gingerly tasted it. "Mm. Actually, not bad tasting," he said aloud. It was true, he was hungry now. It had been several hours since breakfast at the hotel. "Breakfast at the hotel," he said, again aloud. "That seems like a lifetime ago. Shit, Lynne?"

He wondered what was happening back in ..... well, 2000. "*But this can't be happening. This is the sort of event that only happens in movies. It can't happen in real life. It just can't.*" But it was. He was in a cell, behind the German lines, near Polygon Wood, in Belgium, in 1917. He racked his brain now, to think back on all the bits and pieces he had read at the museums and in his notes. "My notes," he said aloud. He stood and patted himself down. Nothing. "I had them in a folder, on the step next to me, on the memorial at the butt," he said. "They must still be there.

Dammit, the obelisk was not there when I woke up. They must have stayed behind in 2000. Don't be such a fool. This is 2000. I'm just somewhere else."

He went over to the bunk which had a wire base and a kapok mattress. He lay down on it in an attempt to get some sleep. It was dank and musty and smelled of.... Heaven only knows what that is. He did not think he would be able to get any sleep. He did however manage to get a little sleep and when he woke, the light was coming through the slits in the door at quite an angle and had a golden hue. "It must be afternoon, late afternoon at that," he thought. He tried peering through the slits in the door. He could see the guard out the front. It looked like a different guard, as he was much taller. He moved to the table and sat down, again trying to work out a way to get out of his predicament. His thoughts just went round and round in his head.

Just then, there was a clank of the slide bolt on the door, and the guard entered with his evening meal. He put it down on the table along with some English language newspapers.

As he left, he got to the door and turned and looked at Frank and said "Schweinehund," then left, locking the door behind him. Frank just sniggered. He did not need an interpreter for that one. He ate his meal and turned the lamp up, to read the newspaper. It was a British newspaper, from several months ago, so the information in it was old, but it was something to read.

Outside, it slowly went dark, as night crawled on. The not-so-far-off noise of battle continued even so. Every now and then, Frank could feel the ground shudder. Later, he grew weary and lay down on the bunk. He fell asleep again. A little later, there was the clanking of the slide bolt in his door again, but this time he was greeted by Lieutenant Rudner. "Good evening, Corporal.

The captain wishes you join him, to experience German counterattack."

"Well thank you, lieutenant. I would be honoured to accompany you," Frank said mockingly, even though he figured Rudner would be unable to realise that he was being mocked.

They wandered back through the trench system, through ankle deep mud and slush. They dodged around men and equipment, with Frank attempting to memorise each turn, each gun emplacement, each point of significance. When they arrived at the command post again, the lieutenant announced his arrival, "Corporal Sooth sir!"

"Thank you, Rudner. Come in corporal. Please take a seat. You look good in a German uniform. You should consider joining us," the captain said with a smile.

"What, and join a losing side?" came Frank's retort. "No way. I will wait to be rescued by our gallant Aussie troops." The smile on von Feldt's face turned to a scowl, but only for a brief time though. His smile slowly returned as he added, "I have brought you here, to see our victorious counterattack. Now we will see how much of a sooth you are, won't we?"

"Alright, let the games begin," said Frank.

"Shortly that will happen, fear not corporal. Do you drink tea, like your British counterparts?" von Feldt asked.

"Yes, thank you. I do," answered Frank.

Von Feldt turned to Rudner and nodded and he left the bunker. The captain returned to the table where Frank was sitting and sat down on the opposite side. He studied Frank's face intently, whilst Frank did likewise. Von Feldt must have been about forty, he thought. Perhaps a little old for the rank of captain. He was dark haired and fair skinned and about 5'6" in height. His hands were quite large and gnarled. Perhaps he was a manual worker with those hands. A captain, who was a worker, with a name prefix von, did not add up for Frank. Usually, in Germany, anyone with the prefix von, was of noble stock, at least somewhere in the past.

"So, what is your story captain? You're from Hamburg and your name is von Feldt." Frank summarised. The captain looked uncomfortable by the question. He went on, "Your hands tell me you are a labourer or similar," (von Feldt moved his hands under the table), "and yet you have the name of a nobleman. What happened?"

"You sir, are very observant and knowledgeable, are you not? Yes, my family was a noble family in the last century, but my grandfather fell foul of the law, a good few years ago. After that, the family struggled for many years to survive. Our name was not well respected after that. In 1910, I joined the army, where the story of my family was not known, and my name managed to get me so far. I fear however, I may not go much further now as my immediate commander knows of my family's misfortune. I am resigned to that, but I am still proud to be a Hauptman in the German army. What about you corporal? You must have a story too. You don't appear to be all that you say."

"Captain, if I were to tell you all of my story you would not believe me. Suffice to say, I grew up with a mother, father and an older brother. He went to war some years ago, and when he came home, he was nothing like what he was when he left." Frank started.

"Ahh yes. That does happen to some," von Feldt commented.

"My Father was an old soldier as well, fighting for his country, as was his father," added Frank. He resisted the temptation to say that in fact, he was over the other side of the butt as they spoke.

"So, you come from a line of soldiers. That explains a lot," added the captain.

"I did my training in architecture and have been doing rather well in it, until I came here, where I found myself in a different world. Quite literally!" Frank laughed at his last comment.

"Yes, Frank, isn't it?" Asked the captain. Frank nodded. "This is really like another world. A world I sometimes do not understand. I am proud to be a soldier of the Kaiser, but I am not so sure this is the right thing to be doing. We are not so different you and I, are we?"

"No captain," replied Frank. "We are not."

At that moment, Rudner broke into the bunker and spoke to the captain. "Danke Rudner." Turning to Frank, von Feldt went on, "Shall we go and watch the counterattack?"

"Sure, if you are sure you want to," replied Frank.

They went out to the front trench and just to be sure, the captain had Frank's hands tied to him. They climbed up onto the firing step to observe. Frank could see many men in the darkness, already out in no man's land. A double red flare went up, and as soon as it was dark again, the men rose and started to advance. Immediately the Allied artillery opened up, and Frank could see advancing German troops flying through the air, silhouetted against the flashes of the exploding artillery. Men were dodging and weaving, left and right, forward and back, until there was a white flare sent up, and all the remaining German troops returned to their trenches. They had not advanced any further than fifty metres before returning to their trenches.

Von Feldt turned and looked at Frank, and Frank just shrugged his shoulders, then added, "I tried to tell you."

"How? Just How? Can you really see the future; or were you just lucky?" von Feldt asked.

Frank took this to be a rhetorical question. At least he turned it into one.

They moved back to the bunker and Rudner removed the restraints. They all sat down. Rudner looked shattered, von Feldt disheartened. Frank just sat and said nothing. Better to be quiet now he thought. Give them time to process what just happened.

"So, if you can see the future Frank, what happens to me?" asked the captain.

Frank thought for a minute, trying to construct his reply without referring to specifics.

"I don't see things that specifically captain, but I can tell you, that you will not retake this wood, this year. Not only that, but you will not win this war. By the end of next year, it will all be over."

"Not true!" yelled Rudner as he jumped to his feet and stomped his foot. "We will defeat you!"

Von Feldt looked up and said disconsolately, "Thank you, Hans. That will be all."

"Mein Herr!" Rudner saluted and left.

"So!" von Feldt commented slowly and deliberately. "What am I to do with you?"

"Well, you could let me go," Frank suggested half hoping.

"That cannot happen, Frank. My men or your men would shoot you out there. And to be quite honest, I do not want that either." Von Feldt found that he genuinely liked Frank, even though he was the 'enemy'. He most certainly respected him for his insight, even if he could not understand it.

"I think I just have to send you up the line, my Corporal Sooth," he smiled. "I will try to get you to a POW camp, without going through the usual channels. I will see what I can do."

"Thank you, Captain von Feldt," Frank said as he stood. "You are a good man. You are not to blame for your grandfather's mistakes. You are your own man. Just remember that. You are you, not your grandfather."

"Thank you, Frank. I know you are right. Good luck to you." He held out his hand to shake, and Frank took it with genuine emotion. Von Feldt went on, "I'm sorry, but I have to send you back to your accommodation for the time being. I will have to try and sort something out for you."

"Thank you, sir," and Frank took a pace back and saluted him. He had been watching the 'Last Post' ceremony closely. The captain returned the salute and then called the guard to take Frank back to his cell. The soldier marched Frank back to his cell, pushing him in. As he pulled the door to, he stopped and looked at Frank. "I know," said Frank, and both he and the soldier chorused "Schweinehund."

Back in his cell Frank reflected on his night's work. He had found that although they were the enemy, they were just men like himself, with the same insecurities and backgrounds. Given a different set of circumstances they would probably all get on. He was now convinced, although his logical brain said it was not possible, that he was indeed in 1917. Somehow, he would have to make the best of this and wait until he could get back to Lynne and the children. What must they be thinking now? It had now been more than 24 hours since he disappeared from them.

He lay down to sleep again, figuring it had to be just before dawn when he heard the artillery start up again, but this time he figured it must be the German artillery firing on the butt. It was not long before he could hear the Allied artillery firing back. This time some of the shells landed awfully close by. He could hear men calling for help and calls of what he thought may have been, "Tragentrager", which he figured must be calls for stretcher-bearers. Shortly there were a lot more voices outside. He figured now that another counterattack had failed. He remained in his cell for the next two days. The meals he received, after his last encounter with the captain, took a turn for the better. He even got a glass of wine with his meal. Not only that, but the guards stopped calling him "Schweinehund".

On Saturday morning, Lieutenant Rudner came to his cell and advised him he was on his way to a POW holding camp, back towards Germany. "Please accompany me, Corporal Bailey." He said in his stilted English. Frank followed him outside into the trench. They were a party of four. Frank, Rudner, and an armed guard in front and behind, with bayonets fixed. *Now was not the time to attempt an escape*, he thought.

He was taken back to what Frank guessed must have been some kind of headquarters, again underground. Once again, the stench was overwhelming. He thought if he was getting further back the area would be cleaner, but to his dismay, if anything it was worse. He figured it must have been about a further five hundred metres back, but this time northeast. That meant he was not yet getting too much further behind the front line. This was good news, he felt. If he was going further back from the front, it was going to be harder going to get back to the allied lines. If his figuring was right, he would still be south of Zonnebeke.

There is not a dramatic difference, between drafting buildings and drafting maps. If you are good at one, then there is a high chance that you have developed a good understanding of mapping. This ability helped Frank to keep track of where he was, in relation to the front line. He loved maps too, and as such, had studied the maps of the area intently when he was trying to work out where his grandfather had been, as well as where he wanted to explore. The pronunciation of the local names, however, was a different game. He had only worked out what he thought the names would sound like. For example, he had thought from the spelling that the town to his north would be pronounced Zon- e -beek, whereas when he got there, he found that it was Zon -e -beck. He decided now, he had to listen intently to conversations, even though they were in German, to see if he could identify any town names.

On arrival, Rudner passed his paperwork to another officer, and the two of them spoke for a brief time. He heard Polygon, so he figured he was explaining where he was 'captured'.

The new officer looked at Frank, indicated for Rudner to stay, and went away, returning shortly with another officer. Frank guessed the first officer must be a lieutenant, as he had similar insignias to Rudner. At this point, Rudner saluted and left with his escort. The second officer spoke to the lieutenant who then said, "The Major here wishes you a happy retirement from this war. You are to remain here for two or three days before being moved to a POW camp in Germany, with some other prisoners we have as our guests." The Major spoke again to the lieutenant who then translated, "You appear to be a valued guest of the Kaiser, corporal. These papers say you have an amazing insight into happenings here on the Western Front. The Major wishes to find out if you have any, shall we say, useful information for us, so we have arranged for you to have private quarters, where we may conduct further interviews with you."

Frank had seen enough WW2 movies to know what 'interview' meant. He was not too impressed with this new commander at this point.

"Tell the Major I will be only too happy to tell him the same information I gave to Hauptman von Feldt. I have truly little other information, either of value, or otherwise," Frank explained to the lieutenant. He watched the Major's face as his words were translated. He could see the major was not impressed by Frank's bravado. Then a smile came to his face, as he gave his reply to the lieutenant, who then turned to Frank and said, "Well corporal, we will be the judge of whether the information is of use or not. We have ways of getting the information we need."

Frank did not flinch one bit as the translation was spoken to him. He then asked the lieutenant for the Major's name, so he could conduct a civil conversation with him. The lieutenant did not worry about translating this, he simply replied, "Major Blick."

An intense conversation then ensued between Blick and the lieutenant, during which, it appeared to Frank, that Blick was not happy that the lieutenant had divulged his name without first seeking his approval. It looked to Frank like the lieutenant received a right royal bollicking. He smiled. At the end of this exchange, the lieutenant told Frank to follow him. As soon as they left the bunker, two armed guards joined them, for the fifty or so metre walk to an extensive dugout network. They descended a few metres, maybe five or eight, into a tunnel that led shortly to a series of large doors, complete with external slide bolts. He recognised the style of door from his time in the cells, just east of Polygon. He was shoved into one of these by the guard and the door bolted. This time there was no light. He quietly called, "Is there anyone else in here?" To which he got no reply.

In the total darkness, Frank felt around and found that this cell was an almost exact duplicate of the one back at Polygon. He found the bed and lay down. He had only just got comfortable when the door unbolted and the lieutenant walked in with a candle. He set it on the table, lit it and motioned for Frank to join him. The guard also came into the room. A particularly uninspiring looking fellow. He had a stern look on his overly filthy face; a square jaw, which could have done with a shave, Frank thought, and looked like he had the sense of humour of a brick. He inwardly smiled. This fellow seemed to fit the archetypal German poster boy of the British media of the time. *Beware the Hun. Lock up your women and children*, was all Frank could think of when he looked at this fellow.

As he sat down, Frank commenced the conversation with, "I take it Major Blick was not too impressed you told me his name?" He figured by asking the first question, he would assume the upper hand.

"I am not interested in that," answered the Lieutenant. "I am Leutnant Erlinger of the 27th Saxon regiment, as you can see, and you are Corporal Frank Bailey of the 55Th Battalion AIF. Is that correct?"

"You're telling the story. Is that what you have been told?" Frank asked. He had been on many Professional Development courses, which told him that he who asks the questions, controls the conversation.

"It is, corporal," Erlinger replied.

"So, what is it you wish to know, lieutenant?" enquired Frank.

"I wish to know everything you know about the Australian Army," replied Erlinger.

"Well, I can tell you they are the best army in the world," Frank taunted.

"Humph!" was the only reply he got from Erlinger.

"I can also tell you; you will not retake Polygon Wood this year, you will also lose Zonnebeke, Broodseinde and Passchendaele, all in the next six weeks." Frank was enjoying this.

"Rubbish! We will retake Polygon shortly, and you will not take another metre of Europe." Erlinger banged his fist on the sturdy table.

"Gotcha!" thought Frank. "You have lost control." He smiled. This smile seemed to upset the German even more.

"So, just what makes you think that the army that just drove you out of Polygon Wood, in one day, where the rest of the British army could not do it in a year, is going to let you just take it back?" Frank again taunted this poor lieutenant.

"The German Army does not surrender, especially to a bunch of colonials," the lieutenant shouted at Frank. Frank just smiled again. He could see out of the corner of his eye the face of the guard. It was cracking; not a smile maybe, but some change all the same. The lieutenant was standing over Frank, from the opposite side of the table at this point. He stopped, stood upright and took a deep breath. This interview was not going the way it was supposed to. He paced the room, as if to measure it, like a captive might do when he first enters his cell.

Shortly he resumed his seat. "Now Corporal Bailey, I wish to know just how many men you have left in your famous 55th Battalion?"

"Beats me," Frank exclaimed. "Do you know how many men in your regiment?"

"I do," replied Erlinger.

"Well, perhaps you could tell me that then," Frank suggested. "You're a lieutenant. I'm just a corporal. How the hell would I know that? I look after fifteen men. That's it. The rest is for officers. Hey Fritz," he called to the guard, "Do you know how many men in your regiment?" The guard just looked at him, but this time his face did not crack.

"He does not speak English corporal. Stop being so impertinent," the lieutenant added.

"Impertinent? To be impertinent, one has to believe that one person in the conversation, is of a much higher status than the other. Do you think you are better than me?" Frank asked him.

"Of course, I am. I am a leutnant in the Kaiser's army and you; you are a pig corporal in some colonial, pretend army," Erlinger again yelled at Frank.

"Ah yes, but a colonial pretend army that just threw you and your army out of Polygon Wood," Frank replied.

The lieutenant instantly stood threateningly, reaching for his pistol, but stopped as his hand was on the holster. In this brief moment, Frank was thinking that his last remark may have been just one too many taunts. At the same time, he knew he had the obviously inexperienced lieutenant rattled.

The lieutenant stood there frozen, for what seemed like an hour, but was of course only three or so seconds, before he again stood straight, smoothed out his tunic and said, "We shall continue this interrogation at a time when you are maybe more prepared to answer. Guard!" The two of them left the cell. Frank heaved a sigh of relief and thought, *"Aussies 1 - Germans nil."*

The meal that was served to him this day was nothing like he had become used to with von Feldt. This was back to unidentifiable slops, with cold coffee. At least he thought it might have been coffee.

Late that afternoon, his door once again opened and this time the officer that entered immediately looked to Frank to be much more experienced. For a start, he was wearing an Iron Cross on his tunic. This guy was for real, he thought. Careful with him.

"Good afternoon Corporal Bailey. I am Captain Gorman, and I wish to ask you a few questions, before you go on to Germany POW camp. This time, however, none of your games like with Leutnant Erlinger."

"Games captain? I don't know what you are talking about. I never played any games with the good lieutenant," Frank replied.

"Hmm. It seems you told Captain von Feldt a few things that I would like to clarify with you." The captain was reading from some notes. "55th Battalion. Australian. Corporal. Amnesia. Shell explosion blew your clothes off, leaving you in your underwear. I would have liked to see that," the captain said with a smile on his face.

"Captain, that is not a very nice thing to say." Frank started in. The smile disappeared and Gorman just glared at him. This one was definitely going to be a harder nut to crack.

"What I want to know, corporal," Gorman started, "is just what were you doing that far in front on your own? You were on your own, were you not?"

"Well, you see captain," Frank commenced, "as your notes clearly tell you, it would appear that a shell explosion nearby blew me over, and I cannot remember much at all of that day.

The medical fraternity say that when a blow to the head causes memory loss it is called concussion. Must have been that."

"So, you still claim amnesia, do you?" Gorman queried.

"Can you think of any other explanation captain?" Frank was swinging around, to asking the questions again.

"Oh yes, corporal. I can think of one or two other explanations," Gorman replied.

"Really?" Frank feigned surprise. "What would they be, I wonder?"

"Well maybe you are just lying, or maybe you are just a fool," the captain answered.

"Ah! I see where you are coming from captain," Frank mocked in his best John Cleese impersonation. "Well for a start, I don't lie and I know I am not a fool, so there must be another reason. Don't you think?" Frank smiled as he answered.

"What is it you find so funny, corporal?" asked the captain.

"Oh, nothing really. It's just that you reminded me of someone I once saw," explained Frank.

"Tell me more, corporal".

"Oh. You reminded me of General Burkhalter, from Hogan's Heroes. You sounded just like him," Frank said.

"A general huh? Yes, I guess that could be true. What is this Hogan's thing?" the captain asked.

"It's a TV show I used to watch as a kid." Frank then explained.

"T V? What is this T V?" the captain queried.

"Oh shit! I've done it again," thought Frank. *"I got too comfortable."* He thought quickly.

"Oh, it's an invention we have in Australia. It's sort of like the picture theatre," he hastily answered.

"Oh, I see." The captain seemed happy with that answer. Frank guessed he would have no knowledge of Australia, or the way of life down there.

"Maybe we should try something a little different. In these notes, it is stated that you knew the outcome of our counterattack before it even happened. Not only the outcome but the reasons for that outcome. How is it that you, a lowly corporal, should have advance knowledge of such things?" Gorman asked.

"You see, it's like this. I read it in the history books. It explained how you lost Polygon Wood, and how you never got it back this year." Frank informed him. He waited anxiously for his reaction to this statement. Initially, there was silence. Frank could see that Gorman was trying to process the statement he had just made.

"History books?" The captain hissed. "This isn't history. It is happening now."

"Oh, I see what you mean," replied Frank. "I thought you knew. I am from the future, from the year 2000, and I know that not only did you lose Polygon Wood, but in the next month or so you will lose, Zonnebeke, Broodseinde, and Passchendaele."

"Don't be absurd man. From the future? What do you take me for? Do you think I am the fool now?" barked the captain.

"Well, you know what they say about the cap fitting and wearing it. Oh, and they will take this place as well, and you will lose the war in November 1918." Frank added the bait.

"Take Molenaarelsthoek? Don't be ridiculous! This place is untakable. As for losing the war, you clearly are deluded. I think you must be mad. Perhaps you have this shell shock thing they are talking about?" the captain started getting annoyed.

"Perhaps, that's what it is my friend, but when you do lose the war, if you are still alive, I want you to think back on this conversation, and ask yourself, who was that man?" Frank felt he had him now.

"I am not your friend, corporal, I am your enemy," Gorman stated emphatically.

"No captain, you are not my enemy," Frank brought the pace of the conversation back down now. "Your country may be at war with mine, but you sir, are not my enemy. You are just another man, just like me. Wrong place, at the wrong time."

"I am not like you. I am better than you, and from a better country than you," Gorman stomped his foot.

"There captain, is the whole reason for war, encapsulated in one short sentence." Frank sat back in his chair now and folded his arms as if to signify, 'that is the end of this interview. You may leave now.'

To his surprise, the captain stood and nodded to the guard. He turned to Frank and repeated, "I think you must be mad. I really do." He turned and walked out. Australia 2 – Germany nil.

"Molenaarelsthoek. I'll have to remember that name," Frank thought.

✦

Chapter 7
Four Mates

**The world is a dangerous place to live; not
because of the people who are evil, but because
of the people who don't do anything about it.**
Albert Einstein

For the next couple of days, Frank had no visitors other than the delivery of his 'food'.

He could hear other men talking in English nearby, but each time he tried to call out to them a rifle butt clattered into his door. On one attempt he did get a return, "Hello Aussie! Are you really mad?" followed by laughter. His reply brought great guffaws from the other cell. "Well, I'm here, aren't I? I must be." Frank yelled back.

"Good on ya Aussie. Give 'em hell," came the reply, before a rifle butt smacked into the other door, followed by a "Schweigen Swein!" Which in turn was followed by "Keep ya hair on Fritz!" and further guffaws of laughter.

In the other cell, were three British POWs. Two of them were from the Royal West Kent's and the third was from the King's Own Scottish Borderers. They had been captured in the days before and were being held, pending transfer to a POW camp.

"Bloomin heck! You'd think these guys didn't want us talkin' to the Aussie." One of the Prisoners said.

"Not very bloody social, these Bosch, are they?" Replied the second.

"Wonder wha' he's done to upset the buggers? That was a few thumps and bumps we 'eard from 'is cell. Hope they didn't touch 'im up too much," the first man added.

"I do not think they hurt him at all, gentlemen. It sounded to me like the Aussie was upsetting the Fritz," the third one answered, in a much more cultured accent.

"Yeah, I think you're right, mate. That's what it sounded like to me too," the second prisoner said. "I certainly hope that's what he did anyway." After a short pause, he continued, "They're a funny lot those Aussies don't you reckon? They seem like they don't give a toss about rank or station or anything like that, but geez can they fight?"

"Yeah mate," answered the first. "Ya wouldn't wanna get on the wrong side of 'em. I go' a few mates, who was wiv 'em in the Dardanelles, in '15. Bloody resourceful lot they are. Makin' bombs from jam tins, periscopes to shoot over the bags, and that bloody water drip firing thing-oh they used to get away from the place, wivout getting noticed, bloody brilliant init?"

"Yeah, funny lot they are," the second fellow added.

Throughout these two days, Frank spent on his own, they were subjected to multiple bombardments from the British, he assumed, artillery. He thought back to the unit diaries he had been reading so intently from the 28th Battalion diaries and laughed at the number of times he read comments like, "subjected to Bosch artillery for a three-hour barrage. Little damage, no casualties." Similar comments were made over many months, so he figured the use of artillery, whilst new to this war, was not particularly effective. He could recall only one case in 1918, where the German artillery had indeed been effective and on that occasion considerable damage had been done to the allied trenches and five ORs were killed. Still, not an effective use of resources, he thought. There were yet other reports in there like, "Our artillery gave the Hun a good dust-up today. Went on for four hours. Looks like it has had a particularly good effect."

Somehow, I doubt whether that would actually have been the case, Frank thought to himself.

He had not been able to work out exactly in which direction his cell faced this time, as it was not receiving any sunlight. This time however, he realised the distant artillery explosions were coming from a direction straight out of his front door, which would mean he was probably facing west, or at least generally in a westerly direction. This barrage from the Allied lines had now been going on for at least two hours. As Frank was trying to gather his thoughts, following a nearby crump that had sent dust into his cell, there was a massive explosion and his front door came careening into his cell. He was fortunate to have been lying on his bunk, which deflected the door, but a large shard of timber, struck him in his right arm, opening up a moderate wound. There was yelling and screaming in the distance and people running in all directions.

He stuck his head outside the door, or what was left of his door, to find the entrance to his part of the dugouts had taken a direct hit. His Guard was dead against the doorframe, half buried in dirt. Frank climbed over the rubble and he was about to do a bolt when he remembered the other cell of Pommies. He looked to his left and saw a similar door to his. It was undamaged. He dashed over and slid the bolt and the door opened. The guard at this door was also dead. His head had been severed and whilst still attached was lying backwards, looking at his feet.

"Poor bastard," Frank commented. as he removed the guard's boots. Frank had been kept in bare feet all the time of his incarceration. The men inside rushed out. "Are you the Aussie?" one of them asked, to which he replied, "Bloody oath I am!"

"Mate your blood's worth bottlin'. Now, 'ow the 'ell do we get out of 'ere?" came the reply from the Brit as he grasped both Frank's shoulders and smiled a huge smile.

Frank intended to use the confusion to affect his escape. "Grab whatever Jerry uniform you can lay your hands on and slide it over your own."

"Jerry? What's that?' came the Englishman's reply.

"Sorry," Frank said shaking his head. "I mean Hun. Jerry must be an Australian name for them." He realised then, that the term 'Jerry' did not come into common use until WW2. *Hun, Bosch or Fritz. I've got to remember that,* he noted, thinking back to the unit diary notes.

There were two other dead Fritz, whose uniforms and gear they acquired, which left one still not disguised. They decided he would be their 'prisoner' if challenged. One of the Brits spoke some German, which would be useful. Frank had picked up a little but did not think it would be particularly useful. They grabbed whatever rifles they could find and a few grenades too. Once they got moving, they just blended in with the soldiers still above ground. They pointed stretcher bearers in the direction of the blow as they went. Their German speaker would add, "Dieser weg" or "Nachster graben". "That way, or Next trench"

The four escapees figured if they could keep moving until sundown, they would be able to hop over the edge, into no man's land and crawl for home. This meant they had about 30 minutes to kill, so to speak. They just hoped that the artillery barrage would continue until then, as most of the forward troops had retreated to the reserve, or fall back trench system. By now they were about two hundred metres to the north of their former position and they found a small cave-like dugout, cut into the front trench wall a few feet below the surface. It was empty.

"This will have to do, fellas. If we can hold out here for 30 minutes or so, and the barrage continues for that long, we may be able to make a break for it across no man's land. Do you know where we are?" he asked the Brits.

"Nar mate," explained the one who seemed to be the spokesman for them all.

"Alright then," Frank started to explain. "We are just northeast of Polygon Wood, at a place called Molenaarelsthoek. We must be about a mile or so, south of Zonnebeke, which is still in German hands. We have the Aussie 55th at Polygon, and tomorrow the 28th is going to take up position opposite us."

"Bloody hell mate. Wha' are you? A bloody general or sommat'?" said the Brit.

"Nar mate I'm just..." he paused and thought for a second, "...I'm just a corporal in the 28th, with some special knowledge. By the way, the name's Frank."

The Englishman shook his head and glanced at his mates. "We've teamed up with a good one 'ere boys." They nodded. "Good on ya, Frank. I'm Geoffrey." They shook hands. This was then followed by "Thanks Frank, I'm Roland," and "Yes, thank you,

Frank, I'm Rupert." This last one was definitely from a different class to the others. He actually sounded like he should be an officer, but he wore no badges of rank. Roland was the one still in British uniform, as Rupert was the one who spoke some German. He would be useful if they were challenged.

Geoffrey then added, "Look mate, I've some bandages in this pack. Let me dress your arm. Looks okay now, but ya better get it covered up before the rats have a go at it."

"Thanks, Geoffrey," Frank answered, then went on, as Geoffrey dressed his wound. "I've been working on this. If we can get up to Zonnebeke and hide out in the ruins, we should be able to move into the forward advances of the 28th in a day or two. I mean why run through that lot out there if they will come to us?" queried Frank.

"Too true ma'ey. Assuming, they actually get through tha' is." Roland spoke up.

"They will. Believe me, they will. I told you I have, special knowledge, didn't I?"

"That you did my Aussie friend. That you did," replied Roland.

Just then a German infantryman rounded the corner and spoke to the men. Frank turned to look, and the soldier immediately recognised him from the captain's dugout. He had raised his rifle to point at Frank when there was a bang and a blast past his ear. The infantryman fell forward and his lifeless body ended up in a heap at Frank's feet.

"Well, that bastard I'n't going to 'urt anybody anymore," Geoffrey spoke. Frank turned to see the muzzle of Geoffrey's rifle pointed at where the German had been standing.

Frank sat with his mouth agape and rubbing his right ear.

Roland spoke up, "Nice shot ma'ey. Anuver notch on the belt."

"Yeah, think I'm going to be deaf in my right ear now though," Frank added, still rubbing his ear.

"Better deaf than dead my friend," Geoffrey replied. Frank just nodded.

"Good anticipation young fellow," Rupert added his congratulations.

By the time night fell the barrage was continuing, so the men thought they had leapt their first hurdle. The Huns were still predominantly underground, with only the occasional passing sentry who did not bother them. Frank had popped his head up a couple of times before dark to survey the scene. His theories were confirmed about the location of Zonnebeke. He could see what remained of it in the distance. Between them and the town lay a wasteland, of shell holes, wreckage and churned-up ground. And Mud, mud everywhere.

"I think our best bet, is to get out into no man's land before the barrage stops and take up in a shell hole, if it's not filled with water. This place will be swarming with Bosch the moment it stops. It looks like there is a firing step, just ten metres, sorry ten yards further on. There's no one there at the moment. Whaddaya think?" Frank asked them.

"Well, wha' I think is, you're the one with the 'special knowledge', so let's do it," Roland said. They all nodded in agreement.

"Let's go then," Frank suggested.

Our four new friends moved up to the firing step and cautiously peered over the top. There were whizzbangs going off, in all directions. Mostly eighteen pounders Rupert said. "It is interesting," he said. "If you listen closely, you can hear the occasional shell hit and not explode. We have been having some problems with our fusing, and we have long suspected that a proportion of our shells are duds."

No sooner than he had spoken, than there was a dull thud in the wall opposite them in the trench. The four men just sat there transfixed, looking at this hole where the shell entered the softer ground and did not explode. A small whisp of smoke or steam was emanating from the hole in the ground.

"I think that may well be the signal for us to go. Gentlemen?" and Frank bolted over the trench wall, heading for the nearest shell hole just five metres in front of the trench. As soon as he lay on his back on the slope looking back toward the German lines, he looked around to see the three others, in like manner, heaving with breathlessness.

"That, my friends, was a bit fucking close for comfort. Thank heavens for Pommie duds." Frank said as he started laughing. The others joined in with a sort of quiet, nervous laugh.

"Well, we are on our way. Over that way," said Frank pointing to his left, "is Zonnebeke. We just need to keep hopping shell holes and hope you poms can't aim right."

"I'll drink to that!" Geoffrey added. "Mind you, right now I could drink to just about anything."

"You said it my friend," added Rupert. "Do I ever have a story to tell when I get back? Yes, that one was one of the one in ten. Wait until I tell my mother about that one." Rupert was lying there with his eyes as wide open as he could get them. Frank wondered if they were about to pop clear out of his head.

"Right, as soon as the next near shell explodes and settles back down, we should hop onto the next hole," Frank explained.

On cue, the next shell dropped about twenty metres short of them. They counted to five then bolted over the top and dived into the next hole. Then silence.

"Shit, that's it. We've gotta move. Quick. Distance men, distance." Frank urged them on.

They were by now about fifty metres away from the German trenches when the air started coming alive, with little white and orange lines through the air. "Down!" yelled Frank as he dived into a hole. When he regained his composure, he found Geoffrey and Roland in the hole with him, but no Rupert. There was, however, a rather ghostly half-skeleton in the shell hole with them. He had one leg missing and the dregs of a German uniform trailing off him. They lay on their backs watching the tracer bullets flying over them. It was then, that he realised these tracers, were in fact going in both directions. "Damn!" he said. "They are both firing at us. Good news is, we can't be too far from the front line. Our front line that is."

"Rupert? Are you there Rupert?" Called Geoffrey.

"Yes, I am. I am just behind you," they heard Rupert reply. "These beastly shell holes, are so difficult to navigate in the half-dark. I have fallen on my face twice now."

The three in the first hole all laughed, a somewhat stifled laugh. Just then the allied artillery re-opened fire, hoping to catch those who had swarmed back to the front line. It sure put an end to the tracers from their rear. This time it only lasted about five minutes though and they were able to hop a further twenty or so metres north. They would lie low now, for an hour or so, to give the impression that they had not survived. From here on in though, Frank explained to them, it would be best if they crawled rather than ran. Rupert, by now, had worked that out and had joined them in their hole, along with an obviously long-dead, half decomposed, horse carcass, sticking up from the lake in the bottom of the hole.

"By now it should only be about fourteen hundred yards to Zonnebeke. I'm sure we can crawl that distance through the night." Frank suggested.

"That shouldn't be too difficult, provided we don't run into many more of these," Roland added, tilting his head toward the horse carcass.

Rupert joined in now, "Don't forget, if a flare goes up, freeze and close only one eye. That way, the closed one will be able to still see at night when the flare has gone."

Frank had not thought about this before, but even his high school science agreed with this practice. Keep one eye closed, to preserve your night vision and one eye open, to keep observing. Sound advice indeed.

By the time the four of them re-commenced their flight north, things had definitely quietened down. This time, their move prompted no machine gun fire. During the next hour, they managed to move, by their estimation, between 100 and 200 metres. They were happy with this progress, given that it was interrupted by seven different flare firings. The other good point was the only machine gun fire they experienced was random searching fire, mostly from the German lines and was nowhere near their position. They had intersected a north-south road, or what was left of it, that Frank calculated should lead them straight into Zonnebeke. If it was the road he thought it was, it should lead up behind the gardens of the Zonnebeke, Passchendaele Museum, although it would not become this for some years; even though it was, last week. *"Bizarre!"* He thought.

At around four am, the four fugitives could just see the glistening outlines of some of the ruins along the eastern edge of the road ahead of them. There was the remains of a copse, to the western side. The trees' ghostly, gaunt, skeletal remains, just visible due to the dew reflecting the available starlight. Frank did have his bearings right.

"Now," he whispered to his friends. "We just have to find somewhere to doss down, for a day or so. It is not going to be light for an hour or so yet, so we have the darkness on our side. Just remember this is a German-occupied town and we do not want to be captured at this stage."

They crept onto the edge of town, avoiding the ruins next to the road. They all figured, that if the Germans had a nest in the area, that would be a logical place to be. Also, there were likely to be trenches through the wooded area to their left. Using the drain alongside the remainder of the road, they crept ahead, inch by inch, stopping and listening every so often. To their surprise, they heard almost nothing in their area at all. At about the second line of ruined houses, they gathered and listened again. They could hear faint noises to the west of them, but nothing in this area. Geoffrey crept into the ruins of this house to see if there was any possibility of concealing themselves in this one. Roland checked out the next, Rupert the next, and all the while Frank kept lookout.

Rupert returned first. The house he had investigated included a small cellar. He figured they would easily fit. Both the others found nothing. By now the sky was showing signs of the approaching dawn. They needed to get out of sight now, so they crawled forward to Rupert's cellar.

"How the hell did you find this in the dark Rupert? It's well concealed," Frank asked him.

"I could say it was by skill, but I would be lying. It was pure luck. I was on hands and knees checking the floorboards, when I thought I felt the floor move. After removing a few blocks and feeling around, I felt a small hole. I placed my finger in it and pulled slowly. Voila!" Rupert felt immensely proud, that he had finally contributed something to their escape plans.

"Well, this should do us nicely lads, I reckon," said Geoffrey. "You've done very nicely here lad."

Rupert smiled.

They all settled back quietly in the cellar and tried to get some sleep. They took it in turns to take watch. Not that they were looking for anything, more like listening. The occasional soldier walked past, but no one seemed to threaten their hideout. With the coming of the daylight, a little light filtered through to their hideout through the cracks in the floorboards. Rupert had been checking out his little find when he found some shelving behind the stairs.

"Frank," he whispered, "There's something behind the stairs, could be food." By now they were all awake, so Geoffrey raised the trapdoor a little, as silently as he could. It let enough light in, for the lads to see some jars and bottles on the shelf.

"Pickles!" Exclaimed Roland. "Pickles. I 'aven't 'ad one o' them since I've been in this damned war. Can we open 'em?"

"Easy," Frank replied. "Screw top lid. There's other snap lock tops here. Holy shit! Is that wine?"

"I would say this is one cellar the Bosch have not found, wouldn't you?" Rupert asked them.

"This, my friend, is the bleedin' jackpot. Oh, my giddy aunt!" Geoffrey was beside himself with joy, albeit in a whisper.

"Don't overdo the wine fellas, we need to be clear thinking when we get out of here, tomorrow." Frank reminded them.

"That my friend is tomorrow. This is today," Roland laughed as he took a swig. A long swig.

Frank immediately took the bottle from him. "You can't do that Aussie," he scowled.

"He can and he has, and I agree," Rupert interrupted. "We have to stay quiet. We have to stay focused."

"Roland, they're right. Ye can't get pissed now. We are so close to gettin' back to our own lines. We 'ave to stick togever; we 'ave to take it easy." Geoffrey tried to console his mate. "Now go and lie down again and get some more sleep. If we can get back to our lines, you know 'ow little sleep you're gonna get there. Make the most o' it man. 'Ere, 'ave another pickle."

"Alright, I get the message," Roland said as he swiped the pickle from Geoffrey.

"Shh! Footsteps," Rupert called to them. They all froze. The footsteps, two lots of them, stopped next to their hideout. Voices were heard. Rupert stood and listened intently. He could not hear a lot, but he did pick up that reinforcements were due here tomorrow, Thursday, he thought. The footsteps shuffled around for a few moments and then moved on.

"Thursday? Tomorrow?" asked Frank.

"Yes, I think that is what he said, Donnerstag. Thursday," answered Rupert.

Frank repeated the date, "Thursday 4th October 1917". He sat down leaning against the wall. "My Grandfather disappeared briefly, 2 days ago," he said.

"Excuse me?" Rupert queried.

Frank realised what he had said, and backtracked. "Oh, don't mind me. I'm just rambling."

As he sat, with his back up against the wall, he was trying to make sense of what was happening again. Maybe this was like "The Matrix", and he was in a simulation. He had seen the movie with Keanu Reeves and Laurence Fishburne almost a year ago, and the plot intrigued him. Maybe that was it. Then again, he thought, that is the movies. Life is not like the movies. But one of his thought processes was nagging at him. It had been playing on his mind all day. Just sitting here, with nothing to do but wait and think. "Nope forget it," he said aloud. The other men just looked at him. Their thoughts were fairly similar all around; *This situation may be getting to him. Just let him be.*

Sleep came fitfully to them all in turn, throughout the day. As the dreamy cloak of night fell over them, they all huddled together for warmth. At least tonight they would not be out in the open. Now being October, the nights were becoming colder, not freezing, but certainly in single-digit degrees Celsius. It was at times like this that they were glad they had managed to acquire some German tunics. They were not perhaps as warm as the British tunic, but they were wool and afforded a modicum of warmth.

At five am, they were all rudely awakened by a massive artillery barrage. It lasted for an hour and their little house took a hit. Not that there was anything left to destroy, but it certainly rearranged the rubble, dropping a load on top of their cellar trapdoor. It sent a stream of dust and dirt down through the floorboards and dusted them all over.

Frank was smiling today. He knew this meant the Aussies were on the advance and should be through here any time soon.

At six am there was shooting outside. Machine gun and rifle fire, interspersed with the occasional grenade explosion. "Grenades! That means they are close lads. Close enough to throw grenades."

The others looked at each other. Roland spoke for them all. "How the bloody hell did he know this was going to happen? Just what is this special knowledge he has?"

Shortly, they heard voices again, but this time they were speaking English.

"That's got the buggers on the run. Piss off ya bastards," the first voice was heard to say.

"Don't get too cocky yet Willie. The buggers have only just left. Probably still a few around so keep ya eyes peeled," the second voice cautioned.

"Yeah, ok Jono. But it's taken a while ta shift them, so I had to give 'em a little goodbye wish," Willie came back with.

Frank put his shoulder to the trapdoor, to raise it a little. It was heavy now with blocks and rubble. Some of it slid off and made a noise as it did so. Frank poked his head out of the hatch, to see two rifles pointed at him, with fixed bayonets. He looked up at the two soldiers and saw the purple-on-blue diamond, from the 2nd Division AIF. "Don't shoot ya bastards," he yelled. "You'd be shootin an Aussie."

"What the fuck are you doing in a fritz uniform, ya dopey bastard?" came the reply.

"Taken Prisoner. They gave me this," Frank wasn't going into long explanations just yet. Just enough to get the message across. "I've got three more Poms with me. They are good ones, so don't shoot them either."

The two soldiers laughed a hearty laugh and one replied, "You're an Aussie alright. Come on give us ya hand."

They assisted all of them out of the cellar and as Roland came out, one of them exclaimed, "Hey, are those pickles? Where the fuck did you get those?"

"Down there. We found one that Fritz missed." Roland replied. "There's some left for you."

Willie bolted down into the cellar and returned with two jars of pickles. "You bloody bewdy," was all he said.

The first one now asked, "So let's have a look at ya dog tags boys,"

The three Englishmen obliged. Frank had not thought about this, so he fell back on the shell explosion blowing off all his clothes, leaving him in only his underwear.

"So, what battalion you with then mate?" asked the first soldier.

"28th mate. White on blues." Frank replied indicating his shoulder patch area.

"Oh, sister battalion. We're 26th, Tasmanians," The first soldier came back with. "They are just waiting to come up now. They are in reserve now." He stopped. Then slowly and suspiciously he continued. "But you would know that wouldn't you?"

Frank had some work to do to convince this bloke. "Nar mate. I've been a prisoner of the Kaiser for days now. I got taken, down at Polygon."

"Oh, I see." It seemed to satisfy the fellow. "Look, if you head back down there," indicating to the west, "you will come across temporary command. They will sort you and your mates out.

"'ow far back mate?" asked Geoffrey.

"Oh, only about 300 yards or so," replied the soldier. "They were to follow us up pretty fast, so they should be there."

"Thanks mate, hope you push the bastards all the way back," Frank motioned east. "You take care now."

The four of them started the short walk back to the command post, the three Englishmen removing their German tunics. No point being target fodder now they were back. As they approached the command post they were once again met by an armed guard. Frank explained who they were, and why he had the remnants of a German uniform to this fellow, who placed a guard around them and then reported to command. Shortly, a young captain came out and introduced himself, as Captain Lloyd, adjutant to Lt Colonel Travers.

"Gentlemen, if you would care to follow me, we will see to your needs," the captain said.

He led them to a tent, where he motioned for them to sit down. "If you would care to introduce yourselves, gentlemen?"

"30234 Private Geoffrey Rainsford, Royal West Kents, sir"

"32325 Private Roland Johnston, Royal West Kents, sir."

"Lieutenant Colonel Rupert Penry-Wright, Kings Own Scottish Borderers, Captain."

All three of them just stared with amazement. They had just spent the last few days with a bloody officer, and a senior officer at that.

"Blimey! That explains the accent then, doesn't it? Ah, sir!" Geoffrey echoed the feelings of the others.

Rupert just smiled, and added, "And a jolly good bunch of soldiers this lot are too, captain. Especially this one." He indicated Frank.

"And you are...?" enquired the captain.

Frank had to think quickly now. He couldn't tell him who he really was, so he used his grandfather's identity for the time being. Just to get him back to the 28th, then, he would have some difficulty explaining his identity.

"Um 3577 Corporal Francis Albert Bailey 28th Battalion, Sir."

"28th eh? Where and when were you taken, corporal?"

"Over at the butt, at Polygon Wood sir," Frank replied.

"The Butt? What were you doing over there?" The captain asked. He was a little suspicious.

"I don't actually remember sir," Frank told him. "They told me I was found in my underwear and nothing else, after having everything else blown off by a shell explosion. Unfortunately, I have little memory of the time before I was captured. I think I must have had concussion, sir."

"You mean shell shock Bailey." The captain corrected him. "Alright, you will all have to be held in custody until your identities can be verified. I hope you don't mind sir?" The captain deferred to the Lieutenant Colonel.

"Not at all captain. I should have been mightily disappointed in you if you had not done so," Rupert replied. He then turned to his escapees and added, "It is correct procedure gentlemen. It has been my pleasure to have spent the last few days with you all. You have all taught me so jolly much and I shall not forget you." He shook hands with each of them and finished with Frank. "And as for you sir, once you confirm your identity and return to your unit, it would be a great shame if you remained a corporal. The leadership you displayed was superb. Good luck Frank."

"Thank you, sir. Good luck back with your men too." Frank then saluted Rupert.

When Rupert had left with the captain, Geoffrey turned to the others, "Well who'd a thunk it eh? Blimey! We was wiv' a bleedin' officer!"

A short while later, an escort arrived to take the two Englishmen to their command area, and Frank was left alone in the tent, with the guard. Captain Lloyd returned shortly after that.

"So, corporal. Tell me all that you can of your time, after when you can remember." There was a sort of disbelief in his voice Frank thought. I have to convince this guy. He told him of his tumble down the butt, of being taken below to Capt von Feldt and Lt Rudner, of the cell he was placed in. He then told him of his transfer to Major Blick and the lieutenant's embarrassing gaff. He told him how, with Lt Erlinger, he managed to evade interrogation by constantly being the questioner and getting him upset, due to them losing Polygon, Zonnebeke and Passchendaele and eventually the whole war. The captain took meticulous notes on everything Frank told him.

"But corporal, they have not lost Passchendaele or the war," stated the captain.

"No sir, they haven't, but they will," Frank explained. "When I spoke with him, they had not lost any of those places, but they have now. It just pissed him off so much, he lost control of the interrogation. Oh, and by the way I was being held at a place called Molenaarelsthoek, about a mile south of Zonnebeke. It had quite a sophisticated underground system."

"Really? Could you find it on a map?" asked the captain.

"I reckon I could get you close sir," Frank told him.

The captain called the guard to go and get a map. When he returned, he laid it on the table in front of Frank.

"Let's see now," Frank said as he looked at the map. "There's the butt at Polygon. After the 55th took it, we were whisked back about five hundred yards, so that would have been about here. No, back here, just before the crossroads." Frank drew a circle on the map to indicate von Feldt's dugout. "That was the road I was taken up after von Feldt, and then north probably by that road. Hm, must have been about five or seven hundred yards, so that would place it about here sir. J 4b 8,6 or 7. Yes, it was on the northeast side, of an old intersection, so that must be it. We used that road to the north as our guide to get up to Zonnebeke."

"Thank you, corporal. We hold all that area now," explained Lloyd, "so I'll tell the Lt Col, and we will see what we can find. Now tell me about your escape."

Frank took him through the ins and outs of the escape, all the way through to the pickles. He left out the bit about Roland wanting to get pissed. He did include the parts where Rupert, the Lt Col, actually did some of the dirty work and came up trumps with the cellar and the pickles. He got the impression, the colonel had not felt he had contributed much to this war until that moment.

"Well Corporal Bailey, I shall be passing this all on to your commanding officer at the 28th and if all this checks out, then I would be recommending, as Lt Colonel Penry-Wright suggested, that you do not stay a corporal for much longer. For the time being, until we get confirmation of your dugout finds, I would ask that you please remain in here. There is a guard on the outside, but I will have some food and drink sent to you in the meantime. How long since you had a hot cup of tea?" Captain Lloyd asked.

"Well over a week now sir," replied Frank.

"Good God man!" the captain exclaimed. "We will have to rectify that immediately. I'll get the doctor to come and have a look at that arm for you too. Oh, and how are your ears now?"

Frank laughed and added, "Thankfully the ringing has now gone, sir."

Frank guessed that he must have convinced the captain with his story, and that of the dugout finds. The difficulty was going to be explaining how there are two Francis Albert Baileys, when he gets to the 28th Battalion. What will happen, if and when, he meets his grandfather? That too, may take some explaining. Captain Lloyd might not be so accepting of his story then. A few minutes passed and an orderly entered the tent with a cup of steaming hot black tea and some hot stew.

"There we go, son. The cap tells me, ye hadnae had a cuppa for over a week noo. So, I put two full sugars in it afore ye. Git tha' lot intae ye lad." Frank barely understood the orderly, with his thick Scottish accent.

"Thank you, good sir. I will enjoy every minute of this," Frank said to the fellow.

"Och, I doubt that laddie. Ye havenae tasted tha stew yet," and he gave out a huge belly laugh as he left the tent.

He was just finishing the meal with the downing of the last of this hot, strong, tea when a medical orderly entered. He checked out Frank's arm re-dressed it with clean dressings and left him to it. An hour later Captain Lloyd re-entered the tent.

"Well, corporal! They have found the dugouts at Molenaarelsthoek. The area had already been surveyed and they were missed. They are going to prove rather useful apparently, so thank you for that. I have already organized for someone from the 28th to collect you, and take you back to your unit. I have no idea when that will be, other than to say it should be soon. They are not far behind us," the captain reported.

"Thank you, sir," Frank replied. "Is there anywhere I can doss down until then? I haven't had much sleep the last few days."

"Of course, lad," Lloyd answered. "Just here. I'll send someone up with a stretcher."

Frank managed to get a couple of hours of sleep in before the bloke from the 28th arrived to take him 'back' to his unit. They left after Frank bid Captain Lloyd goodbye and headed back to the 28th HQ about a kilometre back. They were met there by Major Davis, who took Frank aside once again to listen to his story. When Frank had finished retelling his story to the major, his reaction was one of incredulity.

"Francis, we all had you pegged for dead," the major explained. "You have officially been posted as missing, presumed killed, but to see you back here is nothing short of astounding. You see, there was a witness who said they saw you blown up by a whizzbang direct hit."

"Oh, is that right sir? I really can't remember any of that. My German friends told me that I must have been blown over by something like that because I was found in just my underwear, but up at the butt. I have no recollection of it at all." Frank was not telling any lies here. He really did have no recollection of being blown up. The fact that it was due to the fact that it never happened was just conveniently left out.

"So, Francis, tell me how you managed to frustrate the interrogators so much?" The major asked. "That is one part that interests me."

"Well sir, in my former employment, I attended many instructional courses, on negotiation, amongst other things," Frank explained. "The most consistent point to come out of these courses was, that the person who asks the questions, is the one that controls the conversation. Do you follow what I mean?"

"Er I think so," replied the Major.

"You see sir, I just did that with you. I finished my comments with a question. Do you see that?" Frank asked.

"Oh, so you did. I see that now. So, if I finish my contribution with a question, what you are saying is, I can control the direction of the conversation," the major was latching on.

"Correct," answered Frank. "And if you keep asking the right questions, you can actually steer the conversation away from the inquisitor's intended direction, thus frustrating them. It takes some work to put into practice though. and lots of practice."

"Interesting! We must talk some more about this later," the major indicated. "For the moment, we must get you a new uniform and kit. I have heard from the medic from the 26th, you saw earlier today, and we are going to send you off to the Aid station for follow-up on that, then we can get you back to your company."

"And which company would that be sir?" Frank asked the major.

"You don't know your company, Francis?" the major was confused now.

"I'm sorry sir, I don't remember very much at all," Frank admitted.

"Oh well then, we'd better let the aid station know that too then. They may be able to help. You are in 'A' Company, 3 Platoon, 2 Section," the major advised him.

"A' Company, 3 Platoon, 2 Section. Thank you, sir." Frank repeated.

Fifteen minutes later, a stretcher bearer appeared at the tent entrance to take him to the aid station via the quartermaster store. As soon as Frank was re-kitted with his uniform and equipment, the stretcher bearer walked him the mile or so back to the aid station. There they redressed his wound, put his arm in a sling and queried him about this loss of memory that was mentioned in the accompanying notes. The nurses at the post felt that Frank should be sent back to the base hospital in Etaples for proper assessment. A lorry of soldiers for the Hospital would be leaving early that afternoon and they recommended Frank be in that shipment. He needed proper medical assessment. The lorry would take them to Hazebrouck, where they would be transferred to a hospital train and thence to the combined Red Cross, St John Ambulance Hospital at Etaples.

Frank felt like a huge fraud when he looked at some of the men who were making this trip with him. There were limbs missing, and heads wrapped in so many bandages, he wondered how they were breathing. There were not too many where there was no blood exposed. Those where there was no blood apparent just sat, or lay, staring into the long distance, dazed and glazed. Looking at them all now, he accepted that this was no re-enactment. This was real. Somehow, he was in fact in 1917, using his grandfather's identity, and fearing for his future. Those nagging feelings he had back in the cellar with his British friends, came back to haunt him. He was even more concerned now.

Chapter 8
Francis Returns

If I have seen the future, and I am living the past, just where is my present?

His trip to Etaples was uneventful, if rather slow. He smiled to himself about the truck they first rode in. Everyone here called it a lorry, the English name for a truck, and it was as rough as they come. Solid rubber tyres, and an ineffective suspension. He thought back to his description of trucks to Ellie and wondered if he would ever get to see her again. His eyes were opened even further when the train was being loaded at Hazebrouck. *How the hell are any of these guys going to live?* He thought to himself. *Their wounds are horrific and antibiotics won't become available for another twenty-five or more years.*

Once they all arrived at the Etaples base hospital, he was taken through to a ward where there the men did not appear to have any injuries. No physical injuries, that is. Many of these men just lay in bed motionless, staring into nowhere, just like those on the convoy here. Others prattled constantly, talking to no one in particular. Yet others paced up and down the ward with the strangest of gaits, stiff arms or legs, shaking heads, nervous twitches and absolutely weird body actions, which all added to the strangeness of this place. He immediately realised he was in the ward allocated to 'Shell Shock', a most misunderstood condition. It was the first time Frank had seen anybody exhibiting these strange behaviours. He remembered his dad telling him that the alternative name for this condition was labelled, LMF. Lack of Moral Fibre. In other words, cowardice. He sat there shaking his head. "I don't belong here," he said.

"We'll let the doctor be the judge of that," replied the nurse who took him there. "You just get changed into these pyjamas and pop into bed. The doctor will be along in the morning. There's a good lad. Right now, you need to get some sleep. It's late."

When the doctor did see Frank the next day, he asked a whole lot of questions about what he could remember, and how far back his memory went. Frank had to make a lot of his 'memories' up, knowing that there was in fact nothing wrong with him, but the truth would land him in a mental asylum probably. He tried to persuade the Doctor to let him return to his unit, but the doctor was not prepared to do that just yet. He would need to monitor him for a couple of days just to be sure. Besides, he needed time for his arm to heal sufficiently before he could be expected to be back on the front line. Frank had to agree with that. He was not going to get this one infected here, without Penicillin available. Besides, at this point, any ill-discipline on his part would end up on his grandfather's record. He was, at least only for the moment he hoped, his grandfather.

Over the next few days, the doctors visited Frank, trying to work out what had happened to him and what to do about it. Frank tried to remain as normal and rational about it all as he could. He figured that if he just presented as a normal balanced person, not prone to outbursts of anger or frustration, they would have no option, but to return him to his unit.

"My unit?" he thought. *"It's not my unit. It's my grandfather's unit. Why do I want to go back there?"* He then answered his own question. *"Because if I don't, it will reflect on Francis."* Then, *"But if I do, those nagging feelings I had in the cellar will be realised. Either that, or I will run into my grandfather."* This was a 'Catch 22' if ever there was.

By October 10, Frank had been in the hospital for five days and the doctors could come to no conclusions on his situation. All agreed though, that he seemed perfectly normal and able to continue to fight. They collectively felt that his 'memory' would return in time, so they could see no reason for him to occupy a bed in Etaples any longer. Besides, they needed the space. He was discharged from the hospital and boarded the train for the return journey to the 28th Battalion, once again via Hazebrouck. He arrived back at his unit on October 11, 1917, the day his grandfather had been listed as "rejoined from hosp. Etaples" on his service record. He reported back to Major Currie, who had since replaced Major Davis.

"Well Bailey, how was your stay at Etaples?" the Major queried him, looking for any signs of deficit; anything that would make him unsuitable for service.

"I am fine, thank you, sir," Frank answered.

"How's the memory going?" Currie enquired.

"I still can't remember anything between arriving in France, and my capture at Polygon," Frank told him. He needed to be prepared for what he expected was going to happen next. It had been what he feared since his time in the cellar. "I remember we came over on the 'Themistocles', and got here late March last year, but since that, not much sir."

"So, you don't remember the men from your section?" Currie asked.

"No sir, I'm afraid not," Frank replied honestly.

"Well, I guess, the lance corporal will need to give you a bit of a hand, for a while. I see from the doctor's report that they think your memory will come back in time when you are back into a normal routine," The major advised him.

"Normal? What the fuck is normal?" Frank thought. He no longer had any idea what constituted normal. "Yes sir, I hope so," he dutifully replied.

"If you would like to report to Captain Fredricks at 'A' Company, he will add you back to his strength, then you can report to your lieutenant. 'A' Company is dossed down to the north about one hundred yards. Okay?" Currie had work to get on with. He no longer had time to spend on this unusual case.

"Thank you, sir," Frank took a pace back and saluted his major. He had been watching intently everybody's movements. He needed to make sure he still looked like a soldier in the Australian Army.

He wandered off to the north and found a couple of tents pitched. He was directed to one of them. He introduced himself to the sentry who announced his presence.

"Come in, Francis. It is so good to have you back," called the captain.

The moment of truth thought Frank. Here we go. A couple of deep breaths, then he stepped inside and saluted.

"Thank you, sir. It's good to be here." Frank reported.

The captain stopped dead in his tracks and stared at Frank. *Uh oh*, thought Frank. *The balloon has burst.*

"My God Francis. I think we all better have a stay at Etaples. The food must be pretty good over there. You look much better now." Captain Fredericks had noticed how much extra weight Francis seemed to have put on in the last fortnight. Frank was mightily relieved. The captain believed he was in fact, Francis. Frank took that as proof that he and his grandfather must have looked alike.

"Yes sir. Between those Germans and hospital, they fed us rather well," Frank lied.

"The Germans fed you well?" enquired the amazed captain.

"Yes, well, one lot did anyway," Frank explained. "A Captain von Feldt. From the 49th Regiment. I managed to get under his skin initially, and then broke him down, with my predictions. After that, I even got red wine with my meal. Probably stolen from the Belgians mind you. I think it must have been officer's meals I got."

"Wow, not bad Bailey. What predictions were they?" he asked.

"Oops, did it again didn't I?" he thought. He explained to the captain, "Well sir, I told him the 55th were going to take the butt, and that their first counterattack, would not get further than fifty met... yards. Our artillery would see to that, and that's exactly what happened. He called me Corporal Sooth after that. He was broken. I told him Germany would lose the war next year. I had already seen it. Actually, he was quite a nice man really. Just doing a job, like us."

"Great job Bailey. How did you know all that?" asked Fredericks.

"Oh, it was just calculated guesswork actually sir, using the little knowledge I had. Then I just rubbed it in with the end of war 'prediction'." Frank attempted to downplay his prophecies.

"Well, the reports I have back, from the 26th and Major Davis, indicate to me, Francis, an incredible level of leadership. It has not gone unnoticed either. Who is this, Lt Col Penry-Wright?" the captain asked looking at the report in front of him.

"Oh, Rupert!" Frank laughed. "He was a Pommie Colonel, who was in captivity at Molenaarelsthoek, waiting to be sent down to a POW camp, just like me. He was one of three Brits I managed to bust out, when the artillery hit my bunker. I think he managed to conceal he was an officer, even from his fellow prisoners and me. We used the barrage as cover to escape, after pinching a couple of uniforms."

"Well Lt Col Penry-Wright, has written to our Lt Col Travers, who has now been replaced by Lt Col Collett, giving you the highest recommendation. He seems to think you are officer material. We are going to have to keep that in mind, you see," the captain informed Frank.

"Oh dear, did he really? He too, was a nice man. I felt he was a little lost at the front. Just did not seem to fit," Frank suggested.

"I imagine he did. He is an intelligence officer, not used to being on the front line or in active combat. He had gone forward to gather some intelligence, and got separated from his mates and was captured." Fredericks explained to Frank.

"Ah, that would explain a lot," replied Frank.

"Anyway lad, you had better hunt out Lieutenant Stewart, fill him in and get back to it all. Good luck, Francis," the captain said and motioned for Frank to leave.

"Thank you, sir," and he took a pace back and saluted.

He turned to leave the tent, when the captain stopped him. "Corporal?"

"Sir?" Frank replied as he turned back.

"I know you are suffering memory loss, but an about-turn is to the right, not the left, is it not?" The captain had noticed Frank had turned in the wrong direction when he turned.

"Oh, did I turn left, did I sir? Sorry, won't happen again." Frank took note. It is right, about turn, i.e., clockwise.

The captain smiled. "Off you go lad."

Frank headed towards the bulk of the tents and enquired about the location of the 3 platoon CO. He was directed to an area of further tents. He knocked and waited. "Come in" came the reply. He entered, and the lieutenant and sergeant were studying maps.

"Francis! Well, I'll be buggered. The stories are true. Come in man, come in." Lieutenant Stewart shot around the table, took Frank's hand, and shook it vigorously. "Welcome back. We were sure you had bought it a couple of weeks ago. Harry Williams reckoned you took a direct hit from their arty."

"Yeah, welcome home Francis. Bloody amazing," echoed Sergeant Young.

"Thank you, Sergeant,......?" Frank was about to use his amnesia, not for the last time, to work out who was who.

"Oh yeah, sorry Francis. I'm Sergeant Young. Alfie Young. You don't remember me?"

"Sorry I don't remember either of you, yet," Frank admitted this time truthfully. "The doctors say it will probably all come back to me as soon as I get back into the swing of things."

"Well, we are still very proud of you, corporal. You have done exceptionally well, to get back and bring useful information with you as well as bringing back other captives. All round, a great result," the lieutenant told Frank. "Just thinking Francis, you probably don't remember the men in your section either, do you?"

"No sir, I don't. I have been trying but with no luck." Frank explained to him.

"Right, well, we'll get Lance Corporal Todd to help you through the first couple of days until you get back on your feet. You can take your lead from him.

"Thank you, sir, I will do that. Have we any plans in the next few days?" Frank asked.

"No Francis, we are on a period of rest and resupply at the moment. We have an inspection by Birdy himself, the day after tomorrow. Since you left us, we have taken Polygon and Zonnebeke, which I believe you know about, Broodseinde, Geluveld, Tyne Cot and most points in between. The boys are still working to take Passchendaele. That is proving to be a bit tough though. This bloody mud is stifling any possibility of advance. They keep telling us to move forward, but it is impossible. If only the bloody rain would stop," the lieutenant told him.

"Yes, it is a quagmire out there. Made our progress escaping rather difficult too. Oh well, I suppose we'd better see the boys get that right, hadn't we?" Frank said.

"Yes, we had. Look you are probably down on kit at the moment. We sent all your remaining kit back to the stores. We have an inspection tomorrow and today is about making a list of all deficiencies to send to the QM. So, you'd better get Todd to assist you with that and see that your boys are all up to kit."

"Right then sir. I shall do that. Where do I find them?" Frank asked.

He was directed to the tents for his section and started to walk down there. He stopped for a minute to think. His fears had in fact been realised. His Grandfather WAS killed by that artillery blast that Harry Williams had witnessed, he figured. Frank was now Francis. Francis was Frank. That meant he was stuck here now until.... *Shit! he thought. He ... I, get killed again in October next year. What the fuck? Lynne? The kids? Will I ever get to see them again?* Frank could not get those thoughts out of his mind. *What the hell do I do? Obviously, I play along with it now, but what then?* He thought for a while and then decided he had work to do right now, so had better get on with it and use the time to think. He set off for his section.

He barged into a tent and said, "Lance Corporal Todd?"

Todd spun around and yelled, "Francis! What the hell?" and held out his hand to shake. The others in the tent gathered around as well.

"I'm sorry boys," Frank said sheepishly, "I won't know anyone. I'll have to start all over again, getting to know you. I seem to have no memory of anything or anyone in the Battalion."

"Alan Todd, Francis, sorry Corporal Bailey."

"Bill Nash corp"

"Peter Jones Corp, Jonesy usually."

"James Reid corporal, Jimmy."

"Tom Calder corp."

As each of the men introduced themselves, Frank acknowledged their names and shook hands. Bill dashed next door to the second tent and got the rest of them to come and join them.

"Strewth! It bloody well is the corp. Looks like he's been on a good paddock though. Welcome back corp. I'm Andy Taylor."

"G'day corporal. I'm Ted McLean."

"This seems silly, but I'm Felix Simpson."

"Sorry, Felix. It probably does seem silly to you, but believe me, I have no idea who you all are," Frank informed them. He loved phrasing these statements in such a way as they would not be a lie.

"Bob Galloway corporal."

"John Abbott, with two Ts."

"Peter Jones Corporal, welcome back."

"That means you must be Harry Williams," Frank said holding his hand out. "Sorry to give you such a fright mate. They tell me that shell must have blown my clothes right off me and left me non-compos, coz the Bosch found me at the butt at Polygon, in my underwear."

Harry had been standing back all through the introductions just watching in amazement. He was dumbstruck. Eventually, he spoke. "Corp, I coulda sworn I saw you disappear in a red haze when that shell hit. I'm not looking at a ghost am I, or Francis' twin?"

"Well Harry, I can assure you, that I am no ghost and Francis has no twin brother," Frank explained truthfully.

"Bloody incredible. Bloody glad to have you back though," Harry replied.

"So, tell us what happened to you?" asked L/Cpl Todd.

"Tell you what," Frank said. "I'll tell you all whilst we continue to do the kit checks. These need to be done, or we will miss out on resupply."

"Same old corporal. Some things never change," Toddy laughed.

They all got their kit together and Toddy went through the list and compiled a requisition for the Quartermaster's store. By the time they got through the list, Frank had filled them in on what had gone on during his 'adventure'. The men were all pretty proud that it was their corporal who had been the one who had built up this legend. That is what this escapade was being known as now, even after this short time.

Frank's 'return' to the unit could not have come at a better time. The battalion had been on the front line for a while now and needed a rest. They went through a series of training courses, during which Frank was able to catch up on the regulations and drills that he was supposed to already know. The amnesia became his friend if he ever "forgot" a move or regulation. By the time they got to the end of the month, he felt he had a pretty good grasp of the commands and actions he needed to know.

That evening Frank and Toddy were sitting discussing the current state of play of both the battalion and the war in general. During a lull in the conversation, Frank turned to Toddy and asked, "I know this is going to sound like the weirdest of questions, mate," he paused for a moment to draw in his breath, "but what was I like? What sort of person was I before this incident?"

Toddy was somewhat stunned by the question but he eventually laughed and replied with a long, "Well...!"

"Nar tell me honestly Toddy." Frank interrupted with a smile. "I really don't know. It's like I never knew Francis Bailey."

Toddy dropped his smile now and went on. "Okay, if you really can't remember, I will tell you." He too, now paused to collect his thoughts. "We got on really well from the start. You were, I mean are, certainly a disciplinarian. A stickler for the book. But at the same time, prepared to listen to the men. Um, ya could be a bit grumpy at times if the blokes didn't measure up."

Frank nodded as Toddy spoke, seemingly trying to take it all in.

"I will tell you one thing though corp, I will guarantee the men would follow you anywhere, and now the escapade you have just survived has ensured they will do that to the ends of the earth. Oh, wait a minute, that's where we are now isn't it?" Toddy sniggered.

Frank chuckled softly at this and nodded in agreement.

"Sure is, Toddy," he answered.

The two of them continued talking for some time, all the while sorting out their kits. The whole time Frank was gathering intel on his grandfather that he could take back to his father when, IF, he ever got back home. Toddy also gave him the low down on all the men in his section and the platoon, company and battalion structure. Names, positions, who was worth his salt, who was not worth a pinch of cocky shit (in Toddy's opinion). And who he should steer clear of.

On October 25, the Battalion paraded and the feeling amongst the men was this meant a return to action. It was instead a parade for the distribution of ribbons for gallantry in the field. Four medals were to be presented today by General Sir William Birdwood (Birdy) Commander of the Australian troops on the Western Front. Amongst the recipients of the Military Medal (MM) was one 3577 Cpl Francis Albert Bailey, for 'Shewing calmness, ingenuity and gallantry when faced with capture by the enemy. For ensuring that no information was divulged and for gaining useful intelligence whilst in captivity. Cpl Bailey also managed to effect the release of three other allied troops, one of which held vital information for the advance of the allied forces.'

That day two MMs, one Distinguished Conduct Medal (DCM) and a Military Cross (MC), were awarded to members of the 28th Battalion. It was a proud day for the battalion indeed.

The following morning, movement orders came through. Frank took his brand new MM and tucked it into the pocket of his shorts, underneath his breeches. He was not going to lose this. He would keep it there. The men packed up the camp, climbed aboard the busses and headed to a staging camp, two kilometres southeast of Shrapnel Corner, Ypres. Enemy activity that night was significant, with them being subjected to both artillery and aerial bombardment. Although most of the aerial activity was confined to Ypres itself, they received their fair share of attention, although no casualties were reported. The next morning, they commenced their March to the front line, through Westhoek, then down to an area that looked awfully familiar to Frank.

As they approached this area, Frank started laughing, "I know where we are," he chortled. "We are at Molenaarelsthoek. This is where I escaped from. I'd recognise that smell anywhere."

"What? Where one of our shells hit your bunker?" Asked Toddy.

"Yep!" answered Frank. "This is the place I told the commander of 26th about. They came back and had a better look and found this system. And now we're going to occupy it, that is hilarious. Yep, I'd recognise that stench anywhere."

"Are you going to tell the lieutenant?" Asked Toddy.

"Hell yeah," replied Frank. "I'll even take him on a tour if he wants. Probably let the captain know too, I would imagine. You settle the boys in Toddy. Get them comfortable and I'll go and see the boss."

"No worries, corp, see you soon," Toddy replied.

Frank set off down the trench, to find Sgt Young. "Hey Sarge, need to have a word with you and the lieutenant. You're not gonna believe this."

"Oh yeah? What this time, Francis?" the Sarge queried.

"You'll see," Frank said, as he indicated to the Sergeant to go into the bunker ahead of him.

"Lieutenant, I just want to fill you in on some information," Frank informed the lieutenant.

"What's that Francis?" came the reply.

"Well, this bunker system we're in, is the one I was being held in, when I escaped. It's Monelaarelsthoek isn't it?" Frank asked.

"Sure, is Francis," replied the Lieutenant. "Well, I'll be buggered. So, this is the system you told Davis of the 26th about, is it?"

"Yes sir, it sure is," replied Frank.

"It seems a well-built bunker system, eh? Whereabouts were you held then?" the lieutenant asked.

"Bit to the north sir. Where B Company is now." Frank told him.

"Well Francis, I think you and the Sergeant better wait here. I'll go and tell the captain. He may want to go up there," and the lieutenant left the dugout. He returned shortly with Captain Fredericks. "You're a lucky boy then, aren't you Francis?" laughed the captain as he strode in. "Do you feel like taking us on a tour of where this happened? What is it, about a month ago now?"

"Getting up towards that now sir. I can certainly show you where it all happened anyway. Would be interesting to have a close look at the damage now," Frank replied.

They started their way north, through the system. Each company had the responsibility of looking after about one thousand yards of front, so the area where Frank had been held would be at least that far north. Walking through trenches was a slow process. The trenches did not go in straight lines. They were at best, a zig-zag pattern, but usually a square wave pattern, with right angles every ten metres or so. In order to walk any distance through trenches, they had to walk double that distance. Progress was not helped by the clinging mud. It weighed down their boots and their feet became twice as heavy. It took them about half an hour to traverse the required distance, also slowed down by troops setting up their occupation of this new position.

"That looks like the entrance to the officer's dugout sir, but I will know for sure if we go a little further and find the cells," Frank explained. They walked a further fifty metres and Frank stopped and said, "Yes sirs. This is the crumped area of the cells, so that was the officer's dugout back there. Oh yes, I remember that rat," he joked as a rat ran out of his former cell. "Friendly little bugger." They laughed.

He stood and stared at the mess in front of him. He could see the still missing door area, with only part of the frame still standing. There was not so much dirt piled there now, as they had apparently moved some out when removing the dead sentry and it looked as if they may have started to dig out some more, in order to repair it. He peered inside the room and could see the remains of the door, in the back corner and the bunk he was lying on, where the post was broken by the door implosion.

"I don't remember the bed being broken sir, but that's the door that took a piece out of my arm. The bedpost must have deflected it enough and broken then," Frank explained.

"Well, if that door came at you from a shell blast and you only got a gashed arm, you have done bloody well, Francis," the captain echoed the words of the other two.

"So, I was about to do a bolt out there," Frank said, pointing out the tunnel, "when I remembered there were more prisoners in here. We had been talking occasionally when the sentries allowed us to. They were down here to the left," and he indicated left and started heading that way. "Yes, this is where they were kept. As you can see there is no lock on the door, just this big slide bolt, and a sentry. He was dead, lying just here, with his head almost torn off and hanging there, just looking back at his feet."

"Yes, some of these arty injuries can be pretty horrific," the captain added.

"Yeah, I guess so sir. So, I dragged him out of the way and let the three inside, out. Then, with the barrage still in progress, we headed north, until we found a bit of a funk hole, where we sheltered for about half an hour, until darkness fell. Then we hopped over, expecting to have to dodge our own shells when the barrage stopped, so we hopped it."

"You can remember all of that, Francis, but you can't remember much before it? Is that right?" asked the captain.

"I can honestly say sir, I have no memory of this place before being captured at the butt." Frank truthfully answered the captain.

"So interesting. You're lucky to be alive aren't you now?" the captain enquired.

"I guess so sir," Frank replied.

"Anything you can tell us about the officer's quarters?" the lieutenant asked Frank.

"Not really sir. It was just a dugout, like any other,"

The four of them retraced their steps to the dugout, where Frank first encountered this trench system and Major Blick. He then explained to them about his encounter with the major and Lieutenant Erlinger. He laughed and said, "I learned this conversation technique a few years ago, but I've never had so much fun putting it into practice. I really managed to get under their skin."

"From the reports I have read, Corporal Bailey, you really did well to confuse and distract them. So, you did not give them any useful information?" the captain asked.

"No sir. I was unable to recall any of what they wanted anyway, so that part was easy. Getting them to believe it; that was a little more difficult," Frank replied.

"Well thank you for that little tour, Francis. We will talk again later. I have a feeling we may be seeing a little more of you sooner rather than later, anyway. Oh, and congratulations on the MM corporal." the captain finished with. After the appropriate salutes, he departed hastily, leaving the others to make their way back to their lines on their own.

The three remaining men then set about doing just that. With most of the A and B Company now settled in, their return to their sector was much quicker. The trench system at Molenaarelsthoek had been divided into sections for occupation. B Company occupied the left or northern section of their allocation and A Company, Franks lot, the southern or right section. C Company were in support about one thousand yards behind them and D Company in reserve a further one thousand yards behind them. Their job was to hold this sector from German counterattacks, whilst the Canadians, who had relieved the Australians, pushed on towards Passchendaele. The fresh Canadian troops were definitely advancing on Passchendaele, but it would be another week before they would claim victory there. Over the next couple of days, the men of the 28th were subjected to intense artillery barrages of HE (high explosive), shrapnel and gas shells, at all times of the day and night. The intensity of the situation was all new to Frank. He tried not to overreact around the men when there was an incoming. It took time to become used to it all, but by day two of the bombardment it was all 'old hat' to him. Patrols were sent out regularly to gauge enemy disposition and to occasionally take prisoners in an attempt to gain information.

During this time, the men took the opportunity to bury as many of the dead as possible. Corpses have a habit of attracting rats. These pests need no encouragement, like the presence of dead bodies. There were even examples where the rats did not even wait for death to occur. Any open wound, left undressed, was fair game as far as they were concerned and due to the number of diseases they could carry, death by rat bite was not uncommon. Where possible, the corpses were taken behind the line and buried at least a couple of feet deep. Their graves were marked, regardless of them being English, Australian, New Zealand or German. It would not be until after the war was over that burial parties would exhume these corpses for reburial in a formal cemetery, all of which are now administered by the CWGC (Commonwealth War Graves Commission).

On October 28, Sergeant Young sought out Frank and asked him to accompany him to the lieutenant's quarters.

"Corporal Bailey reporting as ordered Lieutenant," and Frank saluted, as he barked out his introduction. They were in the dugout, so saluting was in order. Above ground, whether it is in the trenches or not, saluting was not expected, as it identifies to any lookout who is an officer, making him a target for snipers.

The lieutenant stood from his table, donned his hat, and said, "Follow me, corporal. Your presence is required at company HQ."

Frank was bemused by this request but dutifully followed the lieutenant. He showed Frank into the HQ where he saw Captain Fredericks and the backs of a couple of Germans.

"Ah Francis, thank you for coming. I believe you may know these gentlemen," the captain said indicating the two Germans.

They turned around and Frank saw Captain von Feldt and Lieutenant Rudner.

"Hello Frank," and the captain extended his hand. "I heard you had escaped from Major Blick's post."

As Frank took it and shook it, he said, "Hauptman von Feldt! Leutnant Rudner! What are you two doing here?"

"Well Frank, it appears one of your patrols got lucky and captured the two of us and two of my guards. It appears you were correct about Zonnebeke and Passchendaele too, my friend. I'm still in awe of your predictions. But it appears, you were not completely truthful about yourself though."

"How is that Captain?" Frank was puzzled.

"55th Battalion?" replied the captain.

"Oh yes, that. Well, the 55th was close by and you knew that. It fitted in with what you knew. It was easier to explain," Frank explained.

"I have to say, Frank, that I am by no means disappointed to have been captured. After our discussions, I lost any desire to push on with this ridiculous war. I mean, what is it all about anyway? I was already disillusioned before that, but you just sealed it for me. I have no quarrel with the likes of you. So, just what are we doing?" von Feldt commented.

"We are upholding the good name of our Kaiser, sir!" interrupted Rudner indignantly. He was not of the Hauptman's mind in this matter.

"Who is a first cousin to the King of England and the Tzar of Russia, although it looks like he has seen his day now; another of your correct predictions Frank." Turning to his compatriot, "No Rudner, this is sheer madness." Von Feldt had had enough of this fighting.

"Sir," said Frank turning to Captain Fredericks, "These men, especially the captain, were very good and considerate to me in captivity. They treated me like a human, not a captive. Is it possible to ask that they be treated likewise by us?" Frank asked the captain.

"They will be treated with the respect they deserve, Francis," replied the captain. "I saw their names when they came in and I recognised them from your report. I thought you might like to see them, this time, with the boot on the other foot."

"Thank you, sir," Frank replied, then turning to von Feldt he added, "Sir, I hope you find the peace you are looking for. I can assure you both that you will be well cared for, as officers and gentlemen. Now, you can be assured you will survive this war. You will be home to your families in just over twelve months. Be assured."

"Is that how long this will last Frank?" asked von Feldt.

"I believe so. Yes, Hauptman, then you will be returned to your families and can live in peace, at least for a while," Frank told them, remembering Hitler's destabilising influence did not start until, around 1933.

"For that Frank, I cannot wait. This madness must end," the captain sighed.

"Good luck gentlemen," and Frank stepped back and saluted them. "And thank you very much, sir, for alerting me to these gentlemen's presence." Again, he saluted and then retired.

"Well Francis, or is it Frank, what did you think of that?" asked the lieutenant on the way back to their positions.

"It was particularly good of the captain to invite me to meet them. I had a feeling we may meet again you know. I'm glad von Feldt is safe now. We got along rather well. As for the name, well I just told them to use Frank as a ploy. You know, to keep them off the track. Even so, I have to say I kinda got a bit used to it, although I still prefer Francis," Frank added.

"Ok. I think we may stick to Francis then. What do you think?" the lieutenant replied.

"I don't mind any more sir" Frank answered. "Whatever you think," and he left it at that.

Chapter 9
Initiative or not?

Wilfred Owen *"Spring Offensive"*

The 28th continued at Molenaarelsthoek until the end of the month. They endured almost constant shelling of one kind or another. H.E. was often followed by shrapnel and then gas was sometimes thrown in just to keep them on their toes. At times like these, the men were glad of the underground bunkers. It afforded them a little more security. Frank was constantly amazed by the seemingly endless supply of shells the Germans continued to send over. The occasional aerial bombardment was added to the mix as well, but that was usually inaccurate and caused little concern. On more than one occasion, a heavy bombardment was followed by an assortment of signal flares from the German front line, but on no occasion did it result in an attack. By the time they were relieved by the South Australian 27th their casualty list read remarkably small. 4 KIA, 10 WIA one later dying of wounds, and twenty-six gassed.

The battalion withdrew to an area only five hundred metres northwest of the butt at Polygon Wood, for rest off the front line, but were that night subjected to an artillery bombardment and multiple gas attacks. This time, the Germans were using a combination of Phosgene, Lachrymatory and some Mustard gas. Phosgene was an odourless gas, which affected the air sacs in the lungs and its effects could go unnoticed for some hours, before oedema set in. By this time, it was too late and the result was usually fatal. Lachrymatory became known as tear gas. Mustard gas, or sulphur mustard, was a fine liquid vapour that caused burning and blistering of the skin where contact was made. If inhaled it burnt the lungs. Large exposure to mustard gas was often fatal. Whilst many of the gases used in this conflict caused fatalities, that was not necessarily the desired outcome. Severe debility was preferable, as it used far more resources of your enemy to look after wounded or injured, or in this case gassed casualties, than outright killing.

That night, the battalion lost a further three dead and five gassed. The following day they were withdrawn further behind the lines, to a camp five km southwest of Ypres, near the village of Dickebusch. Unfortunately for the men, this entailed an eight-mile march, which was a big ask after time on the front line. The men of the 28th accomplished this, without a single man dropping out along the way. The first section of the march, about two kilometres, was marched at almost a running pace, such was the desire to leave the front behind. After that, it settled down to more of a stroll On their arrival at the camp the wonderful people of the YMCA were waiting for them with steaming cups of hot cocoa and biscuits. This was met with great appreciation by the men. The men of the AIF were never so appreciative of the YMCA and the Salvation Army until they turned up at times like this, providing these simple pleasures of life and to boost their morale.

"Will ya look at these guys? God bless 'em all," Tom Calder said as he marched past them. "God bless ya!" he called out and waved to them. "Ya spend weeks on an' off the front line, and when ya get here, they are awaitin' for ya. Bloody magnificent, eh lads?"

"Sure is a wonder of a sight, Tommy. I'll be spendin' a bit o' my time there, even if it's just to get a bit of a sense of home from them," Harry Williams suggested, with a smile.

"I'm just looking forward to a really good HOT cuppa tea, haven't had one for two weeks. Hope they've got some cocoa too," Felix added to the conversation.

"Hope they've got some nice bikkies too," Harry added. "Not those hard shite ones the army gives us."

The men were called to a halt and left turned. Command issued them with the appropriate orders and the men were fallen out to find their tents. Frank followed the other NCOs to find out if there were any special instructions for the rest of the day. He left Toddy to settle the men in. Frank's section all headed off to their allotted area and separated into their two tents. The men entered the tents and flopped on the stretchers, dropping their gear at the foot of the beds.

"Ahh! Heaven at last," sighed Harry. "I think I'll sleep for a week. Goodnight all."

"Yep, the Army will let you do that Harry, you can be sure of it," Ted said sarcastically.

"I don't care what the officers say, I'm sleeping for the duration," Tom concurred with Harry.

"At least here we might get more of a break from them bloody rats, surely," Andy added.

"And the lice. I'm as itchy as buggery," Harry said as he sat up scratching himself yet again.

"We're gonna need a bath and lice powder before that happens lads," Toddy said as he entered the tent. "Surely they'll get that set up for us this time."

"Sure hope so, corp, and the sooner the better I reckon" Harry added.

This relief was to be a large one for the men. They would be off the front line now for six weeks of further training and sports. As it happened the first luxury they experienced in this camp was the following day, on the first Sunday when, after church parade, it was announced that they would all have the opportunity for a bath. To someone who has been stuck in a muddy trench for a week, having bombs dropped on them from above, artillery shells seeking them out to kill them, enduring itching lice and rats for the last two weeks, the sound of a hot bath and clean uniform is pure luxury. Frank was learning firsthand, of the privations of life on the front line.

"This is something they don't teach us about", he thought.

"Well boys," Frank announced as he entered the tent, "they have laid on the Winnipeg baths for us this afternoon. You can all get a good clean up and fresh uniforms."

"Hoo-bloody-ray!" came the reply from Harry Williams. "I was wondering if they were going to remember us."

"They are going to need a bloody huge amount of water to get this lot clean, I can tell you," added Ted McLean.

"Geez guys, don't sound too overwhelmed will you," laughed Frank.

"Nar it's all good, corp. We're just done in," Tom Calder cut in. "We'll feel better after a bath I reckon, don't ya think fellas?" This was followed by general agreement.

Most of the men used the morning to catch up on sleep before the baths, forgoing the opportunity of church parade. There were those who still attended their services, but after a couple of weeks like this, the numbers were usually small. Frank certainly had no intention of wasting his time on a church parade.

The other highlight of their week in the Dickebusch camp was the arrival of the comfort fund packages on the 6th of November. Each man got an issue of a new pair of socks, a new shirt, a singlet (essential under the woollen greyback shirt they wore), a handkerchief, cigarettes and tobacco. These new supplies were always much looked forward to by the men. They were simple and basic things but did a huge amount to lift morale among them. It was also a reminder to them that the people at home had not forgotten them.

After a week at Dickebusch, they moved yet again to Fletre camp, just outside Steenvoorde. The main emphasis of this time off the front line was training in new and upgraded techniques and keeping the men fit. Training kicked off on Monday November 12, a couple of days late due to the seasonally inclement weather. It consisted of field craft exercises, updated gas lectures and the interminable route marches. Frank sat back and watched A Company defeat D Company in Australian rules football two days later in an informal match, but decided that if they were to take on the other battalions he needed to get into the coaching of their team.

Three days later, they were on the march again. This time an overnight march to their new digs at Aldershot camp, two kilometres southwest of Neuve Eglise (now Nieuwkerke). This time they settled in for the long haul.

The training continued apace, but much of their time here was spent in Australian rules football and association football (soccer), with several teams in all grades. The 28th prided itself on being a pretty fair Aussie rules footy team and spent much time in training when they were not training for the war. They felt they had to uphold the honour of the battalion to all comers.

Now being November, the weather had definitely turned towards winter with most days being cold and windy. But weather does not come into it if you have a footy team. It is, after all, a winter sport. They played many different battalions over the next 4 weeks, with some surprising results. Frank had been a reasonable footy player in his time, so jumped at the opportunity to assist the younger guys with their training. He brought with him many of the practices used in the late 20th century, like the use of handball for quick passages of play, and the use of the drop punt when shooting at goals.

"What the hell do you use this drop kick for?" he asked the team. "It is not a long-distance type of kick."

"It's a great kick if you want to get a low quick pass to somebody," came the reply.

"Okay! So, as a stab pass type of kick, I can see that, but it's a lot of wasted effort for when you need to get distance fellas. The drop punt has a better success rate. We should be using that," Frank felt a pang of guilt doing this, as it was all techniques that had not really entered the game yet. He could not stop thinking about Polly Farmer with his next advice. "Also, when you get in a pack or need to switch play, use the handball. Slide it out of the pack to one of your mates hovering around the outer of the pack. If you have your mate running past you and there are opposition players around you, handball it sideways. It confuses the opposition as they do not expect it. Sure, use the kick when you need to get distance and you have a free run at the ball, but use the handball where you can." He then set up some drills for the teams to practice with.

Their first foray into the competition was a match against the 44th Battalion, in which they came out victors, 10 goals 7 behinds (67 pts), to 3 goals 5 behinds (23 pts). Frank was dutifully proud of his boys. They had struggled to adapt to the newly expected skills, but when they did use them they proved their use. Over the next three and a half weeks they took on all comers, including the Corps, undefeated champions, the 2nd DAC (Divisional Ammunition Column), obliterating them 12.10 (82 pts) to 2.5 (17 pts).

(Note: For those of you unfamiliar with Australian Rules Football, a goal (The first number) is worth six points and a behind (The second number after the period) Is worth one point, Thus 12 x 6 = 72 +10 = 82. Polly Farmer was a West Australian footballer who used the handball very effectively. Handballing is holding the ball in one hand (usually the left) and punching it with a closed fist, so it travels directly to your teammate. Throwing it, or using an open hand, is a contravention of the rules. Before Polly popularised it, whilst it was a legal move within the game, it was not used nearly as much as today. It adds a much more rapid transition to the game.)

Sport was not the only activity they accomplished in this period. The training continued as before. Frank, as an NCO, (Non-Commissioned Officer) attended a map reading and topography interpretation school on the 26th and a week later he, along with three officers and sixty-one ORs (Other Ranks), attended a raiding party school at Brigade HQ. Throughout this whole time off the line, their own strength was regained, as well as the battalion strength. Every couple of days, a few more reinforcements were marched in, as well as injured and ill troops returning. By the end of November, the battalion numbers had risen to 855 active, out of a total of 963. This had been an increase of over 100 since their last episode in the trenches.

On December 14, it was snowing and cold, and all the members of the 28th were on the move again, this time back to the fight. They were transported to the vicinity of Ploegsteert Wood and marched the remainder of the way to Red Lodge, less than one thousand yards from Hyde Park corner, on the edge of "Plugstreet Wood". At least the march kept them warm. Red Lodge was the location of a reserve trench line, at the forward base of Hill 63, also known as the Catacombs or Wallangarra Dugouts. These Catacombs were dug by the First Australian Tunnelling Company, between June and October 1916 and had seen many Allied troops accommodated in the many caverns. It was capable of holding in excess of 1200 men, safely underground. The trenches at Red Lodge faced south, looking towards the town of Ploegsteert. They were to lie in wait there, as reserves for the front line, four km to their east. One of the biggest advantages of this position was that they had electricity from 6.30 in the morning until 9 at night, supplied from the Catacombs over the hill.

Whilst in reserve, the troops of the 28th were by no means idle. Each day, three or four officers and up to two hundred ORs moved forward, to extend and consolidate support trenches behind the front line. At the same time, 12 x 6 =72 patrols went out on 'salvage patrols' to bring in any useful equipment they could find. It was estimated that in the second week of December alone, they managed to salvage £7000 Stirling worth of equipment. An extremely useful salvage hunt. They also continued the fruitless task of killing rats.

Late on the 23rd, they got the order to move forward to the front line, in order to relieve the 26th battalion, facing Warneton, on the Belgian/French border, seven kilometres northeast of Armentieres. The relief was achieved in quick time, due to a brilliant moon and by 8.30 everyone was in position. They all lay back and listened to the dulcet tones of 5.9" shells landing to their left on Warn Road and Minenwerfers to their right, onto the 26th Battalion. They received unusually little attention themselves that night, other than from the rats. Their night for bombardment was the next night when they were consistently shelled with shrapnel and pineapple bombs. (They believed chlorine gas smelled like pineapples and pepper). Unfortunately, number seven post took a direct hit two were killed instantly and five were wounded. Of those five, two were to die later at the casualty clearing post.

It had been intended that a raid would be made this evening, by A Company, to gain useful information on enemy disposition, but due to the brilliant moon and high visibility, it was postponed several hours. The raid was re-planned for the following early morning after the moon had set. At five am, an officer, Frank, a Lewis gunner and eleven ORs, all of whom had attended the raiding course whilst at Neuve Eglise, crept out of their sap and moved towards a small patch of higher ground in front of their trench. From this position, they would be able to carefully survey the area in front of them, in no man's land, for any activity. Finding no discernable activity, they moved further north, until they were just out in front of the enemy trenches. It was slow to move through this area, it having been churned up by shells, and many of the holes had partially filled with water, as well as the inevitable bodies, timber and wire. Frank was, by now, used to the stench and hardly noticed it. Here the group split in two, half, under the officer surveyed to the left and the other half, under Frank, to the right. They knew there was a machine gun emplacement nearby but needed to plot exactly where.

Frank signaled to his five men to move close to the German sap, and just lie against its forward slope for a few minutes and listen for any activity. They were unable to detect any nearby noises after a good five minutes of listening, so Frank crept forward on his stomach, to look into the trench. He saw no one. As a matter of fact, he found that this part of the trench had recently been crumped by the artillery, and appeared to be unused and unusable, at this time. He signalled for his men to join him and they slowly lowered themselves into the Fritz trench. Looking both left and right, they saw nobody. Frank further split the group and each trio was to survey twenty yards north and south, then meet back at this spot in three minutes. When Frank returned with his two men the others were already there.

"Corp, there's an MG (machine gun) just down the sap about twenty yards," Andy Taylor whispered to Frank, indicating the direction at the same time. "There's only two Fritz manning it, sitting silently. Couldn't see if there's a bunker behind it though. It's pushed out about six to eight feet forward of the sap."

"Right!" Frank replied and then paused to think for a while. Once he had considered the position, he said to his men, "Change of plan, let's take these two back with us. That way, we will get the info we want straight from the horse's mouth. If all goes well, we can neutralise the gun as well. If it goes tits up, leg it fast and weave back to the mound. The six of us should be able to do this easy."

He carefully snuck forward to check out the layout near the MG. On returning, and after checking the area behind the trench, he sent two of them to crawl out of this trench, behind the line and move quietly past the gunners and slip back down into the trench on the other side of them. At exactly 10 minutes, they would all start to move in on the gunners, with bayonets in hand. Rifles should be briefly left in the trench, with one of the patrol, just before reaching their target. They would need to take the two gunners completely by surprise and silently.

"The German word for them to be silent is Schweigen. Got that, Schweigen." Frank learned that one in the cells at Molenaarelsthoek. "As soon as we get up there, if we manage to surprise them, hold your bayonet at their neck and whisper it, right in their ear. They are machine gunners, so will be armed with a pistol each and maybe a bayonet, but probably no rifle. Disarm them and hold them. As soon as it is safe, we'll go over the top and start making our way back. Felix and Andy, you collect our rifles and I will see if we can disable that machine gun. Everyone got their part?"

The men gave Frank the thumbs up and Felix and Bill slipped out of the trench, behind the lines. At the allotted time they all began the move forward towards the gun. Before long Frank could see the target and a few seconds later was able to see the men advancing from the other side. They moved to within five metres of the firing step, behind the MG, without even a murmur from their targets. The machine gunners were well forward of the trench the boys were in, with the machinegun pit dug out into no man's land by about two to three metres. By this time, Frank could see there was indeed a door opposite the pit, leading to the bunker, for the rest of the crew, he imagined. Crouching low he indicated to the crew on the opposite side the presence of this door. He got the thumbs up from Bill. They moved further forward until they were no more than a metre, from the step to the pit. He indicated to Bill and Felix to go on a count of three. He then counted down by holding out his fingers, counting down. On three, Bill and Frank pounced, grabbing the two Germans around the mouth and holding the bayonet to their throats. "Schweigen! Schweigen!" Frank whispered in his captive's ear, to which he got a vigorous nod in reply. The others quickly disarmed their startled captives and sat quietly for a few seconds, waiting to hear if there was any reaction from anywhere. Their weapons were all aimed at the door of the bunker, waiting for anyone exiting. Hearing nothing, Frank indicated to the men to use two handkerchiefs on each of the Germans, one in the mouth, one tying that into place. He swapped places then with Tom, who took care of his German. Frank got Bill to get some chord from his pocket and they tied the Germans' hands in front of their body, as they would need them in front to be able to negotiate no man's land, on the way to the allied trenches.

He indicated for the men to head back to their entry point and then creep over the top and start making distance to their front lines.

"I'll meet you all on the other side of that rise we first stopped at, okay?" he told them. Once again, he got the thumbs up. Before they left, he tapped the two Germans on the shoulder and motioned with an index finger to their lips, "Shhh" and then drew his bayonet across his throat. He followed this with a tilt of the head and an enquiring look. They understood. Both were kneeling there, wide-eyed and nodding their heads vigorously.

The small party headed back down the trench, sans Frank. Frank then set about disabling the machine gun. He lashed a grenade to the breech of the weapon and tied some of the chord from his pocket to the pin. "Thank you Mr McGuyver," he said as he was tying the last knot. He finished off his little sabotage effort, making sure the grenade was firmly attached to the MG and slipped over the front of the trench, slowly paying out the chord as he went. He figured he had about thirty metres in this little ball, which would give him a reasonable distance as a head start before all hell would likely break loose. At least he would not have to contend with this machine gun, he hoped. Soon, his string ran out, so he stopped there. He waited for at least 10 minutes to give the rest of the crew time to get to their cover. When he figured they would be safe, he gently pulled the string until it was taut, and gave it an almighty pull. Even at that distance, he could hear the clip spring off. At that, he jumped up and ran, as best he could, knowing he still had a few seconds before the grenade went off and signalled to everyone his presence. Seconds passed and he was still running when there was an explosion from the German lines and at the same time, he fell head first into a shell hole filled with icy cold water. Expecting the air to come alive with tracers, he still cursed wildly on landing in the mud. It did; but not in his direction. Everything was directed to the position of the explosion. As soon as he realised this, he jumped up and kept going. Flares started to go up, so he dived and froze each time. Searching machine gun fire raked no man's land periodically after that, which made his progress quite slow. Within 10 minutes, he could see the telltale signs of the rising ground to his front right. Crawling forward he quietly called out, "It's me, Francis. I'm coming in." He was met by only two of the men, Andy and John. "We sent the others on with the lieutenant and the rest of the party. It's just us to get back now."

They made their way back from shell hole to shell hole, dodging the occasional searching machine guns and flares. They hopped back over into their trench system at 6.10 am. What felt like hours to them had only been seventy minutes. They both sat in the trench laughing, deep breathing and in Frank's case, shivering. The rest of their part of the raiding party turned up not long after they dropped in the trench, and they all congratulated each other on a good night's effort.

When they had caught their breath, they got up and Frank went in search of the lieutenant in charge of the raiding party. That was Lieutenant Fraser from No 1 platoon. He found him in the officers' quarters and reported that the machine gun in question was now inoperative, at least until they replaced it.

"Well corporal," Lt Fraser started, "that certainly is an interesting interpretation of gaining intelligence, I must say."

"Yes sir!" Frank replied. "I figured that seeing we had found the MG and there were only two Fritzes there, we might as well kill two birds with one stone, so to speak. I would like to have been there to see their faces, when the rest of their crew came out from their bunker to an exploded MG, but I was face down in a mud hole."

"Yes, well, Company command was certainly surprised, when I turned up with those two. I'm not sure they will see that as following orders though. It was overstepping the mark, corporal, I think you will find. They don't like that, you know."

"Stuffy bastard", Frank thought but decided against saying it aloud. Instead, he offered, "Okay sir. I guess I will hear from them soon enough, in that case."

They left it at that for the time being and Frank walked back to his sap area, to attempt to clean up and get warm. Lt Stewart sought him out, some minutes later.

"Francis, what the hell did you just pull off? I'm hearing stories about two captives. Is that true?" The Lt eagerly asked. He was not waiting for salutes or anything like that, he just wanted information.

"Ah, yes, lieutenant. Two captured Fritz and one blown-up machine gun." Frank answered.

"Bloody marvellous, Francis! How the hell did you pull that off?" The Lt excitedly exclaimed with a massive grin on his face.

Frank went through the step-by-step description of how they achieved their goals that night, adding at the end that he did not think Lt Fraser was too impressed.

"Ha!" The lieutenant laughed. "That's only because it wasn't men from his platoon that did it. You'll see. Company will be smiling today."

"I sure hope so sir. After talking with Lt Fraser, I wasn't so sure," Frank shiveringly added.

"Don't worry about that at all," Stewart reassured him. "Let's head up to Company now and see what's happening."

"Can I get changed first sir? I'm frozen," Frank said with a smile.

"Oh yes, of course. I'll give you ten," the lieutenant offered.

The two of them walked together up to the Company Command post, about fifty metres backward of the line. Frank waited outside while Stewart entered. Shortly, he emerged and asked Frank to enter. On entering he stood to attention before the captain, the senior officer present.

"Francis," the captain said, "I wish to congratulate you, for this morning's fine effort. We have been able to gain some good intelligence from the two Bosch. You had them petrified we were going to gut them. They are currently at battalion HQ, bleeding information."

"Thank you, sir," Frank answered. "We just did what we figured needed doing. The opportunity presented itself and we pounced."

"Jolly good effort, Corporal Bailey. Great initiative man," Captain Fredericks said. "I have heard the basics of what happened, but I want a full report prepared, so can you explain to us now what happened? Here's the map. Can you show us just where you were?"

"Certainly sir," Frank replied and he went on to trace their part once they split with the lieutenant's group. When he had finished explaining the morning's escapade, the captain stood up and said, "Well I can see someone had their eyes and ears open at the raiding party training day. Wouldn't you say, lieutenant?"

"I think the captain may well be correct in that assumption, sir," answered Lt Stewart.

"Well corporal, as you know, Sgt Young has been sent back to the CCP after yesterday's little dust up and the lieutenant and I have been discussing what to do to replace him. How do you feel about fulfilling the role of 3 Platoon sergeant?"

"Me sir? ...Oh dear. ...I suppose someone has to do it sir ... I can give it a go." Frank sort of stuttered out.

"Congratulations Sergeant," and the captain held out his hand to shake Frank's. "Job well done today too. I can tell you, HQ at battalion are well pleased. Better than they had planned."

"Thank you, sir," Frank replied.

"Lieutenant, sergeant, that will be all," the captain ended the conversation as quickly as he had started it.

Once outside, the lieutenant also shook Frank's hand and congratulated him.

"Well done Sergeant Bailey. Congratulations." He was pleased that this morning's efforts had brought praise on members of his platoon. It is always a bit of a challenge, at platoon level, to know if your efforts are recognised and appreciated. Today, Lt Stewart was in no doubt that his boys were doing well.

"Francis, if you want to drop into the quartermaster's store and pick up a set of sergeant stripes and then get back and have a good kip. After a night like that, you need it. Make sure the others who were with you also get a good rest," Lt Stewart advised Frank. "Also, you will need to move your digs up to near the dugout. I need you close at hand."

"Okay, I'll do that straight after a kip and a hot cuppa. What about the section? Do you want Toddy up to corporal?" Frank asked.

"Oh yes, that's right. Yes, I think so. Is he up to it, do you think?" the lieutenant asked.

"Definitely," Frank replied.

"Good. You can tell him, and I will leave the lance jack up to you as well," Stewart advised. "Just let me know who you promote."

Frank headed to the QM store and drew a set of sergeant, corporal and lance corporal stripes. He already knew who he was going to promote. Back at the digs, before he lay down for a rest, he called Alan Todd and Andy Taylor over and said, "Well lads, you're looking at the new platoon sergeant."

Both men quickly shook Frank's hand and congratulated him. He then added, "And I am looking at the new 2 section corporal and lance corporal", as he held out the new sets of stripes to the surprised pair.

"Oh wow, thanks cor... I mean serg." Taylor said.

"Look after the boys won't you fellas," Frank added. "They're a good bunch, all of 'em. Encourage leadership and reward effort. Now I'm headed for a kip and you, Andy and the others on the raid should do the same."

"Yes sir," Andy said mockingly. Frank just glared at him and then laughed. A sergeant does not get called sir, that is a title reserved for officers only.

"Get outta here," Frank said, as he turned and headed underground for a sleep.

As he lay down to sleep his mind raced with all the happenings of the morning. As his mind slowed down, he realised that he had been so caught up in the moment, he had forgotten he was not from this time. *"Crikey Moses,"* *Frank said to himself. "It's December. That's the month* *Francis got his sergeant stripes."* A chill went down his spine.

It confirmed, in his mind at least, that he was definitely filling Francis' role. "Until next October anyway," he muttered aloud. Then he sat up in his bunk. "Shit! Today is Christmas Day," then he slumped and said aloud but slowly, "Merry Christmas Lynne. Merry Christmas Tim. Merry Christmas Eloise. Merry Christmas Mum and Dad," he paused for a moment then added, "Wherever you all are."

Chapter 10
Onwards and Upwards

Opportunity is missed by most people because it is dressed in overalls and looks like work.

Thomas Edison

For the next week, the men of the 28th rotated their companies through the front line, support and reserve lines. The artillery was incessant. Frank figured he may have been responsible, at least in part, for the increase in artillery attention. Still, they endured HE, shrapnel and gas, as well as the freezing temperatures at night. By the time they were relieved by the 26th battalion on New Year's Eve, the 28th casualty list read, 4 KIA, 6 WIA, all ORs, 3 DOW, 6 frostbite. Nineteen men in one week. It was a heavy toll to pay.

The battalion moved back to Red Lodge, for just one day. Following a good sleep, they were off to the Romarin Camp a few kilometres to their west. That meant BATHs for all the men. They relished their days on bath parade. They could finally get clean, if only for a day or two, before working parties or training or both. This time, in the afternoon, they had a special treat waiting. As was the tradition in the army, at Christmas, the officers would cook the meal for the troops. Because they were on the front line through Christmas, this did not happen, so it was set up for their first day off the line. The men walked into the mess that day to be greeted by festivities, decorations and some of the officers in cooks' aprons. The men were seated and the officers served them a traditional roast meal, complete with Christmas pudding and custard. The men were beside themselves with joy and celebrations. After the meal, gifts purchased from the battalion funds were distributed amongst the men.

The rest of January saw a few moves to new locations, ending the month at Le Wast, only fifteen kilometres from the coast at Boulogne, well behind the front line. Here, the men could give their ears and their nerves a well-earned rest.

Their time at Le Wast was for resupply, reinforcements, rest and training. The men had some onsite training, as well as going to brigade school, which covered such topics as, musketry, bombing (grenades), navigation, Corps and transport. During this time, they also competed in competitions with the other battalions, in range shooting and some sports. It was during this time that Lieutenant Stewart approached Frank one day early in February.

"Sergeant," he said. "We are needed up at Company. Coming?"

"Yes sir," Frank replied. "What's up?"

"No idea really. Could be anything," is all Frank got as a reply.

"Come in gentlemen," the captain said on greeting them. "I'll get straight to the point fellas. As you know, we have taken a bit of a beating in strength and I certainly hope that this time here will help that situation. However, I can't sit back and rely on that. Our officer list keeps shrinking and good officers don't come by easily, so Frank, I would like to send you back to Blighty, for an officer training school. How would you feel about that?"

"Oh, oh really?" Frank stuttered out. "Um, yeah, I suppose so sir. If you think it's appropriate. I haven't been here as long as some of the others though."

"It's not about time, Francis. It's about leadership," the captain explained. "And leadership is what you have shown in spades. Both the lieutenant here and I think it's entirely appropriate."

"Yes, Francis. I agree. You realise that you won't stay with this platoon or company though. If you are successful, you will be placed in a different company. You can't have my job!" The lieutenant spoke with a huge smile on his face.

"Of course, I understand that. Thank you, sirs. It would be an honour," was all Frank could say.

"Right, well, I'll get the necessary papers drawn up and you should be on your way to England by the end of the week," the captain advised him. "Keep up the good work Francis."

"Thank you, sir," Frank replied and they stepped back, saluted and left.

On the way back to their digs, Lieutenant Stewart expanded. "As you know Francis, companies are commanded by captains with a full lieutenant as his 2 I/C and platoons have a 2nd lieutenant like me. At the moment we are seeing companies commanded by lieutenants, as we just can't keep up the supply of officers."

"Yes sir. I had noticed. It's a tough situation, isn't it?" Frank replied.

"It is, but it does offer opportunities for the promotion of good people, like yourself. I've been meaning to ask for some time Francis, but the man before me now is a little different from the Francis before your escapade at Polygon Wood," the lieutenant commented. "The Francis of old didn't often put himself forward, but you, now? It's like you're a different person."

Frank swallowed hard. The lieutenant was the first one to notice anything different between him and his grandfather. At least he was the first to say anything. It had been obvious to him, that he looked and sounded like his grandfather, but Francis must have been more content to sit back a little. Mind you, he had made it to corporal.

"I must say, I feel like a different person," Frank answered. "Not that I can remember what I was like. I suppose something happened to change my outlook. Maybe it was finding myself in that situation and working my way out of it. I have to say, I find things a bit different to before Polygon. I have had to adapt and learn or perhaps re-learn." Frank, sure as hell, was not lying on this point. There had been a lot of adapting and a lot of learning. Now he was going to have to do a lot more learning.

"We really need more men like you, Francis; ones who think outside the normal and use initiative. This, blindly charging across open ground into machine gun fire, has to stop. It's like they at the top think the only way to win, is just to keep throwing good men to the slaughter. It just can't keep going, 'to the last man' so to speak."

This was the first time the lieutenant had spoken to Frank like he was an equal. In the Army, one does not complain down the line of command. It is bad for discipline and morale. Frank understood this. It is the same principle in business.

"Agreed lieutenant," Frank responded. "I can see a different way to deal with these situations, due to my experience in a previous life, so to speak. But don't worry, we have an ace up our sleeve yet. I think you will find things are about to change, down on the Somme. The coming Aussie commander down there is a thinker and I believe he is about to make a huge impression on this war. Just you watch."

"Who do you mean, Monash or White or Birdwood?" the lieutenant queried.

"Monash sir. He has had a lot of time, since the Dardanelles, thinking and planning and once he gets his opportunity, I guarantee you, he will make the difference. History will be made," Frank told the lieutenant. He did not want to say too much more, so quickly changed the subject.

"So, what will I need to take to England with me?"

"Well 2nd Lieutenant Bailey, I suggest you take your high falootin' ideas with you and show them how it's done here," the lieutenant was laughing now.

"Hey, I'm not there yet sir. Gotta get through the course first." Frank replied.

"You will Francis. You will have no trouble with that," replied the Lieutenant.

Frank spent a couple of days on platoon training, then departed by battalion transport to Boulogne-sur-mer, along with two other sergeants from B and D Company. They took accommodation in the town down near the harbour for the night. As was the custom amongst the men, they found one of the local photographic houses and had their photos taken together in front of a painted backdrop of an archway, adorned with what looked like wisteria. The men enjoyed their leisurely afternoon and evening, without the pressures of the army, the war or the camp life. The following morning, they walked down to the ship and boarded for the short trip across the channel, before catching the train from Folkstone to London and then down to the training grounds of Salisbury Plains.

Frank spent three weeks in camp learning about the duties of an officer and how to go about the same. He felt their training was a little on the basic side but tried to remember this was 1918, not the year 2000. With the knowledge he already had on leadership, this course was a breeze. Sure, there was stuff he did not know about, particularly pertaining to the Army system, but mostly, the knowledge was adaptable from what he already knew. The one situation that disturbed him was the preponderance of upper-middle-class Englishmen there; purely because they were, upper-middle-class Englishmen. He could see why the progress of the war had been slow, to this point. The Australian Army, he thought, promotes on merit. The British Army promotes predominantly on class. Not really an effective way to progress your military prowess. The best part of this course though, was the absence of rats and lice.

They did have some time off during their course, and apart from quantities of warm English beer, he got the chance to see some of the countryside. Of course, in this area of Salisbury lay the famous Stone Henge, which all the Australians on the course wanted to see. Being 1918, and at this time privately owned, Frank got to go right into the Henge, not like in present day Frank figured, where it is all fenced off and access is restricted. He was in awe of the size of these stones. "They are massive," he thought. He was talking to one of the other officer cadets and explained to him, "Apparently the stone for these comes from a quarry over near the west coast. Imagine having to get these all the way from the quarry to a boat, then sailing them here and then getting them across the land again to here. Then you have to stand them up."

The reply he got stunned him at first, "Really? How do you know where the stone comes from? No one seems to know according to the literature."

"Oh shit, I've done it again," he thought to himself. *" Late 20*[th] *century knowledge again."*

"Um, well, I believe there has just been some new research on it and they think they have found the source," Frank tried to explain. "It's still to be confirmed though. I was reading something in London just the other day." Frank figured he had better not be an authority on everything. *"Maybe time to shut up,"* he thought.

During the course, the men were all measured up and fitted out with their officer's tunic, Sam Browne and cap. On successful completion, they were issued with their shoulder Pip. One pip for second lieutenant. They also received their Webley .38 revolver.

Frank returned to Le Wast at the end of February. The battalion was still in residence at the camp and, having received a few new recruits and men returning from hospital, the numbers were on the increase again. Still, there was a long way to go to get back up to full strength. Frank immediately reported to Battalion HQ.

Lt Col Currie was back at the helm of the battalion and warmly welcomed Frank back to the camp.

"Well 2nd Lieutenant Bailey, I have heard good reports from Salisbury on your course, I was just reading it. You have done well. Congratulations."

"Thank you, sir," Frank replied.

"They say here you have some good ideas, albeit a little different to the usual. From what I have heard from A Company, that doesn't really surprise me either. So, what are we going to do with you now? You realise you won't go to A Company, don't you?" the colonel explained, somewhat matter of fact.

"Yes sir, I do," Frank replied dutifully.

"What we are going to do is attach you to C Company command, just to get the ropes of that company, before allocating a platoon to you," the colonel stated.

"Yes sir, that sounds good," Frank kept the conversation to a minimum. Less chance of a slip up then.

"Good. Take yourself over to C Company and Captain Dunkley."

"Yes sir. Thank you, sir," Frank saluted and left the headquarters.

Frank took himself down to C Company and introduced himself to Captain Dunkley.

"Ah, yes Francis. It is Francis isn't it, 2nd lieutenant?" the captain asked as he surveyed his paperwork.

"Yes sir. You have been well informed," Frank replied with a smile.

"As I dare say you have been informed we will hang on to you, here at company HQ, so you can catch up with the personnel here, and our 'modus operandi', so to speak. I will leave you with Lieutenant McDonald to take you around and introduce you to the others," the captain informed Frank. He turned to McDonald and nodded.

"If you would like to come this way Lieutenant," McDonald indicated.

Frank saluted the captain and left with Lt McDonald.

"Congratulations Francis on your promotion. Well deserved, from what I'm hearing," the lieutenant said as they walked over toward the company tents.

"Thank you, sir. I must say I was a bit surprised by it all," Frank responded.

"Not at all. You shouldn't have been. That was quite a stunt bringing in those Bosch down near Warneton," McDonald quipped with a wide smile on his face.

"Oh, you heard about that did you?" Frank asked.

"Heard about it?" The lieutenant queried raising his eyebrows. "Everyone knows about that. It's a legendary tale now."

"Oh dear. Really?" Frank was unaware of this.

"Everyone thinks you're a legend. Well, everyone except for Fraser, anyway. Stuffy ol' bugger. He's too much of a one to stick to the book, predictable. That's his English background. Nope, you are right. We are in a different kind of war now and it needs different ways of thinking. The old stand and deliver, is over, we need to be able to think on our feet, not just do as we are told. We're all pretty much all of the one mind here. The lieutenant was being unusually forthright. "Oh, and by the way," he stopped walking and turned to face Frank, "we are both lieutenants, so the name's Bruce."

"Oh, I thought you, with two pips, would be next rank up," Frank queried.

"True, but 1st or 2nd lieutenant, there's really not much difference. Except when we are around the men of course. Better keep formalities then," McDonald added.

"Sure, no problem here," Frank answered eagerly.

"So, what's your take on the situation Francis? What do you think will happen now?" the lieutenant asked.

Frank smiled to himself. He couldn't resist, so he made this prediction, "I've made a bit of a name for predicting things recently, so here's what I think. We're nearly done here, in Flanders. Fritz has something like fifty divisions freed up from the Russian front now that lot is over, so he will be able to reinforce, both here in Flanders and down the Somme. I'm guessing he will make a push, fairly soon. If we are clever, we will let him advance, give him minimal resistance. If he gets a taste of success, he will push too far and his supply lines will become too long. That's when we need to strike. Strike him when he is vulnerable and can't respond adequately. If we can keep the pressure on, he will fold and head for home. Be over by the end of the year."

McDonald started laughing, "Home by Christmas, eh? Seem to have heard that before."

Frank chuckled, "Yep all over by Christmas, but home early next year."

"So, this big push, here or Somme?" The lieutenant asked.

"My best guess Bruce, is Somme," Frank stated emphatically. "And we'll be there."

"Interesting take. Somme, eh? You think we'll relocate?" Bruce questioned.

"Yep. Next month." Frank was getting bold now.

As their conversation concluded, they arrived at the first of the platoon leader's tents.

"Lieutenant Farquharson, please meet Lieutenant Francis Bailey formerly 'A' Company," McDonald said.

"Hello Francis. I'm Max. I've got 6 Platoon. You'll like it here in C." Farquharson held out his hand and shook Frank's.

"Thanks, Max. I'm looking forward to a change and the challenge," Frank answered.

"Quite a stunt you pulled down at Warneton, that was," Farquharson added, smilingly.

"Oh, that. Yes, I am beginning to see that," Frank laughed.

"Stuffed up old Fraser, didn't you?" Farquharson laughed too.

"Well, that wasn't the intention. I just thought I was doing my job," Frank was getting embarrassed now. He had no argument with Lt Fraser.

"Jolly good show though eh?" Farquharson added.

"Okay, Francis we'll keep moving down the line," McDonald could see this was getting to Frank.

"Next, will be Lieutenant Skevington. Skev to his mates," McDonald indicated. As they walked into the next tent, he continued.

"G'day Skev. I want you to meet Lieutenant Bailey. Francis. He's come from 'A' coy,"

"How do you do Francis? Good to meet you. Heard a lot of good things." Skev was an outgoing type and it showed in his manner of speaking.

"Glad to meet you too, lieutenant," Frank replied.

"Nar, enough of this formality man, it's Skev. That is if there's no grunts around." Skev laughed.

"Okay Skev it is then," Frank replied. "Which platoon do you have?"

"Oh yeah," answered Skev. "I've got 5 Platoon. As good a bunch of reprobates as you could get, I reckon. Bloody good sergeant too. Sergeant Harris. Dean Harris. Keep your eye on him."

"Sergeant Harris. Okay I'll do that," Frank wasn't sure why he was keeping an eye on him, but he agreed to. He thought Skev would be a bit like his speech, jumping around all over the place, keen, eager.

"If you're ever looking for a tipple on the side, Skev's your man. He can find it anywhere," McDonald advised Frank.

"That, I shall have to remember," Frank added.

"Right, on to the next platoon, my lad. See ya later Skev," McDonald said.

"He seems like a lively sort of character, Bruce?" Frank queried, as they moved towards the next lot of tents.

"Lively!" Bruce laughed. "Yep, that's one way of putting it. Skev's trouble is not shutting up sometimes. You'll find that out. Salt of the earth though." Bruce laughed again.

"Last one is Folley. He's the quiet one. Every company has one. Deep thinker. You never know what he is going to come out with. One thing is for sure, he has given it a lot of thought before saying it though."

"Lieutenant Folley, this is Lieutenant Bailey. He's new to us from A Company," Bruce said on entering this tent.

"Lieutenant," Folley held out his hand.

"How do you do Lieutenant Folley?" Frank asked.

"Fine thank you. I'm Ed," Folley said rather softly.

"And I'm Francis," Frank added.

"Oh, Francis Bailey. Well done sir. Good job at Warneton," Folley remarked.

"It seems like everyone knows about that," Frank commented.

"Yep!" Folley answered. "When initiative pays off everyone notices. Look forward to working with you."

"Likewise, Ed. See you later," Frank replied.

Folley nodded and went back to his paperwork. Frank and Bruce exited.

"So, there you have it Francis," The lieutenant explained. "Ed has 8 platoon and I have 7. Still sort of doing two jobs at the moment. It will be up to the captain, but I think you will probably take seven, once you're settled in. A good bunch, on the whole. There's always the troublemaker. It wouldn't be an Aussie platoon if it didn't have a troublemaker in it, would it?" Bruce slapped Frank on the back and laughed.

"No, it wouldn't, would it?" Frank replied rather sheepishly. He didn't think that was necessarily the case. Sure, there were a few troublemakers around, but his feeling was that it was usually a reflection of leadership. He guessed he would find out soon enough. It would be a little more difficult if the previous leader allowed the situation to occur though, he figured.

"Right let's head back to HQ and see what needs doing," Lieutenant McDonald suggested.

Frank spent the next few days copying out reports and filling out returns and requisitions. He did enjoy the somewhat casual atmosphere around C Coy, but wondered how that would be reflected in their performance in the field. He held some reservations in this area. For the moment, he just got on with the tasks in hand, making sure everything was in order for the coming transfer to the Somme region, not that anyone else knew that was going to happen soon.

The middle of March saw the Battalion move back to Le Romarin camp and that would only mean one thing. More time on the front line, on the border between Belgium and France. The battalion was split up on this rotation with only one or two companies required at a time. For the rest of the battalion, not on the line, it meant more training, more drills, more working parties. Trenches always need maintaining and expanding. Frank was detailed on a couple of occasions to lead some of these work parties, as a way of easing him into the platoon commander role. In the third week of March, he took over 7 Platoon from Lt McDonald, as suggested. His first job was to try and get them all thinking along his lines. They were mostly aware of the incident down at Warneton, so Frank had a bit of an image even before he took the platoon. He trained them, along with his Sergeant Martin, and tried to instil his attitudes and values into the men. Due to his 'legendary' status, most of them came on board fairly smartly. There were a couple of those 'troublemakers' that McDonald alluded to, but Frank had already decided these two would be simple enough to crack. Responsibility, Frank figured, would be the key to these two. Responsibility at the appropriate time.

The appropriate time arose, when on a working party for wire laying, Frank took one of the men aside. He had planned that the corporal and sergeant were off on another detail, so that this opportunity would arise.

"Henschell!" He yelled out.

"Yes sir!" Henschell answered as he came over to Frank.

"Henschell, we don't seem to have any NCOs in this party, so I would like you to please take charge of Group 1 there. I will supervise Group 2. You know what is required don't you?" Frank asked him, knowing full well that he had explained it all to them previously.

"Yes sir I do. Are you sure you want me to look after this group?" he answered.

"Yes, I do. Is there any reason why I shouldn't?" Frank threw the ball back into his court.

"No sir. Not at all, sir. Thank you sir!" Henschell replied to Frank and he left to do the job with a smile on his face.

Gotcha number 1, Frank thought to himself.

In the last week of March, the battalion was advised that all leave was cancelled, and they were on 'short notice for movement' status. By now, the strength of the battalion was back up around the one thousand mark, although not all of them were present. Some were still in hospital and some were still on courses, here and there. To prepare for the move stores had to be returned, kits to be inspected, parades to be inspected and all soldiers had to have the required equipment. Working parties still went out but on short recall notice. On the 2nd of April, the movement order came through. They were posted to the Somme, to Corbie to be precise.

Corbie was located, 94 km south of Romarin, on the northern banks of the Somme River, at the confluence with the Ancre River, about 15 km east of Amiens. The transfer would take them four days by foot, bus and train. When they arrived in Corbie, the townsfolk were unaware of their impending arrival.

"Monsieur Le Mayor. We need to put all these men somewhere for the night. Have you not been forewarned of our arrival?" The adjutant asked the Mayor of Corbie.

"No, my good sir, we have not, but do not fear, if you give me an hour or so, It will be my pleasure to organise it," the mayor excitedly replied. "It will have to be mostly floors for this many men at such short notice. We are so glad that we can be of service to our great allies. Please, I will organise now."

"Thank you, good Monsieur. I am so sorry no one told you of our stopping here."

"No sir, it is fine. We will see it done."

The mayor left and spoke to his staff who immediately dispersed around the town to ask for assistance.

The men needed billeting just for the one night, so the townspeople just left their shops and businesses and raced home to prepare for the troops for the night. Businesses were left wide open by the locals, just to prepare for the Australian troops. At this time, Corbie had been spared the devastation that had been inflicted on many of their nearby towns. There was little evidence of the war here, yet. The townsfolk, however, were extremely glad to be of service to the troops and the men of the 28th settled down to a comfortable night.

The following morning, the men marched again, eastward to Bresle, and A and C Companies, immediately moved to the front line, northwest of Dernancourt, on the Ancre River. Thankfully, their first day on the line was a breeze, as it is a tough ask to complete a march of that magnitude and then hit the front line immediately. There was absolutely no activity at all, that first full day.

"Let's hope it continues like this for a while sergeant," Frank said to his new Sergeant McLean.

"I figure that will be a vain hope, don't you think sir?" the sergeant asked in reply.

Frank laughed. "Yeah, I think that may be the case, Peter. Still, one can live in hope, eh?"

The following day, they had the answer to that question when the German artillery opened up on them, with a two-hour gas bombardment. For two hours plus the men of A and C Companies sat in their claustrophobic gas respirators, underground, just waiting and praying for the barrage to lift. Frank tried moving around his troops in an attempt to keep morale up. He had noticed that several of the men were not handling the barrages particularly well, particularly the HE whizbangs, which made their subterranean hideouts shudder with each explosion. Every time a bomb exploded, dirt fell from the roof of their hideout and the less seasoned of the men felt certain the roof was about to cave in and bury them. Frank could hear in the distance, a man crying out for the barrage to stop, so he made his way along to where the noise was coming from and sat down beside the offending private. He was one of the few men who had been unable to fit in the underground bunker, so was in a funk hole in the trench. Frank could not afford to have the morale of the company undermined by any one person's whining.

"How are you doing son?" Frank asked him.

The soldier stopped and looked at Frank with a fearful expression. "Can't you make 'em stop sir?"

"I wish that I could, lad. They don't give up do they?" came Frank's reply. "But I'll tell you what. They miss their target, nearly all the time. Have you noticed that?"

"Miss, sir?" the terrified soldier replied, still cowering in the corner of his hole.

"Yes. Have you ever noticed how many actually land in our trench? Bugger all son. We had that one up at Warneton, but that was pretty much it. They are wasting their time and energy bombing us, coz it just is not working," Frank explained to him in an attempt to calm him down. "How many have you seen that have landed in the trench?"

"Well, um, none sir!" he replied after a moment's reflection.

"There you go, son. So the trench is probably the safest place to be, don't you think? Okay, it's loud and hurts the eardrums a bit, but that's gotta be better than getting hit." Frank was digging deep now and just then, another shell landed just in front of the trench, spraying them with dirt. They both ducked down, but the young soldier buried his head in his knees and covered his head with his arms and whimpered again.

"See, they missed again." Frank grasped him by the shoulder with one hand. "You can make it, son. We are about to give these Hun bastards a hiding to nothing. You just watch and I want you to see the results of that, first hand. You can do that, can't you?"

The private lifted his head from his knees and looked straight at Frank. "Do you really think so sir?"

"Think so? Son, I know so." Frank leaned in and looked about before quietly whispering in the soldier's ear. "Just between you and me, I have seen the future of this battle and we beat the crap out of them," Frank explained to him. He had no fear telling the fellow this. It would just be seen as an officer reassuring a private if the comment ever saw the light of day.

"If you think so sir, I can make it. I still want the noise to stop though." The soldier replied.

"It will, son. Fairly soon too. They will burn their guns out if they don't." Frank added with a big smile on his face.

The young fellow smiled back. "That would be amusing to see, would it not sir?"

"That it would, son," Frank answered. "You just hang in there and when we beat the pants off them, you remember this conversation."

"I will sir. Thank you, sir,"

"Keep up the good work, son. You're in number 1 Section aren't you?" Frank asked him quietly.

"Yes sir!" He smiled again. The lieutenant must have noticed him before to know that. "What's your name son?" Frank asked him.

"Anderson sir. Henry Anderson," the lad replied.

"Well Henry, you tell Corporal Goodman, that we had this chat, okay?" Frank patted him on the shoulder and stood to leave.

"Yes sir, I will. Thank you," the now, much-relieved soldier, replied to Frank.

Shortly after his chat with the young private the barrage did indeed lift.

As soon as it did, they had to 'stand to', in case of an enemy charge. Nothing eventuated, to their relief. That evening, B and D Companies relieved them on the front line and A and C fell back to the reserve line. The action here at Dernancourt saw the beginning of the reduction in numbers for the battalion once again. Two lieutenants were severely wounded and one OR, killed.

After only 4 days on the front line here, the 28th was relieved by the 26th. Unlike their previous relief operations, this one proved fatal for two of the men and two others were wounded by machine gun fire. The dark nights at this time had assisted the relief operations, but tonight, the Germans got lucky. As the men were making their way back to the support trench line, a couple of kilometres behind the line, German machine guns began firing indiscriminately in the dark. Usually, this was totally ineffective, but tonight they were on target. The firing did not last long, so after a short time, they continued their way back to the reserve line. Even here, they were not safe really. The enemy had a habit of targeting the rear areas with artillery. This did cause the 28th to lose another dozen or so men in the six days in the support trenches.

Life in the support trenches was no picnic. This position was supposed to be a relief from the front line, but with artillery and work parties, life was just as dangerous. Every day in support, 3 or 4 work parties, sometimes up to one hundred men, were called for wiring parties, ammunition carriage, food delivery to the front line, expanding trenches, digging further trenches and many other sundry tasks. These parties had to contend with just as much fire as those on the front line. Also, it was not just a matter of moving forward on the roads. That would bring instant death. It was shell holes, water, dead horses, smashed equipment, mud, trenches that may not have been dug deep enough yet, and rats. Progress was always slow and, depending on visibility on any day, the journey could take anything from one hour to four hours. The hot food was cooked behind the line and taken forward, so on those days where progress was slow, the food was often cold by the time it reached the men on the front. In these areas, in winter, a kerosene tin full of hot, black tea, would leave the rear areas, piping hot, delivering along the way and by the time it got to the front line, not only could it be cold, but frozen. On those occasions, the men would chip a few chunks out of the tin, into their cups and try and thaw it over a candle or small lamp. If that was not possible, they would just take a chunk and suck on it.

Back at the support camp, the men endured frequent, indiscriminate shelling. Sometimes there seemed to be no logic to the artillery targeting. On one occasion this week, the artillery was targeted on a particular road nearby but contained no HE, meaning there would be no damage to the road.

"Have you noticed, sergeant, that today's arty targeting the Albert – Amiens Road, is only gas and shrapnel?" Frank asked. The road in question was about a kilometre north of their position.

"I have sir. Rather strange isn't it, if they want to disrupt our progress?" The sergeant asked in return.

"Yes. However, I'm thinking they don't want to damage it, possibly so they can use it themselves on a counterattack. Watch out for that, Peter." Frank replied.

"That makes sense, actually. Do we need to advise Company?" Peter asked.

"They will more than likely have worked that out too, but let's not leave that to chance. I'll make a note, if you can get a runner to take it back to company HQ. Thanks," Frank ordered. "Actually Peter, if you can find Ward, use him, but tell him it is an important message that can only be given to a trusted person. I want to see how he reacts."

"Ward sir?" queried the sergeant.

"Yes, sergeant. I know he's been a bit difficult, but I want to see how he goes if he realises he is valued," Frank explained.

"Certainly sir," and the sergeant turned to find Private Ward.

"Gotcha number 2," Frank muttered to himself.

They had worked it out at Company as well and had advised battalion HQ of the same. It was a case of being prepared for the inevitable. On the 17th, the battalion was once again to go forward and relieve the 26th battalion near Dernancourt. Once again it was A and C up front, with B and D in reserve, three days on three days off. In the officer's dugout, Lt McDonald and Frank were sitting drinking a cup of tea.

"You know Frank, I think that nickname given to you by that Hun captain, might have to stick," McDonald began.

"What one would that be?" Frank asked him.

"Corporal, but now Lieutenant Sooth," McDonald replied.

Frank laughed. "Oh yes! Why is that, Bruce?"

"Do you recall a conversation we had back at Le Wast, about the future of this war?" McDonald asked.

"Oh vaguely. What in particular?" Frank feigned. He remembered alright but wasn't going to acknowledge that.

"You said something like, Fritz will attack and gain a lot of ground that we should let him take, until he overstretches his supply lines. Then, we should drive him backwards. Ring any bells?" McDonald asked with a querying eye tilt.

"Oh, that! Yeah. Looks like he might have just done that, don't you think?" Frank teased.

"How the hell did you work that out? Are you a general in disguise?" McDonald appeared incredulous.

"Oh well, to my way of thinking it was an obvious tactic," Frank replied. "You know, let him think he is doing well, wait for him to start congratulating himself, and then wallop him when he least expects it. It's an age-old tactic. It seems to me we are at the holding stage right now. Soon we will counterattack and, boom, that will be the end of Fritz."

"I see. So, what else do you see happening? Anything I should know about?" He asked Frank.

"Oh, lots of things," he teased. "Who do you think is the best General in our army?"

McDonald thought for a few seconds and then answered, "It would have to be between White, Birdwood and Monash!"

"Agreed!" Frank replied. "I think Birdy is getting too old for command and White is too conservative, so my best guess is Monash will head the Australian corps. So, who do you think is going to make with the different tactics? Monash or Haig?"

McDonald laughed. "Oh yes, Haig for sure. I can see him altering course and making a huge difference; never," he replied sarcastically. "Monash of course; and I think you are right that he will be our next commander. Do you think he will even get a say though?"

"Well, he is next in line to command down in this region, so I reckon it will be he that makes all the difference," Frank explained. "Once Monash takes charge, a whole different kind of war will commence. None of this sitting in bloody trenches all day, playing tit-for-tat. I'll throw one at you and you can throw one at me. It simply is not working. Look at how many arty shells Fritz sends over, compared to how many casualties it causes. What an absolute wasted effort not to mention the cost."

"I have to agree with you on that one, but do you really think Haig will let an Australian take command?" McDonald asked.

"He will have no choice. You watch. Have a look around you. What are we using in this war, which is a first?" Frank asked Bruce.

"Well, there's tanks," he replied.

"And?" Frank re-asked.

"Oh, machine guns. And aeroplanes of course," he added.

"And modern artillery, gas, grenades. But let me ask you this Bruce; when have we used all these advances in technology in a fully coordinated attack? All those things working together." Frank went on without waiting for an answer. "We haven't. Not properly. Not yet. That's where Monash comes in. He has a plan to use them all together."

"How the hell would you know all that? Despite the fact that it does actually make sense. Where do you get this information from?" Bruce was clearly frustrated now.

"Trust me, Bruce," Frank assured him. "I know a few people. Let's just leave it at that."

Just then Skev burst through the door, "Them bloody Bosch planes are outside again. Come, look." They all donned their tin hats and headed outside, to watch the 'show'. There were bombers just to their north, headed for Amiens again. They were flying too high for any of the machine gunners to hit them, but the anti-aircraft gunners were engaging them, with little success. They were being circled by several fighter aircraft as escorts when a squadron of British aircraft approached from the northwest. A series of dogfights ensued, with each side scoring hits. One British and one German aircraft spun out of control and crashed about one km to their north. Another was forced down just to their south and the men rushed and captured the uninjured pilot. The fighters were getting lower as they fought, when Frank called out, "Anyone got binoculars, I mean field glasses, handy?"

Skev called back, "Yeah here. What's up?"

Frank took the glasses and peered up at the dog fights above. Two of the escorting fighters he recognised as red Fokker Tri-planes. The type used by the Baron von Richthofen. He also knew there were not really as many of these planes as the movies would have you believe, so he said to the others, "I think you will find that one of those two on the left is the 'Red Baron, von Richthofen. They are Fokker triplanes, that's what he flies. There are not many of those planes in use."

Bruce spoke up, "Here, let me have a look," and Frank passed the glasses.

After a few seconds, he spoke again this time slowly, "You know, I think you may well be correct, lad. I think they are triplanes. Bit hard from this distance, but it does look like they are." He put the glasses down and passed them back to Skev and added, "Might sound poor form, but ya have to admire the bloke. He's a real Ace, regardless of which side you're on."

Frank responded with, "Well put, Bruce. He is indeed."

That night the intercompany relief happened, as B and D moved forward and the others moved back to reserve. Both these companies reported seeing the Baron active over the area over the next couple of days. On the 22nd of April, news came through that von Richthofen had been fatally shot down the previous day, by Australian machine gunners in action, in the area of Morlancourt, two km to their south. That saw the end of a legend of the sky, with a tally in excess of eighty enemy planes downed. The men of 3 Squadron Australian Flying Corps saw to it that the baron was buried with full military honours on the 22nd, such was the reputation and the esteem this man was afforded.

The following day the battalion was withdrawn from the front line, in order to rest and recuperate. The battalion numbers had dropped by over eighty since arriving in the Somme region. At the end of the month, these losses started to rise even further as men began to fall victim to what appeared to be some kind of severe influenza. Men started reporting extremely high temperatures, aches, pains and congestion.

In the officers' mess, they were sitting having a 'therapeutic tipple', courtesy of Skev, and they were discussing this, due to the fact that it could have a really significant impact on their fighting strength. Frank was thinking about the timing of this outbreak. Something stirred in in his mind.

"Spanish Flu?" he muttered, almost under his breath.

"What was that, Francis? Spanish? Spanish what?" Skev asked.

"Oh, I was just thinking out loud," Frank said trying to back down again. "I have heard something about a flu epidemic that may be starting to take hold. It is considered extremely dangerous, so we need to all take care not to spread it. It has the potential to decimate our men. We should get these men off to hospital as soon as possible and keep them separate from the others. Tell the hospital to isolate them as well."

"Where do you get all this information from Francis? You seem to be a fountain of knowledge," Ralph asked him.

"Well, it's not so much what you know, but who you know. I have a lot of contacts that I get information from. Plus, I do a lot of reading," Frank needed to divert the conversation, so he added, "I think I will go see the MO, to discuss the matter. I'll see what he knows."

He took himself off to see the MO, Captain Harper. Along the way, he was thinking to himself about the Spanish Flu pandemic. It lasted from 1918 to 1920, but his understanding of the pandemic was that it started later than this. *"Whilst it is called the Spanish flu everywhere, except in Spain, it did not start there,"* he thought. *"I wonder if it was actually already going here in France, before the reports of it raised a few eyebrows."*

Up at the CCS, Captain Harper was talking to one of the nurses.

"This is the third case for the day and the tenth we have seen this week. I am a little concerned we are seeing some kind of outbreak here."

"Yes, Doctor. It seems to be some sort of influenza, do you think?" the nurse answered.

"Yes, it does," the Doctor replied. "I don't know whether we need to isolate all these cases to try and stop transmission through the rest of the men," the doctor added, looking around.

At that point, Frank walked into the Company Medical Officer's tent and sought out the captain.

"Captain Harper. Lieutenant Bailey sir," Frank started.

"What can I do for you lieutenant," came the reply.

"Sir, I wanted to talk to you about what appears to be the beginning of a potentially serious outbreak. A kind of flu like illness. Have you seen much of it?" Frank enquired.

"Interesting question, lieutenant. As a matter of fact, we were just talking about that very subject only a few minutes ago, as you arrived. We've seen three new cases today and it does appear to be a particularly severe kind of influenza," the MO answered.

Frank then asked, "Have you heard if any of the other companies or battalions have seen similar cases?"

"Indeed I have. There appears to be a much higher rate this month than one would expect in April," the Doctor added. "Why do you ask lieutenant?"

"Well, I have a sneaking suspicion that this may well be the beginning of something way more serious, than 'just a flu'," Frank tried to explain. "From information I have, this could turn into one of the biggest natural disasters the world has seen so far. I would not want to tell you how to do your job of course sir, but I think that isolation may well be advised for these men, if we are to reduce the spread of this influenza."

"Very interesting, lieutenant. And just what is this information that you have? Asked the MO.

"I can't go into all the details sir, but information is currently emerging in England, Spain and other countries, about the possibility of a pandemic," Frank wanted to play down his part but encourage the doctor to take all the necessary precautions.

"I have not heard anything like that yet, lieutenant, but I will say one thing. We have already been discussing what to do to prevent the spread of this influenza. I have been wondering if we need to set up separate accommodation for those patients. We don't wish to lose all our troops to it now, do we?" The doctor asked.

"No sir, we do not," Frank answered. "Now if you could just send it across no man's land, to our Fritz cousins, that would be lovely."

"Not a bad idea, lieutenant," the doctor laughed. "Interesting though. I wonder if they have it already? Now, that would lend weight to your argument, wouldn't it?"

"It would at that sir," Frank admitted.

"I think I will go and see the QM and see if we can get another tent set up, just to deal with these fellows. That way, hopefully, we can stop this spreading. I will also talk to the colonel, about looking out for it amongst the men," the captain replied trying to decide what to do next.

"Thank you for your time, sir. I just thought I would check with you on your thoughts." Frank bid him goodbye and returned to the officer's quarters. When he arrived only Lt Folley was there, the others having gone to check on their platoons.

"Well Frank, what did you learn at the Mos?" Folley asked him.

"The MO says that he is seeing an increase in the influenza cases right now Ed. More than he would expect. I think he is going to isolate them for everybody's benefit," Frank explained.

"Wise move, I think. Especially if you are right," Ed replied.

"I think, maybe we should let the men know that the moment they feel anything like a flu coming on they need to report it. We need to isolate these guys for the benefit of the company," Frank suggested.

"I have to say, Frank, I am intrigued by your predictions. It's like you have some knowledge, of what the future holds." He stopped there and just studied Frank's face.

Frank tried not to react too much. "Oh, I don't know Ed. Sometimes, you just have to look at the available information, and the future predicts itself, if you look at it logically."

Frank liked Ed. He was not prone to leaping to conclusions, or exaggeration. He analysed situations rationally and made his decisions based on sound thinking, rather than adrenaline or emotion. He also knew he would have to be extra careful around him for the same reasons, not that for one minute he thought Ed would work out he was from 80 years ahead.

"That is very true Francis, but it is still uncanny, all the same," Ed replied.

"Guess I've had a bit of luck too. Not everything works out the way you think it will. I think I will go and see Sergeant McLean and see if there are any sickies in my lot. Cheerio." Frank terminated the conversation there and left.

At the end of the month, the battalion got orders to move to Camon, on the outskirts of Amiens, at the confluence of the Somme and Avre Rivers. April had seen the battalion lose thirty-eight men to sickness, twenty-nine wounded, ten killed and one died of wounds. Not to mention the four who were sent to prison for desertion. If these men had been in the British army they would have faced the firing squad. The view within the Australian army was different. All Australian troops were volunteers. Every one of them. Australian leadership felt that, whilst desertion was a serious crime, it should not be punishable by death as the men were there voluntarily in the first place. These four men were sentenced by Court Martial, to ten, ten, seven and five years penal servitude. A penalty, no doubt lifted on conclusion of the war. They would, however, have been unlikely to qualify for service medals, pensions or any of the other benefits due to returned servicemen.

The first week of May, at Camon, was spent shoring up the last fallback line for the Australian troops. This was the last line that would be defended if it came to that. The German "Spring Offensive" had come to an end in April/May, after their supply lines became too long to sustain, and as Frank had explained to Lt McDonald, that was the time to mount a counterattack. Major General Pompey Elliot had already predicted that the Germans would take Villers-Bretonneux, a few kilometres to the southeast of Amiens, and was prepared to let them do that, in order to mount his counterattack, which was successful on 25th April 1918. This was the first setback for the Kaiser's army, for the year. It would not be the last.

With the last line of defence set at Camon, training commenced on the new tactics of coordinated, integrated attack, under the advisement of Maj. Gen. John Monash AIF. The men of the 28th and other battalions were trained at night in the use of tanks for cover for advancing infantry. At this time, the casualty list amongst the officers was climbing alarmingly. In one week, with Lt McDonald off on a course, Farquharson on secondment and Folley on other duties, Frank was the most senior officer in the company. He knew, however, that the sergeants were the men who really ran the platoons, so he allowed them to do just that.

Chapter 11
Tell Your Children

They went with songs to the battle, they were young.
Straight of limb, true of eyes, steady and aglow.
They were staunch to the end against odds uncounted,
They fell with their faces to the foe.
For the Fallen
(Ode to Remembrance 1st verse)

Laurence Binyon

By the time it came for their next move forward, C Coy had a full complement of officers again. The three weeks in reserve had been well timed for the battalion. They had managed to regain several of their troops from both illness and injury and the numbers were on the rise again. This move took them to the small village of Treux, on the south side of the River Ancre, into the positions previously occupied by the 21st and 22nd Battalions, as they had moved forward and captured the town of Ville-su-Ancre, five km southwest of Albert.

With A and C Companies in the front line and B and D in reserve yet again, the positions at Treux were held on to, despite daily artillery barrages, including on one day four-hour barrage of gas, which yet again yielded no casualties. In one of these barrages, the enemy artillery concentrated on their rear areas and, in doing so, cut all lines of communications to the front line. Linesmen were sent out in the barrage to try and restore communications, but it was some time until they could accomplish this. The officers were hunkered down in their bunker yet again and discussing the situation.

Skev opened the discussion with, "I wouldn't be those line repair guys for quids."

"Nup, me neither," echoed Max.

"They've gotta have nerves of steel, to be out in that lot I reckon," Skev replied.

"These communications tools are bloomin' marvellous though, aren't they?" Frank entered the conversation. "Damn site better, than sending runners all the time wouldn't you think?"

"Too true my lad," Skev added.

"Mind you, we can see limitations with it. I reckon before too long, I don't know, say 20 or 30 years, all these comms systems won't need wires. The signal will just travel through the air and be picked up by someone miles away on another unit," Frank explained.

"Oh, you're talking about the Marconi contraption, Francis. The big problem with that is the size of the transmitter and mast required. It can't be portable," Bruce entered into the conversation.

"At the moment, that is certainly true," Frank agreed. "But they also said he couldn't send signals across the Atlantic either. Now it's common. Fear not, they will be working on making this smaller, more compact and portable. It will happen."

McDonald chuckled, "Ah here's our resident sooth, predicting the future again. I guess Francis, that means it will happen."

Frank chuckled too, "Yes Bruce, it most certainly does." They all laughed. They were getting used to Frank's predictions coming to pass.

At that moment, their acting company CO, Lt Dunkley dashed into the room shaking dust off his helmet.

"What are we discussing this time boys?" he asked.

Again chuckling, Bruce answered, "Oh just more of Francis' predictions."

"Oh yes? What does he reckon this time?" Dunkley asked with a smile and a sideways glance at Frank.

Skev jumped into the conversation again, "Just that all communications will be wireless soon, and all our talk will go through the air, person to person."

"Oh, is that all?" Dunkley replied turning to Frank, "I completely agree with you Francis. Marconi has done some amazing work on that since arriving in England. What you predict is not far away at all."

Frank smiled and then his eyes lit up, "Hey are those captain pips on your shoulders, Ira?"

Bruce jumped forward, "Hey old man, congratulations, Sir."

Skev jumped to his feet and saluted the captain. "Well done Ira, I mean Sir."

All the men congratulated him and shook his hand.

"It's only a temporary promotion at the moment, boys," Ira added.

"Yes, but you know how they have a habit of becoming permanent, what with the current attrition rate and all," Frank stated gloomily.

"Downside is, Captain Brown from D Company has been taken out by a machine gun shot to the leg. He'll survive, but he'll be out of action for some time yet," the new captain said.

"Bugger!" Exclaimed McDonald. "We're losing officers too fast. Makes you wonder when it will be our turn?"

"They'll have to shoot fast to get me," Skev added with a laugh.

"Yeah, they'll struggle to hit the bee in a bottle," Dunkley laughed. "Seriously though guys, don't take any unnecessary risks. I recon, we are getting close to the end of this lot."

"Agreed," Frank answered.

"Oh, and by the way, if you see any stray-looking Yanks hanging around they are two 'lootenants' from the US Army. They will be with us for a week or so, to get the hang of what goes on. They've come to learn," Dunkley added. He made a point of emphasising the American pronunciation of the word.

Skev scoffed. "I didn't think anyone could teach the Yanks anything."

"You be civil to them, Skev. They are genuinely interested in learning," Dunkley directed.

"Don't worry captain, we will look after them. What's their names?" Frank asked.

"One's Cosgrove and the tall one is Frasier," Dunkley answered. "Francis, can I see you outside please." Captain Dunkley stepped outside and Frank followed him. "Francis it is beginning to look like you may end up with a transfer of company. We are back to full strength, and you may be needed either at Nucleus or transferring to one of the other companies. It is not certain yet, but I thought you had better be warned that it is up for consideration."

"Oh, I see," replied Frank. "I guess I could see it coming, so I'm not all that surprised. How long 'til we know?"

"Probably about a week, I guess, unless something untoward happens in the meantime," the captain advised him.

"Thanks for letting me know, sir," Frank replied.

At midnight, on May 26, the battalion was relieved and took up position in the reserve trenches back on the Ancre River. One company got lucky and received permission to go swimming in the river that afternoon. The rest of the battalion put the pressure on the following day and were all granted a swim. The men were heartily relieved to be able to swim after a week on the front line. In fact, it was so well received that, command allowed them to swim almost every day. In the afternoon, they all watched, as multiple aeroplanes fought each other overhead. One enemy aircraft was seen to spiral towards the ground, in flames. At around the 1000' mark, the pilot and his observer were seen to fall out of the aircraft and plummet to the ground. They were of course both killed. A party was sent out from the battalion to assess the two Germans, and they buried them both where they fell. Once they were buried the Aussies erected two crosses at their graves. It was not uncommon, when faced with a choice of perishing in the flames of a burning aircraft, or from the fall, that pilots would opt to leap from their aircraft and die in the fall, rather than be burned alive.

The battalion had a noticeably quiet time in reserve and were successfully relieved by the 22nc Battalion at midnight May 31. The men were marching, in companies, the seven kilometres to their rest area at La Houssoye that morning, when an enemy aircraft flying overhead, spied the column marching. The pilot banked the plane to his left and dived down, toward the now scattering column, safe in the knowledge that there were no anti-aircraft batteries to contend with this far behind the line. He dropped his two bombs. They exploded amongst B Company. 27 ORs were killed instantly and one officer and 39 ORs were wounded. Three horses perished in the blast as well. Lt Col Currie, battalion commander, was no more than seven yards from the blast, but somehow survived uninjured, probably protected by other bodies between him and the blast. The fallen were buried at the nearby Franvillers Cemetery.

This event certainly cast a pall of gloom over the entire battalion, which up until that point had been in extremely high spirits, having finished their stint up front. They were all looking forward to a rest, well away from the action. Never before, had the battalion lost so many mates in one day. This really was a wretched war.

Their time off the front line was spent quietly, even though there was fairly regular shelling of the rear areas. The shelling was of all kinds of artillery, but resulted in no casualties of any significance. Halfway through the second week of June, it became obvious that things were building up to another "push". Captain Dunkley sought out Frank.

"Francis, you remember I mentioned about changing companies last week?"

"Yes sir, I do. Where am I going?" Frank got in first.

Chuckling the captain replied, "You've probably heard of another action soon, and A Company is short, due to leave in England for a couple of their lieutenants. We'd like you to fill in over there for this action."

Frank smiled, "Back to A Company, eh?"

"Yes, so if you want to head over and report to Captain Hammond, he will allocate you as required," Captain Dunkley told him.

"Back to the boys of A Company again," thought Frank. ""That's where I belong. Wait a minute, I don't belong anywhere here. What am I thinking? These thoughts were followed by a frustrated sigh. He often thought of Lynne, Tim, Eloise and his parents. He made a point of this every day, but with the growing list of officers, particularly lieutenants, getting killed, he wondered if he would ever see them again.

"Lieutenant Bailey reporting for duty with A Company sir!" Frank barked out as he entered the command tent.

Captain Hammond looked up and laughed. "Hello Francis. You finally made it back here, eh? Welcome back."

Frank looked on Captain Hammond with great admiration. Since he last had dealings with the then Lt Hammond MM, the year before, Lt Meysey George Hammond MM, MC, had again been wounded in action. He had first been wounded as a sergeant back in November 1916, when he received a GSW (gun shot wound) to the left elbow. It had rendered his left arm completely useless, locking it at a right angle and the useless appendage lay supported in a permanent sling. This is when he was awarded his first gong, that of the MM. On his recovery, he had somehow persuaded the powers that be that he could usefully continue his duties in the battalion, so was returned to duty. In October 1917, he led a charge at the enemy, despite only having the use of one arm, and captured a trench from the enemy and gathered a plethora of intelligence which led to further advances in the following days. He was a fearless leader and inspired fearlessness and gallantry in his men, During this action he received his second GSW, this time to his leg, which led to his evacuation to hospital in England yet again. For this action, Hammond had been awarded the MC. (Some thought, and many still do, that it should have been the Victoria Cross.)

As Frank looked at the captain, he noticed the useless arm and now the cane that he used for assistance when walking. He could only wonder how these injuries could have been sustained and yet still allow him to continue as the battalion intelligence officer, let alone his position as company commander of his old A Company.

"Thank you, sir. You weren't a captain when I left though sir, and congratulations on the MC too sir," Frank said with a smile.

"Thank you, Francis; and no, I suppose I wasn't. Stuff happens when you least expect it though, eh Francis?" came the reply from the captain. "I'm going to allocate you to your old bunch, 3 Platoon, much as I know it's not normally done like that, but needs must at the moment."

"Thank you, sir. I don't think it will be a problem, sir. It's been quite a while now since I was with them. There's bound to be a lot of new faces by now." Frank said to the captain.

"I sure hope not," Hammond replied. "You go and get reacquainted, I'll call you back when it's time for the briefing. Okay? Now the company is on the front line today, in the left sector. You've just come from the east sector, haven't you?"

"I have sir," Frank replied.

"So, you'll know where I'm talking about. Sgt Todd will be able to fill you in on all the gossip from your area. Right then, see you shortly," the captain finished.

Frank smiled, as he headed through the saps. He relished the thought of being back with Toddy. As he walked through the front trench, he passed by men on watch, snipers trying their luck, apparently with a little success today it appeared, and plenty of men asleep in their funk holes, rifle clutched across their chests, ready to stand to if called to do so. All around in the distance was the sound of artillery explosions and the occasional sniper shot. After wading through the interminable mud, he found Toddy, about three hundred metres down the front line. He was facing the other way, talking to someone else. Frank walked quietly, up behind him and slapped him on the shoulder, balling in an authoritative voice, "Just what do you think you're doing, sergeant?"

Toddy immediately sprang to attention and spun around. He drew in his breath to reply, when he realised who it was. "Francis, it's you, ya bastard. Oh, I'm sorry, I mean it's you sir ... ya bastard." They both laughed and Toddy's previous conversant stood with mouth agape.

"It's alright private, we're old mates," Frank explained to him, as he and Toddy shook hands.

"Lieutenant Bailey, this is Private Dawson," Toddy introduced them.

"How do you do Dawson? So, they made you a sergeant, hey Toddy?" Frank asked.

"Yep, the army does recognise good people," replied Toddy.

"Not so sure about that," responded Frank. "I'm your new platoon CO."

"Oh, fantastic. Just like old times, eh?" Toddy replied.

"What happened to Lt Stewart?" Frank asked cautiously.

"Knocked last week," Toddy replied. "Taken off to the CCS but I don't think we will see him back. Reckon he's got a Blighty."

"Bugger. It's happening way too frequently, Alan. We will have to have a go at the boys, to take care. We're nearly there. Would hate for them to get knocked now," Frank explained, becoming serious now.

"Do you really think we are nearly there?" Toddy asked him almost hopefully pleading.

"Yep, sure do. We've got 'em by the balls now," Frank made the usual upward palm-grabbing motion with his right hand as he said this. "Just a few more days of pushes and consolidations and we'll be done."

Toddy gave a half laugh and added, "Well, I sure hope you're right, mate. I hate seeing all this carnage. Not sure just how much more of this I can put up with."

"Yep, I know what you mean," reassured Frank. "But hang in there. Not long now. Now we have our next push coming up in the next day or so, although I don't have any details, as yet. Can you get the platoon together in the one place, please? I want to talk to them all."

"Sure, give me ten. Will you be in the officers' dugout?" asked Toddy.

"Yep. Where is it?" Frank asked with a chuckle.

"Oh yeah. Three more doors down. I'm not sure who's in today though," Toddy advised Frank.

Frank opened the hessian drape across the doorway and walked into the officers' dugout. Three lieutenants were sitting drinking tea and looked around as he entered.

"Hello Cobbold," Frank said on entering.

"Well, I'll be buggered. Hello Francis. You come to replace Stewart, have you?" the lieutenant asked.

"Yeah, I have Walter. It's a real bugger that, Toddy tells me he probably won't return either," Frank replied.

"Yeah, he is a good man that one. Meet Lieutenants Blythe and Hardwick." Walter introduced them to Frank.

"Gentlemen!" Frank replied.

"Hello, Francis. Percy Blythe 2 Platoon."

"Francis! Jim Hardwick, 4 Platoon."

They each shook hands on introduction.

"Jim's been a part of the battalion probably longer than you have, but has had a pretty bad run of luck, what with wounds and sickness, I reckon he has spent half his time in this war on his back." He laughed heartily at this point. Jim just glared at him. "Do you remember him, Francis?"

"No, I'm sorry I don't," Frank answered.

"Did you ever get any of your memory back, mate?" Walter asked.

"Still have nothing before Polygon," Frank answered truthfully.

"Oh, you're the one who got taken by the Bosch over at Polygon Wood and got away are you?" enquired Percy.

Frank chuckled, "Yep! The very same."

"Damned good show that, Francis. Damned good," Percy added.

"Thanks. Seems like a million years ago, now though," Frank reflected on all the water under the bridge since then. It was only eight months ago, but it did feel like years. "Anyway, there is a new stunt planned, for a couple of days off. It will give us a chance to push these Hun bastards back where they belong."

Just then Sgt Todd knocked and entered. "The men are assembled, sir."

"Thanks, Toddy," and turning to the lieutenants, Frank continued, "So the captain will be calling us to explain fairly soon. See you again shortly," and then turning to Toddy, "Let's go Toddy."

As he entered the men's dugout, Toddy called the men to attention. Frank told them to relax. He stood there looking at the assembled men; some sitting on the floor, some on the bunks and some at the tables. He recognised quite a few of them and nodded to them in recognition, but there were a lot of new faces too. He studied them, as they studied him. They looked a bit ragtag for Frank's liking. He could see the ravages of the last three years in the faces of many of the men. They looked tired, but not half as tired as they were going to get in the remaining four months of action for them. He also knew that some of them would not be going home. He drew in his breath.

"Well gentlemen; for those of you who don't know me, I am Lieutenant Bailey. For those of you who do know me, I am still, Lieutenant Bailey." There were a few chuckles around the group. "Sergeant Todd and I have worked together before, as I have with a few of you." He paused at this point. "I have been assigned to this platoon now and it is my intention to get you all through to the end of this damned war. We have the Germans on the run now, whether you know it or not. In the next couple of days, you will see evidence of that. I don't as yet know exactly what we will be doing, but I can assure you, we will be shoving curry, fair up the Bosch's arse!"

At this point, the room erupted in laughter. Frank waited until the din had died down.

"Now, what I want from you guys is a full-on effort. But, we are getting close to the end now, so I do not want you taking unnecessary risks. Each of you has a mate or two in this platoon. I want each of you to watch each other's backs like a hawk," At this point, Frank could see many of the men turn to each other and give a nod of acknowledgement.

"We know these Hun have a habit of popping up behind us sometimes when we advance, so do not forget to watch your rear." Again, he paused, to collect his thoughts. "I know some of you are currently at rest phase, even though we are all on alert, but I will not accept anyone turning up for the advance in anything but full uniform, properly prepared kit, tin hat, fully cleaned and serviced weapon and a determination to give it to these Hun bastards."

He got cheers for that last remark. "We are coming into a new phase of this war. One where we are going to be much more mobile and not relying on digging into one location. We will be shortly commanded, by Major General Monash and he has a different idea on tactics to the British. You will need your wits about you. I want you working in at least pairs but preferably threes or even fours when we move forward. This way, you should be able to keep each other safe. Under my leadership, there will be none of this, as I call it, 'advancing in line of machine gun fodder'. One of the great things about our country is the reliance on looking out for your mates. Our country would not have survived if we did not have that creed. Now, more than ever is the time to ensure that continues. We here are a kind of brotherhood and together we can make it through." Turning to Toddy, Frank asked, "How many men do we have now sergeant?"

"Thirty nine sir," answered Toddy. "Including us," he added.

"Okay, thirty-seven, three sections; so we are about twelve each section. Not ideal is it, but we will make it work. Four threes or three fours per section. That will be up to each section to work out. When we get a chance, I want to take you all through some of our own training, to make sure this works for us. NCOs make sure you are spread. I would love to say that I will get all of you through this next four months, but we all know that is not really going to happen, but if you look out for each other, most of you will. The more you watch each other's backs, the more of you will make it through. Thank you all, and good luck."

Frank broke off here and went and caught up with those of the old crew who had made it this far. Of the eleven men there when he was a corporal, only seven of them remained. They talked for a few minutes before he bid them goodbye and walked back to the officers' dugout.

"Four months, Francis?" Toddy asked Frank after the meeting broke off. "Is that what you see? Four months?"

"Yeah, mate! November all over, red rover." Frank advised Toddy as he grasped his left arm. "That's all we need to survive I reckon."

The next day, all the lieutenants got the call to attend a briefing on the coming action. At the same time, the German artillery opened up a five-hour artillery barrage of HE and gas. Yet again, there were no casualties from this barrage. The intensity of this barrage indicated that the enemy was either planning an action or figured the Australians were planning an action. Brigadier Wisdom, CO of the 7th Brigade, briefed all officers of the Brigade. The Brigadier gave an overall description of the coming action, leaving the specifics to the battalion level.

"Gentlemen, tomorrow evening, we are going to attempt an action, just on dusk. We haven't attempted this since Pozieres, two years ago. I would think Fritz will not be expecting this at all. General Monash is concerned about the Germans assaulting the rail head at Amiens. We are going to attack around Morlancourt tomorrow evening. Our 7th Brigade will bear the brunt of the attack. 28th Battalion will be on the left, 25th in the centre, 27th on the right and some elements of the 51st will be protecting your right flank. The 26th Battalion will be in support and once the advance has commenced, they will move up to our present frontline. Tonight, you need to get all your men up to the front line, under the cover of darkness and to stay as quiet as possible throughout tomorrow, to avoid alerting the enemy to the buildup. Zero hour for the assault will be at 2145, with the artillery opening up on the German frontline, at 2100. At zero hour, you will advance under a creeping barrage, which will advance at the rate of one hundred yards every two minutes. Machine-gun sections have been issued with orders to set up, firstly to support the advance and secondly to mitigate any counterattack on the part of the Germans. Your orders have been handed to battalion and company commanders and you are to drive the Germans out of this sector and take as many prisoners as possible. Gentlemen, timing and surprise are everything in this operation. Fritz has overstretched his resources with his recent advances and we are going to take full advantage of that situation, here and now. Thank you, gentlemen."

The briefing broke up and everyone headed back to their own areas. News went out to all at platoon level to prepare for this attack and move forward during this evening. The rest of the day was devoted to preparing tactics and ensuring everyone was kitted out appropriately. Machine guns and mortars were to move forward during the night as well as the infantry. Back at battalion level, it was decided that C Company would take the left position, D would be in the centre and A on the right. B Company, having recently been decimated by the aerial bombardment, was to be placed in the support role of carriers. They would be responsible for bringing forward ammunition and other supplies, as well as assisting to remove wounded and any prisoners taken.

As night fell on the evening of the ninth, those members of the battalion not already on the front line moved forward and occupied whatever space they could find. Fortunately, this time of year was warmer in the evening and many of the men slept outside. The following day, the men tried to keep up the appearances of the frontline, the same as any other day. This worked for most of the time, but in the afternoon the Germans must have become suspicious that something was happening. They sent up an aircraft, to observe what was happening on the Australian frontline and shortly afterwards an artillery barrage commenced, but it only lasted ten minutes and produced few casualties despite the packed frontline.

Right on time, at 9 pm, the artillery opened up on the German frontline for a 30 minute barrage. During that time, frontline troops prepared to go over the top and drive the Germans away.

"Now remember what I said, fellas," Frank reminded them, "we only have 15 minutes of light, after zero hour. The temptation will be there to rush forward, but to do so will put you straight into our own artillery, so resist the urge to rush. Listen to my call, we will be there soon enough. Remember what I told you two days ago about looking after each other? Right, get ready. As soon as we get the call, we go." He glanced at his watch, then closed the cover.

"One minute to go." That was all he needed to say. Men climbed onto the first rungs of their ladders, waiting for the order. In the trench, they checked each other's pack behind and waited.

They could hear the whistles blowing down the line.

"Go! Give it to them!" Frank ordered, and the men immediately started pouring over the front wall of the trench. Those of them who were not near a ladder had dug footholds in the front wall and used those to go over the top. Others had used ammunition boxes, stacked to give them a start up the wall. These walls were about seven feet high. Some started to run, falling into old bad habits. Frank immediately called out to them, "Slow it down boys, slow it down. Remember the creeping barrage. Don't let the adrenaline drive you. Save it for the fight. You still have a thousand yards to go. When the machine guns start, use whatever cover you can find."

There was only sporadic machine gun fire, due to the barrage keeping the enemy's heads down. After about 20 minutes, the men came upon the remains of the defending Bosch. They jumped in and assailed them with every device they had at hand. They shot some, coshed others, bayonetted those that resisted and the new Mills grenade saw to some others. Many of the defenders turned on their heels and fled.

"Remember we need prisoners," Frank called out to his men. There were those that willingly laid down their arms and surrendered. They were mustered together and sent back with the members of B Coy, some with smiles on their faces and chattering agreeably in German. They were happy to be out of this war. The 27th Battalion had the toughest time, with the strongest resistance, but even they managed to achieve all of their objectives by 10 pm. A green flare was seen soaring high into the sky around then. This signalled that all objectives had been achieved. At that point, those machine guns and Lewis guns held in reserve and fallback positions, dashed forward to consolidate the forward positions and prepare for the inevitable counterattack. The objective they had taken was on the backslope of a spur, now a forward slope of the new front line, so for once, they now held a position of superiority. The counterattack was not long in coming, but due to the rapid consolidation, it was repulsed in quick fashion.

Frank checked around his men to see how they were. A quick count, found he had lost only two. One killed and one wounded. Two more than he had hoped for, all the same. As soon as he had established this, he went to confer with the other lieutenants from A Company. To his dismay, he found Cobbold and Blythe had both been killed in the attack. There was only Hardwick and himself left. In the immediate short term, Frank took the added responsibility for 1 Platoon and Ron Hardwick took 2 Platoon, on top of their own platoons. Further enquiries revealed D Company had lost Lt Goolee, and his old C Company had lost Bruce McDonald, "Skev" Skevington and Max Farquharson, all wounded quite severely. That left C Coy with only Captain Dunkley and the 'quiet one', Lt Folley. He also learned that his old platoon had unfortunately lost Henry Anderson, the young soldier Frank had comforted in the trenches when they first arrived in the Somme area. It turned out that this lad was only 16 years old too. He was apparently one of the many lads who had tried to escape from some aspect of their lives, back in Australia. The total casualties, however, only added up to fifty, which for an action of this kind was extremely light. It was just heavily laden with officers, evidence that they led from the front. Frank recalled Skev's words, "They'll have to move fast to get the old Skev." They did indeed get the 'bee in a bottle'.

B Company and Lt Edmonston came in for special mention for their activity during the battle, following the attack with all the essentials. They kept up to the advancing troops with ammunition, bombs (grenades), wire, hot cocoa and rum. B Company was down to around half strength, so it made for useful and essential work, without taxing an already devastated and demoralised company any further.

Throughout the following morning, it was noticeably quiet until just after noon, when the enemy artillery managed to range in on the new front line and gave it quite a pasting. In return, the British artillery retaliated with their own creeping barrage, in which elements of the 28th charged the German trenches. During this charge, Captain M G Hammond MM MC, again took the lead and led his men forward under the barrage, walking stick and revolver in hand. Most of this time he was walking backwards, exhorting his men to keep up and give it to the Hun. Late in the advance, he turned and rushed forward into one of the German trenches and held the Germans there at gunpoint with his revolver. He held about twenty of the enemy prisoner, until men of the battalion caught him up. While he was holding the men hostage, he took a bullet to the abdomen from a sniper and died of wounds three days later. He was later awarded a bar to his MC for this action. Many felt it should have been the VC and many still do.

On Hammond's initial evacuation, Lt Hardwick took over A Company, leaving Frank as the only lieutenant, until Lt Henry Smiley was transferred in. The upshot of the action was that the AIF took 175 prisoners, including 2 officers, 10 machine guns and

2 light trench mortars. Command were well pleased with the outcome.

Whilst this was really only a minor skirmish, Frank knew it was only a practice for the upcoming assault on Le Hamel, three weeks hence. All the same, for the rest of the push to be effective, all the men and equipment needed to be in ship-shape order, right here. The trenches were previously occupied by troops of the German 54th Division and elements of the 24th reserve division, but they were not suited to the requirements of the Australians. Frank, being the only A Company platoon officer remaining at that time, got busy.

"We need to improve these trenches. You can be assured Fritz will send over plenty of arty on us. He knows exactly where we are so we need to build protection, underground. I know you are tired," he paused, "we are all tired, but I'd rather be tired than dead."

He gave each platoon sergeant specific instructions on what was needed. Each of the four platoons was assigned different areas and they started expanding. On their second full day in the new trench, an incoming shell took out yet another officer. This time from D Company, Lt Wood sustained a serious head wound, as well as a broken leg and was evacuated to the 61st CCS and eventually, England.

At 4 am on June 15, the battalion was relieved and marched back to La Houssoye and the following day a further ten kilometres back to Cardonnette, about four kilometres northeast of Amiens. Here, it was figured, the men would be far away from any firing and should be able to have a good rest and recuperation. Whilst there were the inevitable training exercises as well, most of their time was spent on sports, particularly cricket and swimming.

In fact, the only enemy activity they witnessed in that ten-day period was one enemy aircraft, that flew over and shot down an observation balloon.

On the 27th, A Company occupied the forward position, as relief for the 34th Battalion, two kilometres west of Villers Bretonneux, at Bois-de-l'Abbe. Their time there was also fairly quiet, with only the occasional artillery incursion and only one minor injury. The event that Frank was waiting for was to commence on the 4th of July, however. This was a date that would demonstrate to the British command what could be done with a fully coordinated attack.

Maj General Monash had been tasked with the job of driving the Germans further east, out of an area known as Le Hamel. It was only a small village just northeast of Villers Bretonneux, but occupies a crucial area, south of the Somme River. Monash's plan involved a coordinated attack, using aircraft, artillery, tanks, machine guns and infantry, each working with the other and providing cover for each other. For example, using tanks going forward, with the infantry sheltering behind them to allow them to get close to the action before exposing themselves. This was a total departure from the previous method: advancing in line abreast, into enemy machine guns, unprotected. The use of the aircraft was not only in an offensive role but also as a means of dropping much-needed ammunition and supplies to forward troops as well. This battle was also the first time that US troops were commanded by a foreign leader. The date of US Independence Day was chosen deliberately by Monash, in deference to the first use of US troops in the battle. There were supposed to be six US companies, assisting in this battle, but the day before the attack, US General Pershing learnt of the plans and ordered the removal of US troops. He was not going to have US troops, commanded by anyone but Americans. The Australians had been in this war for almost four years at this time, and had only just now been afforded the luxury of being commanded by their own leadership. Up until now, they had been subjected to, in their view, inept British command despite constant requests from both the Australian Prime Minister and the Australian commanders in the field for their own command sector. The Americans had been in five minutes and were demanding their individual command. Such arrogance. Four companies did withdraw from the coming action, but two remained in defiance of orders, stating that they were not informed in time to withdraw. Their leadership at the face understood that by remaining in this action, their troops would gain invaluable experience. This reduction in numbers did have an effect on the planning, but General Monash insisted it went ahead anyway.

Monash told his commanders that if everybody did their job the battle should last ninety minutes. Many scoffed at his wild and ridiculous prediction, given that battles of this nature, had taken days previously and had not always worked anyway. The battle took ninety three minutes, and all objectives were taken in that time. Those Germans that did not run, were either captured or killed. The Australians lost 1062 men, with around 800 dead and the Americans lost 176 including around 20 killed. The Germans, however, lost 2000 killed and 1600 captured, out of a total strength of around 5600, a 64% loss.

The 28th battalion took no part in the battle, other than to supply carrying parties, taking up vital supplies, both during the fight and in the immediate aftermath. The 28th suffered no casualties that day. German counterattacks continued into the evening but were continually repulsed. Resupply was often a problem when an action like this moved forward but, yet again, using modern technology proved the winner. Aerial drops of equipment and supplies took place for forward troops until German fighter planes joined the affray. The men were not content to just sit and stay, however. That evening, they continued to press the desperately defending Germans. In fact, the Australian troops advanced further that evening and took an additional five hundred prisoners.

Back at 28th Battalion, A Company HQ the following day, Lts Hardwick (CO), Smiley and Bailey were talking about the day's events.

"Now we have them on the run," Hardwick said.

"That we do, Jim. They won't stop now. That is the beginning of the end for the Kaiser," Frank told them.

"How can you be so sure of that, Francis?" asked Harry Smiley.

"This is the beginning of a new type of war," Frank explained. "You mark my words. Gone are the days of static trench warfare. The Bosch will not adapt to the new system, yet for a while. They haven't even worked out what happened yet either."

"I'd like to believe you Francis, but I have difficulty with that, after all this time," Hardwick disconsolately replied.

"Nup. Definitely the beginning of the end. Le Hamel today, next is Morcourt and Albert, followed by Mont St Quentin and Peronne, then the Hindenburg Line, Sombre Canal and home. All over, red rover." Frank joyously described.

"You are very specific there, Francis. What do you know, that we don't?" Jim asked him suspiciously.

"I know what I know fellas," Frank replied. "And I know, it will be over by Christmas this time and I do mean, this Christmas." His tone dropped a little, before carrying on. "I also know that I won't see it."

"What the hell are you talking about, Francis? Are you some kind of psychic or something? Did you bring your Ouija board with ya?" Jim was incensed by Francis' last comment.

"Well, all I can say now is, just wait and see. Next month, we will be battling for Albert," Frank advised them.

"I guess that would be a logical next move," Harry joined in. "That area to the south of Albert is crucial to seeing Fritz back to his Fatherland, Jim."

"True enough," Jim replied. "But I still don't understand where you're coming from, Francis?"

"Don't worry about it, Jim," Frank said with a laugh. "I'm just having a lend of ya."

"You bastard," Jim sighed. "This prediction stuff is getting out of hand."

"Yes it is, fellas," Frank laughed again. "And the more people talk about it, the more it sets in concrete. Still, it will be interesting to see what happens from here though, won't it?"

"Yeah. I do hope you are right about having them on the run though," Jim added.

"Yep! I am," and Frank smiled, thumped Jim on the shoulder and started to walk out. "I'd better go and check on the fellas. Give them a bit more of the news. They'll like that." He walked out of the dugout smiling. He had had fun, teasing them with his "insight". His demise was sealed and he preferred not to dwell on it. There was work to be done in the meantime. Three months of work to do. In that time, he had to get as many of his men through to the end, three months and one day away.

He checked on all his boys, making sure they were all organized and comfortable. He filled them in on the news to date, and whilst most of them were aware of yesterday's events, there had been some exaggeration in some quarters. He put them straight and advised them that they would be in the thick of it for the next move, so they had better be ready for that.

On the morning of July 9, Brigadier Wisdom suggested a plan to the 28th to take the enemy trenches, directly in front of their present position. The South Australian 27th Battalion had executed a successful operation the previous day and Wisdom proposed that the 28th should do the same in their sector. A Company was chosen to carry out this action. Two officers and 40 ORs were selected in two parties of 1 officer and 20 men. Lt Cockburn MM was chosen to lead the party on the right, and Frank the party on the left. This raid was to take place, in broad daylight, at 3 pm.

At 2.30, the forty-two men crept out of their trench and crawled their way forward on their bellies, through the crop, which was growing in no man's land. This area had not suffered the same artillery destruction, that they were used to having to cross, and still contained a standing crop. Crawling slowly and carefully, using the crop for cover, they made it to within twenty metres of the enemy front line. The plan was for the party on the right to enter the trench at a predetermined point and rush the occupants to the right. 1 NCO and nine men from each party, were to act as moppers and to watch the backs of the attackers. The left party were to enter the trench at the same point and clear the trench to the left. Additionally, one officer and four ORs were to enter the trench on the far left flank and drive towards the others. Frank was assigned to the left flank party. Once it was evident all were in place, at exactly three in the afternoon, the signal was given to attack, with lots of noise. There was so much surprise in the German trench, that the majority just up and ran. Those that did not, were either eliminated or raised their hands and were captured. The left flank party had a little more resistance, but this was overcome shortly with bayonets and grenades. Being an officer, Frank did not carry a bayonet, to his relief, but a revolver and grenades for this job. Several of the retreating Germans came racing at Frank's party, but in a well-rehearsed move, they took up separate positions to separate the enemy fire and hurled grenades and poured rifle and pistol fire into the troops. In a matter of minutes, the action was over, with complete success. A call was put out to the previous front line and A and C companies moved forward to occupy the twelve hundred yards of captured trench. It was instantly reinforced, to prepare for the inevitable counterattack. This section of trench was captured in fifteen minutes by two officers and forty ORs. The counterattacks did eventuate but were halfhearted affairs and instantly repulsed.

Over the next few days, the men endured sporadic shelling, but for a change, the enemy scored a few direct hits. This led to the death of Sergeant Fred Cramb. On the 11th, Toddy came to Frank after the cessation of the artillery barrage.

"Hey, Francis, I think you need to come and have a look at this. Bring your field glasses," Toddy said. Providing no one else was around, Frank was happy for Toddy to be informal. That's how they were before.

"Sure Toddy. What's up?" Frank replied as he exited the bunker.

"Not sure if it's anything yet. There's some strange things happening out there." Toddy answered.

"Look over there," Toddy said indicating the direction. "Cart and a few men. What does it look like to you?"

Peering through the binoculars, Frank summarised what he saw. "Several horses and carts ... Maybe twenty men ... boxes. What are they doing?" Frank asked rhetorically, but slowly. "They are placing the boxes beside the road in our sector ... There's enough crap lying around there that you would not take a second look at them lying there. I have a fairly good idea what that is. Do not let anyone near them. I'll go and organise the engineers to check this out."

"Sure boss, do you recon it's bombs?" Toddy asked.

"I do, Toddy. I do." Frank replied and he took off for company command at the trot.

The engineers arrived an hour or so later and carefully examined the boxes.

"Yes, they are bombs. Actually, anti-tank by the size of them. Well spotted, we've found thirteen of them here," the engineer told Frank and Lt Hardwick. "We've not seen these tactics before, down here, so it is rather fortuitous to get these first. Quite crude really, but if they went off, they would be highly effective. We'll get the message out about this. I would think we are about to see a lot more of things like this as the Fritz retreat."

"Well, I think you can thank the eagle eye of my sergeant and the lookout for this one captain," Frank told the engineer captain.

"Ah, yes lieutenant, but if they are not trained to be this observant, what do you have? A lot more dead people. Thanks all the same and pass on my thanks, to the men concerned," answered the captain.

"I will be sure to do that sir," Frank turned and moved back to his men. He sought out Toddy and the lookout and passed on the thanks of the engineers.

To his men, he said, "So this is looking like a new tactic, to slow or stop an advancing enemy. These roadside bombs will become more common, as we drive them further back. Be careful what you touch, be careful what you move. Anything could be mined. And I do mean anything. They are getting desperate."

For the remainder of this fortnight, the 28th were on and off the front line, but not directly involved in any of the actions. There was a successful push to the east of Villers Bretonneux, but the 28th were held in support only, except for D Company, which provided carriers for the other battalions of the 7th Brigade. In one of the retaliatory artillery barrages, it was estimated that over a thousand gas shells were fired into their area, as well as the accompanying shrapnel. No casualties resulted from this action against the 28th.

Slowly, ever so slowly, the allied armies were moving forward, little by little and the Germans were definitely on the back foot. They were not beaten yet, as their artillery persisted in reminding them. However, it did seem like they were sending over less. Barrages were getting shorter and less frequent, with some days going by with no artillery action at all. The men figured their efforts were having some effect on Fritz's ability to wage war.

On the 19th, the men got a full relief, being sent well back to Blangy-Tronville for a rest again. Being camped on the banks of the Somme, much of their free time again was spent swimming, as it was still summer. They began to pick up a few more replacement officers, with Captain Cyril Pugh taking over the reins of A Company and Lt James Hopkins rejoining them from the hospital in England. Frank also noticed that Lt Max Farquharson from C Company had returned from hospital as well.

The rest of the month was allocated to training and re-training, but Command also realised that what the men needed most, was rest. The training schedule looked rigorous but was more prone to letting the men rest. Essential training was still undertaken. This included a rather interesting demonstration/practice on the 30th. The men were bussed an hour and a half west, to Vaux, to a tank demonstration. The demonstration was performed by the demonstration unit of the 5th Division and was used to show the best methods to utilise a tank for cover during an advance. Some work had gone into this since Le Hamel, as although it had been a successful action, the use of the tanks had been a little haphazard. The powers that be got together and came up with a refined procedure, to best utilise the cover. The men were only there to observe, but they were so keen to give it a go, that all four companies were given the opportunity to practice the procedure.

"There you go, Jim," Frank said, "They are preparing us for the coming attacks on Morcourt, Albert and Mont St Quentin. What did I tell you?" He was really living dangerously here. He knew he would get a bite from Jim Hardwick on this, as it was, 'one of his predictions'.

"Yes, I see what you mean, Francis," Jim answered. Jim's reply took Francis completely by surprise.

"Damn," he thought. "He's not biting."

"Bet you thought you would get a bite on that, didn't you Francis?" Jim chuckled. "Thing is, even if you were just getting a rise out of me last time, I've had a good look at the situation, and whilst you may have been joking, I think you may be right. Especially after these couple of minor actions of this month. Morcourt will be next for sure. No point taking what we have and then stopping there. Morcourt area is a dead certainty, as far as I am concerned."

"Yeah. That will then ensure the right flank is secure before trying to take Albert. What do you reckon?" Frank replied more seriously this time.

"Yep. You should have been a tactician you know, Francis," laughed Jim.

"Nar, I just wish they had put Monash in there sooner," replied Frank.

"Not so sure, Frank. I think it's a case of right man, right time." Jim mused.

"You could well be right there, mate," Frank replied, "And by the look of this today, I'd say we're about to put this lot into practice," and he left it at that.

August came round with the news; they were going back to the front. This time to the eastern edge of Villers Bretonneux, to relieve elements of the 22nd and 23rd Battalions.

"Max! What the hell are you doing here?" Frank called, as Max Farquharson walked into their new dugout.

"Well, ol' Francis, I'm your new 4 Platoon commander," Max replied laughing. "How are you, old mate? Still predicting?"

"I heard you were back after your injury, but I didn't expect you to end up here. I think you know everyone here, don't you?" Frank asked him, ignoring the second part of the question.

"G'day fellas. Not everyone." Turning to Ridley. "G'day, I'm Evelyn Farquharson, but everyone calls me Max."

"G'day Max, I'm Harold Ridley."

"Harold. Pleased to meet you," replied Max.

"The irony Max, is that Harold here has been part of this unit for longer than any of us. Started at Gallipoli in fifteen," Frank informed him.

"Holy shit! Really? How come I don't know you? I was there too." Max was puzzled.

"Oh well, I started with the 11th, but since I transferred to the 28th, I've spent a fair bit of time in the hospitals around, what with injuries and illnesses," Harold explained. "Then I spent a fair bit of this year in England at Cadet school. I've only been a 2nd since June, and I was in D Company originally, so not really surprising."

"Well, well done, son. Well done indeed, for sticking at it," Max shook his hand. "Hey, did you hear Colonel Currie has been recalled from leave?"

"Yeah. Guess that's a clue as to the next couple of day's work," Hopkins remarked.

"Yep! Sounds like a big one this time," Max said.

Max was correct in his assumption, that this was a big one. The German "Spring Offensive" had been halted and turned, and as was expected had overstretched their supply lines. The recent smaller actions, in retaliation, had shown that Fritz was vulnerable, and indeed was stoppable. This coming action would see the commencement of what would become known as the One Hundred Day Offensive, which would see the end of this war.

The following day, A and C Companies were withdrawn from the front line, back to L'Abbe wood assembly area. This was able to be done in daylight this time, as the weather had turned rather wet and miserable, reducing visibility to less than a kilometre. Also, due to the visibility, it became easier to move men and equipment up to the assembly points. That evening Lt Col Currie called all the Officers and NCOs to a meeting to discuss the following days' action.

Frank walked into the briefing tent with Max and Harold. As soon as they entered, Frank could feel the excitement in the air. The normal banter was replaced by a heightened sense of expectation. "We've got these bastards now," was how he described the feeling in the room. It was rare to have a briefing of this size, including the NCOs, but Frank recognised the enormity of the occasion, and he felt the inclusion of the NCOs was critical. He felt they should always be included. After all, it was they who were about to execute the plans. Lt Col Currie entered the tent and someone called "Atten...tion!" Everyone sprang to their feet.

"As you were gentlemen," The colonel called, and they all sat down. Once the noise died down, the colonel continued. "The day after tomorrow, we intend to start to drive the enemy back to his damned fatherland. We have had a couple of practices now, putting into play some new tactics. They have been refined and now we are ready. At Zero hour minus thirty, you will hear, and probably see, many British bombers travelling eastward at reasonably low altitude, the height of which will depend on the weather. These will be British Handley Page bombers. They have been chosen for two reasons. Firstly, and the obvious one, is that they will be able to bomb rear areas before our advance, but more importantly, the sound of their mighty engines is not too dissimilar to that of our tanks. Whilst they are flying around, our tanks will move up, hopefully undetected, their sound being masked by the aeroplanes, and when they pass by our positions we will slip in behind them, as per the training you did last week. Our objective is three thousand five hundred yards to the east, so it will be a long march. You will be partnered in this area by the 3rd Divvy. On your left will be one division of British troops and on your right will be three divisions of Canadians, whilst on their right will be a French division. On the north side of the river will be a combined division of British and US troops. Once our objectives have been reached, we will dig in and will be leapfrogged by the 5th Divvy, who will continue to drive the Bosch east. The aim of this action is to completely clear the area to the south of Albert, of Bosch."

At this point, Frank glanced across at Jim Hopkins, sitting two up from him. He was quietly shaking his head and must have realised Frank was looking at him, as he turned and looked back at Frank, smiling and still shaking his head. Exactly what Frank had suggested would happen. Frank thought it was a pity he could not tell Jim how he knew all this. Even if he did, he knew Jim would not believe him anyway.

The Colonel continued, "We expect to take many prisoners, so have your men ready to escort them back. Our Tunneller boys will be ready to follow you to assess any dugouts found for their suitability for our use, so if you find anything please mark it with some kind of flag. They will be looking for it. Gentlemen, this is the beginning of the end for the Bosch. This will be an Australian commanded operation, south of the Somme. Lt General Monash is the CO of this operation. General Rawlinson will take care of the north sector. Some of you were privileged to be part of both of Monash's previous forays, at Le Hamel and nearby. They were very small operations, compared to this. Seven divisions will step off together on Thursday. This is the biggest operation we have been involved with. Let us show these Germans and the Brits how good we are." This last comment brought a cheer from the assembled men.

"Company commanders, your orders are here, on my right. Please collect these before you leave and good luck to you all. Thank you."

"Atten...tion" was once again called and the men all sprang to their feet again. Colonel Currie departed, and the men broke up and commanders collected their orders. Each of the platoon officers gathered around their COs.

"Okay boys," started Jim. "28th will be centre with 26th on our right and 27th on our left 25th support. Jump-off will be at P 2 b 2 5. Jump-off time is 0425 on August 8th. White tape by 0330. Ah, objective, ridge at P 11b to P 11c, 3500 yards, near Record Wood. Dig in. 5th div take over. Prisoners to dugout P 1 c 5 2. Planes ... Tanks ... Infantry ... carriers ... resupply. Right, let's head back and sit down and work all this out."

They all went back to the A Company HQ, sat down with the maps and plotted their points of interest and direction of progress. Each of them was given their tasks. It would be A, B, C and D in that order from the left. The sergeants and corporals were to go out tomorrow afternoon and survey the route, to the jump-off point. No good everyone following the same route to the jump-off. The Intelligence officer was responsible for placing the jump-off white tape across their path. It was literally a length of white tape, stretched across their start line. That would be done as soon as night fell tomorrow night.

The following day, as usual, was spent ensuring everyone was kitted and ammunitioned appropriately. The NCOs surveyed the route to the jump-off, as arranged. Frank spent much of his time travelling back and forward to the men of his platoon and a few more, to make sure they knew what they were doing. He also made sure they knew to stay as safe as possible, telling all of them this was the beginning of the end. He told them they would all be going home soon, so keep your head down. He encouraged them to hit the sack early, to be good and rested for the inevitable long day, tomorrow. At no time did he say, 'if' we are successful. That was a foregone conclusion, only they did not know it.

As Frank lay on his bunk that night, he pondered his situation. *"So, if the outcome of this battle has already been decided, because it has already happened, how much of our life; that is, the life I had in the year 2000, had already been predetermined, because it had already happened somewhere before?"* he thought. *"That makes for an interesting philosophical discussion if only you could get people to believe that this travelling through time really is possible. Hmmm. I suppose I am not dreaming."* He reached down and pinched himself. "Nope, not dreaming." He laughed, considering all the different pains he had experienced in the last ten months; "The door of my cell; that piece of shrapnel that knocked my helmet off; the multiple dives into trenches; the experience of blood on my face from my victims. "Nope! This is not a dream." He rolled over, but sleep would not come. He was a part of history now, the end of which was nearly two months away. He thought back to his time with Lynne and the kids. People used to say, ' Live every day as if it were going to be your last.' He had often wondered what that would be like, knowing that on a particular day, it would be your last. "Guess I'm beginning to know what that feels like," he thought. Eventually, he drifted off to sleep.

Two o'clock the following morning came around way too quickly. He rose and prepared himself. He decided today he would not wear his officer's uniform. That was too much of a giveaway. It made him more of a target. He donned the same tunic that the troops wore, but still with his officer rank on the shoulder. On arrival at the initial muster point, Toddy was already checking platoon members off. "All present, sir," is all he had to say. The men were busy checking each other's packs, to make sure nothing would clank, rattle or fall out.

"Thanks, Toddy," Frank replied. "Ready, are we?"

Toddy nodded silently, as did the rest of the platoon.

"Okay then NCOs, lead the way," and Frank pointed toward the front.

Toddy and the corporals led the way, with Frank bringing up the rear. When they reached the secondary assembly point, Toddy stopped and waited for the men to catch up. As soon as Frank arrived, he squatted down and the men did the same. In a whispered voice he informed them that the white tape was one hundred yards further on.

"No 1 Section, ten yards to the left of centre, corporal, you take the flank. Remember your spacings. Right go!" Frank ordered. 1 Section moved out, slowly crawling forward on their belies.

"No 2 Section, you're next, corporal, you on the left of your lot. Go!" Frank waited for them to depart and get a good distance out before he turned to Toddy, and said, "I want you on the right flank of No 3 Section. I'll go between 2 and 3. Ready, let's go." They commenced their crawl forward. One hundred yards is not that far, but when you are crawling on your belly, loaded up with a full pack, carrying a rifle and ammunition and trying to do it silently so as not to alert the enemy who will shoot you, it takes ages. Some managed it in fifteen minutes, whilst those behind, who had slower ones in front of them, took thirty minutes. By 3.15 am, all troops were in position ready and waiting. They still had over an hour to wait, or so they thought, for not long after getting settled on the tape, the enemy commenced an artillery barrage. Not due to them being aware of the impending attack, but simply in retaliation for an earlier British feint. The only casualty from the thirty-minute barrage was the signal officer, Lt Kell, who was severely wounded and died of his wounds the following day. He was replaced, immediately it became known he had fallen.

At 4 am, an unseasonal morning fog descended on the waiting troops. Whilst this would make for good cover for the attacking troops, it made life exceedingly difficult for the newly formed RAF. Flying in fog was not a desirable activity, in these early aircraft. The British command made the decision not to force pilots to fly in it but to make it optional. As this was likely to reduce the masking effect of the twin-engine bombers, two of the pilots agreed to continue with the plan.

At 4.20, the artillery opened up with their creeping barrage and the tanks could be heard approaching the jump-off line. As they passed, the men jumped up and followed them as instructed. Within five minutes of jumping off, the first of the prisoners was marched back to Allied lines. They were from the 43rd Infantry Regiment and they were more than a little surprised when Australians started jumping into their trenches, en masse. They just threw their arms in the air and surrendered without a fight. The men continued further, but by now the news of an advance had broken, so more Bosch were ready for a fight. The buddy system Frank had tried to instil in his men worked well, for as one was attacking an enemy, his back was being watched by his mate. The adrenaline of the fight can induce a kind of tunnel vision, which can mean you can be taken from behind in the action of taking out an enemy combatant.

In one trench the men entered, a fight to the death was already in progress between one of the men and a German infantryman. No one was behind him and another German came around the corner and was about to attack. Frank came over the top in the nick of time and shot him without even thinking. His compatriot was shocked by the shot behind him and stopped to look, just as his opposition regained footing and charged. Frank instinctively pulled the trigger again and the German fell. "Where's your partner, Fred?" Frank immediately asked.

"Knocked sir," was all he got in reply.

"Right together son, let's get 'em," Frank responded, as another Fritz, with bayonet attached, rounded the corner. His eyes were wide open and his gasping breathing could plainly be heard. It sounded to Frank, like a fire-breathing dragon on the attack. Crack! Down he went. "Eyes and ears open, lad. Follow that trench." Frank was just as surprised to see this German soldier crumple and fall, right at his feet, even though it was he who had shot him. It had clearly been an instinctive move. He had no time to think about what he was doing.

The two of them continued down this communication trench, now being joined by four more from their platoon. This trench zig-zagged its way eastward and terminated in what appeared to be a reserve trench. The air came alive with bullets as they tried to enter the reserve trench. They pulled back quickly and

Frank drew a grenade and removed the pin. "Bombs boys." As he waited three others did the same. Frank indicated two to throw left and he and one other to the right. Frank lobbed his grenade across the corner to land about twenty feet up and the others did likewise. Following four almost simultaneous explosions, the men jumped into the intersection of the trenches watching left and right. There were moans and groans from both directions. "Aufgeben! Hande Hoch!" Frank yelled. (Surrender! Hands up).

"Nicht Shiessen! Nicht Schiessen!" (Don't shoot) came the reply, and several bloodied and tattered Germans came through the smoke and dust toward Frank, with their hands in the air. As soon as the men on the other side heard the troops surrendering, there were calls of "Nicht Schiessen" from that side too.

"Komm," Frank called to them and they moved cautiously toward the party.

"Check them over for weapons, and Fred can you take them back to muster please?" Frank ordered.

"Sure can, sir," Fred responded with a smile on his face. That would keep him out of the firing line, at least for a little while.

"As soon as you can offload them, buddy up again and rejoin us. But do not try and come back on your own. Okay?" Frank told him.

"Thank you, sir. I will do that," replied Fred.

Fred departed with his little cache of seven prisoners. They seemed happily cooperative, with their hands on their helmets, once again, like they too, were glad to be out of it now.

"Okay lads, just hang on a minute," Frank told them. He needed to consult his compass to work out which way to proceed. The fog made it difficult to see anything, even though the day was now half-light. "Okay, we proceed to the right. Oh, hello Rob. Didn't realise it was you." Rob Galloway was in his original section when he was a corporal. "Do you want to lead us ahead? Take it carefully though."

"Sir," and Rob headed off down the trench, carefully. In the next fifty metres, they encountered no enemy. Rob stopped at another trench junction and waited for Frank. "Left or straight ahead sir?"

"We'll go left," and as Frank said it, a figure loomed out of the fog in front. All rifles came to bear on the figure. It was Toddy, with a whole section behind him.

Frank laughed, "Ya nearly got shot, ya dopey bugger."

"Not if I didn't shoot you first," came the reply. "How's it going with you lot?" Toddy asked.

"We've knocked a few, captured about ten and I think we may have lost one. You?" Frank asked.

"About the same, but we haven't lost anyone yet," Toddy replied.

"Okay if we join up, we should be able to move through here and out of the trenches soon, I would think," Frank said. "The trench map has this as a communication sap ending about one hundred yards further east. Rob, you ready and willing?"

"You bet!" Rob replied and off he went.

They continued for about a hundred and fifty yards and the sap did end. They were back above ground now, but still in fog. Frank knew the bearing he had been on until now and where they were. He recalculated the new bearing to around 135°. They were about two-thirds of the way to their objective, so set off at pace. At 6.55 am, they arrived at their objective and commenced to dig in. They had quite a ridge to shelter behind, so it was not difficult to do. The rest of the battalion was with them within fifteen minutes. They all prepared for the expected counterattack.

As they were preparing, Frank was made aware that two of the casualties were Max Farquharson, again, with a gunshot wound to the neck, and Jim Hopkins again, with a serious GSW to the leg and elbow. Hopkins would not return to the fighting and would be RTA in December. Frank then realised he was now the most senior officer in the company, making him now the company CO, at least temporarily.

An hour later, the 5th Division passed through their position to further the attack. The whole attack had been such a surprise to the Germans, that a group of divisional staff officers, were taken prisoner as they sat at breakfast. Imagine the looks on their faces as they sat waiting for their eggs, and in walked a bunch of Australians armed to the teeth. A troop train was also captured as it arrived at Harbonnieres, south of their position, complete with five officers and a full complement of infantry. By 7 am, the fog lifted and the beautiful sunshine allowed the attacking troops to drive further and further east. By day's end, a hole, twenty four km wide, had been blown in the German defences. General Eric Ludendorf of the German command later described this day as "Ein schwarzer Tag fur die Bundeswehr", "A black day for the German army". Not just for the ground lost, but for the loss of morale of the German troops. It was clear that many were surrendering without a fight. These soldiers had had enough. They were done.

By 8 am, the 28th was relieved and the men returned to the safety of their bivvies, where a hot meal awaited them. That day, they managed to capture three thousand five hundred yards of ground, many hundreds of POWs, countless machine guns and three field artillery pieces, all of the 77 mm type; all for the loss of 1 officer and 1 OR killed, and 4 officers and 16 ORs wounded. An incredibly light casualty list.

The British on the north side of the river did not have such an easy time of it unfortunately. They had much more difficult ground to cross and only one squadron of tanks in assistance. The enemy were well and truly dug in, around the area of Chipilly, occupying a tight bend in the river, so there was really only one way in. From that position they were able to keep up withering fire on both the British troops, attacking them and the Australian troops across the river, near Le Hamel. By the late afternoon, the British were exhausted and withdrew. The US 33rd Division then stepped forward and attacked. They were not going to be defeated by these Bosch and pushed home the attack, despite the hail of shells and machine gun fire pouring down on them. By that evening, the Doughboys (nickname for US infantry from the Mexican-American war, 1846) had taken the majority of the Chipilly spur. The following morning, they pressed home their advantage and took the remainder of that spur. By the same evening, they had completely routed the German occupation, taking 700 POWs, over 100 machine guns, 1 aircraft and 30 artillery pieces. This was just the tonic the Americans needed. Finally, a success, and an important one at that, was the feeling in the American camp. Until now, they had experienced little success, but this, this was marvellous.

On return to their base, Frank gathered the whole of A Company together and spoke to them all.

"What you have achieved today is nothing short of incredible and I for one, am incredibly proud of you. This, however, is not the end; but it is the beginning of the end. Today we showed the world that the Australian digger is not to be trifled with. We are not just those 'bloody colonials'. We are Australian soldiers and if you want to trifle with us, then let it be at your peril." There were murmurs of agreement from amongst the group.

"We are not finished here yet. There is still a way to go. We have yet to take Albert, Mont St Quentin, Peronne and St Quentin town. When we have done that, we will be done." A murmur of approval ran through the men. Today we lost three good men; Lt Hopkins and Lt Farquharson were both wounded and Private Tom Walker was killed. We will grieve their loss, but this is an incredibly light casualty list for such a huge operation. You were a part of a seven-division attack. That's around seventy thousand men. Who knows how far forward we will be by nightfall? You have been a part of something to be proud of. Something to tell your grandkids about." Frank paused at this point, realising the irony of the point he just made. He was thinking of his father and his son.

He continued with a lowered voice, "When this is all over, they are going to tell you to go home and forget about all this. Yes, that's right. Forget about having been part of the best army in the world. Not bloody likely!" Everyone laughed at this. "I am going to tell you something different. Do tell your grandkids and your kids about this. Maybe not straight away, it will probably be too raw for you for some time. But, when the time is right, and the opportunity arises, do tell them.

They need to know, just how much you gave, to ensure that the world is a safer place to live in. Tell them about the mates you lost; the ones that paid the supreme sacrifice. Tell them of the things you did." At this point he paused. "Hmm, well maybe not ALL the things you did." Again, the group erupted with laughter. Frank could see men pointing the finger at their mates and some of them looking decidedly sheepish. "Men of A Company, 28th Battalion, I salute you," and Frank saluted them. To a man, they sprang to their feet and returned the salute. They then broke off and made for the hot food. They were left to rest for the rest of the day.

Chapter 12
The Last Advance

It may be he shall take my hand
And lead me into his dark land
And close my eyes and quench my breath—
It may be I shall pass him still.
I have a rendezvous with Death
On some scarred slope of battered hill,
When Spring comes round again this year
And the first meadow-flowers appear.

Alan Seeger 1917

The following day was thrown into confusion, when mid-morning, a communication came through for the battalion to 'stand to' and be prepared to move at one hour's notice. Hurried preparations were made to re-supply all the men. Bedlam ensued, given the time normally allowed to carry out the resupply. It had been decided by Command that due to the overwhelming success of the previous day's operation, to capitalise on the presumed confusion within the German ranks. A few minutes before midday the order came through to move.

Frank called the only other officer and all the NCOs together, "We have a follow-up to carry out to yesterday's action.

I realise now you were all told you were coming back to rest, but Command has realised Fritz is in complete disarray and is going to make good use of that. We are to be moved down to a muster point, just west of Bayonvillers and will move forward to a position north of Harbonnieres. At least we will be in reserve for this action, with our sister battalions doing the deed today. With a bit of luck, that's all we will have to do eh? Get the boys loaded and we will be off."

He was met with a chorus of "Yes sir!" but during the loading, the murmurs told a different story. They were tired. They were worn out. They needed rest to rebuild their strength.

They were bussed down to their muster point and then marched across country, to Harbonnieres. The men took up position, on the left of the defensive line, just to the west of Framerville. The action to take both Framerville and Vauvillers kicked off at 4.30 pm and was once again a complete success and was over by 5.30. Their sister battalions had captured a further one hundred and eighty five prisoners, many machine guns, copious quantities of ammunition and several field guns. Once again, the casualties were exceptionally light, but B Company lost their CO, Captain G S McTaggart DCM, who was wounded severely in the attack and later died of his wounds at the CCS. (Casualty Clearing Station) The men of A Company set themselves up here for the night and the following day, which they were advised would be for rest. The men were not convinced.

At 4 pm that following afternoon, orders were received, once again, for an attack the following morning. They were to continue to push Fritz further and further east. He was completely unsettled now and they needed to take full advantage of his confusion and weakness. This action would be the next stage in pushing them back across the Somme, and clear the way, south of Peronne.

The men were on their line by two the next morning. Currently, they were one kilometre east of Framerville, awaiting the signal to advance. This time, the 5th Brigade were on the left. The 7th Brigade on the right had the 28th Battalion left of the 26th battalion and the 25th and 27th in reserve. At 4 am, the artillery opened fire on the German front line, with all calibres. The enemy replied in like fashion, including a considerable quantity of gas shells, but without any effect. At 4.15, the advance began across a two km wide front.

"Right A Company, let's go. Remember to stay under the creeping barrage," Frank called out to his men.

They had not advanced particularly far, when the air sprang to life with a hail of metal. Tracers and lead, coming from everywhere.

"Stay low, advance as you can," Frank yelled out. "Watch your backs when we get there."

Quite soon it became extremely difficult to advance at anything but a crawl; to stand would have meant instant death by a thousand bullets.

"Bugger me!" yelled Toddy. "They must have every machine gun in the country here."

"Yeah! We can't make much progress at this rate. How far to the nearest MG do you reckon Toddy?" Frank asked.

"About fifty yards I reckon, in that direction," he replied, pointing slightly left of straight ahead.

"Yeah, that's what I thought," Frank said.

"Choose three men to meet me here. Make sure they have grenades. We need to make a path." Frank ordered.

Toddy crawled back a few feet and got the first three he could find.

"Toddy, you look after the mob. We are going to neutralise that bastard," Frank turned to his three 'volunteers'. "Right lads, what we will do here is this. We are still below his line of fire and sight, provided we stay low enough. It's still dark enough for us to crawl closer, but remember he has the dawn behind him, so he sees us better than we see him. You two, move to the left side of his bunker, you, son, go up the centre and I'll go to the right."

He finished explaining to the three of them and they commenced their crawl forward, keeping pace with each other. As they inched painfully slowly forward they fanned out over about a ten yard wide line and crawled to within seven yards of the bunker. He signaled to the other three and they pulled the pins on their grenades. Frank waited until the sweep of the machine gun was away from him, then he jumped up and fired two shots from his revolver into the pit. He saw one of the men fall backwards and as the MG swung his direction, with all eyes following, Frank dropped to the ground and the other three men lobbed their grenades into the pit. This was followed by three explosions. All four of the assailants jumped up and rushed forward, rifles at the ready, but there was no need to mop anything up. All the Germans lay dead in their bunker. This was an outpost bunker MG, so there was no trench attached for reinforcements to come from. Frank called back to Toddy, and the men again started their advance, still at a crawl.

As soon as they were satisfied the MG pit was cleared, fire started in on them from the right side, again about fifty yards away. A quick check with his three men and they commenced the same tactic on that MG, this time from the side and rear. It was equally effective and this opened up a wide path for A Company to advance through. Once they were through the machine gun belt, progress was easier. Similar antics were taking place all the way down and up the line, resulting in the elimination of all the outpost MG installations. Lieutenants Galey (D Coy) and Loveday (A Coy), were both killed neutralising MG posts and Lieutenants Maskiel (B Coy) and Stokes (B Coy) were wounded.

By 4.45 am it was all over, with all objectives taken, along with 2 Officers and 67 ORs taken prisoner and 16 machine guns. It came at a cost though. Over the last 2 days the battalion lost 2 officers killed and 3 wounded, and 7 ORs killed and 68 wounded. The men were mightily relieved when they were told they were being sent back to the reserve lines, one and a half kilometres behind Framerville. Not that they trusted the brass about this revelation yet, but they gladly marched the three kilometres back to this line. The rest of the day was spent resting, finally.

The actual fighting strength of the battalion was now down to just 449 men, less than half full strength. In the afternoon Frank was pleased to welcome Lieutenant Ken McIntyre as CO of A Company. Having to endure the new direction of his life was one trial, but having to command this company too made for a heavy load. He was glad to be rid of that responsibility.

For that week the men were kept in reserve but faced no action. With all this added action the men were completely exhausted. They had been a part of so much action, with such long distances to cover, back and forward and they needed a rest. What they really wanted, was to go home. But whilst Frank had a fair idea when that would happen, the men did not. The week was spent on repairs and re-equipping, whilst dodging the occasional artillery barrage, which seemed to be somewhat indiscriminate, sometimes forward lines, sometimes rear areas. It was felt they were searching for the artillery and reserve areas. At no time did they hit either. One aspect that was noticed about the artillery was that it was all heavy guns. No light guns, anymore. They must have been drawn backward to protect their rear. Yet another sign of the Bosche retreat. There was also the occasional reconnaissance flight over the top too, but they were certainly becoming less frequent. All signs pointed to an enemy that was running out of men and equipment.

During the night of August 17, the battalion was bussed all the way back to Busy-la-dour, near Amiens. Here, there would be no chance of artillery barrages. Here, the men were in billets as well, so were comfortable and much more contented. Here, they got rejuvenating hot baths, hot food, fresh uniforms and played Cricket. They still had some training to do as well, but the emphasis of this relief was rest. The battalion canteen was set up and the YMCA was set up as well. Concert parties were on the agenda too, which drew the men right in. It had been a long time since they had had the opportunity for a hearty laugh.

On the 20th, Frank, Harold and the new CO Ken McIntyre were sitting chatting, when in walked a familiar face. "Hello, 'ello, 'ello. What's all this then?"

"Well bugger me dead, if it isn't the invincible Max bloody Farquharson. Haven't they killed you yet?" Frank said as he rose and warmly shook Max's hand. "Welcome back old fella."

"Thanks, Frank. G'day ... Harold isn't it?" asked Max. Harold had not been there long enough to get his name set in Max's mind before departing again.

"It is, Max. Welcome back," replied Harold.

"I take it you're Lieutenant McIntyre. How do you do sir?" Max greeted Ken.

"Ken, please Max. Welcome back. You've had a pretty rough time I believe," the CO commented.

"Oh, I wasn't too bad this time Ken. Just a scratch," Max answered. They all laughed.

"So, what's the tally now, Max?" asked Frank.

"That makes four, three GSWs and a bomb," Max explained tapping the four wound stripes on his lower arm. "That bomb nearly did for me. Got that in Gallipoli. They sent me home after that and I had a year off in the middle. The three GSWs were right thigh here first," he indicated the place. "Then the bomb, the 2nd GSW was with C Company, just here," indicating his arm, "and the third, here in the neck. I'd only been back two bloody days when that one hit me. I'm like a lead magnet."

"Moral of the story is, when going into battle, stay away from Max," Frank added and laughed.

"It's alright for you buddy, but there won't be much left of me by the time this lot is over," Max complained.

They all laughed.

"So, is anything in the pipeline yet?" Max cautiously asked.

"Nothing yet, Max. Time to settle back in," Ken answered.

"That's good. I might actually get to spend some time in a unit other than a hospital, before being sent away again," he scoffed.

Max ended up with a week to settle back in and this time to get to know his sergeant and men.

It was not until August 27th, that the next operation was announced for them. They were to take over from the 20th Battalion, twenty kilometres away, back in the area they left two weeks previously.

That evening, the battalion loaded onto busses and travelled the bulk of the distance, being dropped off at a position five kilometres north of Harbonnieres and two kilometres south of the Somme River. They set up there in the open for the night, after arriving at 11 pm. The following day, they marched across the country to the Marley Woods, north of Chuignolles, on the edge of the Somme, a distance of a little over four kilometres. Here, they took over the position from the 20th and set up camp again, awaiting orders for the following day.

Frank watched the men of the 20th moving off the line. It was disheartening to see their disposition. They looked all in. There were many injured troops that had refused to leave the front line until relieved. It was obvious to all that they had had a tough time here. There were injuries of all types, from head and torso wounds to limb wounds by either bullet or shrapnel. Some were weeping and seeping blood. Others were more bandages than uniform. Some were being supported by their mates. Yet others had that faraway look in their eyes; the thousand-yard stare, of 'shell shock'. It was like they had no idea anyone else was there, just staring and walking. How they managed to see where to put their feet, Frank could not understand. They reminded him of that far away time he spent in the hospital at Etaples.

At 4.30 am the following morning, the men marched forward six kilometres, to the jumping-off line. They waited here, between the villages of Dompierre and Herbecourt, for the zero hour of 7.30 am. When the signal was given the men jumped up and advanced eastward toward the Somme. Their aim was to reach this section of the river where it turned right and ran south–north and drive the Germans out of that area. Enroute, they had to pass through and take the village of Flaucourt. To their surprise, they encountered no resistance there. The Germans had left, so they kept moving forward. Approaching Biaches however, was a different story. Here they met fierce resistance, as the Hun was backed up against the river and controlled the high ground to the right. It was with pure dogged determination to not lose the ascendancy, that the battalion kept nagging away at the enemy here, and eventually demolished the resistance. Extensive hand to hand fighting ensued and yet again, the system of buddies saw the men successfully through this episode. The Germans had disintegrated into a large group of individual fighters, with no defensive structure. It was like they had no upper level structure to guide them anymore. Once they had taken Biaches, it was a simple matter to turn right and continue the few hundred yards south to La Chapelette. All objectives were achieved by 9.45 am, with exceptionally light casualties. By the time they had achieved their objectives, they had captured 1 officer, 23 ORs and 16 machine guns. The fact that they captured only the one officer, seemed to the men to explain why the defence was so haphazard. To them, the officers had mostly left them to it. With this action completed, the men dug in once again. That evening, the 28th was relieved and moved back to their jump-off position from that morning. They enjoyed their rest, whilst also realising, that they were not done with yet.

Now, Peronne and Mont Saint Quentin were just on the other side of the river to their north. The town of Peronne was nestled at the base of Mont St Quentin, immediately north of the bend in the River Somme and the town of La Chapelette, that they had just liberated. They were now just two kilometres from the centre of Peronne. This would obviously be the next target. This would be a much more difficult and dangerous task. They had a river to cross first, and the Mount, one and a half kilometres north of the town of Peronne, had significant high ground, from which to pour withering fire down on any assaulting troops. Several attempts had been made to capture this feature in previous years by divisional sized assaults, (around 10 000 men) but had been unsuccessful. This time, it was to be attempted by a half strength brigade sized force (about 2000 men). This hill, was one hundred metres higher than all the surrounding area. Not particularly high in normal terms, but with its situation on the major bend in the river, it commanded a magnificent observation point, and was capable of observing activity for many miles. The Germans always knew that this was a critical position and further attempts would surely be made to wrest it from them. By now they were well aware that this would be the next target for the Australians, and heavily reinforced it with several defensive lines.

It was expected that the 28th would be required for the inevitable assault on Mont St Quentin, so they were not surprised, when, on the evening of the 31st, they got orders to move to a new position north of the river. They would cross the bridge at the village of Feuilleres, six kilometres to the west of Peronne, move through Clery-sur-Somme and take up a position one thousand yards to the east, facing the mount. Whilst on the march they received orders to halt, wherever they were at that time. The men settled in for the rest of the night in a trench system on the western outskirts of Clery-sur-Somme, three and a half kilometres from the mount.

It was obvious to Frank and many of the others that they were about to move on Mt St Quentin, and they would not be moving on until dark. The company officers were all together at one point.

"It's pretty darn obvious what we are about to do, Frank started. "We will have to move up tonight, ready to assault tomorrow. Why don't we use this time to move forward, just us, and check out the route and the roads we have to use? We should be able to gain some pretty good intelligence, don't you think?"

"Fair call I'd say, Francis," Ken answered. "But I think perhaps, we should involve the NCOs too, don't you?"

"Great idea," replied Frank. "Who knows, after this lot, some of them may be our only leaders left. I for one won't be here."

Max Farquharson spoke up, "What the fuck are you talking about, Francis? Given my track record, it's more likely to be me, wouldn't you think?"

Frank laughed, "I see what you mean Maxxy, but you see, my time here is almost done. I have found out what I came here for and that's all there is to it."

"What the hell are you talking about, Francis?" asked Ken.

"Well, Keith, you see it is like this," Max started. "Francis here, has been predicting our future actions all the way since Polygon wood, with remarkable accuracy I might add. It's almost as if he knows in advance what is going to happen." He turned sideways and winked at Francis. "Francis believes his time is up, soon. So, then we will know one way or the other, just how much shit he is full of." Then Max laughed, Frank smiled and Keith gave them both a quizzical look.

"What balderdash. Utter rubbish, was all they got in reply from Ken.

That afternoon, the officers and the NCOs all crept forward, as far as the trench system would allow and then through the ruins of the village, to observe the mount and the pathways to it. Each of them discussed the best way through. When night fell, they all moved forward to the trench system halfway between Clery and the Mont St Quentin. They had to contend with sporadic machine gun sprays throughout the night. Not specifically directed at them, so much, as just searching and firing to keep heads down.

During the night, a conference of senior Brigade officers modified the plan a little. The 28th, which was to be support for the action, was split into two halves. A and B Company formed what was known as the right half of the battalion and C and D Company the left half. The right half of the battalion would act in support of the 26th Battalion to the south of Mont St Quentin and the left half would act as support for the 27th, to the north of the Mont. Each would assume positions one thousand yards to the rear of the attacking force, and not approach the front until requested.

Zero hour of 5 am saw attacks on all sides of the mount commence. The 26th advanced to the base of the mount and both they and the right half of the 28th took exceptionally heavy machine gun fire and artillery, including a substantial proportion of gas. No injuries occurred, due to either the artillery, or gas. The biggest impact of the gas was that troops had to don their service respirators and try and fight in those. That was exceedingly difficult and inconvenient. The respirators (gas masks) significantly reduced their peripheral vision. If the gas comes close enough to the defending forces, they also had to don the masks to protect themselves, so it is usually reserved for approaching troops.

The 26th took heavy casualties in the first few hours, and the call was made to the support troops to reinforce the front.

"Okay, lads. We have the call to join our sister battalion at the front," Frank told his platoon. "Our aim is to sweep the front part of the Mont, cut the main road and bunker down in the quarry trench, over that road. Let's go. Good luck."

They rushed forward to assist the 26th. By the time they got there, troops of the 26th were taking cover on the lower slopes to the southwest of the road. Frank took his boys around to the left side of the 26th along with Max Farquharson's platoon.

"If we can move up that little gully there," Frank was explaining to Max and Toddy, "we may be able to get close enough to either charge or send over some bombs. Staying low may be enough to give us the cover we need."

"Agreed," said Max. "If you like I can take twenty of these fellas around there and give it a crack."

"Okay!" Frank agreed. "I'll back up from here."

Frank and Max drew the nearest twenty, which included men from both platoons. The battalion strength was down to less than half the usual number, having received no reinforcements since March. Between them, Max and Frank commanded no more than a platoon, about fifty men. Max indicated the direction he wanted the men to go and they headed off. They had not gone any further than ten metres when Max fell. Frank crawled over and dragged Max back to the safety of the cover.

"Stay there," he yelled out to the party. "I'll join you in a minute."

"Max, you dopy bugger. Number five? You really must learn to duck." Frank was holding Max, while one of the men got a dressing on his arm. From the position of the wound in Max's right arm, Frank figured this would have hit the bone as well. This was a serious but not life-threatening wound. Frank got the men to organise medical evacuation for Max, but he was having none of it. Wounded or not, he was staying right there until he was no longer required. There was precious little command remaining in the company and he was not about to make it any less. Frank left them to it and crawled over to the attack party. They had made it into the slight gully and were hiding there, waiting for Frank to arrive.

"Right men, were any of you with me on any of the previous machine gun stunts?" He asked them. All of them shook their heads.

"Right, it's a ploy that has worked for us before," Frank explained to them. "We will get a better idea of what to do when we get closer. It will depend on how close we can get to them. So, if it goes to plan, we will break into three groups. I'll lead a group of three as close as we can get. The rest of you, break into halves and stop in two different places, up the depression, at least ten to fifteen yards apart. On the signal, the highest of the two groups will distract the machine gunner and before he bears on you drop down and the lower group will then provide a second distraction, then quickly drop down. Hopefully, they will be confused enough for us to drop a couple of bombs on them. That is if we can get close enough. If not, we will just have to open fire. When you hear us execute the plan, charge forward, but watch for other fire. Got it?" He received nods and yeses from the group.

He led off with the party of the top three and a minute later half the remaining men followed. They slowly crawled their way up the gully, in their three little groups. This 'gully' was no more than a slight depression running up the hill, but it did provide them with a small amount of cover. Enough for them to stay below the machine gun's line of fire. When they got to the point where Frank thought they would be exposed if they went any further, he stopped and signalled for the others to do likewise. He slowly raised his head to find they were nearly at the same elevation as the MG post. It was about twenty yards away and firing down the hill at the bulk of the company. He dropped down lying on his back. There were mortar bombs going off all around the hill, mostly without causing too many problems for the Germans.

"Right, the post is about twenty yards away, Can you three lob grenades that far?" Frank asked.

"Easy, Yep and No worries," were the three responses he got.

"Sweet. Draw your grenades, but don't pull the pin until I say so," Frank ordered.

Frank checked back down the gully and saw that the men were all keeping an eye on him.

"Right pin out, and hold. Throw on GO!" he said. He gave the thumbs up down the gully and the first group jumped up and fired a shot each at the MG. Fritz swung his fire around to their area, but they had already ducked down. The lower group jumped up and fired and dropped down. As the German fire and attention swung back down the gully, Frank called "Go", then the four of them leaned up and they all threw, then immediately dropped back to the ground. Four explosions followed, and then they jumped back up and charged. Four grenades had done the trick. Frank immediately jumped on the MG, swung it left, and checked to see that it still fired. The others took cover behind the sandbag sangar. He loosened off the friction knob and let off a volley of fire onto the next MG around the slope and it too fell silent. He then swung the opposite direction and did likewise, with similar results, although they rapidly got the idea about what was happening and were, by then, preparing to shoot first. Sometimes, it is only a matter of parts of a second that decides who will live and who will die.

The elimination of these couple of machine gun posts was the signal for the bogged down troops to advance again. At least there was now an alley to advance through. Having already dealt with the first line of defence, before Frank and his boys arrived, they were now through the second line. Now they could spread laterally and clear this line. They managed to progress slowly around to the right until they made the Peronne road. Frank smiled as he crossed the road as he realised it would later be named the Avenue des Australiens. A few more grenades and a lot of rifle fire saw the battalions advance eastward until they made the quarry. Night was falling as they arrived at the quarry and temporary safety.

"This is it for the moment boys," Frank said. "Settle down and dig in for the night. We're not there yet." At this point, they were only a paltry ten to fifteen metres below the summit, so tomorrow would be more like moving across, rather than up the mount.

The men prepared for a predictably lively night of it, making sure they had plenty of protection. To their surprise, they had a rather quiet night. A few mortar shells dropped nearby but nothing hit their trench.

"We have the bulk of the job done, lads," Frank explained to the combined 3 and 4 Platoons.

"How many have we got, Toddy?" Frank asked.

"Only forty-five others, sir. Two Sergeants, four corporals and forty privates," Toddy replied.

"Alright. We make do with what we have, don't we? How was Farky, when you left him by the way?" He again asked Toddy.

"Typical Lt Farquharson sir. Looking forward to getting his fifth wound stripe. Silly Bugger. He hung on until we were well underway, refusing to leave until there was no more he could do.

I don't think he will be coming back this time though," Toddy told Frank.

"Yeah, that was my impression," Frank agreed.

"So tomorrow, lads, we will drive these bastards off the Mont, make no mistake. I would think Fritz is already making plans to withdraw to the Hindenburg Line. Tomorrow when we charge, Monash wants us to yell and scream, with all the lungs you've got. Scare the bejeebers out of those Hun." He smiled as he told them this. "They sure as hell won't be expecting that. Also, this road we are charging up will forever become known as the Avenue of the Australians, so make it a good effort."

"What are you talking about Francis?" Toddy asked Frank when they were alone. "The Avenue of the Australians?"

Frank laughed out loud. "Yes, Toddy! We become legends tomorrow my friend. These frogs will not forget us for a very long time."

"You are seriously weird, Francis. Do you know that?" Toddy chuckled as he said this.

"Yep!" Frank replied laughing. "And a lot weirder, than you will ever know."

The following morning came around and the fellows all lined up for their zero hour final charge. Of his original section, all he had left was Toddy, Harry Williams, Felix Simpson and Peter Jones. The others were all either dead or incapacitated. He called them all together and together they would advance on this objective. At 4.45 they lined up together to the left of the quarry, lying low until the whistle.

As soon as they heard the whistle, they all jumped up around the mount and charged forward with blood-curdling screams. A few machine guns fired up and a few mortars started raining in on them as they raced forward. Many of the Germans immediately stood up and raised their arms. "Nicht Schiessen" was heard in many areas of this lightning advance. It appeared to Frank now that the whole of the German occupation had decided that surrender was the best way to get out of all this. The men pushed forward and, in the matter of a few minutes, had secured the whole of Mont St Quentin.

To their south, the 5th Division took the town of Peronne as well. This whole sector was now back in Allied possession.

It was, however, a costly action, with the battalion losing 2 officers killed, Lts Ed Folley (The quiet one) and Edmonstone, 4 wounded, including Farquharson, 11 ORs killed and 72 wounded. This was a large loss, given that the battalion was already below half-strength.

General Henry Rawlinson, commander of the British 4th Army, described the final attack on Mont St Quentin as "The greatest military achievement of a war." Big praise, from a leading British General.

By the evening of September 5, they were relieved by the 3rd Battalion, Shropshire Regiment, which had been attached to the Australian Corps. The exceptionally weary men were marched back to their rather comfortable bivvies, at Clery-sur-Somme.

"Well fellas, looks like the Army appreciates your efforts. Hot food awaits you," Frank managed to raise a smile as he said this. The men did not even have enough strength to raise a cheer. They just dropped their equipment and tucked into a really good feed. After this, they turned into their riverbank holes, their home for the night. Here they slept the sleep of the dead.

The next morning the men all indulged in the wonderful swimming hole this position afforded them. Three days ago, they had watched as artillery shells raised massive plumes of water as they landed and exploded in this part of the river. Today they were using it for relaxation. The irony was not lost on them.

"Crazy isn't it, Toddy?" Frank pondered. "Here we are enjoying a swim and a frolic today in the same place as we were dodging getting killed only three days ago."

"It certainly is Francis. I didn't think I was going to get out of this one you know." Toddy replied.

"Nar, you'll make it mate. You're tough," Frank tried to reassure him as he sat watching the remaining men of the battalion frolicking in the river.

"Might be tough Francis, but I'm not sure how much more of this stuff I can take. I'm starting to lose my nerve."

Frank sat and mulled Toddy's last statement over in his mind. If only he realised this lot really was nearly over. He only needs to hang in for one more month and he will be on his way home soon enough. He considered the position they were in and decided to give Toddy some year 2000 advice.

"What if I told you for a fact," Frank began slowly," that this was only going to last another two months, and we only need to do one more month?. Do you reckon you could make it?" Frank watched to see Toddy's reaction. Toddy just shrugged his shoulders and disconsolately replied, "One more month? I could probably do that. Is that how long you reckon we've got?"

"That's what I reckon, mate. I would say, the Hindenburg line next, at the end of the month, and then, it's off the line and it's all over bar the shouting. You know Billy Hughes wants us to be taken off the line. He knows we've had enough. Come on, mate. You can do that." Frank encouraged him.

"Hindenburg line, eh? Yeah, they will give that up easily, won't they? That will be a shit show." He paused at this point and then added, "You actually do know what is going to happen, don't you Francis?" Toddy stood and ran into the water yelling back, "Come on, you sooth. Come in and enjoy the water, for tomorrow we may be dead."

Frank smiled and thought Toddy, was closer to the mark than he realised.

That afternoon, the men were reassembled and marched about ten kilometres, across the river and west, to a camp just northeast of Cappy. When they set up residence in this rest area, battalion fighting strength was down to 347, about one-third full strength. They spent the next three weeks here resting, playing sport, training and swimming. During this time they did regain some of their earlier numbers with returns from hospital and a few reinforcements.

One evening at the camp, the remaining officers, Ken McIntyre, Harold Ridley and Frank, along with Alan Todd, who was considered as good as an officer now, were sitting talking about their experiences so far, when, after a pause in the conversation, Harold asked, "Well chaps, Frank appears to be correct in his assumption that this will be over fairly soon. Do you think it was all worth it?"

"Absolutely!" Ken immediately replied. "Why do you ask? Do you not think so?"

"I was just thinking about the cost. Look at all the officers alone that we have lost. Dead. Let alone the rank and file. And for what? Why did they have to pay that price and not us?"

"It's not over yet, Harold." Frank reminded him.

"Nar, I know. We are only a small country and what are we, 12,000 miles away? Why are we here? We only have four million people and about ten percent of us came over here of which probably 60,000 have died. How will a country like ours, rise from that loss? The effects of this will last for generations. Not to mention the devastation of these beautiful cities, towns and people all over France and Belgium."

Ken jumped in now and answered, "Harold, what would you have us do? Sit back and watch the mother country go down. No Harold, we are a part of this world and it is our duty, even our obligation, to see that this kind of tyranny does not dominate our world, despite our size. In fact, I believe it is because of our size that we need to be a part of any defeat. We need to show the rest of the world, that our nation will not tolerate oppression."

"But couldn't this be showing the world that we support war?" Toddy put his tuppence worth in now.

"I don't see this as supporting war, Toddy," Frank explained. "Unfortunately, when diplomacy fails and these things descend into war, the only way to say we do not agree is to enter war. It's a bit of an anachronism, I understand that, but I see it as showing the world that we do not countenance war. By trying to stop it as quickly as possible."

"Agreed Frank," Ken added. "By employing the types of tactics we have in the last few months, we have shown the warmongers that we will not tolerate their wastage strategies either."

"Unfortunately, lads, even though we may drive the Hun into submission this time, it won't be the end of it," Frank explained quietly. "There are those on the other side who will see defeat here as just an intermission. There will be a rise of nationalism in Germany over the next few years, that will see this all start over again."

"This has been called the war to end all wars, and you think it will happen all over again?" Harold asked Frank.

"Yes Harold, I do," Frank replied. He glanced across at Toddy, to see him nodding almost imperceptibly.

"I know you have a habit of accurately predicting the future Francis, but this time I most desperately hope you are wrong," Ken said determinedly.

"It will be the sons and daughters of these men around you who will have to face the next onslaught though. These Germans will not lie down. They are a proud race and do not take defeat lying down. They will be back." Frank stated. "So in answer to your initial question Harold, I don't know if it is ever worth it. I guess it depends on where you are looking at it from. Ask Mrs Hammond, if she thinks it was worth it. Ask Mrs Stewart, Mrs Folley. I think they would tell you it was not worth it." Frank paused for a moment. "But Ken is right. We cannot just sit back and watch. It is as good as condoning tyranny. We have to be counted, and we have been."

Frank raised his glass and finished with, "Here's to all our mates, alive or dead. You made a difference."

All four stood and drank the toast to their mates.

At about this time, Lt Gen Sir John Monash was concerned about the brigade's fighting strength and proposed collapsing some battalions into others. Most of the men of the AIF resisted this, so in the end, most of the battalions contracted the number of companies to three. For the 28th it meant the loss of D Company, with the officers and men being divided up between the other three companies. In the last week of September, the men resumed training and preparations for what would be their final action. The assault on the Hindenburg / Beaurevoir line. By the 27th of September, the battalion received orders to proceed to the forward area.

On this same date, the British and then the US troops were to carry out a small action on the left of the proposed advance, in order to take some lost ground, leading up to the proposed start line. Unfortunately, they were both unsuccessful in accomplishing this. Gen. Monash was already committed to the start date of the 29th for the full action, so he had to go with the start line on the left, backward of the planned start point. The US 27th was to attack on the left and then to consolidate position whilst the Australian 3rd Division would leapfrog them and carry the battle forward. The US 30th was to start on the right and the Australian 5th Division would leapfrog them. The British 46th would attack over the St Quentin Canal, to their right, and the French further to their right.

The US / Australian attack would take place over the only underground section of the St Quentin Canal, known as the Bellicourt Tunnel, between Vendhuile in the north and Bellicourt in the south. This was the only land bridge over the canal and was six kilometres wide. Needless to say, the Germans had several lines of defence in this section. It was felt that no army could effectively cross the open canal in the above-ground parts, as the canal itself was probably one hundred feet below the surrounding ground level and thus extremely steep and wide. No tank would be capable of crossing it. They certainly did not, however, expect the tenacity of the British 46th (North Midlands) Division, nor the fact that they would capture the Riqueval Bridge intact. This was the only bridge across the canal in this region and was around three km south of Bellicourt. The British troops were the first to cross the canal, which was a massive boost.

The action in the centre went much to plan, with the US 30th and Australian 5th, but the action in the north did not. The American 27th Division failed to do what they were trained to do as they advanced. Rapidly advancing is one strategy, but if you do it too quickly and do not "mop up" as you go, ensuring an area is completely cleared of enemy troops, you end up with enemy enclaves popping up behind you. This means making sure the ground you have just taken is actually cleared of enemy troops, and that you have left no enemy behind you. If you just keep moving forward, you find you are fighting in front of you and behind you. Because they failed to do this, the Australian 3rd Division was forced, instead of leapfrogging the Americans, to join in the initial battles for their area. As they were now fighting for ground way behind the advance in the centre, The US 30th and the Australian 5th, in the centre, found themselves fighting off Germans on their left now, as well as in front, as the action on their left had not kept pace.

It was at this point that the plan fell into one big hole. Monash realised this, and tried rather unsuccessfully, during the first night, to bring the US troops back to some form of attack line. By day two, he just had to leave it up to the individual commanders to work their troops, to the best advantage. At least he had the confidence in his men to let that happen. News came through on this same day that Bulgaria had surrendered to the Allies, and that gave the men a boost. The end was definitely in sight now.

By day three, the northern sector was taken and the advance continued. Back at the 28th Battalion, they, being in support now, were waiting for orders to take on the front line. They were still a few kilometres behind the action, having just arrived at Templeaux de Guerard, at 1.30 pm on the 1st of October. This had been a previously unoccupied position.

"Righto, lads," Frank called out to his men, "this is where we are to spend the night so dig in. Get yourselves comfortable and try and stay dry." To this point, the last few days had been cold and showery, with the coming of winter. By 5 pm they had all dug in and were quite comfortable.

At 8.30 a runner came to each of the company and platoon commanders with a message.

"Ok fellas, sorry about this, but obviously there has been a cock up at the front. We have to advance to the front line, right now," Frank informed them all. There were groans all around. "Bugger me! We've only just dug in," was a fairly mild form of comment fired off in his direction.

"Don't shoot the messenger boys," was all Frank could say in response.

They trudged forward and arrived at their muster point at 3 am. It took forever to cover the distance, as the night was particularly dark and finding your way was almost impossible. Along the way, they got shelled and lost three of their team, one of them killed. On arrival at their destination, they dug in again, although this time it was already mostly done. For the rest of the night, they endured artillery shelling and aerial bombardment, mostly aimed at Bellicourt, just to their west, but many of the shots dropped short on their position. They were now over the Hindenburg line and all that remained was to take the Beaurevoir line, which was the rear line of the Hindenburg defences.

At 5 the following morning, October 3rd, a hot meal was brought around to the troops and they were told to drop all their surplus equipment at battalion HQ, in order to lighten their load. All the supplies they needed would follow them quickly. The men were a little worried by the fact that although this whole stunt was a major action, everything was so unnervingly quiet.

At 5.20, the men formed up on their tape, about three kilometres northeast of Bellicourt, awaiting the barrage. At 6.05, the barrage commenced and the men rose and commenced their advance, under the creeping barrage.

"Hold your line boys, we're in no hurry here," Frank called out. They advanced in a northeasterly direction and had only travelled a kilometre when they had to hold up, whilst some enemy resistance was overcome in a small copse to their left, after which they continued. A further kilometre forward, they commenced fairly heavy hand to hand fighting as they came upon the Beaurevoir line itself. Here, it was a mass of artillery, mortars, bullets and bayonets, but before too long the battalion had the ascendency.

"Remember what I said, boys, keep an eye on each other's backs. In pairs, look after your buddy." Frank was barking out instructions, left right and centre. Prisoners started to flow toward the rear with escorts now. The men were dodging bodies, animals, timber, weapons and each other as they went. Progress was difficult over this churned-up landscape and once again, Frank noticed the stench of human waste and death that lay all around them.

They were facing three machine gun nests on the rise above them. Assaults on the two on the left were rapidly successful and the machine gun fire was definitely reduced. This gun on the right though; that was proving problematic. It was set up in the ruins of an old farmhouse, now no more than a pile of rubble, but that rubble provided them with solid cover. Frank had stopped to consider the situation when he realised where he was. This was the Boulanger's cottage remains, where the family had enjoyed coffee with the as-yet unborn son of the present owner, on their first day of exploring the battlefield.

He looked up, to see Toddy run his bayonet through an attacking Hun, about to throttle Harry Williams, about twenty yards away. He smiled briefly at Harry and gave him the thumbs up.

Just then, everything stopped. No movement, no sounds, nothing. Then Frank heard a voice. "Well, Frank. Do you have the answers you sought when you came to Europe?" It was the Gentleman from atop the butt in Polygon wood. He was still so impeccably dressed, only now, he looked totally out of place.

"What the....?" Frank started and he looked around him at the stationary world. "What is going on?"

"Well, you didn't think I was going to leave you here, to perish, did you?" The gentleman said.

"Who are you?" Frank demanded of him.

"Haven't you worked that out yet Frank? Actually, it matters not who I am, it only matters who you are now," he answered.

"You look very familiar I have to say, but no," Frank replied.

The gentleman removed his hat and glasses and looked at Frank.

"Are you ready to go home now Frank?"

"Oh, my lord," Frank exclaimed. You're ..." As he said this, there was a massive explosion, which shattered the tree next to him.

Harry Williams looked across at Francis, just in time to see the thumbs up, and then saw him disappear behind a tree as the tree was hit by an artillery shell. He dashed over to check on his lieutenant, only to find he was not there. "Oh lord! Not again!" he said. "The shell must have hit him directly. This time he really is dead." He charged on, with the rest of the boys and took the trench and the line. By the end of the day, they had taken a large slice of the Beaurevoir line and were positioned just to the west of Beaurevoir town. On this day they had taken 50 prisoners, 6 machine guns, 1 x 77mm gun sight and 1 full signaling set. However, this action came at a hefty price. Three officers and eleven ORs killed and four officers and 66 ORs wounded.

It was now the 3rd of October, and in a little over five weeks, it would all be over. At least until 1939.

The following day, all Australian infantry were withdrawn from the front line, for rest, following orders from the Prime Minister, Billy Hughes. They never returned before the Armistice was called.

Chapter 13
The Last Post

They shall grow not old, as we that are left grow old:
Age shall not weary them, nor the years condemn.
At the going down of the sun and in the morning,
We will remember them.
For the Fallen
(Ode to Remembrance 2nd verse)
Laurence Binyon

"Frank! Frank! Where are you? Have you kids seen your dad? Lynne asked trying not to look too panicked.

"No, not for the last hour. Mum you really should read some of these headstones," Tim said to her.

"Maybe later, Son. I haven't seen your father for at least an hour. I'm getting worried. I last saw him sitting on the cenotaph up the top of the butt. I found his folder and papers up there, but he wasn't there," Lynne said waving her arms around.

"Maybe he's gone for a walk, or maybe he's looking for a coffee shop," Tim replied.

"Maybe, but I don't think there is anything around here. The closest is back at Zonnebeke," Lynne replied, still searching from side to side.

"He'll be somewhere alright. You know he likes to wander off," Tim told her.

"Yes," and then to herself, "But not without telling me first."

"Maybe he's gone for a walk in the woods," Eloise chimed in. "Maybe he's gone to pick some wildflowers for you," and she smiled.

"Maybe, baby. Maybe," Lynne was getting really concerned. She went back to the steps and climbed up the butt again. She stood on top and cast her eyes around. He was not to be seen in the cemetery. She had already been back to the car and he was not there. She slowly scanned her eyes through the woods but could see no sign of him there. "He said something about bunkers in the butt. Maybe he's found something like that," she thought to herself. She walked back down the steps at the end near the cemetery entrance and wandered around behind the butt. All the way along the base she walked, but there was no sign of anything like that. It was all meticulously kept. Mowed regularly and bushes were neatly trimmed. She called out his name a few more times, wary not to disturb the atmosphere. No reply. She walked around the southern end of the butt and reclimbed the stairs to the top again. As she approached the cenotaph again, she stood and scanned the cemetery once more. Still nothing. She continued walking past the cenotaph yet again. Just then, Frank appeared from around the corner of it.

"Oh Frank! There you are. Where the heck have you been? I've been worried sick," Lynne admonished him. He just stood there, looking around himself, at the butt, at the cenotaph, at the cemetery, at himself, at Lynne. He suddenly looked down the back face of the butt, like he was looking for something.

"Frank, are you alright? How did you get so filthy?" Lynne again asked him. Still, he did not answer. He just kept looking around, like he was stunned.

"Frank!" Lynne yelled at him as she took him by the shoulders. "Frank!"

"Lynne? Is that really you?" Frank asked.

"Of course, it is. Who did you think it was?" she asked him sarcastically. She was now getting annoyed.

Frank patted himself down. "I'm here. I'm back!" He threw his arms around her and gave her a huge hug.

"Back?" Lynne queried. "Back from where? Where have you been? Why are you so dirty?"

Frank seemed to be snapping out of it now. "Um, 1918."

"What the...?" Lynne started to say.

Frank cut her off. "The kids. Where are the kids?" and he started to look around.

"They're up in the memorial at the far end. Frank, what the heck is going on? Where have you been?" Lynne demanded to know.

"You wouldn't believe me, if I told you right now," he said, as he started towards the children. "Let's go. I'll tell you all about it later." He raced off to get the children. When he found them, he called them over and gave them the biggest hugs.

"Daddy, not so tight. It hurts," said Eloise with a wince.

"Where have you been, Dad? Mum was worried. And why are you so dirty?" Tim now asked.

"I will tell you, all about it, Son. But not just now. Come on let's go," and they all headed for the car.

"Frank you are behaving very strangely," Lynne commented on the walk to the car. "What has happened?"

"I know exactly what happened to Grandfather, Lynne. He died right here, in 1917. Remember the papers saying KIA 1.10.17? Well, that should not have been crossed out. That IS when he died." Frank explained quickly. He had a big smile on his face as he walked and looked at his children and Lynne.

Lynne smiled back but was really puzzled by this weird behaviour. "But the papers said he went on until September the following year."

"They got it wrong," Frank indicated. "That wasn't him. It was me."

"Frank, stop that," Lynne stated emphatically. "This is weird, you're weirding me out. Stop it." She stopped walking. There were tears in her eyes now. She was scared again.

"I'm sorry my love, it is a lot weird, but if you wait a bit, I will explain it all. There is so much more research to do now."

"Frank, where's your shoes, your Crocs?" Lynne asked him as she started walking again.

This time Frank stopped and looked down at his bare feet. He started laughing, "Oh they're probably buried about six feet under the butt I guess."

Lynne just shook her head. He was making no sense.

"Come on you lot. I'm starving. Who's for lunch?" Frank was in top spirits now. He had his answers and he had his family back.

In the car Frank said, "I think we will go back to Ieper and have lunch there," he then turned to Lynne and added, "It will take a long time, a very long time, to explain everything to you. Please be patient. Trust me, what I tell you will be the honest truth. You will not be able to believe me I think, but it will be true." He grabbed a few wet wipes and gave himself a bit of a cleanup. He still had Somme mud on him.

At lunch, they sat the kids at one table and Frank and Lynne sat at another. Over lunch, Frank started to tell Lynne what had gone on. He was right, she would not believe him, at first. She tried to convince him that he had fallen asleep and dreamt it all. Then he asked her if he was asleep at the Cenotaph. "Well no, you weren't, and your papers were just left there."

"And where did you find me?" Frank asked her.

She sat and thought for a bit. *"His papers were there and he wasn't. I looked many times. He was not there. Then he was. Surely not!"*

Then Frank looked at his arm. He lifted the sleeve of his T-shirt and there was the scar from the door of the cell at Molenaarelsthoek. "Look at this. Have you seen this before?"

"No. Where and when, did you get that?" Lynne asked.

"A little place called Molenaarelsthoek, about a mile, I mean a kilometre and a half northeast of the butt. In 1917."

Lynne sighed. She had to give this a lot of thought. *He didn't have it before.* "That I do know. *It is too significant to have missed before. He certainly looks skinnier than this morning, but I just put that down to ... well, I don't know what I put that down to. It can't be true. But what other explanation would there be, for it?"*

"Here I'll show you," he said as he reached for the maps in the folder. He spread the 28 NE map out on the table. "J 4 b 8 5, just there. That's the bunker I was held in when the shell blew the door in and did this," he said pointing to his arm. "I got three other British dudes out as well and we made our way up this road here, overnight and into the south edge of Zonnebeke, behind the lake that we sat and had an ice-cream at last year. Damn, I mean this morning." He started laughing.

"What's so funny?" asked Lynne.

"One of the guys, who turned out to be a British lieutenant colonel, Rupert Penry-Wright was his name, found a cache of pickles in the cellar we were hiding in. Pickles! Everyone thought they were gold. He was the guy who wrote a letter to command, praising my leadership and saying I should be promoted. They gave me a medal for that. Medal! The bloody medal," and he sprang to his feet and began searching in the pocket of his shorts. He stopped and a smile came to his face. He gently pulled his MM from his pocket and handed it to Lynne.

"This," he said, "is the original that grandma couldn't get. Look at the edge."

Lynne looked at the medal and read 3557 Cpl F.A. Bailey 28th Batt. A.I.F. She just looked at Frank and she teared up. "This will mean so much to your father."

"Except grandfather didn't win it. He was already dead." Frank quietly said.

"Bloody Hell," Lynne replied. "What are you going to do?"

"I have no idea sweetheart. I haven't had time to think about everything yet. I'm just overjoyed to be back. You believe me now, don't you?" Frank asked her.

Lynne waited for some time before answering him. "It goes against everything I know and understand about this world, but ..." She did not finish her sentence. She couldn't.

"Remember when we were at the Boulanger's cottage?" Frank asked Lynne.

"Yes, I do," she replied.

"Well, we weren't far off where Francis was killed," then Frank paused. "Except it wasn't him, was it? It was me. Damn, I can't process all this. Anyway, that was about 50 metres down the hill from their house. It was when I recognised the MG post was in their house that everything stopped and I came back." Frank spent some time, trying to process what he had just said.

"I think we need to do some stuff for the kids," Frank said changing the subject. "Preferably, before we drive poor Ellie nuts. I do want to trace back through some of the places I was at and check them out. I have to say that right now, it does seem like a dream. I need to determine just what happened. If I can find these places that I was then maybe I can settle things in my own mind."

"So, where does that mean we need to go?" Lynne asked Frank.

"Right here is the best place to start. I need to write down everything I can remember of the last year." Frank laughed. "The last year! For you, it was what, an hour?"

"Yes, you were missing for about an hour," Lynne replied.

"You see, for me, that was a full year. It's weird. It's like time is completely relative. I don't try to understand what happened, I just know it did and I have the scars to prove it, so to speak," Frank laughed as he spoke and looked at the scar on his arm.

Lynne smiled, still not quite sure how to take all this. She too, did not understand. Everything in her education told her that this was not possible, but here it was, right in front of her. A husband that she loved and trusted implicitly, who only this morning, was completely 'normal', looking for answers about his grandfather and now has come forward with this weird story. That was just as unlikely as his story was.

"So where to now then, Frank?" Lynne asked.

"I think this afternoon, you and the kids should go shopping or whatever you, or they, want to do. I'm going back to the hotel to start writing notes while it is still fresh in my mind," Frank suggested.

"Sounds like a plan," Lynne answered. "What do you think you will tell the kids about this?"

"Mm, I haven't got an answer to that yet," Frank admitted. "Leave that one with me. I might get an idea while writing it down. Tim will be alright, but Ellie's probably a bit young to understand."

"Too young?" exclaimed a laughing Lynne. "I don't even understand."

"Too true darling. Maybe one day we might get answers to it all." Frank sighed.

"Dad! What are we doing this afternoon?" Tim came over and prodded his father.

"Well, Son, I thought I might turn you three loose on Ieper, to do whatever you like. I have a little work to do," Frank explained to Tim and Eloise.

"Sweet, Dad. Sure you can't come too?" Tim queried.

"I will tomorrow, don't worry, it's just that I have some pretty urgent stuff to get organised this afternoon," Frank explained to them, as he gathered Ellie in his arms and gave her a hug. "So, no museums this afternoon, my sweet." Frank rubbed her nose with his forefinger and smiled a big smile.

"Good. Can we go shopping?" Ellie asked expectantly.

"I am sure your mother would love to take you shopping," Frank laughed.

"And Dad? Can we try the Last Post again tonight, but get there early?" Tim tentatively asked.

"What a great idea, Son." Frank agreed. "We will most certainly get there early this time. I have some special business there, this time."

Lynne and the children left for a walk around the town and Frank walked back to the hotel. He sat down with pen and paper and started noting all the places he had been in the last year and the people he could remember. By the time he had progressed to the present day, he had six sheets of paper, with notes and arrows and diagrams, going in every direction. It started off in a nice, neat fashion, line by line, and then after a while, as he would remember earlier events, small side notes were added and linked to whatever. It ended up looking a right mess, but he was happy. He could now rewrite it all, in a manner that both he and anyone else would be able to follow.

Once the notes were completed, he sent an email to his father, explaining that he had learned a lot about his grandfather. He was bringing home so much information on him, he could not explain it all here. There was still more information to gather, but his investigations to date had turned up some exceptionally interesting facts and figures. He did tell his father that Francis had been in Polygon Wood, Zonnebeke, Passchendaele, Corbie, Le Hamel, Morlancourt, Amiens, Villers Bretonneux and Mont St Quentin, as the unit diaries had indicated, as well as the fact that he had more detailed information on his part in those campaigns. He finished the email by saying that he also had a really special memento for him, without disclosing to him the nature of that item. Frank sent off the email and sat back and smiled. It was a smug smile. The kind of smile one might make when one knows they have made a difference for somebody else.

Frank was sitting back in the lounge chair when the room came alive as the children dashed in.

"Oh Dad; we saw all sorts of different things this afternoon," Ellie started. "There were some lovely shops and we bought a few things for back home. There was a lovely chocolate shop too. Oh, it was so nice, and ice cream. I like Belgium, Dad."

Frank laughed, "Yes, it is a very nice country isn't it, Sweetie? What about you, Tim?"

"Well, I have to say again, it is amazing that they have rebuilt this town to look the same as it did before the war, only better and more modern inside. It will last another thousand years now." Tim said matter of factly.

"So, what did you buy out there, Son?" Frank asked him.

"I bought this Dad," and he held out a little wooden cross with a poppy in the middle. "I can write great grandad's name on this and put it on a grave. Just not sure where, yet."

"I have a suggestion on that, Son. I would like to go back out to Zonnebeke and Polygon, to check a couple of points. How about we find a grave out there and put it on his headstone?" Frank could not have been prouder of his son.

"That sounds like a great idea," Tim replied with a smile. "Can we do that tomorrow please?"

"It's a date, Son," Frank said. "Now, if we want to get to the Last Post early enough, we need to go and get some dinner. Hungry yet?"

"Famished," replied Tim.

"You bet," answered Ellie.

Frank looked at Lynne, who had been watching this interaction from a distance and smiled. She smiled back. Yes, they were growing up, were they not? At 7.30 pm, they walked the two hundred metres to the Menin Gate, to find it already closed off to traffic and the crowd starting to gather. The children raced forward to get a front-row place and Frank and Lynne joined them, standing behind. Before too long there were probably two hundred people of all nations there. They listened carefully to all the accents around them. They could pick the English and the Australian accents easily. There were a couple of Americans there as well. Many of the rest were speaking in foreign languages, so they figured they were mostly Belgian and French.

At 8 pm sharp a local dignitary stepped forward and gave a brief call to attention, followed by a short prayer. The next step in the procedure was the playing of the last post by the Last Post Association Buglers. Tonight, there were four of them. Frank was not prepared for what happened next. The buglers played beautifully, and Frank found he had tears in his eyes. Not just wet eyes, but full-blown tears streaming down his face. He remembered his grandfather, and all the wonderful men he made friends with in 1917-18 and lost. He remembered their faces, their jokes, their issues even. He remembered the men from his 2 Section, 3 Platoon, all of them gone by now of course. He wondered what happened to Toddy, Max, Keith, and even von Feldt.

Lynne looked over to Frank during the following silence and saw the tears. She reached over to him, took his arm in hers and drew him close, then reached into her pocket and drew out a tissue and handed it to him. He just held it until after the silence, when he wiped away the tears. The wreaths were laid and the Reveille played and then the national anthems of Australia, New Zealand and Belgium were played. It was only then that both Lynne and Frank realised how many Australians were there. They could actually hear people, all around them singing their own National Anthem, 'Advance Australia Fair'.

After the short service was over, the family walked over to the steps and inspected the wreaths laid there. Wreaths from organisations here in Belgium and from home in Australia. Wreaths from individuals. Wreaths in memory of family members. Frank stood silently reading them all, one by one. He decided then if he was allowed, to return to lay a wreath of his own. He sought out the official who opened the proceedings and asked him if it were possible for him to lay a wreath and was told, "Of course it is, sir. Just come and see us tomorrow at the office and we will register you as a wreath layer, for whatever date you prefer." He gave him the address and Frank was now determined to lay that wreath for his mates. He also realised that the same way he found out about his grandfather he could find out what happened to his mates.

On the way back to the hotel, he explained to Lynne what thoughts he had and that he needed to research the fellows he served with.

"Well, at least this way," Lynne explained, "I will be able to see if this really did happen."

"What do you mean?" Frank asked with a quizzical look on his face.

"You have a list of names I take it that you believe you served with?" Lynne asked him.

"Yes! I do. I wrote most, if not all of them down this afternoon," Frank explained, still not understanding what Lynne was getting at.

"Okay, so now if you find them all on the NAA site, there is little doubt what happened to you. If you can't find them, well it really was a dream," she explained.

Frank did not react immediately. He just thought about what he had heard. *"She still is not sure whether to believe me or not,"* he thought. *"Mind you, it is a lot to accept really."*

"Yes, I see what you mean, but the way I put it is that I am about to show you that it really did happen. No doubt whatsoever," Frank stated emphatically. Lynne said no more.

As soon as they returned to the hotel, Frank stopped in the hotel foyer and opened up one of the computers in the internet café. He brought up the NAA site and started the name search. One by one he entered the names of those he fought with that were still alive when he left, or those he didn't find out what happened to. He got paper and a pen from the reception desk and started to compile the list.

*Lt Col Currie survived and re-enlisted in WW2 in Queensland. Toddy survived and was RTA 5.2.19. He remained a Sergeant. Lt Stewart DOW 4.6.18

*Max (Evelyn) Farquharson survived 5 WIAs and RTA 18.1.19. He was awarded the MC.

Both Harry Williams and Felix Simpson survived and both RTA.

Peter Jones was KIA the day after Francis. 4.10.18

*Captain Dunkley survived his wounds and RTA, 1.6.19.

*Lt Hopkins RTA 5.2.19.

*Lt Flanagan RTA 5.2.19 and re-enlisted in the militia in WW2.

*Lt Skevington survived his wounds and RTA 16.12.18.

*Lt Tozer received GSW and RTA 9.19.

*Lt McIntyre survived and was promoted to Captain 26.10.18. He RTA 3.3.19 and received the MC on 8.9.19.

*Lt Hardwick RTA 15.1.20.

*Lt Stokes RTA 2.19.

*Lt Maskiell RTA invalid, 2.3.19

Of the original ten in Frank's No 2 section, that he met, only three survived.

(* indicates the actual outcome for this real person)

On completing his list, Frank closed the computer down and started slowly upstairs. He could not help thinking about what a waste this all was. It all boiled over again, twenty-one years later. He opened the door to their room and the children were already in bed. Frank went over to Lynne and sat next to her. He went through the list one by one with Lynne.

"These are only the boys who were still alive when I left. There are dozens of others I knew didn't make it. They were killed whilst I was there," Frank attempted to explain to Lynne. "Look at this, Hubert Tozer must have been pretty seriously wounded the day after me. He did not come home for nearly a year. And this, one of my original boys shot in the head the day after me." Frank sighed. "And for what? Just to have that megalomaniac half-wit start it all up twenty-one years later. Sheer bloody madness."

Lynne just sat there and held his hand. She looked at the list and was now convinced the impossible had actually happened. These were the names of real men from the 28th Battalion AIF and Frank had been Francis, with them. "So Frank, who was the man you saw on the butt at Polygon?"

"He looked very familiar, well, I remember thinking that he looked very familiar anyway," he replied hesitantly. "I thought I worked it out just before I came back, but I never got the chance to find out for sure and I can't recall who I worked out it was. That is the really weird thing; if I worked it out, why can I not remember? At this stage, I simply don't know."

"Maybe he didn't want you to remember, for some reason. So, Francis was killed back in '17 you think?" Lynne asked him.

"Yeah. Harry Williams, swore he saw him vapourised in a pink haze, by a Hun shell. Oh Hell! He was there when I disappeared, in another shell explosion. Poor bugger. He'd probably be wondering what he had done to deserve this sight, twice and for the same victim?" At least now Frank was smiling. "I can't get my head around it, but if I left 1918 this morning, it must still be going on there now. The war, hasn't finished there yet. Try and figure that one out. Oh, my brain hurts."

"Nope! Not going to try and figure that one out," Lynne replied laughing. "If you want to go visiting some of the places that you were at tomorrow, what are you going to tell the kids?"

"Mm, well I suppose I had better try explaining it to them in the morning," Frank sighed. "In the meantime, I need sleep, in a nice comfortable bed."

"So, what's on the agenda for today, Dad?" Tim blurted out at breakfast.

"Well, I would like to go back to a few places briefly today, some of which we have already been to because I need to check on a few things," Frank explained to them. "But first I need to talk to you both about something a little strange." "Ooo, sounds exciting," chirped Ellie clapping her hands.

"Yes, well, maybe. Do you remember yesterday, when we were at the Polygon Wood Cemetery, I disappeared for a while?" Frank asked them.

"Yes! Where were you? You still haven't said. Mum was really quite worried. You left behind all your papers and stuff." Tim queried him, almost with an air of disapproval.

"I don't know quite how to explain it and you are going to find this exceptionally difficult to believe, but here goes. When I was sitting up on the monument at the top of the butt, a man came up to me to talk. He seemed to know an awful lot about your great grandfather, even though he could not have been alive then, to know him." Frank started.

"Yes, that would make him pretty old now, wouldn't it?" laughed Tim.

"Yes, it would," laughed Frank. "This man asked me a few questions and then asked if I would like to see exactly what happened to my grandfather. Naturally, I answered, yes. Next second, I am tumbling down the butt, in the dark, to be greeted by a German soldier pointing a gun at me."

"Okay?" Tim said, rather suspiciously and oh so slowly.

"Anyway, it appears that, although it is so exceptionally hard to believe, I was transported back to 1917 just before my grandfather died," Frank stopped there to gauge the reaction.

"You are saying then that your grandfather did die, in that first KIA entry?" Tim suggested to his dad.

"Yes, that's right," Frank replied. He was somewhat taken aback by the question. It was not questioning the time travel, but the war records entry.

"So, what was the next year's entry for him then?" Tim quizzed.

Here we go again, thought Frank. He continued, "Well, it turns out that all that stuff in the records after that date, ... was me. I have been back there for a year and I did all the stuff, that he was supposed to have done. It turns out that not only do I share his name, but I must look identical to him because no one queried that." Again, Frank sat silently, allowing the story to sink in.

"I don't get it, Dad," Eloise had been sitting quietly up until now. "You went back to 1917? For a year? In one hour?"

"When you put it like that, it seems impossible doesn't it?" Frank smiled at her.

"Difficult, yes. Impossible, no," Tim added. "Einstein talked about this sort of possibility, and whilst we haven't found any evidence of it yet, it remains theoretically possible."

Frank looked at Lynne and she was already smiling and slowly, almost imperceptibly, shaking her head. "Where did this kid come from?" They were both thinking similar thoughts.

"Hey Dad, this now means you have fought in a war!" and Tim started laughing.

"Yep, Son. That's where this all started, isn't it?" Frank laughed too.

"Sure is. What did you do there then, Dad?" Tim eagerly queried.

Frank went through the basics of what happened to him over the course of the year. He explained why he wanted to go to these places again and told them he would add any further explanations when they got there. They all set off back to their room to prepare for the day. The children took the elevator and went up alone. Frank said he had some quick business to attend to on the other side of the square. He returned shortly and he and Lynne took the stairs back to the unit.

"How's that darn kid of ours, just accepting the possibility of what I said without question?" Frank said to Lynne.

"I know. It wasn't like he didn't understand or grasp the situation. He genuinely believes it's a possibility. Well actually, we now know it's not just a possibility, don't we?" Lynne replied.

"Yep. Still damned hard to believe though," Frank added.

"I just thought of something," Lynne started. "What were you thinking when you first realised that you were kind of Francis? I mean, you knew he was killed in October 1918."

"Yeah! That was difficult," Frank admitted. "I tried to put it out of my mind mostly. I had no idea what was going to happen. I didn't know if I would ever get to see you or the kids again. After a while, I just became Francis and just went about his daily chores."

"That must have been horrible," Lynne added softly shaking her head.

"I try not to remember those feelings, Love," Frank replied sullenly.

When they got to their room, the children were waiting for them. "First stop Polygon Wood, Dad?" queried Tim.

"It is, lad. Then Zonnebeke and Molenaarelsthoek." Frank replied cheerfully.

"Where?" Tim asked, turning his head sideways at his dad.

"Molenaarelsthoek. Where else?" Frank laughed. "It's a place a couple of Ks south of Zonnebeke. It's where I was held prisoner."

"Oh okay," Tim replied.

Frank looked across at Lynne, where Ellie was chatting quietly to her, almost secretively. Lynne was half smiling as she whispered back into Ellie's ear. Ellie nodded and went about getting her things together for the day. On the way down to the car, Frank asked Lynne what that was all about.

Lynne smiled and said, "She was saying she can't understand all this talk of travelling through time. She wanted to know if you have been watching too many sci-fi movies recently."

Frank laughed and just nodded. He did not expect either of his children to understand, especially as he did not completely understand himself, but he was surprised at Tim's accepting reaction.

Once they were at Polygon, they all headed straight up the stairs to the cenotaph atop the butt. Frank sat down where his journey had started.

"Okay, so this is where I was sat when I was approached from over there by that gentleman. I did not see him come up, he was just suddenly there. He was probably in his forties or maybe early fifties, and so immaculately dressed. He was wearing the Flanders Poppy on his suit, right here, over his heart." Frank indicated with his hand, above his left breast.

"He sat down beside me, just here," pointing to the place next to him. "He spoke as if he knew Francis. He knew everything about him. What he had done, what he was like, when he had died," Frank paused for a moment as a wave of realisation came over him. "Oh yes! Now I understand what he meant." Frank became excited and jumped to his feet. "When he asked me if I had any family buried here, I said that I didn't think so. He answered, 'You might be surprised.' That probably means Francis IS buried here, as an unknown soldier."

Tim had been listening to his father intently and now spoke up. "Dad? You know how I said about the little wooden cross I bought yesterday?"

"Yes, I do," Frank replied.

"How about we write his details on this cross and place it on one of the unknown soldiers' graves?" Tim suggested slowly and reverently.

Frank looked at Lynne now. Both of them had tears in their eyes. This kid of theirs was way ahead of them.

"Tim, I think that would be an amazing thing to do," Lynne managed to get out. Frank was by now unable to speak lest he break down.

They all walked down the stairs into the cemetery and looked around. Frank turned to Tim and said, "How about you decide which grave it should go on son." Tim nodded and cast his eyes around the cemetery, trying to decide which of the many headstones in front of him he should place it on. He started zig-zagging his way through the pristine rows of white engraved stone until he was standing in front of one grave, on which was engraved the rising sun at the top and the words, "An Australian Soldier of the Great War" and then down below it, "Known Unto God". Tim reached down and reverently placed the cross at the base of the headstone and pushed it gently into the Flanders soil. "Thank you, Great Grandpa" is all he said. All of them now had tears.

They all sat down on the grass around this grave and talked a little to Francis. Frank finished with, "Well Granddad, we can now go home safe in the knowledge of your contribution and commitment. I will tell your son of your bravery. I guess by now you have already met up with Grandma and you are both at peace."

At that moment, a lark flew around them and settled in the tree alongside them. It flitted from branch to branch and sang. It then flew down and sat on the gravestone stone for a few moments and looked at them before flying away to the woods. Frank put his arm around Lynne and she sobbed.

"I think that may be a sign to get back to our quest," Frank quietly said.

The four of them walked around the base of the butt to the other side. They walked past rows and rows of unknown soldiers, a testament to the ferocity of the battles fought in this area.

"Over three-quarters of the men in this cemetery are unidentified. Imagine that in this one cemetery alone, over 1500 families who have no idea where their loved ones lie," Lynne reminded them.

Once they made it to the reverse side of the butt, Frank looked at the cenotaph and worked out where he must have come to rest.

"I think this is probably where I landed when I rolled down the slope. I was walked along this way a few feet and down into a dugout about here," he explained pointing to a place at the base of the butt.

"Actually Frank, I think you can see from here, what seems to be a slight depression at that point," Lynne was a few metres behind the others, along the base of the slope. Frank walked back to where she was and looked with a critical eye.

"You know, I believe you may be right," he commented. "So here I was taken underground and introduced to Hauptman (Captain) von Feldt and Leutnant (Lieutenant) Rudner. I liked von Feldt, but Rudner I think would have been a good Nazi in the 2nd war. When the 55th attacked, we all went back to the rear via trenches, I would say, next to that road there. We ended up in Molenaarelsthoek. If you look at this trench map you can see where that is. I have marked it."

"Okay, so is that where we are headed now, Dad?" Tim asked him, once he had studied the map.

"Yep! To the batmobile everyone," he said, mimicking Batman.

They took the car and drove the eight hundred or so metres to where Frank thought the old dugouts were. There was no sign of them now of course. The farms had all been rebuilt over the ruins of their former glory. He showed them where they were, on the northern corner of the two roads where a farmhouse and sheds now stood. There was nowhere for him to pull over here so he continued up the road towards Zonnebeke until he could park. Once he had stopped, he explained about Blick, Erlinger and the escape, with the three Englishmen. He also explained that the road they were parked on was probably the road they followed to get to Zonnebeke.

"Next challenge," he informed them, "is to try and determine which house cellar we hid in."

He drove on slowly and the road curved around a wooded area. "We should be behind the museum we went into in Zonnebeke the other day. You should see a lake on your left soon."

After a couple more turns, Tim called out, "There's your lake, through there."

"Right, so that means the house should be around here. There were nowhere near this number of houses then, I might add. We were right on the edge of town, or what was left of it. Probably here," Frank indicated to his right, "but I couldn't say for sure."

"Well, you tried Dad. But everything has been rebuilt hasn't it?" Tim asked.

"Yep, it has. Oh well, let's move on to Red Lodge, down by Hyde Park corner, just north of Plugstreet".

On the way down to Ploegsteert, he told them of his adventures with the three Englishmen and in particular the story about the pickles. Also about the time they spent in the cellar and their rescue by the Aussie soldiers. He also backtracked to his 'predictions' he made to disillusion von Feldt because he already knew not only the outcome of the battles they were about to fight but the outcome of the war itself. He added that this would only work on someone who was already looking for a way out of their predicament. They drove back past Ieper, then down through St Elois and Mesen (Messines) and on toward

Ploegsteert Wood. He told them of the usual name they gave to this place; Plugstreet Wood. As they approached the wood, he explained that all it was in 1917 was a stand of sticks, as most had been destroyed by bombardment. As they exited the wood, they turned right.

"This corner used to be called Hyde Park Corner. The Poms had all sorts of English names for places over here, often because they were unable, or maybe unwilling, to pronounce the local names. It's only about eight hundred metres along here on the bend. There we are, right where I said it would be. We had miles of trenches and dugouts in the hill there, and the electricity came from over the other side of the hill, from the Wallangarra dugouts. Our 1st Australian Tunnelling Company dug that in 1916."

"Wow, that is amazing, Dad. How many of you were there in there?" Tim asked him.

"The whole battalion, which at that time was about eight hundred," his father replied.

"Eight hundred living in holes in the ground. That sounds incredible, doesn't it?" Lynne commented.

"Wasn't it dirty under there, Dad?" Eloise asked.

They all sniggered and Frank answered, "Yes dear, it was a little dirty at times. Especially when you only had a bath maybe every three or four weeks."

"Oo yucky," Ellie replied, screwing up her face.

"Hey Dad, is that some of the leftovers of the trenches in there, under those trees?" Tim asked.

Frank gazed over in the direction of Tim's observation and answered. "Actually Son, they might be, mightn't they? Maybe they have kept some of them. There should be a cemetery around here somewhere too, from memory, unless they moved them."

They drove on a short distance past the farmhouse around the corner and found the cemetery. They parked the car and walked over to the cemetery.

"There should be a couple of blokes here from the battalion. They took a direct hit on one of the posts over there at Warneton. Two blokes from C Company were killed instantly and five, I think, were wounded. Two of them died later at the CCS," Frank explained. Lynne was now convinced of his travels. There was just too much specific information that had been verified one way or another for him to have either made this up or dreamt it.

"Anyone see anything here from the 28th?" Frank called out to them as they looked.

"Nothing Dad!" Tim called back.

"Sorry Hun, nothing," Lynne replied.

"I thought they would be here," Frank sighed. "Maybe they got moved later. That happened a lot apparently. Oh well, better move on. Let's see if we can get anywhere near the Warneton trenches, eh?"

This was not going to be quite as easy this time. A motorway had since been built right through the middle of the trench system, just outside Warneton. By comparing his current-day map with the trench map, he was able to navigate a way to the area. On turning right onto the Messines Rd again, they found almost immediately a massive memorial and a cemetery.

"Oh wow, I didn't know about this," Frank exclaimed. "I tell you what. Let's go and have a look and maybe I can explain a few things to you, then we can go and have lunch over the road, and maybe some more of that Belgian ice cream."

"Great idea, Dad," Tim answered.

"Oh yes please," Ellie added.

On walking up the pathway to the memorials, Ellie turned to her mum and said, "They always look after these places very nicely, don't they Mum?"

"They most certainly do, Sweetie," Lynne answered.

They walked along the rows of headstones again, Frank checking for any of the 28th boys as he walked along. Lynne did likewise.

"Here they are," Frank called out. When the others got over to him and looked down at the headstones, Frank spoke again. "I didn't know either of them. They sure would not have known a thing. It would have been instant." Frank just stood there reading every detail on the two headstones. He knelt down next to Ellie and spoke to her directly. "Do you understand what this is all about, Sweetie?" he asked her.

"I think so," she replied hesitantly. "These were friends of yours when you were in the war. Is that it?"

"That is about the best way I could have described it, Sweetheart," he answered as he gave her a hug. "I didn't really know them, but they were there helping us all beat the nasty people. It takes a lot of people to fight in a war and lots of people die. These two men were just a couple of them."

"Just like your grandpa huh?" She added.

"Yes, just like my grandpa, your great-grandpa," Frank replied with a faint smile.

After lunch, they continued their journey to the Warneton area. Turning left at Ploegsteert, they continued northeast for a little over three kilometres before encountering the motorway. Lynne guided Frank along a sideroad and about two minutes later, he cried out, "There it is. That's the Douve River there. Well, to call it a river is a bit of a stretch; more of a creek really."

"Yes, not a particularly significant river, is it Frank?" Lynne commented.

"Oh, it is, if you are on foot and trying to cross it," Frank chuckled. "Was as boggy as heck in there. No grass like now. Let's see now; if that's the river, and that's Warneton over the other side of the motorway, then ... yes, up there is where we were."

"Actually, there is a track that goes around there. See here," Lynne said as she showed him the map.

"Yep, that's good. We'll go around there then," he replied, then he turned the car around and drove the few hundred metres around this track.

"This is about spot on," Frank said, as he got out of the car. When the others had done the same, he explained, "Trenches must have been about here, and do you see that little rise over there?"

"Yes," answered Tim and the others.

"That's where we crept to, before crawling down to the German trenches, which would have been just the other side of that motorway. It has been built right through the Hun trenches there.

"What is this Hun dad? Were they sweet, like honey?" A confused Ellie asked.

Frank chuckled again. "No, Sweetie that was one of the names given to the Germans. It's a very old term that describes one of the tribes that make up the German people. During the war, we didn't talk so much about Germans but Huns or Fritz or Bosch. It's just a name that was used."

"Oh, I see," Ellie replied.

"Anyway, it was down there that I decided to capture two German machine gunners and blow up their machine gun. It is all probably buried under that freeway now," Frank explained with a bit of a smile on his face. "Became a bit of a legend after that actually."

"Did you really blow up a machine gun Dad?" Tim asked excitedly.

Frank laughed. "Sure did, Son. I got a grenade and tied it tightly to the side of the gun. Then I tied a length of string that I always kept in my pocket to the gun and crawled away up that slope. When I pulled the string, the pin came out of the grenade and started it. I ran like the wind until it went off. Unfortunately, I stumbled at the same time and fell head-first into a shell hole full of freezing mud. Was that ever so cold? I must have looked a sight when I got back. With the explosion all the machine guns along their trenches started firing everywhere in that area. They had no idea I was a hundred metres away by then. Have to say, that was kind of fun. All I could think of was that TV show, McGuyver."

"That's funny," Lynne added laughing, "because that's exactly what I was thinking. He's turned into bloomin' McGuyver."

"So, we got the two prisoners back to HQ and they spilled a lot of information, apparently." Frank stopped there and gazed around in silence then. The family had worked out when to stay silent.

"Good men lost their lives right here, and families lost their loved ones. And for what?" He just left it there.

"But you can't stand back and let them get away with it, Dad. If they have to be stopped, what choice do you have?" Tim asked his father.

"Yes, I know Tim," Frank replied quietly. "But what I can never understand is why the people that cause these wars sit back in their palaces and send ordinary men, and women now, to do their dirty work. They remain safe at home and the likes of us do the fighting and lose their lives."

"Yeah, it isn't fair, is it?" Tim said looking out, just like his father.

Lynne just smiled looking at the pair. Frank and mini Frank.

"You know how big a battalion is, don't you Son? Frank asked Tim.

"Yes. You said about a thousand men, didn't you?" Tim answered.

"Correct. The 44th Battalion was another Western Australian battalion but in the 3rd Division. They fought with us at Broodseinde and along the Hindenburg line. When the AIF was withdrawn from the fighting on the 4th of October 1918, have a guess how many men walked off the front line, to have a rest."

"Oh, I don't know Dad, three hundred?" Tim shrugged his shoulders.

" Eighty! Eighty, out of probably fifteen or sixteen hundred men, including reinforcements. The rest were either dead or wounded."

Tim looked up at his dad to see he had tears in his eyes. "Only eighty?" He repeated in amazement.

"Yes, Son. Tell me how that is right." Frank was now talking not so much to Tim or either Lynne or Ellie, but to some kind of almighty war organiser. Lynne took a pace over, slipped her arm around Frank and held him tightly. Tim then did the same, and Ellie joined in. The four of them just stood there in a family hug, staring at the area. Peace at last.

After a minute or two, Frank suggested that they move on, back to Ieper. He took this opportunity to tell them he had organised to lay a wreath at the Menin Gate tonight, on behalf of his mates from the 28th. The wreath would be delivered to the organisers at the gate by 7.45 pm. He expected he would be attending on his own tonight, as it would be the third time at the Last Post service for the family. He figured they would have had enough of it by now. To his surprise, they all wanted to go again. It now held a greater significance for them all and they all wanted to be a part of it.

They arrived at 7.30 again and spoke with the organisers. Frank did not tell them he was laying the wreath on behalf of his mates he served with. That would be a stretch too far, so he told them it was on behalf of his grandfather and all his mates in the 28th Battalion. Frank asked Lynne if she would accompany him, for the laying of the wreath, but she suggested that he and Tim should lay it. Frank just nodded his head. *How was it, that it seemed everyone else in his family, was wiser than him?* He turned to Tim.

"Tim, would you like to help me lay this wreath tonight?" Frank asked his son.

"Are you serious? Can I?" Tim answered eagerly.

"Of course, you can. You are why we are here today," his father suggested.

"Thanks, Dad. I'd love to." Tim beamed from ear to ear.

When the time for the wreath laying came, Tim watched intently how the people ahead of them acted and tried to do the same. Eventually, it was their turn and the two of them marched forward, laid the wreath reverently on the steps, took a pace rearward and placed their right hand over their heart, then turned and marched back to their place. Tim tried so hard to keep a solemn face throughout and he managed to do so until he saw his mother and sister waiting for them when they came back and his smile crept through yet again.

Throughout the process, Frank was thinking of not only those men he knew who made the ultimate sacrifice but those whose lives were undoubtedly changed forever through the suffering they experienced. Men like Max Farquharson, who must have been impacted for the rest of his life by five woundings. Men like Toddy, who survived, but after witnessing the things he saw, and remembering the things he did, had to return to normal life and was supposed to forget about it all. He thought about the cliché phrases, often used to describe the fallen. *"They died for their country. What rubbish,"* he thought. *"They died trying to preserve a way of life, free from oppression. A natural right of every citizen on this earth"*.

When the last post was played, Frank was in tears again. Never had it meant so much. The remainder of the service was a blur for Frank. He could not get the pictures out of his head of his mates and fellow fighters.

Frank and Lynne were talking, once they got back to their accommodation, about the remainder of their time in Belgium and France.

"My intention was to go back down to the Somme region and look around there again, but after tonight, that is enough. I can't achieve anything more than I have now. I would like to stop off briefly and get some more photos, but that is all. We only have a couple of days left, so how about we find out what the kids want to do." Frank suggested.

"I already know," replied Lynne. "I have asked them if there is anything they wish to do. Ellie has heard about Disneyland Paris and would love to go there. When I mentioned this to Tim, he agreed. So, what do you think?"

"I think," began Frank slowly, "that they have had to put up with being dragged around here, the last week or so by me, that it is the least we can do. Go and enjoy it as a family, eh?"

"I couldn't agree more. I understand that this trip has been about finding answers about your grandfather. I think we have done that now, even though there is probably still more to be learned, but now it's time for the kids," Lynne answered.

"Done. Tomorrow we should head back to Paris then." Frank stated.

"Agreed," Lynne said.

After taking advice on which route to take, they headed south the next morning. Frank started laughing, not long after leaving, when the route took them straight through the very place they had stopped at yesterday, at Warneton. The motorway they saw yesterday that cut through the old battlefield, was the motorway they were now driving on. Once they approached Lens, they left this motorway and commenced the longer route to Paris. This way avoided the tolls and they got to see more of the countryside as well. More coincidences happened when they drove straight over the top of the St Quentin Canal at Bellicourt, just near Frank's last day on the Hindenburg Line. Here they left the main road and crossed west to Peronne, Clery-sur-Somme, Feuilleres, Herbecourt and Biaches for Frank to get some more photos for his album. When he had what he wanted from there, they drove across through Cappy to Corbie.

Just before arriving at Corbie, Frank stopped the car when they could see both the Somme River on their left and the Ancre

River on their right. He left the car and wandered around for a minute then called the family to join him.

"You've no doubt heard of the Red Baron or Baron von Richthofen, have you not?" He asked them.

"Yes, of course," said Lynne.

"Sure have," said Tim.

"Um, Nope," Eloise said.

"He was a very famous German pilot, Sweetie. It was a really early time for aeroplanes, and he was very good at his job," Lynne explained to Ellie.

"Well just over there is where I think he crashed. We were in trenches just through those trees there, over the river, when he was shot down and crashed about there," he indicated, pointing in the direction he figured it was.

"Interesting," Lynne commented. "I believe there is a lot of dispute about just who got him in the end, wasn't there?"

"Yes, there was, but it was the Aussie machine gunners just through there," again Frank indicated the direction, "that got him. He had been forced down low in a chase and there was definitely a fighter behind him, but the guys from B Company said it was definitely the ground machine gunners that got him. We were back in reserve at that time. I missed it by a day, but I did see him flying around up there, the day before."

Tim had been off wandering around looking for signs of anything that might indicate the crash site and called out to the family from about 50m up the road.

"Come up here. There's a sign telling about it."

They all walked up to the sign and read it. It was indeed the site Frank remembered.

Once Frank was satisfied he had what he wanted they continued their southward journey towards Paris and stopped at the airport to drop off the car. They would no longer be needing it. From the airport, it was the train back to their lodgings in Paris again. The following day, they all caught the train out to Disneyland Paris and enjoyed a wonderful day. The children had an absolute ball. Lynne and Frank did not exactly dislike it either. At one point, they were sitting whilst the children were on a ride.

"Well Frank, I think this trip has been a bit of a revelation as far as Tim is concerned. He has grown so much, in so many different ways, don't you think?" Lynne asked as she sat back in the seat.

"Sure has," Frank answered. "I cannot believe some of the words and ideas that have come out of his mouth this week. The sudden maturity, and like, his behaviour last night at the Menin Gate. Amazing, to say the least."

"Not that I have had any experience at bringing up a boy before, but it is strange. I never expected a kind of quantum leap in maturity, like this. Between you and your father, and maybe even your grandfather, you have done a number on him, haven't you?" Lynne smiled and turned to look at Frank.

He turned to her and replied, "Maybe we have. But I like it." He leaned over and kissed her. Here sat two enormously proud parents.

The following day was spent just walking around Paris, the city of love, watching the various artists along the Seine, the array of street performers and picking up little mementoes here and there. Frank hailed a taxi to take them up to Sacre Coeur. High up on the hill at Montmartre, it afforded them all a wonderful view over the expanse of Paris.

"Look Mum, there's a windmill down there," Eloise pointed it out to her mother.

Lynne smiled and explained, "That is called the Moulin Rouge. It's like a famous dance club.

"I've heard of that place," Ellie replied feeling proud of herself.

They wandered around the shops and stopped for lunch in one of the many boutique restaurants, before walking down the steps and slopes below Sacre Coeur and along past the Moulin Rouge and more shopping. The children marvelled at the gaiety of the district and the variety of people they encountered.

Back at the accommodation that night, they prepared for their return journey to Perth, Western Australia. It had been a long trip for them all, but for Frank, it had been a year, something he still was unable to get his head around. After the children had gone to bed, the two adults were sitting, and talking.

"Have you worked out what you are going to tell your dad yet?" Lynne asked.

"I swing from telling him everything to very little. I still don't know," Frank admitted.

"The way I see it, if you tell him; first, he won't believe you, second, even if he does, he will know his father died earlier and it wasn't him that won the bravery award. If you don't tell him; well, you know what he is like, he will know you are holding back on him," Lynne's reply wasn't all that comforting.

"Yeah! The problem is that the truth is just so unbelievable. I'm still not 100% convinced myself," Frank admitted. "I keep wondering if I am dreaming or dreamt it all up. I mean, I know it happened, there is just so much stuff that has been verified, but ..." He couldn't even think how to finish the sentence. He just sat there shaking his head.

"I guess you have tomorrow on the flight to think about it, with not much else to do," Lynne added cheerfully.

"Gee thanks, Love. That's a big help," Frank answered with a smile.

"You never know though, he may surprise you with what he knows and understands," she went on to say. "Plus, there's your mother to think about here too. If you tell them, she will believe you. You know that."

"That's true enough normally, but with this kind of information? It's a tough ask for anyone to believe," he responded with his hands raised, palm up.

"Well, I believed you, didn't I?" Lynne suggested.

"Not immediately. Not until I showed you some kind of verifiable proof," Frank was remembering the interaction as he arrived back at the butt after his experience.

"Maybe so, but I do believe you and so will your parents eventually," she replied taking his hand in hers.

"Maybe!" he admitted. "I have a few hours tomorrow to think about it. Let's sleep now."

"Our last night in the city of love and you want to sleep? I think not." Lynne said with a twinkle in her eye and a smile on her face.

Frank just smiled back and chuckled. He took her hand now and they went to bed.

✦

Chapter 14
Homeward Bound

**Until all mankind, without exception,
undergoes a great change, wars will be waged,
everything that has been built up, cultivated
and grown will be cut down and disfigured,
to begin all over again after that!**

Anne Frank

Patsy and Alby were there at the airport to meet the family when they arrived back in Perth, two days later. They were standing in the arrivals hall, somewhat impatiently waiting for them, when they cleared customs. Tim and Eloise rushed forward and hugged them both.

"Oh, Grandad and Grandma, we have so much to tell you," Tim eventually got out.

"I am so glad you had a good time, kids," Patsy said with a big smile.

"Hello Lynne. Welcome home," Alby hugged her.

"Hello Dad," Lynne answered.

"G'day Son," Patsy gave Frank a hug and a kiss.

"Rather than compete with all these people trying to leave, how about a cup of coffee and a milkshake?" Alby asked them.

"Oh yes please," sighed Frank. "Would love a good coffee. We've just had a day of airline coffee." Everyone laughed and they headed for the coffee shop.

"Well, Son," Alby eventually asked, "what did you find out?"

Frank glanced at Lynne. He still was not sure what to say.

"We will go into all the details when we get home," Frank told them, "but we managed to get to several of the places your father was. I managed to find a series of trench map reproductions and using the references in the unit diaries we were able to pinpoint, almost exactly, where the different actions happened."

"Really? That must have been quite an experience for you to actually be there," Alby replied.

"You can say that again," Frank answered, giving Lynne a sideways glance. "Yes. We followed on from the Polygon Wood entry and saw the places the battalion was at after that, right up to the Hindenburg line. We even met the owners of the farm where Francis' final action took place. We had sort of worked out where it was and we were parked on the side of the road when the farmer came up to us to see if we were in need of help. Lynne explained to him why we were there and he warmly welcomed us and asked us to all go back to his cottage, for coffee with him and his wife. They were profoundly grateful for Francis' service and asked us to pass that on."

"They were lovely people," Lynne added. "They were able to pinpoint where the particular actions took place, and a lot of it happened from the remains of their cottage. Monsieur Boulanger's father had to rebuild it after the war. It was demolished in the battles."

"Yes, almost everything was destroyed, poor buggers. Imagine coming home to that," Alby replied rather glumly.

"We worked backwards from there, to Mont St Quentin, Peronne, Villers Bretonneux, Amiens, all along the Somme then we went up to Ieper," Frank explained.

"Yes, Grandad!" Tim added. "The French and the Belgians are very grateful for the work of our soldiers. There is more recognition for them over there, than there is here at home."

"They even have roads named after the Australians, Grandma," Eloise excitedly jumped in with.

"Is that right, Darling?" Patsy said, leaning down to her.

"Funny name though. Something like 'Rude Australians'. Strange, isn't it?" Ellie said with a screwed-up face.

Everyone laughed. "Yes, Rude Australians is probably about right," Alby threw into the conversation.

"Sweetie, it's Rue D'Australien," Lynne explained. "It is how the French say Road of the Australians. Rue means road and the d' means of. Actually, it is the Avenue des Australiens, but that is by the by."

"Oh, that's why Rue was everywhere." Ellie seemed satisfied with that response.

"And speaking of roads, it was interesting that although it was almost a hundred years ago, the roads have not changed positions except for the construction of motorways, so it was easy to find places from the trench maps. The roads are still where they were then. They just rebuilt them," Frank explained.

Patsy then added, "Yes that's the presence of an old culture for you. Did you see any really straight roads?"

"Yes, we did see a few. One in particular, from St Quentin to Amiens through Villers Bretonneux went something like fifty kilometres, dead straight," Frank mentioned.

"That will likely be an old Roman road then. So that's two thousand years old," Patsy explained.

"Is that right?" Frank queried.

"Yes, the Romans liked to build straight roads. Makes our culture in this country look tame, doesn't it?" Patsy replied with a smile.

"That it does mum," Lynne added. "Why don't we all head home now eh? We can continue there and show you some of the things we found."

On the way back to the Cottesloe house, the children told Alby and Patsy all about Disneyland and the sights of Paris. They regaled them with all the fun of the park, all the rides and exhibits they saw, as well as the characters they met like Mickey and Minnie Mouse, Donald Duck, Snow White and a few more. When they got to the house, they carried all their luggage inside and sat down to talk about their experiences.

"I need to show you something, Dad. I think you will find it's rather special," and Frank reached into his pocket and pulled out the MM. He handed it to Alby who instantly recognised it for what it was.

"Yes, Son. I have one of these at home. Don't you remember?" Alby told Frank.

"Have a close look at it, Dad," Frank suggested.

Alby again studied the medallion including the edge. "How the hell did you get that engraved Frank?" Alby asked having noticed the imprinted information around the rim.

"I didn't Dad," Frank said slowly. "It's the original."

"The original?" Alby was confused. "How the heck did you get that? Where did you find it?"

"I didn't find it, Dad. It was given to me. By General Birdwood."
Frank held his breath waiting for the answer. "What do you mean,
by Birdwood? That's crazy" Alby asked. He was more confused
than ever now.

"Well, Dad. It's a long, rather fantastic story. But I won that
MM. Your father Francis, was indeed KIA on October 1st, 1917."
Frank waited for his father's reply.

"But you showed us where his service records told of his
exploits after that date. I don't understand. What do you
mean, you won it?" Alby responded. He was sitting there with
a furrowed brow, one eye half shut, the other wide open, head
cocked to one side.

Frank then went into a detailed explanation of what had
happened to him after sitting at the Cenotaph on Polygon Wood,
right through to his return a year, or an hour later. Throughout his
explanation both Alby and Patsy sat and listened, both unable to
believe what they were hearing. Once he had finished, he added,
"I know, it is almost impossible to understand, but I can assure
you, it is the truth."

"I ... I don't know what to say. Are you sure it wasn't a dream?"
Alby asked.

"Absolutely positive now," Frank replied. "I have had so many
events to verify it all. The medal, names, records, and happenings
that aren't in the unit records. There is just way too much stuff
I now know."

"I know, it is hard to believe, Dad and Mum," Lynne spoke
slowly and directly to them. "I too, took some convincing. But
having seen these things that Frank talks of as verification, I too,
believe it happened,"

"Well, I for one believe you Frank," Patsy spoke up now. "This is not the sort of thing one makes jokes or lies about. If you say you have these happenings to verify your story, then it must be. There are strange things in this world that we know nothing about and sometimes we just need to have faith."

"Here's something else. I haven't shown you guys yet either," Frank said looking at Lynne and the kids. "I found this in my luggage that came back with me. I didn't see it at first, but found it just before we left Paris. I thought I would keep just one more surprise." Frank reached into his pocket and drew out a postcard. As he showed the picture on it, he said, "I had this taken at Boulogne-sur-mer, on the way to England for the officer's course in January 1918. That's me with Sergeants Ernest Hurst and James McGowan from B and D companies, the day before the ferry to Folkstone."

"Oh, my lord," Patsy gasped, as she grasped her mouth with her hand.

"Bugger me!" Alby unapologetically let slip.

"Wow," uttered Tim, and Lynne and Ellie sat silently staring.

"Strange things alright, Mum," Frank chuckled. He paused for a few seconds to let this sink in. "So, I can tell you, exactly what it was like there. It is not something one would choose, but I am glad I experienced it. I now have such an admiration for what all those blokes endured. Of course, that goes for you too, Dad. Oh, and now I can say without any shadow of a doubt, that General Monash was the biggest single factor in turning the tide and winning that war. He showed everyone exactly what needed to change, to win that war, and he showed them how to do it."

"I'll not argue with you on that point, Son. I have always believed that," Alby agreed. "The English will tell you they won the war, the Yanks will tell you they made all the difference, but the reality is, it needed a different type of command from Haig to make the difference. Monash was that difference. At least they learnt from it and kept it up." He paused for a few moments then went on. "So, from what you are saying, Dad was actually killed, October 1917," Alby stated slowly.

"Yes, I'm afraid so, Dad. There was a witness who saw it happen. He was stunned when I walked in as Francis. I had to try and pass off as Francis, otherwise I would have been arrested as a nut case or an unidentifiable spy. You know what happens to them. I'm guessing he and I must look pretty much the same. Anyway, this poor guy probably thought I was a ghost," Frank explained.

"Poor bugger!" Alby chuckled.

"The really sad thing for him was that he was nearby and saw when I 'died' again," Frank told them. "He saw me blown up a second time. Can't imagine how that affected him through the rest of his life. He was one of only three of my, ... sorry, Francis' section, that made it through. Oh, that's another thing, Dad. Artillery. What an absolute waste of time and money that was. Many a time we endured an hour, or four, of concentrated HE or gas, and not a single casualty. Not even a scratch."

"Really? Not very effective then, I take it." Alby queried.

"About the only effect it had was it made you keep your head down, so you weren't shooting at them. Either that or simply churning up the ground," Frank laughed. "Our unit notes often said that our artillery barrages on them were 'with good effect', but I have serious doubts about that. Although I do have to admit when we started advancing in the last 3 months, we could see that a lot of the dead were from our artillery."

"Not all artillery is aimed at hitting troops though, Frank," Alby explained to him.

"True enough, Dad. There was wire cutting and smoke screening with the creeping barrage driving troops backwards. But gas is definitely anti-personnel, and many times there were simply no casualties," Frank added. "Definitely not cost- effective at all. Up at around Zonnebeke, millions of shells were sent over between the two sides and really, all that achieved was to make the ground an absolute quagmire. Impenetrable in places. It was completely counterproductive, slowing down the attacks and helping the defenders."

"Yeah, I've seen photos of that," Alby stated.

The conversation stalled for a few seconds as the situation sunk in. Frank restarted it when he explained to his parents, "What I can tell you, for a fact, is that Francis was a well loved and respected corporal. Sounds like he was a little more conservative than me, but that's to be expected, given the era. Because I was using the amnesia excuse for not knowing anything before Polygon, I was able to find out that sort of information, not only from the men but the officers too."

"That's good, Son." Alby appeared a little dejected at this point. "Kinda puts a whole new light on everything though, doesn't it?"

"To a degree, but he was still the same person who accomplished some really positive things, Dad," Frank told him. "Don't lose sight of that."

"That's right, Alby. Nothing really has changed, other than the date of his death," Patsy consoled Alby. She took hold of his arm and squeezed it in support.

"I suppose so," Alby sighed. "Oh, I've just realised; that would be why the letters to mum, stopped when they did. She said she wrote after that, but they came back, unopened."

Frank laughed, "Probably, no one told the Army postal section that he was raised from the dead. They probably had him KIA and they changed only the unit records back, when I turned up."

"Still can't get used to you being my father," Alby added, laughing.

"Oh, my lord," exclaimed Frank. "I never thought of that."

"And thank heavens you didn't, Frank," Patsy added.

They all had a good laugh about that. Frank tried to explain all the different philosophical aspects he had thought of regarding this situation, and that he had not been able to get his head around some of them, and they discussed this for some time. After a while, Patsy stood and announced that they should go home and let the family unpack and settle back in. Alby agreed and stood as well. He stopped and held out his hand toward Frank, still grasping the medal, and said, "Well, Son, I think this better go to you then."

Frank shook his head and replied, "No Dad. Keep it with the others. They belong as a set. There will be plenty of time for me to admire them, after you have gone."

"True enough. But you're not getting rid of me just yet," Alby advised him, with a smile.

"I sure hope not, Grandad," Tim cried out.

"Ah Tim," Alby said. "I want to thank you so very much for having an enquiring mind and asking questions. Due to your inquisitiveness, I now know a lot more about my father. I will never know everything, but this, is a thousand per cent better than what I knew before."

"Thanks, Grandad." Tim hugged him and added, "I have learnt so much this last two weeks too. Things I had never even heard of and didn't know that I didn't know them."

"What do you think about history now, young Tim?" Alby asked him.

Tim thought for a few seconds before answering. "It's a bit like being a detective, Grandad. You have to ask lots of questions and listen to all the answers before building a picture of what it was like. It is really interesting. It helps you to work out who you are, I think."

"Very true, Son," Alby agreed with Tim, and then added, "Well family, I think we two should leave you all to unpack and settle back in. How about you come round tomorrow for lunch, and we can talk some more."

With that, Alby and Patsy bid them all goodbye and drove home, leaving the family to unpack.

"Well then, Darling. What did you think, about all that then?" Patsy asked Alby, on the drive home.

"Sounds a bit far-fetched doesn't it? It is clear that he believes it happened though." Alby replied cautiously, eyes fixed on the road ahead.

"Yes. It's true that it does sound way out, but there's no way in the world he would intentionally make up untruths," Patsy said in his defence. "Also, Lynne really believes it and that scar she said was an old one, but not there that morning. I sure, have never seen it before."

"Yeah, and if he was able to name all those blokes, very few of which are even named in the records but were real people; I mean how the hell would he know?" Alby was more than a little confused. "The detail of everything. The experiences. The stuff we didn't know. How else would he find out? It beggars belief but seems to be the truth. That Military medal too; it's not a reproduction. You can tell a reproduction. I really don't know. I want to believe it, but it's kinda, outta this world.

"I understand dear, but this is Frank. Our Frank, we're talking about. He would not mislead us," Patsy reassured him.

"Yeah. I guess we just have to accept it, regardless of how illogical it seems," Alby replied.

"I think so," Patsy paused. "Well, did you get the answers you were looking for though?" Patsy asked him.

"Not the ones I was expecting, but I do now have a lot more answers," Alby admitted. He was slowly nodding his head. "I am happy with that. I just wish we had some answers for Mum, before she passed away."

"I understand that Honey, but I think she has them all now. Probably more than we do," Patsy added, patting him on the leg as he drove. Alby just nodded.

The following day, the Bailey family gathered together at the East Fremantle house for one of Patsy's sumptuous lunches. All four of the travellers had brought some of their mementos with them to show to Alby and Patsy, as well as quite a few of the photos that they had taken. Frank and Lynne were able to show photos of all the places they had talked about. Places like the Hindenburg line area, Riqueval Bridge, Mont St Quentin, Villers Bretonneux, Zonnebeke and of course the now infamous Polygon Wood. At least it was infamous within the Bailey Family. Frank left Tim to show his grandparents the photo of the headstone in the Buttes New British Cemetery, at Polygon Wood, where Tim had placed the little wooden cross with his great- grandfather's name on it.

"I bought this little wooden cross with a Flanders Poppy on it, Grandad. It didn't cost much, but I wrote your father's name on it and looked around the cemetery to see if any particular headstone stood out to me. I fixed my eye on one quite a way off and we all went over to it, and it was an unknown Aussie soldier. I placed the cross in the ground at the bottom of the stone and said thanks to him. We all sat down there for a few minutes and said, what we wanted to say. And do you know what, Grandad?" Tim turned and looked directly at Alby as he asked.

"No, what is it, lad?" Alby replied, choking back his emotions.

"A little bird came down as we sat there and played in the tree next to us, then it flew down onto the headstone and looked straight at us. Then he just flew away into the bush." Tim made the hand movements describing the actions of the bird as he explained this to Alby.

"Well, that must have been pretty special, Tim," Patsy said and she smiled.

"Yes, it was a very pretty bird, Grandma," Ellie added. "It was just like she was talking to us."

Alby was unable to add anything to this conversation at this point. He was so choked up with emotion, that anything he said now would result in him breaking down. Lynne defused the situation by moving on to the next photograph, which was a view of the cemetery, from on top of the butt.

"Oh, it looks so peaceful there doesn't it?" Patsy commented.

"It truly is a beautiful place, Mum. It is peaceful, there is no doubt," Lynne added.

"Somewhat of an irony though, given its history," Frank chuckled as he spoke. "It was vastly different eighty-four years ago. The butt itself was like a beehive. Holes all over it, through it and under it. When I first got there it was in German hands, but not for long. I heard the Hun took it back in 1918 for a short while, but were shoved off it, back to their Fatherland pronto."

"So, when was that compared to when Dad copped it, Son," Alby had regained his composure and now wanted to know more.

"I got taken by Fritz about two days before Francis was killed, which incidentally must have been in the retaliatory barrages sent over by Fritz after losing Polygon," Frank answered. "In fact, I remember it was the day before I escaped from the Germans at Molenaarelsthoek."

"Wow that's a mouthful of a name isn't it?" Alby said.

"Yes, it is. The town nearby is Molenaarelst, and apparently, the hoek suffix on the end means corner or junction or something like that. So, we got out of there, ..." Frank was interrupted by Alby.

"We? Who's we?" Alby asked.

"Oh yeah!" Frank backtracked. "When the shell blew my door in and clobbered me, that's when I got this." Frank pointed to his arm scar. "Then, before I started my escape run, I remembered some Pommie prisoners nearby that I had heard, so I went and let them out too. The guards were both well and truly kaput. We grabbed some Fritz uniforms and donned them over our own clothes and in the confusion that followed the shell blast, we managed to get away. It was when we were hiding in a cellar, later on the next morning I think, that I realised, that it was when Francis was KIA. At that stage, I didn't know that I would be replacing him. I still expected him to turn up a few days later. I wasn't sure how that was going to pan out if I actually met him.

Once I realised I was Francis I couldn't stop thinking that in a year's time he would be killed again, only now it was me. That had me a bit worried."

"I can see how that would cause you a bit of grief'" Alby chuckled as he said this.

"Once we were found by the Aussie 26th boys, I had to come up with a strategy for getting out of the predicament I found myself in. In the short term, I posed as your father just to get me to the 28th, because I had no dog tags or ID," Frank explained.

"Oh yes that would make it rather difficult I suppose. So how did you convince them you were friend not foe?" Alby asked him.

"I told them what was happening up front, who I had been found by and how we got away and then I showed them on the trench maps, just where Molenaarelsthoek dugouts were," Frank went on to describe that morning. "They hadn't found them at this stage, so were grateful for the information. They passed me on to the 28th command for further follow-up. When I walked in, the fellas there recognised me instantly, so I did not then have to prove anything, thankfully. From that, I took it that I must look just like your father."

"I have often wondered that, Frank. From the one poor photo I had of him, I thought you looked a lot like him," Alby said, with a smile.

"So, for me began a hasty education, in Army etiquette, rules and regs. I was able to fall back on the amnesia excuse a few times, thankfully, but mostly, I just watched. They sent me off to the hospital in Etaples for assessment, due to the arm wound and the "amnesia", but after a week they thought I was completely sane. Huh! Little did they know!" Frank let out a big laugh, echoed by his father.

"So, how then did you manage the promotions?" Patsy asked him. She had been sitting listening intently to the exchange between Frank and Alby.

Frank went on to explain about Lt Col Penry-Wright and his letter to Frank's CO, which had put him in front of the eyes of Command. Then, with the raid on the MG trench at Warneton, he had all but cemented the view at Command that this man was command material. After Frank had explained about that raid, Alby had a huge smile on his face and said, "My word Frank! You'd have done McGuyver proud."

Frank and Lynne both laughed. "That is exactly what we thought," Lynne added.

He told them all about Ypres, as it was then, and the mud of Passchendaele, his time back in England on officer training and his faux pas about the stones' place of origin, at Stone Henge. He went on to include the transfer to the Somme and the build-up to Le Hamel.

"I tell you, Dad, these old aircraft they were using, it was a sight to behold. Those men probably had little idea of what they were doing I imagine, but they threw these things around like there was no tomorrow, which for some of them was true. I remember down near Corbie, watching a Hun plane falling in flames. It was spinning out of control, then at about a thousand feet, the two men in it came out and fell to the ground. I don't know whether they fell, or jumped."

"Yes, I understand some of them chose to die from the fall, rather than the flames. Takes guts that," Alby commented.

"Oh, and I saw the Red Baron too, from the same place. There weren't many of those Fokker triplanes were there?" Frank asked his father.

"I believe not. They were not as common as folklore would have us believe, I understand," Alby replied.

"That's what I told the guys there. Plus, only two days later, our machine gunners downed him, in that area. He was a very well-respected aviator, that one. Our flyboys gave him a full military funeral," Frank explained.

"Yes, even to this day, the Red Baron is classed as the best fighter pilot of the Great War," Alby sighed. "Sad isn't it, that the best way to get fame, is to kill more people than anybody else?"

"Sad?" Echoed Patsy. "Insane, would be a better description."

"True!" echoed Frank. "The day after the two Hun pilots parted company with their burning plane was a dreadful day for us though. We were heading back, well behind the lines, for R & R. We were marching in companies, with about five hundred metres between companies, when a blasted Hun bomber came over and found us on the move. He swooped and dropped two bombs on B Company, killing and wounding heaps. We lost more men that day than any other single day of the war. It was devastating. We ended up with sixty-seven casualties and two dead horses out of that."

"Wow, that's quite a loss. How many of them were fatal? Do you remember?" Alby asked.

"I think it was high twenties dead, from memory," Frank answered.

"That is a lot, without even being on the front line," Alby commented.

"Yeah! That was a month before Le Hamel," Frank informed them sadly. He went on then rather more upbeat. "It would have been nice to be a part of that historic action, but we were relegated to support for that stunt. We were part of the actions that evaluated the manoeuvres beforehand though. Monash refined them after our actions and the result was complete success at Le Hamel and a month later, at Morcourt, which we were heavily involved with. We followed that up, with variations, along the southern edge of the Somme, through Chuignolles, Herbecourt and on to Biaches and La Chapelette, both just over the river from Peronne. By this time, Fritz was well and truly in the retreat phase."

"That's interesting, because all we ever hear about the Somme is how stagnant the battle was there and how muddy it was," Patsy remarked.

"That was true of the earlier years along the Somme, Mum. 1915, '16 and '17 were indeed like that. That was mostly the Poms and French along the Somme at that time, although there were a few of our battalions there too. They were still using Haig's 'strategy'. I'll give you an example of the difference in tactics. Five days after the action at Le Hamel, forty-two of us were chosen to try a sneak attack on a twelve-hundred-yard section of trench in front of us, not far from Le Hamel. Remember that number, forty-two men. In thirty minutes after zero hour, we had the trench taken, reinforced and ready for their inevitable counterattack. Previously this position had been assaulted by two battalions, that's anywhere from one to two thousand men, and they failed. So, this was the dawn of a new type of war. A mobile one."

"Yeah, I heard Adolf Hitler was somewhere near there, at the time, and he learned the value of that kind of attack. He used those tactics in the 2nd war and called it Blitzkrieg," Alby added.

"Is that right, Dad? Do you mean I was right near Schicklgruber and I didn't know it? Huh! I could have changed the course of history if I'd known that," Frank exclaimed.

"I doubt it, Hun," Lynne commented. "I've thought about a lot of aspects of this. All this had already happened with you there. There is no way you could have changed anything, as you had already done it."

Frank sighed, "I guess so. Gee, it does your head in trying to understand all this."

"You're telling me, Son! Struth, I still don't get it all. Probably never will," Alby said rather frustratedly.

They all had a bit of a chuckle about this. They were all in agreement, there was no way they were ever going to be able to understand how this happened.

Frank finished off by telling his mother and father the rest of the story, right up until he was transported back to the year 2000. He then added what he had found out about his grandfather, from the other men. This was mostly information that he gleaned inadvertently, from the others, under the assumption that Frank was unable to remember anything from before Polygon Wood. There was not a lot, but it let Alby know a little more of the man, that Francis was. Over lunch, Alby was quiet, obviously processing the information Frank had given him.

Over coffee, at the end of the meal, he finally spoke up. He spoke slowly and deliberately.

"Frank, as hard as it is to swallow this story it is obvious to me now that you were there. That you made it back alive is miraculous, given the average lifetime of a soldier on the front line as much as you were. I have to add a huge thank you for bringing back the information you have. Now I can understand a little more of what he was like and what he went through. I guess in the not-too-distant future, I will get to meet him and then I can compare notes, so to speak. Thanks, Son, and thanks Tim for asking that vital question that started this all."

"No worries, Dad. Yes, it is interesting isn't it when such a small thing like a question, can change the whole course of one's life." Frank replied wistfully. "And while the circumstances were entirely different, I now have much more understanding of Ted's situation. I saw enough blokes with shell shock to know that it really is all PTSD. That will be the next challenge, telling him."

"I think you can leave that to me, Son," Alby said looking for reassurance from Patsy. "I'll choose the time and place for that. No doubt he will then approach you about it all."

Patsy nodded in agreement, and they left it there.

The afternoon passed pleasantly with them all sitting around talking about Paris, Ieper and the other sights they had seen, and the activities they had been a part of together. Around four, they decided to head home, finish the unpacking and make a start on their photo album.

Back in Cottesloe, they put everything away, displayed their new mementoes and started the inevitable washing chores. After dinner, they were sitting around the table putting photos in order. They had started their journey at the end of Francis' supposed journey, so now they had to rearrange the photos in order of Frank's experiences. They made two albums. One of the family's travels and one of Frank/Francis' journey through the year, at least of present-day photos of the places he was. They all participated in the family album, but Frank had to compile his experiences on his own. After all, he was the only one of them there. He had the photos laid out, in chronological order, starting at Polygon and finishing with the Boulanger's farm, on the old Hindenburg Line. Tim was sitting alongside him as he started putting them into his album. He had about a third of them in the display album when Tim spoke up. "That one is in the wrong place, Dad."

"No, Son. That's just east of Villers Bretonneux, before the move on Morlancourt.

"Yes, Dad, that is true, but that one of the trench areas you were there before the Red Baron was shot down, not after. You were just forward of that area after that." He turned and looked at a stunned Frank. "How the hell would he know that?" Frank thought.

Tim just winked at him.

Glossary of Abbreviations

2 I/C	Second In Charge
AIF	Australian Imperial Forces
AWM	Australian War Memorial
Capt	Captain
CCS CCP	Casualty Clearing Station (Post)
CO	Commanding Officer
Coy	Company
Cpl	Corporal
DCM	Distinguished Conduct Medal
DOW	Died Of Wounds
Gen.	General
GSW	Gun Shot Wound
HE	High Explosive
HQ	Headquarters
KIA	Killed In Action
L/Cpl	Lance Corporal
Lt	Lieutenant
Lt Col	Lieutenant Colonel
M.	Monsieur (Mr)

Maj	Major
MG	Machine Gun
MC	Military Cross
MM	Military Medal
Mme	Madame (Mrs)
MO	Medical Officer
NAA	National Archives of Australia
NCO	Non-commissioned Officer
QM	QuarterMaster
OR(s)	Other Rank(s)
POW	Prisoner Of War
RAF	Royal AirForce
RAAF	Royal Australian Air Force
RFC	Royal Flying Corps
RTA	Returned To Australia
Sgt	Sergeant
WIA	Wounded In Action

Units of troop disposition WW1 infantry

Type of unit	Commander	2 I/C	Numbers	Total Number
Section	Corporal	L/Corporal	Up to15	17
Platoon	2nd Lieutenant	Sergeant	3 sections	54
Company	Captain	Lieutenant	4 Platoons	App. 220
Battalion	Lt Colonel	Major	4 Companies + Ancillary coys	App. 1000
Brigade	Brigadier (Gen)	Colonel	4 Battalions + Ancillaries	4-5000

Rank Insignia
used in this story

L/Cpl	One stripe upper arm
Cpl	Two stipes upper arm
Sgt	Three stripes upper arm
2nd Lt	One pip on shoulder
Lt	Two pips shoulder
Capt	Three pips shoulder
Maj	One crown shoulder
Lt Col	One crown one pip Shoulder
Col	One crown Two pips shoulder
Brig	One Crown Three pips Shoulder
Maj Gen	One pip crossed sword and baton
Lt Gen	One crown Crossed sword and baton

✦

About the Author

The Time Gentleman is the second book by the author. The first "Whatever It Takes" was written under the name Ewen Hill. It is the story of my grandfather's time in the first AIF. I have a passion for education, believing knowledge is useless unless shared.

The Time Gentleman is a fiction based around real events during The Great War and is a novel way of describing real happenings through fictional people. It is an opportunity to learn and to enjoy. The Time Gentleman is the first of three stories.